FLORENCE GRAHAM.

OR,

THE PIRATE'S DAUGHTER.

BY THE AUTHOR OF

"THE LIFE OF NELSON;" "THE BLACK PIRATE, OR THE PHANTOM SHIP;" "THE ROBBER CHIEF," &C.

Come, sit thee down by me, love ; come, sit thee down by me,
And I will tell thee many a tale of the dangers of the sea ;
Of the perils of the deep, love, when the stormy tempests roar,
And the raging billows wildly dash upon the groaning shore.

The skies are flaming red, love, the skies are flaming red,
And darkly rolls the mountain wave, and curls its monstrous head;
Whilst clouds and ocean blending, and loud howls the bitter blast,
And the daring tar, 'twixt life and death, clings to the shattered mast.

THE OLD SAILOR.

LONDON :

PUBLISHED BY E. LLOYD, AT THE OFFICE OF THE ILLUSTRATED EDITIONS
OF STANDARD WORKS, 12, SALISBURY SQUARE, FLEET STREET.

1847.

FLORENCE GRAHAM;

OR, THE
PIRATE'S DAUGHTER.

BY THE AUTHOR OF "THE LIFE OF NELSON;" "THE BLACK PIRATE; OR, THE PHANTOM SHIP;" "THE ROBBER CHIEF," &c. &c.

CHAPTER I.

When winds breathe soft along the silent deep,
The waters curl, the peaceful billows sleep,
A stronger gale the troubled wave awakes,
The surface roughens and the ocean shakes.

More dreadful still when furious storms arise,
The mounting billows bellow to the skies;
On liquid rocks the tottering vessel's toss'd,
Unnumber'd surges lash the foaming coast.

WEBBE.

MORNING had advanced nearly into noon, and the bright rays of the sun were reflected in the ocean. The marbled clouds lay motionless far and wide over the deep blue sky, and all memory of storm and hurricane had vanished from the

No. 1.

ignificence of that immense calm. There was but a gentle fluctuation on the
bosom of the deep, and the sea birds floated steadily there, or dipped their wings
a moment in the wreathed foam, and again wheeled sportively away into the
sunshine.

One ship—only one single ship—was within the encircling horizon, and she
had lain there, as if at anchor, since the morning light; for although all her
sails where set, scarcely a wandering breeze touched her canvass, and her flags
hung dead on staff and at peak or lifted themselves uncertainly up at intervals, and
then sunk again in motionless repose. The crew paced the deck anxiously awaiting
coming breeze.

The vessel was the captured merchantman, now under the command of
Malcolm Graham, which had long left the island of Cuba, bearing the hapless
man to the native land of her father.

She sat in the cabin listening to him attentively; he was relating to her that
portion of his life, which suited his intentions of keeping secret from his daughter,
real character. He told her of his marriage with her mother, of her melancholy death, occasioned by an earthquake, and of the supposed loss of her child,
of his uncertainty of her fate, until he recognized her, from the great
likeness she bore to her mother, in the hut of Mary Adams, which he had left so
suddenly in consequence of a false charge made against him, upon which he had
been imprisoned, and had made his escape, when she found him in the forest
most frozen to death.

He had proceeded thus far, the breeze having in the mean time sprung up,
when he was interrupted by a sailor entering the cabin.

The man reported a strange sail in the distance, Graham hastily left the cabin,
door of which he carefully closed, and ascended the companion-way : upon
gaining the deck, he cast a piercing glance around the horizon.

"Ha! a sail, and dead a-head!" he exclaimed, as his practised eye rested
on a scarcely visible grey speck upon the horizon, in the direction of the
vessel's course.

"Another—two! Keep her away a point, and let us reconnoitre them," he
called, taking his glass, and closely surveying the distant objects.

The vessel kept steadily on her way, closed hauled to the wind, while the
strangers came down upon them, with the wind nearly aft.

As they approached nearer, the foremost one shewed the square rig of a large
vessel, with royals and studing-sails set. In less than an hour from the time they
caught the eye of Graham, they were within half-a mile to leeward of his vessel,
at such a disadvantage had he cautiously thrown her, by altering his course,
and distinctly displayed the tall and majestic apparel of a ship of war.

"The Rattlesnake sir !" said one of the seamen, after gazing at the ship for a
moment, from the top of a gun carriage, through a focus formed by his large
hands ; "her teeth glisten like the black's here," and he looked towards the
ungainly figure of negro, who, with one long arm clinging to a stay, his head and
body went forward. and his lips drawn back with an admiring gaze, was inspecting,
with much curiosity, the noble and warlike spectacle which the strange sail
exhibited.

"Indeed !" said Graham, looking for a moment steadily at the passing ship, "I
expect you are right—but do you know the other vessel?

"I do know her, captain, by the length between her mizen and main-mast,
and the rake of her main royal mast, as if it had been sprung. Yon vessel in
company with the Rattlesnake is the good ship the 'Phantom.'"

"You have a seaman's eye, Mizen ; and you are right too," Graham quickly
added, "the British flag flies at her peak—Stromberg I expect then has been
captured, and his vessel is now returning to England with the Rattlesnake. Well,
well," continued Graham musingly, "Stromberg was a brave fellow after all—
is a pity his career has been so soon cut off, for he would still have been useful
me. Hold to your course again, sir," he said to the helmsman.

The ship came close to the wind, and rapidly held on in the direction from

which she had diverged to avoid the strange ship, which, silently and majestical
with her companion moved onward, apparently standing for the island, fro
which Graham had so fortunately taken his departure.

Graham's vessel continued steadily on her course, and evening was closing in
when Susan sought the deck with her father. Mizen was sitting on a gun carriag
relating some portion of a tale to his messmates. Susan drew near and lent a
attentive ear to his narrative.

"Cleave to the staunch oak, my son, were the words of my old father," sai
Miven; "cleave to a tight ship, my boy, as long as the wind bloweth, and whi
she lives upon the waters, she'll aye be a mother to thee. Pine not upon a dow
pillow ashore wix' pale maids and wrinkled beldames bewailing about thee
—but when thee diest, die like a true heart—the white foam for thy windii
sheet, the roaring voice of the ocean for thy death lament, and a noble bark fc
thy coffin. What can mate with the great sea? Look thee, my son, it's beautifi
at all times—when it beats against the beach-rocks that hem it in foaming an
raging like a madman with his fetters, as well as when the waves be one and a
asleep, moving as gently as slumbering babies with the broad moon poring like
fond mother above them. What though thee diest, as the Hollanders had lik
to ha' died an hour aback, in a cockle shell smack! even then thee goest out c
the world like a man. You shall hear, mesmates," continued the stout seama
raising his voice to the men around him—

"The brig was scudding away like a sea-bird above the breeze, and we, afearin
nought, though 'twas dark as death, having those aboard that knew the course a
well as the way to their hammocks, and warranted coming athwart o' little 'po
that tack, while the wind spoke nor' about. Anow the forward look-out,
whistling time after he'd howl'd out his dismal 'All's well,' jump'd upon th
cable-coil and shouted wi' all his breath, 'Vast! avast! mates, helm a-lee an
about ship! a sail a-head here—all hands, yohoy!' Ben roar'd but 'twas to
late. A sloop of a thing with all aboard snoring under hatches, lay just 'neat
our bows. We crushed upon her about midships, and rode her down awfully.
demurrage for a second succeeded the shock, and then on we went again as
nought had happened. She proved to be a Dutch swab, lurking about the sea fc
fish, or something richer mayhap. To put about, or bring to, in time for help wa
impossible—moreover, every sand in the glass was gold to us. But the yawl wa
out, and three hearties, with the captain himself and me, were aboard her in
snatch. It got light in the nick, the moon having struck out from her black cloud
harbour into the broad blue sea of heaven. We tugged aback with heart an
sinew, but all was quiet and silent above and about the place where she went down
as a grave at midnight, and nought visible but the trailing feather o' foam whic
the strong brig left astern. I thought I heard a deep screech in the waters belov
us—'twas fancy mayhap, but it hit me hard like a bullet. 'Twas just as if m
heart heard it afore my ear. It reminded me against my will o' the night whe
my old father sunk abaft the keel (as we say) long ago. Presently up sho
a cask and a few spars, then a shoal of hake, skate, and your beggarly ling, som
gasping, others quite dead with their white bellies and glazed eyes glittering in
the mooonlight. We heard a dash and sputter windward, and upon looking abou
to our awful wonder, eyed a little out-o'-sorts creature kicking and spluttering
amid another troop o' floating milk-bellies, and laying among 'em wi' his arms
like a windmill in a hurricane. His face was lean, hard and tawny. It looke
like old gold horridly tarnished by time, but age could not wrinkle it. Sometime
he stood aloft, and clamouring knee-deep in the sea; then he sunk fathoms, an
we saw nought of him for a time again. We were one and all mortally gallied a
the sight, but the captain. The yawl lay like a log upon the waters, while we
stood to gaze at the wonder. Anon, however, the captain doffed wollens, an
dashed among the pieces of wreck that now covered the sea's face, grappled th
tawny one, and towed him manfully alongside. Upon hauling him aboard, smit
me, messmates, but there was a thumping bag of leather hanging at the waist o
the yellow devil, from which the eloquent voice of gold emanated at every jerk

We soon loosened it from the side of the strange fellow, who uttered a loud screech, and again jumped into the sea. 'Never mind him, my men, let him go,' said the captain, 'I warrant I don't try again to save him,' and he attempted to sever the thongs which bound the mouth of the bag. His knife was keen, but the tough hide altogether defied its edge, and the irritated captain growled forth a tremendous oath, as he suddenly drew his blade awthwart the bellying side of the gorged bag. My eyes, messmates, there was a sight! a flood of tarnished silver and gold mingled with precious stones, some of which were naked, and others richly encased, streamed from the gash. The captain was overjoyed at the sight of so much treasure; we returned to the ship with the prize, and the whole of the crew were handsomely rewarded by he lucky captain."

"Well, but, Mizen," said one of the seamen, "who was the little yellow fellow?"

"Why, messmates, that I never could learn, but the captain said it was a desperate smuggler, who was conveying the gold from France to some one in England, for some treasonable purposes; but I never troubled my head about it when I'd spent the gold, and that was not long after I got ashore."

Susan now retired to her cabin, as the sky began to be overcast, and heavy clouds rose slowly from the horizon. Here and there a solitary sea gull soared lazily over his shadow in the water, and then, bending downwards, dipped his wing in the smooth sea, rising up again with a sharp, quick turn, and a shrill scream which sounded rather ominously, particularly as there was a kind of bright hazy indistinctness hanging over the whole scene, and a close suffocating oppression in the atmosphere, foretelling change and storm.

The wind seemed to be awaiting in silence and reserving its strength for the approaching conflict of the elements; for there was not a breath stirring; the sea birds shrieked around them, as if to warn them of approaching danger. At length the fore-runner of the squall appeared in the shape of a broad bright sudden blaze of lightning, followed by a rattling peal of thunder, which seemed to have burst open the flood-gates of Heaven, for the rain descended in torrents from the overcharged clouds, while flash followed flash, and peal followed peal in rapid succession.

"We shall have a smart blow," said Mizen to his mates, and he had scarcely spoken the word, when the crash of falling spars and a shout of the helmsman caught his ear; at the same moment an alarming lee-lurch of the ship threw them sprawling.

In an instant Graham was on deck—the cabin seemed turned upside down—the vessel was on her beam ends.

The helmsman, who was one of the worst hands in the ship, had been knocked down at the wheel, and the vessel all but thrown up in the wind—a second blast and their destruction would have been inevitable. However, she happily righted after the first violence of the squall had passed over them, and Mizen with three able hands went aloft to cut and clear away the wreck of the fore-top-mast, which had snapped like a reed on the first burst of the tornado.

Graham seized the wheel, and boxed her about like a boat obedient to his masterly helm, and the vessel whizzed her away through a sea of foam and fire, for the whole surface of the wide water seemed to flash with liquid flame, while her wake, resembling some mighty monster, fresh from his native hell, seemed to chase her through the boiling flood in burning inflections.

The wreck all clear, main-top-gallant mast struck, and the ship put under snug sail for the night, the bold Mizen descended to the deck, and, after a watchful look cast over the taffrail, in which he swept the whole horizon with his keen and anxious eye, he turned to the captain at the helm, and wiping the salt water from his dripping face, begged he would relieve any anxiety, under which his daughter might be in consequence of the storm, while he took the helm.

Graham, accordingly resigned the wheel; joined Susan in the cabin, and entreated her to discard all fear, since the danger was happily over. "Upon account of the almost dead calm," continued Graham, "we had crowded too much sail, and the sudden squall arising, carried off some of the rigging that was not in a very perfect condition. But my brave seamen have repaired the injury, and we are, it seems, in a better state than we were before this accident. However, Susan, I must remind you of the caprice of those elements to which fate has at present, consigned you; and should this prove a squally of tempestuous night, as some of the seamen portend, I doubt not from the fortitude you have evinced, that you will not suffer much alarm, particularly as the seamen are all experienced hands."

Susan promised to exert all her heroism, if necessary, and Graham again left her, and repaired to the deck.

A strong breeze had sprung up from the south, the flashes of lightning became less and less vivid; and the low grumbling of the thunder was heard afar off, as the clouds slowly and unwillingly retreated before the wind which had freshened up rapidly, and blew fresh the whole night.

CHAPTER II.

Loud roar'd the dreadful thunder,
　The rain a deluge showers !
The clouds were rent asunder,
　By lightning's vivid powers !

Now dash'd upon the billow,
　Our opening timbers creak,
Each fears a watery pillow,
　None stop the dreadful leak !　　　Song.

A FAINT tinge along the eastern horizon announced the coming dawn; the night breeze had lulled, and the sails, at every lift of the vessel upon some larger sea, flapped heavily against the masts. The watch were sitting or standing, with their hands thrust into their bosoms, around the windlass; the officer of the deck paced his lonely round ; the helmsman stood at the helm, and, like its master-spirit, directed the course of the yielding vessel steadily towards the invisible point of her destination. Naught was to be seen but the broad heaving ocean and the bending blue sky, in which here and there twinkled a solitary star, and the pale western moon, like a timid novice modestly veiling her face at the approach of the morning sun.

The ocean had lost its turbulence; but at long and irregular intervals, immense masses of its waters were elevated into a mountainous swell which first appeared undulating near the horizon, and gradually rolled onwards, increasing in height and magnitude, till it approached the ship, and raised it on its lofty ridge far above the level of the surrounding sea.

The sky was still lurid with fragments of clouds, which bore little affinity to each other, either in density, form, or colour, and seemed to have been torn, dispersed, and thrown into confusion by the tempest of the preceding night. The horizon, though clear, was of leaden hue, and the newly risen sun appeared contracted in dimensions, and shed a cold and brassy light upon the ocean.

The vessel continued on her course, with a steady breeze, fine clear weather by day, and brilliant nights. Week after week had passed, and Graham expected daily to behold the white cliffs of Albion. The breeze was light and fair, and the waves were breaking short and crisp, curling their little white crests as they rose and fell in rapid succession; but there was a long heavy under swell from the southward, which gave rise to many an ominous shake of the head from the experienced mariners.

There was nothing to be seen but sea and sky; but it was beautiful and boundless nature—nature in her solitude and strength. There were no crowds of human beings jostling and hurrying past each other, as in the haunts of men and of art ; but there was the glorious sun, shining in almost unclouded splendour ; the sea, with its playful waves, dancing and smiling in the sunbeam, and teeming with life and energy.

Susan was looking over the side of the vessel, as she was sailing through St. George's Channel into the Irish sea, watching the shoals of flying fish quivering their little wings, glittering like silver in the sun, and then dropping fluttering into the waters ; while those " hunters of the sea," dolphins and bonitoes, darted, leaped, and plunged in pursuit of them, sometimes rising five or six abreast, and making immense flying leaps together, as if emulating each other, and putting to shame the steeple-chasing "lords of the creation." Her attention was diverted from the water by the gradual heeling over of the vessel, and the creaking noise of the blocks, as the freshening breeze gave additional tension to the tacks and sheets ; at the same time, she heard one of the men muttering to another, as they stood close by —

" This here breeze is a freshing fast, Tom. I doesn't like to see them beggars a galloping round the ship like so many mad horses; and look how the cat's a whisking about. There's a gale of wind in her tail, I'll take my oath."

Susan retired to her cabin to offer up to the throne of mercy supplications for protection through the expected tempest.

The face of nature was no longer smiling ; the heavy masses of clouds had risen from the southern horizon, one dense body seeming to push another upwards as it rose from the gulf of darkness, till the whole surface of the heavens was covered with a veil of gloomy and wildly-driving clouds. The waves were no longer " like playful lambs on a mountain's side," but were rushing after each other like wild beasts in search of prey.

The night came on impenetrably dark, and the angry elements, after jarring for some time, at length burst out into a degree of tremendous violence, the ship plunged and rolled heavily, and the white foam of the long tumbling seas looked doubly ghastly through the gloom, while their roaring formed dismal harmony with the howling of the wind.

During the whole of the long, and to Susan, miserable night, all hands were kept constantly at work; and she heard the loud orders of her father, and the cries of the answering seamen, confusedly and at intervals, through the roaring of the wind and the rushing of the seas. She half envied the seamen who were exposed to the pelting of the pitiless storm ; they were actively employed, the excitement of the moment left no time for reflection. Besides, storm, tempest, and danger were their elements ; but she sat idle and helpless, knowing just enough of the danger to imagine it to be much greater ; brooding over the chimeras of her own fancy, and anticipating she knew not what of approaching calamity. The continual creaking of the bulkheads—the pattering of the thick shower of spray upon the decks, following the dull heavy " thud" of some giant sea which made the ship reel and tremble through every timber—the cries of the seamen, heard indistinctly and at intervals, and then borne far away to leeward on the gale, as if the spirits of the air were shrieking above and around them—formed altogether a fearful medley of wild sounds.

At length, towards morning, nothing was heard on deck but the deep moaning voice of the gale and the roar of the sea; but new and more ominous sounds arose from the lower deck ; there was the monotonous clanking of the pumps, and the rush of water from side to side of the ship, as she rolled heavily and deeply.

Susan could stop in the cabin no longer ; her nerves were worked up to a state of dreadful excitement, and she rushed on deck to breathe the fresh air. It was to her an awful sight. Again the howling and ungovernable wind rushed with headlong fury to the bottom of the deep, to stir up rage and strife, while the indignant sea, agitated to convulsive foam, arose in boiling surges to the clouds, to dare the bold disturber of his serenity. The heavy sable clouds hurried im-uously along; all clashed in discord, and rolled in awful peals their most emendous thunder, whilst vivid lightning flashed almost incessantly, and the whole expansion of the sea now appeared like columns and rocks of flaming fire, except when, at intervals, the most horrible darkness rested on its surface, shutting out for a moment even the foaming billows from every mortal eye.

The ship looked almost a wreck to her eyes. The top-gallant masts had been got on deck, the booms were crowded with wet sails and rigging, the small ropes aloft bellying out with the wind, and then striking violently against the masts with the roll of the ship, the hatches were battened down, life-lines were stretched along from the poop to the forecastle; heavy seas were striking the bow, every now and then pouring volumes of clear blue water over the decks, while the spray flew like a thick shower over head, nearly half-mast high. The horizon all around was pitchy black, except where a dull, hazy, fiery gleam marked its eastern verge; the surface of the water was one wide sheet of white foam, glistening through the gloom, and the strength of the gale seemed absolutely to blow the tops off the giant seas, and scattered them abroad in showers of drift.

Her father was standing under the lee of the weather bulwark, holding on by the main-brace, looking pale and exhausted; near him, with his arm round the poop ladder, stood the officer of the watch, Mizen, muffled up in his pea-jacket, his eyes red and inflamed, and speaking in a low husky whisper, his voice being completely broken with the exertions of the night.

Susan asked one or two questions of her father, which he evidently evaded answering. She accordingly desisted from her enquiries; but a dark and undefined presentiment of evil came over her, which she strove in vain to shake off. Finding her father so uncommunicative, and the spray that was constantly dashing over the decks anything but comfortable, she again returned to her cabin.

She had not long returned to her cabin, when the masts and rigging were shattered to pieces, and borne away from time to time, by the unpitying winds; whilst the raging billows attacked her with equal violence, hurling her from hill to valley, which the surges made without mercy or respite. The door of the cabin was suddenly opened by Mizen, whose countenance betrayed the agitation of his mind, for Susan instantly exclaimed—

"Is there any hope? Tell me the worst! I am prepared for it, and can bear it calmly!"

Mizen hesitated.

"You need not speak," said Susan, "your silence tells me there is no hope."

"There is indeed none," replied Mizen, "but in the mercy of an over-ruling Providence! In another hour, our doom, whether for life or death will be sealed."

"It is a painful trial," exclaimed Susan, "but His will be done;" and her heart and lips devoutly breathed forth prayers to her Creator, into whose presence she now each moment expected to be summoned; and Mizen's attention was divided between those serious thoughts which sincere piety inspired, and the most tender, affecting care of our poor heroine.

Disaster upon disaster had succeeded through this night of horrors, and the morning's dawn found them completely dismasted, deprived of their rudder, and the shattered hulk nothing better than a wreck. Whilst there remained anything to be done for the general safety, the mariners had been indefatigable in their exertions and toil; but when dreadfully convinced that the possibility of being useful was past, they threw themselves, certain of inevitable destruction, upon the deck, in desponding hopeless groups. In this moment of awful inaction, thought acquired full dominion over all. The days that were passed recurred to some in terrible array, and told them a tale they had long refused to hear. Those who had scoffed at the existence of a Deity, now felt conviction, unbidden, arise, and, as the delusions of life were passing off, believed and trembled; whilst those who, through their existence, loved and revered their Creator, found the ties that bound them to him draw closer round their hearts as they believed themselves approaching to his presence.

The scene altogether was one to appal the bravest—to make the boldest " hold his breath." Scarcely a mile to leeward lay the coast—dark, frowning, precipitous, and apparently inaccessible—its lower line completely hidden from their view; but at intervals, the dark and rugged summits of the rocks were seen through the sheets of white foam dashed over them by the breakers.   To windward the prospect was as cheerless ; darkness was again beginning to settle upon the waters, and, in the distance nothing was to be seen but the foam of the crested seas flashing indistinct and ghastly through the gloom.

Viewed by that uncertain light, and rising in such various waving forms, they seemed as if the sea had given up her dead, and the spirits of the departed were assembling on the waters, to witness their approaching fate.   The ship was already a wreck ; the mizen-mast was still hanging alongside, having smashed the poop, hammock nettings, and bulwark, in its fall; the stumps of the fore and main-top-mast were all that remained aloft, the giant seas were dashing over the sides, deluging the decks, fore and aft, and blinding the seamen with their thick showers of spray ; the lower yard-arms dipped into the water, as the half water-logged ship rolled heavily and deeply, groaning and trembling in every timber, like a living creature in its mortal agony.

And then the accompaniments !—the hollow, ominous moaning of the gale, mourning, as it were, over the wreck of its own violence ; the roaring of the waters as they rose and rushed, and dashed against her sides ; the dull, mournful, dirge-like sound of the guns which were fired as signals of distress ; the shuddering cries of the timid ; the curses and imprecations of the hardened and the desperate ! oh, if the recollection of it be so appalling, what must have been the reality ?

At length one of the seamen, an Irishman, suddenly disencumbering himself of his upper garments, exclaiming :—

"By the powers, I could swim, for a wager, with any lubberly fish of the deep, so I'll be after towing myself into safe harbour, by Jasus, but I will, so here goes." He plunged into the sea and made for the shore.   This break upon the general silence of the crew, by restoring 'the soother hope, roused at once the faculties of all to action, and many of his messmates. on the instant, instinctively followed the Irishman ; while others, more wary, paused to observe the fate of their pre-cipitate companions before they ventured.   The bold mariner and his companions were seen to buffet successfully with the waves, for a time, and to emerge constantly, unsubdued, from the foaming whirlpools ! the mighty waves bore them unharmed towards the land, and then, rising up with awful grandeur and impetuosity, curled and burst in myriads of particles within a few yards from the shore, overwhelming them in an abyss of foam, bruising them against the shingle, and, ere they had time to make sure their footing, the receding eddies tore them back with irresistible violence beneath their vortex; then was heard a shout, a shriek, as of human voices, and the next moment they sank to rise no more

The ship did all that a gallant vessel could, rising trom the trough of the sea, and shaking the water from her, as she was occasionally buried fore-castle under, cleaving the huge masses of the element with her sharp stern, and trembling fore and aft with the violence of the agitated waters.   But the mountainous waves took her with irresistible force from her chesstree, when the vessel rose upon the crest of an enormous sea, and seemed to be balancing herself for a moment, as if loth to meet her doom, another instant, and she struck with a shock which threw the men off their feet as they raised an appealing cry to Heaven, which was mocked by the howling of the wind, and the roar of the waters ; again she was lifted by the sea, and dashed on the rocks nearer the shore ; and a crash as if the noble fabric were falling to pieces beneath them.   The loud voice of Graham was heard exclaiming : "Look to yourselves, my lads—look to your own safety."

The clouds of night already gathered round them, vnd the wild scud flew past the dark clouds, that seemed to sink down with their heavy burdens till they nearly touched the sea.   The waves still followed each other mountains high ; the wind blew with the same violence ; and as the stormy petrels flew over the billows, indicating by their presence that the gale would continue, the unfortunate survivors looked at each other in silence and despair.

"Going down !—going down !" was spread with dreadful rapidity throughout the ship, and all discipline and subordination appeared to be at an end, when the men threw themselves into the sea, and were swept towards the shore; not one lived to reach the land, an enormous surge curled over them as they went down, and, as if disappointed at not being able to wreak its fury upon the vessel, drove it in revenge several yards further upon the rocks.

Mizen had refused to quit the vessel with his messmates:—" No," he said " I was born on the sea, it rocked my cradle, and he who raised the storm, will, in his own good time, save me if he thinks fit."

The violent striking of the ship on the rocks threatened every moment to stave in

her side. The moon burst through the clouds in brilliant splendour; the tide was at its height; and the eyes of Susan were fondly bent towards the shore; pale, with clasped hands, she was kneeling; and her pitiful looks implored the Mercy of the most high. A sudden wave threw her against the mast of the vessel. She clung closely to this protecting support; and, calm as virgin purity, she did not

No. 2.

tremble; she still prayed to to the Ruler of the wind and waves. In the midst of this terrific confusion, she looked like the angel of mercy, beseeching Heaven's grace for earth.

Graham, with burning and haggard eye, contemplated the terrific scene of the conflicting elements, inanimate as a block. Immovable and silent he seemed an indifferent spectator of the commotions of nature, a strange guest of the spirit of the storm.

The raging sea now roared over the vessel on every side with deafening noise, and rising above this war of sounds, the loud and distant voice of the unsubdued Northern made itself be heard. The ship had taken a partial and unsteady heel to the starboard, to which side the wreck of the foremast inclined in its fall. The ever watchful Mizen, perceiving that another heave of the sea would change her position, requested Graham and Susan to proceed aft, out of the reach of the wreck of the falling foremast; at that instant a lofty ground swell threw the hull of the vessel with a sudden shock on her larboard bulge, when the foremast thundered over the lee-side, with a horrid crash, sweeping in its ruin the unfortunate Mizen.

A shrill cry of agony came, mingling awfully with the hoarse dashings of the breakers: and, here and there, the boatswain might be seen still struggling with his fate, and attempting vainly to stem the roaring current, which was carrying him rapidly from the wreck, and at last ingulfed him, beneath its swift and sparkling eddies. Graham stood for a moment as if paralysed, as he looked towards the shore, which was now thronged with men seeming anxious to render assistance. His eyes seemed to dwell particularly on the black and decayed hulls of two vessels, which, half immersed in the quicksand, still addressed to every heart a tale of shipwreck and desolation. "Ha!" he exclaimed, "there's the 'Spectre Hulks of the Solway.'"—he then addressed his daughter:—

"We are here alone: none of human kind are privy to our converse. But the omniscient, the omnipresent Being, whose altar is all space, he listens to the vow which I exact: he views the heart, sincere or hypocritical, of which I claim obedience! Are you—will you swear before that Being that you will never without my previous consent, divulge to any human creature, should we be preserved from this doomed ship, your real name or that of your father's. I have reasons for your secrecy—still answer to the name you have so long borne."

"Implicitly I bow to your directions," said Susan; "and solemnly invoke the heavenly registers of our inmost thoughts and words, to record my voluntary oath of inviolable secrecy."

"Enough!" replied Graham, "should our lives be saved, I will tell you why I request this silence on your part, at present I dare not appear in England under my right name; call me Adams."

At that instant a giant wave washed the deck, and bore Susan as its prey towards the beach. She tossed her arms wildly over her head, gave one shrill and piercing scream, and was borne away and hidden from the view of Graham by the following sea.

He dashed fearlessly into the sea, which was to him a familiar element. A few vigorous strokes, and the friendly elevation of a rising wave gave him a sight of Susan; he immediately swam towards her, and by partly supporting himself on a floating spar, and directing it towards the shore, he was fortunate enough to succeed in bearing his lovely burthen in safety to the beach, against which they were dashed with great violence.

CHAPTER III.

"As he spoke,
A sea burst o'er them, and their cables broke!
Then, like a lion bounding from the toil,
The ship shot through the billows' black recoil ;
Urged by the howling blast—all guidance gone—
They shuddering felt her reeling, rushing on—
Nor dare to question where ; nor dared to cast
One asking look,—for that might be their last."   •

ON the Scottish side of the sea of Solway, is seen from Allanbay and Skinverness the beautiful old Castle of Caerlaverock, standing on a small woody promontory, bounded by the river Nith on one side, by the deep sea on another, by the almost impassable morass of Solway on a third ; while far beyound may be observed the three spires of Dumfries, and the high green hills of Dalwinton and Keir.   It was formerly the residence of the almost princely names of Douglas, Seaton, Kirkpatrick, and Maxwell ; it is now the dwelling place of the hawk and the owl ; its courts are a lair for cattle, and its walls afford a midnight shelter to the passing smuggler ; or, like those of the city doomed in Scripture, are places for the fishermen to dry their nets.   Between this fine old ruin and the city of Dumfries stood the castle of Lochallan, in a sweet and romantic nook, such a one in which tradition says, the priesthood of the Romish Church love to erect their altars, and set up their carved images, and collect the riches of the earth. The valley was a good arrow flight across, the sides slope up into hills covered with verdure as soft, and, by the nibbling of sheep, as short as the down of velvet ; here and there a stray garden flower, and a plum or wild apple tree contrived to struggle for existence, and told, with the return of the spring, the story of the ancient glory of the place. In the bosom lay a lake deep and cool, and so clear, that without seeing the bottom, which the peasants placed at the distance of many a fathom, you might see the whole shaggy outline of the pastoral hills reflected quietly on its bosom.   Many green shrubs, bearing fruit or flower, flourished along the water's edge, and the chafing of the lake freaked its weedy borders into innumerable little nooks and tongues, where the wild ducks, an orange tawney brood, moved half seen among the water-grass, and the broad leaves of the lake lily.

Eastward, the vale expanded, and between two green and conical hills, covered half way to the summits with natural wood, which seemed never to have felt the axe, might be seen a long narrow vista of the ocean, with the waves leaping and rolling ; and the chafing of the waters against the cliff and promontory, and that kind of hollow and mournful sound which waves raise when they fall on a rocky and caverned shore, could be distinctly heard at the castle.

Having thus briefly described the locality of the place, we will proceed to describe its present inhabitants.   It was an old fisherman and his wife, with whom was staying William Maxwell, the second son of the present possessor of the estate.

Miles Lawson, the old fisherman, entered the room, (with his halve-net on his back,) where sat Maxwell listening to Dame Lawson, who was narrating to him the tradition of the Spectre Hulks of the Solway.

The fisherman was an old weather-beaten man, whose hair, which seemed to have refused all intercourse with the comb, hung matted upon his shoulders : a kind of mantle, or rather blanket, pinned with a wooden skewer round his neck, fell mid-leg down, concealing all his nether garments as far as a pair of hose, darned with yarn of all conceivable colours, and a pair of shoes, patched and repaired till nothing of the original structure remained, and clasped on his feet with two massy silver buckles.

He threw his net to the ground, at the same time exclaiming :—" I must back again to the shore, for there's a storm brewing in the heavens."

William Maxwell sprung from his seat, and proceeded with the old man at once to the shore, where they found a numerous party of fishermen assembled.

The mid-day sun had been unusually sultry, accompanied with hot and suffocating rushes of wind; and the appearance of a huge and dark cloud, which, hung like a canopy of smoke and flame over a burning city,—betokened to an experienced eye an approaching storm. One of the old fishermen shook his head, and combing the hair over his forehead with his fingers, said :—

" Woe's me ! one token comes and another token arises, of tempest and wrath on that darkening water. It comes to my memory like a dream." As he said this the tide wheeled and foamed around the two black hulls of the haunted ships; creeping inch by inch up their sides, and at last fairly threw its waters over the top, a long and hollow eddy shewed the resistance which the liquid element received. The moment they were fairly buried in the water the old man clasped his hands together, and said :—

" Blessed be the tide that will break over and bury ye for ever ! Sad to mariners and sorrowful to maids and mothers, has the time been you have choked up this deep and bonny bay. For evil were you sent, and for evil have you continued. Every season finds from you its song of sorrow and wail, its funeral processions and its shrouded corses. Woe to the land where the wood grew that made ye ! cursed be the axe that hewed thee on the mountains ! the hands that joined ye together ! and the bay ye first swam in ! and the wind that wafted ye here ! Seven times have ye put my life in peril, three fair sons have ye swept from my side, and two bonnie grand bairns; and now, even now, your waters foam and flash for more victims. I see by that ripple and that foam, and hear by the sound and singing of the surge, that ye yearn for another :—I recollect when I was but a boy then groping trout in Ellenwater—that it was on such a day as this, some fifty years ago, that the Buxom Bess of Saint Bees, was wrecked on that spot, o'er the top of which the tide is whirling and boiling,—and the father and three brethren of Randal Forster were drowned. How can I forget such a sea ? It leaped on the shore among these shells and pebbles, as high as the mast of a brig; and threw its foam as far as the corn ricks of Walter Selby's stack yard,—and that a good half mile." " I'se warrant," interrupted a squat and demure old man, whose speech was a singular mixture of Cumbrian, English and Border Scotch,—" I'se warrant, Willie, your memory will be rifer o' the lovely lass of Annanwater, who whomel'd keel up ard, on the hip of the Mermaid rock, and split her rare wameful of brandy into the thankless Solway. Faith mickle good liquor has been thrown into that punch-bowl; but find a drop of grog was ever made out of such a thriftless basin. It will aiblins be long afore such a gude send comes to our coast again. There was Saunders Macdonald, was drunk between yule and yule—for by—" " Waes me, well may I remember that duleful day," interrupted the former speaker ; " it cost me a fair son, my youngest and my best—I had seven once—alas ! what have I now—three were devoured by that false and unstable water, three perished by the sharp swords of those Highland invaders,—who slew so many of the gallant Dacres and Selbys at Clifton and Carlisle—but the Cumberland ravens had their revenge! I mind the head and yellow hair of him who slew my Richard, hanging over the Scottish gate of Carlisle. Aye, I was avenged no doubt. But the son I have left has disgraced for ever the pure blood of the Selbys, by wedding a border Gordon, with as mickle gipsy blood in her veins as would make plebeians of all the Howards and Percies. I would rather have stretched him in the church ground of Allanbay, with the mark of a Heilandman's brand on his brow, as was the lot of his brave brothers; or gathered his body from among these rocks, as I did those of my other children ! But oh, sirs, when did man witness so fearful a coming-on as yon dark sky forbodes."

While this conversation went on, the clouds had assembled on the summits of the Scottish and Cumbrian mountain, and a thick canopy of them, which hung over the Isle of Man, waxed more ominous and vast. A light, as of a fierce fire burning, dropt frequent from its bosom, throwing a sort of supernatural flame along the surface of the water, and showing distinctly the haven, and houses, and shipping, and haunted Castle of the Isle. The old men sat silently gazing on the scene, while cloud succeeded cloud, till the whole congregating vapour, unable to sustain itself longer, stooped suddenly down from the opposing peaks of Criffel and Skiddaw, filling up the mighty space between the mountains, and approaching so close to the bosom of the ocean, as to leave room alone for the visible flight of the seamew and cormorant.

The waterfowl, starting from the sea, flew landward in a flock, fanning the waves with their wings, and uttering that wild and piercing scream, which distinguishes them from all other fowls, when their haunts are disturbed. The clouds and darkness increased, and the birds on the rock, the cattle in the fold, and the fishermen on the beach, all looked upward and seaward, expecting the coming of the storm.

"William Maxwell," said the old fisherman, as he approached his side, and stood gazing on the sea, "I counsel thee, youth, to go home, and shelter these young hairs beneath the castle roof. The mountains have covered their heads—and hearken, too,—that hollow moan running among the cliffs! There is a voice of mourning goes along the sea-cliffs of Solway before she swallows up the seafaring man. Seven times have I heard that warning voice in one season, and it cries, Woe to the wives and the maids of Cumberland!"

The experienced mariners on the Scottish and Cumbrian coasts appeared busy, mooring and double mooring their vessels. Some sought a securer haven, and those who allowed their barks to remain, prepared them, with all their skill, for the encounter of a storm, which no one reckoned distant.

The sea presented one wide sheet of foam, with here and there a dark object driven like the ocean weed upon the waters. Night now closed in upon them and the rain poured down in torrents; it blew a perfect hurricane; the scud drove furiously across the sky, while now and then the broken beams of an angry moon darted on the ocean a wild and scattered light from under dense masses of the blackest clouds, which sped athwart the heavens as if bent on some message of destruction; the waves rolled mountains high, and dashed with wild impetuosity upon the rocks, roaring in thunder as they approached the shore. Gun after gun was fired, but at such a distance that they despaired of being useful.

They knew not how or whither to direct their efforts, but stood close together, trying to resist the force of the tempest, and endeavouring to catch any sound that might guide them to the scene of distress, when the report of a gun was again heard much nearer; the flash pointed out her position, but nothing could yet be seen.

The storm came more heavily, and vivid lightnings rent the dark clouds; then, when the glaring flash threw its stream of awful splendour on the feathery foam, that fated ship was seen struggling with the waves, like the soul of the mighty struggling with despair. Another gun—and yet another—but help was hopeless. From the shore no assistance could be given, every attempt to get through the raging surf was useless; and the brave fishermen were compelled to be sad spectators of the scene.

The ship rode heavily as the long rolling waves came foaming in, and the streaming lightning flashed so vividly, and so frequently, that the wide and agitated expanse of Solway was visible from side to side—from St. Bees to Barnhourie. A very heavy rain, mingled with hail, succeeded; and a wind accompanied it, so fierce, and so high, that the white foam of the sea was showered as thick as snow on the summit of Caerlaverock castle. Through this perilous sea, and amid the darkness and tempest, the ship was observed coming swiftly down the middle of the sea. The carry, as it is called, of the tempest was direct from St. Bees to Caerlaverock; and those on shore could see that the vessel would be driven full on the fatal shores of the Scottish side, but the lightning was so fierce that few dared look on the approaching ship, or take measures for endeavouring to preserve the lives of the unfortunate mariners.

Still onward she came through the hissing foam. Still onward she urged her desperate course, till a tremendous crash, a loud yell—proclaimed that her stout timbers were shattered, and many a stouter heart was buried in the waves.

The ship had struck on the part of the shore where the rocks were steepest; and the wreck remained wedged in firmly between two craggy knolls not more than one hundred fathom from perfect safety. But even that was a fearful space; for the heavy breakers rolled over the sunken rocks, and dashed with wild fury. Body after body came on the surge, and was throw upon the land; but life had fled, and no effort could restore animation to the mangled and disfigured corpses.

The lightning still flashed vivid and fast, and the storm raged with unabated fury; for between the ship and the shore, the sea broke in frightful undulations, and the waves leaped on the greensward several fathoms deep abreast.

The ship still continued grinding between the rocks, and victim after victim was hurried into eternity. At length, part of a mast, with several seamen clinging to it, was seen floating from the wreck, and lifted by a mountain surge clear over the craggy rocks. Another wave came rolling in; but just before it reached them, it raised its awful crest, and with a tremendous roar, like the famished panther when seizing his prey, dashed furiously upon their heads. They were seen for a few moments hurled confusedly amongst the bubbling eddies, and then disappeared.

The vessel bore for a time the fury of the elements, but a strong wind came suddenly upon her, and, crushing her between the wave and the freestone bank, drove her further in upon the rocks. Then was seen upon her deck the figure of a girl kneeling to Heaven for supplication, while a man stood by her side; the next moment the two were seen buffeting the waves, which rolled landward as far as the place where the fishermen stood; one large wave threw them fiercely upon the beach, and the men sprung forward, exclaiming, "They're saved! They're saved!" Graham received but little injury, and upon recovering his senses he perceived the insensible form of Susan in the arms of Miles Lawson; she lay so still and pale that at first his heart died within him; he thought she was gone for ever.

"Don't be afeared, sir," said the old fisherman, as Susan uttered a faint sigh: "don't be afeared. Her cheek is a little pale or so; but my auld woman 'll soon bring the colour intill it again. Bless her auld heart she's a famous doctor!"

"Hout, hout, ye'll a' mad thegither," said a young woman; "ye'll be a' long ganging to the castle, and the puir lass maun have speedy succour. My house is here: see the door's open—a warm fire's glowing on the floor. I'll make my ain son, start out of his ain warm bed; and we'll just pop the puir half-drowned creature intill't. Auld Nannie here will help me; there's no the like of her in the land for handling ailing folk; and ye can jist send us something nourishing frae the castle."

"For Heaven's sake, be quick, my friends," said Graham, "and you shall be handsomely rewarded for your trouble."

"Reward, sir!" replied the woman, "I look for no reward for doing my duty. Mair's the luck, there's a gude fire in the house; bring in here the puir lass."

In half an hour, thanks to blankets, hot water, and Hollands, Susan was in a quiet and placid slumber; and Lawson and Graham, accompanied by young Maxwell, after having fortified themselves with a glass of good Schiedam, hastened again to the beach. The storm was still raging in all its fury; lights were flashing along the shore, and parties of men were running up and down—some in search of plunder, others with the more benevolent wish to afford assistance in rescuing from the waves aught valuable that might be thrown ashore, to restore to the rescued Graham. The beach was strewed with broken spars and ship timber, and every now and then the fisherman's light flashed upon a dead body laying extended partly on the sand and partly in the water. As they were hurrying along, Graham stumbled, and nearly fell, over something hard, which he could not distinguish in the darkness, the fisherman being some paces a-head of him with the lantern. He stooped down and found it was the casket, which he had brought with him from America, by the side of it lay a bag well filled with Spanish dollars, and around lay the fragments of his chest.

He uttered an exclamation of joy upon finding these treasures, which brought the old fisherman to his side with the light, and who now for the first time looked steadily in the face of Graham. He took him by the arm, and again fixing his eye upon his face said:—"Your name is—"

"Adams!" replied Graham suddenly, and then looked confused, and seemed to know not what to say next, as he recognised the features of an old dependant of his fathers.

The acute observation of Miles Lawson would have detected a much better attempt to deceive him than this; and as he possessed an uncommon boldness of character, he now looked him full in the face, and said, " Do you think, sir, to deceive me ? or that I, who was born on the very estate that should have called you master, do not know a Graham? I know the family features as well as I know my own face. Let me see but one of their kindred in the most distant corner of the globe, and their air of pride, their haughty, unbending brow, their eye that, in the soberest of them all, could not be mistaken, I could tell a Graham, even if I looked upon him as he lay coffined in the earth, by the very form and size of his bones."

" If you know so well who I am good man," said Graham, " you cannot be ignorant that I have no desire to make my name so public, as you would seem to think, by thus loudly repeating it. Take this and be silent," and Graham offered him a handful of dollars from the bag.

" No!" said Miles Lawson, rejecting the proffered money, " No! you are the first of your name, that ever offered Miles Lawson a reward for secrecy. I can keep a silent tongue to serve him, whom these aged arms have so often carried in years bygone. Hark ye, Malcolm Graham, I know more of your affairs than you may think I do, Take my advice, and do not linger here, I know that there's a reward lately offered for the Pirate Graham, who has committed some ravages on the coast of America in company with a pirate still more notorious. This information has been communicated to the government, by Captain Elliott, the son of Lord Dalwinston; and the result is that the reward has been offered for your apprehension. Your family estates are now in the possession of Lady Helen Maxwell, your mother's sister, and whose youngest son stands there ;—you might be safe here for a short time, but still suspicion would be created—therefore take my advice and quit Caerlaverock at once."

CHAPTER IV.

" Sweet Auburn! loveliest village of the plain,
Where health and plenty cheer'd the labouring swain,
Where smiling Spring its earliest visit paid,
And parting Summer's lingering bloom delay'd.
Dear, lovely bowers of innocence and ease."
                                        GOLDSMITH.
" A stranger ! say'st thou ? Is she young and fair?

IN a remote corner of the beautiful county of Northumberland, at no great distance from the river Tyne, stands one of those picturesque and unassuming mansions, which, more perhaps than any other class of buildings that are to be found within the compass of the four seas, give their peculiar character of civilization and refinement to almost every English landscape. The traveller who may chance to visit that part of the country to which it is the ornament, will not fail, if he keeps his eyes open, to recognise it. Thrown back from the bank of the stream so far, that by him who stands upon the lawn the brawling of the water will scarce be heard, the house lifts its modest head just beneath the slope of the hill: a small portion of which being included in the globe, and tastefully planted, forms a background to the little scene, which can be rightly estimated only after it has been seen. In front, and sloping down towards the water, are the lawn, the shrubbery, and the kitchen-garden, all of them fenced in by well-trimmed hedges, and each separated from the other by screens of laurestinas.

At a short distance from the mansion, and on the road which led to Allendale, stood a neatly white-washed cottage, known as the village inn, by the painted sign-board suspended from a post near the door. It was at this inn, late in the evening, that three travellers arrived, the one a tall man, enveloped in a large cloak, who evidently sought to conceal his features, he was accompanied by a beautiful young girl, and an old man, apparently a seaman.

Their uncommon appearance could not fail of attracting universal attention among the rustics who had assembled in the tap room, among whom had lately arrived a pedlar from the city of York, who suggested to the inquisitive hostess, that they might be suspicious characters, and "Indeed," said the pedlar, "who knows but what that tall man may be the pirate, for whom I hear there is a handsome reward offered."

"Very likely, good Mr. Pedlar," replied the hostess, "very likely that a pirate should come to my house. I suppose you would have me go and inform the Squire, that I have a suspicious character in my house, because a party of travellers happen to stop for the night?"

"God forbid!" ejaculated Black Will the pedlar, in something of a hypocritical tone of sanctity—"Only, as I was observing just now, you had better just inquire something about your customers."

"And where would ye have my husband enquire?" exclaimed the hostess. "Would ye have him go to the market-place of Newcastle, and proclaim to the good people that he has got a world of custom, and, like a fool, does not know how to make the best use of it? It is seldom I trow we have so much to do, that we need turn money away, because we don't like the look of the customers."

"Peace! peace! my dear," said her husband, afraid that, in her zeal for the new comers, she should offend the pedlar—who added to his profession the character of smuggler, and often supplied the landlord with contraband spirits. "Will means all for our good; he is only fearful we should lose by harbouring suspicious people."

"Just so, just so, Christy; and I have something else to tell you, which will prove I don't want you to lose a chance of getting money, as your wife seems to think. Suppose you to find that out this man is the pirate, as I hear he has left America, it is supposed for his own home in Scotland. Suppose, I say, it was so, and you were to give him up to the magistrate of the county; then, my good fellow, what a handsome sum you might gain by way of reward," said the pedlar, with significant shrewdness, as if well convinced of his own superior sagacity in the method of getting money.

"And so you would have my husband turn informer, and give up the man, upon the supposition that he is a pirate! No, no, William Amos; though we are poor, yet we would scorn to get rich in such a pitiful way—no, should we be mistaken in the man, what character should we have from our neighbours? our house would be deserted and we should be ruined—no, no, he shall never do such a villanous action while I am Margaret Christy," said the hostess, with decisive vehemence, in which her husband himself seconded her, to the no small mortification of Black Will, who walked off, after having bid them beware how they entertained those who had not the means of paying for what they ordered. "At all events," he added, "be certain that they have money."

Upon this hint from the pedlar, Mrs. Christy thought it advisable to have a consultation with her husband, as they had frequently been taken in by less suspicious looking guests. The very small portion of luggage with which they were provided, occurred to her, and she felt convinced that their departure had been suddenly undertaken; it likewise tended to increase the suspicions created by Black Will, and, in her judgment, it not only bespoke scanty finances, but likewise precluded every hope of indemnification by other means, should pecuniary deficiencies render the dentention of their trunk a necessary measure.

Mrs. Christy, from the preceding conversation, might have been considered a charitable woman, and was so considered by the villagers; but they were entirely mistaken in her real character, for she was selfish in the extreme, and only appeared charitable to preserve the custom of the house.

Having duly scanned over the apparent circumstances of her guest, she proceeded to enumerate the incalculable losses sustained on similar occasions by the easy temper of a husband, who, but for her interposition would speedily ruin both his poor wife and child, by that eternal and nonsensical propensity to assist others at the expense of his own interest.

Christy, who was really a worthy fellow, had been too long and too well accustomed to what is vulgarly styled petticoat government, to think of contesting the matter with a woman of so selfish a disposition; he therefore, usually let her

talk on without interruption, and not venturing to increase the evil by open opposition, generally contrived to practise in private what he dared not speak when humanity called upon his exertions in its favour.

The result of this consultation was, therefore, if the strangers were not well supplied with cash, to clear the house of its present guests without delay.

Her husband swallowed a glass of rum and water, in silence and tacitly acquiesced in her sentiments, though resolved to counteract them, if they militated too much against the feelings of his own honest heart when put in execution.

No. 3.

Determined to commence her operations with caution, lest the supposed adventurers should prove quality in disguise, and the biter be bit, a circumstance which had more than once occurred before the present juncture, Mrs. Christy repaired at once to the room occupied by the strangers, and, opening the door, frequested to know if anything was wanted, at the same time glancing her eye upon the table, upon which lay a bag apparently well filled with coin ; her countenance underwent an instantaneous change.

The stranger immediately upon the entrance of the hostess, rose from his seat, advanced towards her, and taking her in the passage enquired if she could direct him to a respectable boarding-school, as he wished to place his daughter with a person competent to complete her education.

This information was furnished by Mrs. Christy, who having received orders for the evening meal withdrew.

On the following morning, the stranger accompanied by the young girl, made their appearance at the boarding school of Miss Glenroy, the mansion described at the commencement of this chapter.

Upon Miss Glenroy entering the parlour, he immediately addressed her, saying that he wished to place his daughter under her care to complete her education.

"You will find her untutored," he remarked, "for she had no mother to watch over her infancy, and I fear she has been sadly neglected, as my avocations have been such that I could not keep her with me."

There was something in the appearance of the girl, which insensibly interested Miss Glenroy, and she assured him, that every attention should be paid to his daughter.

"I leave her entirely to you, madam," replied the stranger. "My habits are so desultory, that it is impossible for me to say when I can have her with me. I have now brought her from America, where she has been residing with an aged nurse, who has totally neglected her education. Indeed so much so, that I was obliged to bring her to England, to learn those accomplishments, which are so necessary for a girl of her station in life. I am now about returning immediately to America, and it is probable that I shall not be able to see you again for some years, I will, therefore, pay you for the first two years in advance, and at the end of that time, if I should not be here, I will send you an order for any additional expense that may be incurred during that period, and after it has expired. It is my wish, madam, that my daughter shall have every advantage your establishment affords."

Preliminaries were speedily settled, and the daughter of the stranger (Susan Adams) was received as a pupil in the school.

Susan soon became a general favourite among her companions, but there was one among them who claimed her most devoted friendship.

Edith was the only daughter of General Trevanion, who was by birth, by education, in sentiment, in principle, in person, in manner, in all his habits, a Scotchman. Cautious and prudent, slow to adopt an opinion yet inflexible in his support of it, the rigid notions that he entertained of honour and morality caused him to condemn and, where he possessed the power, to punish with unrelenting severity, any infringement of duty, or dereliction from virtue. Yet Trevanion, with all his peculiarities, was brave and generous, sincere and scrupulously just. He had very early in life entered the British army, where his invariable good conduct, and skill in military tactics raised him, before he had attained the age of fifty, to the rank of general. He married an English lady, of tolerable fortune, which with the economy that he had always observed in his expenditure, enabled him, not long after his arrival at this last step of promotion, to retire from the army, and devote himself to the quiet enjoyment of domestic life.

With this intention, he had chosen a comfortable cottage, near Allendale, directly opposite to the residence of the Glenroys. It was of pure white with corresponding wings on either side, shadowed by two imperial elms, and looking down upon a sloping lawn, of a verdure so deep and bright, it recalled the evangelical description of those sweet fields "beyond the swelling flood," arrayed in living green. The living green was again dazzlingly contrasted by a neat railing of the same spotless hue as the mansion, which marked the enclosure, and at the same time shut out the encroaching cattle. But the most graceful feature in this rural habitation was an artificial drapery of green lattice work, arranged in regular festoons around the piazza, and so much resembling the inter-wreathing tendrils of the vine that gamboled about the columns which supported it, it was somewhat difficult to separate the work of nature and art.

Here General Trevanion lived in a mode of unsocial seclusion which might have been found irksome and dull, had not the incessant toil and hazard and fatigue of his former life, given a zest, by force of contrast, to his present state of comparative solitude.

Edith Trevanion, at the period of Susan's introduction to the school, had just attained the age of sixteen ; her figure was tall, and her deportment graceful; but a finely arched brow, an open forehead, and a placid smile, that ever hovered on her lip, constituted the only charms of a countenance possessing more of intelligence than beauty, Her disposition was a softened resemblance of her father's; his obstinacy, was in her perseverance ; his pride, her-self-respect ; the power which he felt gratified in exercising over others, she exerted to command herself; he was violent and implacable in his animosities, she was constant and devoted in her attachments.

Two years of happy tranquility flew rapidly away. Susan, under the tuition of Miss Glenroy, aided by Edith's patient co-operation, had attained to a tolerable complement of knowledge of polite accomplishments ; she could paint prettily, and in all the lighter branches of education was well skilled. In music and singing she transcendently excelled ; and her taste and execution in both called forth the enthusiastic commendation of her teachers. She was of an obliging temper and amiable disposition, that could not fail to endear her to every one with whom she associated. To Edith, in particular, she was an object of the most unbounded affection ; the predilection which the former had conceived on their first meeting, had ripened into a firm and everlasting attachment, and having no home of her own to go to, she spent her vacations with her friend.

The two years had expired, and Susan began to look forward for the return of her father, but he came not, and she could not help wondering at his silence, even in not writing to her.

Edite Trevanion was to return to school no more, and she was anticipating with eager delight her introduction into society.

" I wonder if ever father thinks of me !" said Susan to her friend Edith. " I remember the kiss he gave me when he left me here. When he turned away there was a tear on my forehead. That tear comforts me now, amidst all his neglect. It tells me he had for me a parent's feeling ; and often I dream he is again clasping me to his heart, and that hot tear falling on my brow. Edith, you cannot know how desolate I sometimes feel."

Edith threw her arms round her friend's neck, and kissed away the tear that slowly rolled over her cheek, as she said,—" Dear Susan ! while I live you can never feel the want of a friend."

"Never, I hope. Were your friendship to fail me, Edith, I should be lost indeed.'

CHAPTER V.

"This world has not a feeling given,
　　So holy or so fair,
So like the intercourse in heaven,
　　Which blessed spirits share.
As those sweet friendships which entwine
　　Young kindred hearts around,
And make an earthly Eden shine
　　In home's delightful bound."—
STRICKLAND.

IT was a bright evening in autumn ; one of those glorious sun-sets where the rich tints of the western clouds seem to throw into still broader beauty the varying colours of the forest foliage, and to clothe the earth in a panoply of splendour :— It was not one of those still and noiseless evenings, whose almost death-like silence fills the mind with a feeling resembling awe, if not awe itself; when the heart ashamed of its own emotion amid such an unearthly calm, yields to the dreamy softness of the scene—or, wretched and repining itself, quarrels with the rebuking calm, and

"To stillness gives
The cold, harsh names of brutal apathy."

No! it was an evening the very reverse of such an one. It was like life, all change—half hope—half fear—mingling and mixing, till it would have been difficult to tell which had the mastery. It seemed formed to delight :

"Who would not view
The green earth always green,
Or the blue sky always blue ?"

The bustle of the day was over, but the birds were not weary yet of singing ; the labourer whistled as he sought his humble but happy home ; the mother sat at her cottage door, singing to the crowing baby in her lap ; and the merry children laughed and shouted as they joined in the animated game, or chased each other in the fields.

The scene was beautiful—a cone-like hill, feathered even to its summit with stately trees ; clumps of ash and elm, majestic oaks stretching their wide and shadowy arms far across the green sward, and groups of the weeping birch waving in the wind its fragile and feathery boughs—here and there a stately chesnut tree, broad and bright in the sinking light—and at intervals a trembling aspen turning up the snowy lining of its leaves to the breeze in which they shivered; this was the rich background of the picture ; while on either side a stately park swept far into the distance, its soft undulations of surface, relieving and deluding the eye into the belief that it was of almost boundless extent.

The house stood, or rather nestled, under the shadow of the hill ; it was a square, solid, substantial structure of stone, undistinguished by any beauty of design, or architectural elaboration. A broad flight of steps led up to the principal entrance, and the wide doors fell back so vastly as to impart an heir of stateliness even to their simplicity. Involuntarily, as the eye rested upon Hexham Hall, the mind, in seeking to pourtray its days of ancient splendour, reverted to other and earlier times ; and the impression was a correct one ; where herds of stately deer had once swept through the sunny glades, or clustered in the shadows of the tall trees ; flocks of sheep, and groups of cows now browsed quietly on the sweet herbage ; and the curious eye might detect through many a vista, patches of corn ripe for the sickle, and small stretches of land whereon were reared clover, and other crops calculated to supply food for cattle. These were, indeed, skilfully fenced off from the main park, and so disposed as to be altogether invisible from the house, though on traversing the road which led to it, and which, although partially bordered by chesnut and beech trees, was yet too open at intervals to be strictly denominated an avenue, the eye rested occasionally on the rich corn-patches which stood out, gay and golden, in striking relief from the fresh grass-land by which they were surrounded. As it neared the house the road wound abruptly through a thick shrubbery of evergreens, its direct line being broken by a small lake, upon whose surface floated a pair of majestic swans, while patches of the undulating lotus opened their waxen blossoms to the light, upborne upon their leafy canopy, and the banks were fringed by pensile willows, and the most rare and beautiful flowering shrubs.

Such was the scene to which the last touch of beauty was supplied by the appearance of two figures, that suddenly emerged from the shelter of the dense shrubbery to which allusion has already been made, and stood out in the rich light upon the margin of the lake. They were those of two females, the elder of which was Griselda, the daughter of Sir Reginald Willoughby, the owner of the mansion.

To this young lady nature had been somewhat niggard of her bounties; but fortune, as if to indemnify her for the parsimony of her rival, lavished upon her her golden gifts. Independent of the reversion of her father's unencumbered wealth, she was the heiress of an opulent maiden aunt, and well had she earned the dowry, by bearing the rueful name of Griselda, in honour of her relative.

Her companion, Alice Cameron, was her cousin, and exceedingly beautiful; she was an orphan, and a ward of Sir Reginald Willoughby's. She had just finished her education, in the fashionable sense of the expression: that is, was just released from a fashionable boarding school, and received as a future inmate of the family.

Griselda Willoughby had hoped to be safely reposing in the myrtle shade of courtship before this formidable rival should enter the lists for public admiration. But she saw the myrtle leaves waving around without offering to shelter her with their perennial verdure, and was doomed to see this junior beauty a fixture in her household, whose personal attractions might justify the fear she entertained of a personal eclipse.

What kind of a spirit animated this lovely mixture of earth's mould, may be better understood from her own conversation and deportment, than from the most studied description.

"My dear Griselda," said Alice, "when shall we have those delightful riding and sailing parties, you have so often described as so pastoral and romantic? I begin to be tired of this monotony, and long for some excitement, some interesting event, to break in on the provoking sameness of our every-day existence."

"Why, this is a sudden fit of ennui, Alice," exclaimed Griselda, "it is no later than last evening, on this self-same spot, I heard you talking in raptures to Herbert Glenroy, of the charms of a country life. But I suppose there *is* more excitement when your companion is a handsome young man, instead of your humble cousin."

"You may spare your sarcasms, Grizzy," replied Alice, who, when displeased, always addressed her in this manner; "you, who have such boisterous spirits, can make no allowance for the alteration of feeling, to which persons of sensibility are ever subject. They are happy without knowing wherefore, and sad without knowing why. The shades of sensibility are too delicate to be analysed, at least by the vulgar eye."

"I hope you would not insinuate that *my* eye is vulgar," retorted her cousin, "it does not require a microscopic vision to discover that you are happy when Herbert Glenroy is near, and dispirited when he is absent. Can you deny it, my fair sensitive coz?"

"I scorn to deny what there is no shame in acknowledging," said Alice assuming the dignity of a Minna Troil, when avowing her love for the Pirate Cleveland; "I do admire Herbert Glenroy. He is so different from the poor working mortals of the present day, he is one of those ethereal beings"—

"I don't know what you call ethereal, Alice," interrupted Griselda, "but I am sure he doesn't live upon air. He did ample justice to our roasted turkey and plum pudding the other day, and he likes a good glass of wine in the bargain."

"I am astonished at your coarseness, Grizzy," replied Alice, withdrawing her arm as she spoke, "you always come like a blighting mildew over the flowers of sentiment and feeling. But I shall soon learn to conceal every emotion in the deep foldings of my own heart."

"Well, do not be angry, my gentle coz, and I will promise to be more senti-mental in future. I do not think he eats more than is necessary for existence, or drinks wine but for the pleasure of drinking to you with his eyes, while he asks you to partake of the sparkling glass. Admire the brother as much as you please, but do not, if you love me, extend your admiration to the sister. If there is one girl I more cordially hate than another, it is Margaret Glenroy."

"You should not suffer your prejudices to be so violent, Griselda. I cannot say that I exactly like her myself; she is too self-possessed, too *unimpulsive*, if I may use the expression, to be congenial to my taste. But why you should *hate* her, I cannot imagine."

"There are a thousand reasons. I disliked her the first moment I saw her. She has such a look of conscious superiority; then she has constantly slighted all my attentions—condescensions, I might call them, considering the vast difference in our situations, for if they were not very poor, she would never have engaged in the mean employment of school-keeping, yet she carries herself with such an air, when she walks through the town with her train of pupils, you would think it was some princess with her retinue. I wonder her brother permitted her to undertake such a thing, he is so very proud. Then there is Mrs. Trevanion, who has always been cold to me, treats her with such marked distinction; constantly inviting her to her house, presenting her books, and vaunting her talents to her friends, in short, making as much fuss about her, as if, to speak frankly, she had my wealth or *your* beauty to boast of."

"Oh! Griselda, I am sure she is handsome, and then her younger sister, the sweet Constance, is a perfect angel."

"She might be an interesting child, if everybody didn't spoil her, by making such an idol of her. Her family make themselves ridiculous by it. Indeed, they think too much of each other ever to care much about anybody else. Don't blush so angrily, Alice, I can't help speaking the truth at least. They are too selfish, too shockingly domestic. But see—whose carriage can that be that glitters through the shady trees? It is a very stylish one."

The carriage, whose approach interrupted this edifying conversation, was evidently a travelling equipage, from the dark colour of the body, and the trunks lashed on behind; and it was evident that it was occupied by persons of conse-quence, from the brilliancy of its rich ornaments, and the two out-riders which preceded the carriage. As it passed they could discern the figures of two females, the one young and beautiful, and the other an elderly female, apparently her mother.

"Who can they be?" exclaimed Miss Willoughby, with irresistible curiosity, "I am sure they must be travellers of distinction. Did you see any gentleman in the carriage? Oh! here comes Dr. Rovington, perhaps he can tell us who they are."

The gentleman in question opened the gate and sauntered up the steps, with an air of easy familiarity and indifference, which marks the security of the consciously welcome guest.

Griselda, in her eagerness to pursue her inquiries, ran down the steps to meet him.

"Doctor, do you know whose carriage passed you? Did you see the lady? Was she young? Was she pretty?" were questions which assailed him in one breath.

"I know one thing," replied the doctor drily, "that a pair of young bright eyes sparkled on me, from the carriage, and they dazzled me so I could not see any thing else distinctly."

"Were her eyes," said Alice "of the light azure of sunny day, or the deep blue of starry night."

"I could no more tell their colour," answered the doctor, "than that of a shooting star. They were bright and heavenly, but they're passed."

"They certainly resembled a shooting star, in one respect," said Miss Willoughby who prided herself upon her brilliant repartees, " they reflected their rays on a midnight expanse."

" Very good, Miss Willoughby, I owe you one ; but who do you think were the inmates of the carriage ?"

" I cannot tell, I'm sure ; if you know, doctor, tell us at once, and end all suspense ?"

" It is Lady Helen Maxwell and her daughter returning to their seat at Hexham," replied doctor Rovington.

" I am glad of that," exclaimed Alice, "now we shall have a little more life for I am heartily tired of this dull place."

CHAPTER VI.

His was the port—the distant mein—
That seems to shun the sight, and awes when seen ;
The solemn aspect, and the high-born eye,
*That checks low mirth, but lacks not courtesy.—*BYRON.

AND who was Herbert Glenroy, that *ethereal being* admired by the beautiful Alice Cameron !

Herbert Glenroy, to speak in the touching language of Scripture, "was the only son of his mother, and she a widow," he was, moreover, the only guardian of two orphan sisters. But let us not be so unjust to departed worth, as to introduce this interesting family without paying a passing tribute to the memory of that husband and father, who was, in the most emphatic sense, what Pope describes as the "noblest work of God."

He was the only son of a rich lawyer, and no sooner had he become possessed of the property of his father, which the law placed at his disposal at the death of his parent, then he left the land of his birth, in company with a gentleman of ancient family and considerable wealth—for whom, from his earliest childhood, he had always entertained the warmest affection.

This youth, whose name was Lovell, was by no means of an ordinary character. Gifted by nature with talents of the first order, he devoted himself to the improvement of them, and, unlike the generality of the English youth, employed the whole of his time, until he sailed for the continent, in intense and arduous application, not only to the accomplishments (as they might be called) of a literary education, but to the more difficult and abstruse studies necessary to philosophical investigation. He was left an orphan at an early age, and doubtless no small share of credit was due to his maternal uncle, a gentleman of distinguished eminence in the learned world, under whose care and superintendence he acquired the larger portion of his information.

The companions were well suited for each other ; the enthusiastic and head-strong disposition of Glenroy received a salutary check in the more sedate, though not less ardent, mind of his friend Lovell ; while the unsuspecting ingenuousness of the latter (originating in his trifling intercourse with the world) was shielded from harm by the observing, or rather more initiated, character of the formed.

Very contrary to his intention, or expectation, at the expiration of the third year, Reuben Glenroy surrendered up his liberty into the hands of a fair enemy, whom he encountered in France of English family, but who was induced by peculiar circumstances, to reside with some distant relatives in the neighbourhood of Paris.

After spending another year in an excursion through the varied attractions of Italy and Spain, he returned with his lovely wife to England, and Lovell was left to continue his travels alone.

Repeated assurances of his happiness were transmitted by Glenroy to his friend, who now located himself in Italy, where for two years he resisted innumerable solicitations to return to England. The reason, however, for this apparent obduracy was sufficient; for, at the expiration of that time, he married an Italian lady of some family and great beauty.

The two friends now seemed to be completely sundered; as the wife of Lovell was entirely unwilling ever to leave her native land, and as the affection of her devoted husband was two ardent to endure even the thought of a separation. Their happiness, however, was of short duration; Mrs. Lovell died in giving birth to her first child, and the afflicted man, leaving his infant in the charge of the only sister of his wife, fled from scenes, the associations with which were beyond measure torturing to his wounded spirit.

Receiving continual account of the health and prosperity of his son, and having his grief soothed by the affectionate attention of his friends in England, he protracted his stay there, much longer than he had intended; while an accession to the family of Glenroy, of a daughter, (named Margaret, in memory of the departed wife of Lovell) tended to strengthen the bonds which were already too powerful to be broken.

Living in the most unreserved intercourse with his friend's family, it was natural that he should contract the sincerest affection for all its members, but more especially for the amiable Mrs. Glenroy, with whose society in France he had been particularly pleased, and who, in former days, had been acquainted with his beloved Margaret. He continued to reside with them for several years, and used every endeavour to seduce the affections of the wife from her husband, who continued in the closest friendship with one who was using every method to injure him. Lovell had induced him to speculate largely to improve his fortune, but he was unsuccessful and almost ruined himself through listening to the false advice of his friend; he was obliged to borrow a large sum of a friend to meet the demands of his creditors, and after satisfying them, he was reduced to absolute poverty. Lovell continued his overtures to his friend's wife, and urged her to fly from poverty to wealth, she spurned him from her, and disclosed to her husband the villany of his friends.

The astonished Glenroy sought a meeting with this cold-blooded and deliberate villain; but he fled from England, not daring to hazard a rencontre with one whom he had so greatly injured.

Through the influence of his friends, Glenroy procured a situation of high public trust at Newcastle, by which he was once more enabled to support his family, nearly in the same style and comfort which they had formerly enjoyed; and, thinking that the years of our pilgrimage are few and short, he wished his resting place from the turmoils of business to be somewhat aloof from the gay and encroaching many. To him Allendale appeared at Eden, without one trace of the primeval curse; but he was driven from it, not by the flaming sword of justice, but by the cold hand of death. By one of those dark Providences, which must ever be inscrutable to human penetration, he was suddenly snatched away in the unwasted vigour of his manhood, and meridian of his usefulness.

The salary, which had afforded him a liberal support, ceased at his death; and as he had no real estate, independent of his house at Allendale, which he had purchased several years after he had obtained his lucrative situation, he left his widow dowerless, and his children portionless, save the portion of an honoured name, and the inheritance of an irreproachable example.

The ruddy bloom and sunny brightness of adolescence, still mantled on the cheek and revelled in the eye of Herbert Glenroy, when he was invested with such sacred responsibilities. Passing through a cloudless boyhood, the conscious object of pride, hope and affection, his character had never been tested by that ordeal, through which, if it had no other influence than developing the latent energies of man, the pilgrims of earth should unmurmuring pass.

The friends of the widowed Mrs. Glenroy doubly compassionated her, that she was left with so oppressive a charge as the education of a wild impetuous youth, just placed in the very heart of temptation, though it were the cherishing bosom of the most venerable Alma Mater of our country. They knew not the mine whose yet unfathomed treasures were to pour their lustre to the day, and unlike the dark caverns of nature, which remain chill and unenlightened while they lavish their gems upon the world, was destined to feel the reflection of all the beams it imparted.

Had no unusual solemnity attended the circumstance of this bereavement—had he merely lost a father, however venerated, it is probable that after the stunning

effect of the blow was past, his feelings might have rebounded from the pressure, with the usual elasticity of his age. But a circumstance occurred, which had as commanding an influence as if the voice of his dead parent had addressed him from beneath the sods of the valley. While he was examining some of his own papers which he had left in his father's secretary when he entered the university,

No. 4.

he found a sealed letter, directed to himself, in characters now more than ever sacred in his eyes. With a strange feeling of awe and curiosity he broke the seal and read, what we may be pardoned for transcribing at length, as it has so important a connexion with the history we are relating :—

"My beloved, my only Son,—I am ill; my friends believe it a transient indisposition, but though the cold fingers now only gently touch me, I feel that it is the hand of death. Something whispers that you will soon be summoned to the bedside of a dying father, to receive the holiest trust that ever devolved upon a poor untried boy like thee—the guardianship of such a mother and two young orphan sisters. Herbert, as you hope for an inheritance in the kingdom of heaven, be faithful to this trust. As you hope to lay your head in peace, on the death-pillow I soon may press, remember my parting words. But it is not alone to give you this solemn injunction I triumph over the weakness of disease, and trace these trembling lines. An event, which took place some years back, I am about to leave in your confidence, as it may hereafter have consequences of weight. Through the advice of a false friend, Richard Lovell, I was induced to enter into speculations, which entirely failed, and they brought me to the brink of ruin. Poverty, and its most appalling attendances, appeared in dark perspective. I could not break your mother's heart by telling her that I was undone; but I disclosed the secret to a friend, who had ever been to me as a brother. The sum of five thousand pounds, lent me in a timely hour, by that kind friend, rescued me from unknown miseries. This benefactor is Mr. Henry Montford, whose son is now your class-mate and companion. The salary received for my labours has liberally supported my family, and that is all. I have never been able to refund the debt; but whenever I spoke of it he turned from the subject, and avowed his determination never to demand it, promising the same on behalf of his son after his own decease. He is now on the continent. In a few years his son will be of age, for he is much your senior. I know not that he is the heir of his father's virtues, but I fear he is mercenary. Should Mr. Montford be taken from his family, and Charles, upon his majority, demand his due, I cannot give another pang to your mother, in addition to those she must soon bear. She knows it not. To you, my son, young as you are, I confide the honour of my name and everything dependant on a link, which has never yet been tarnished. Should evil days come when I am low in the dust, which God in his mercy avert, be thou, my son, all, and far more than thy father would have been, had he been spared on earth. Sacrifice everything but integrity, for the sake of her who bore thee, and who loves thee with a love even passing a mother's fondness. Forsake everything but truth, rather than leave thy young sisters unprotected and alone. Keep together, my children, and may the home of your parents never be taken from you. Bind closer and closer the silver cord. Let filial devotion, strengthened and sanctified by Christian piety, be the directing, sustaining principle of your life. Shun the name of Lovell, and ever avoid the descendants of that false friend, who has so basely injured me. May everlasting blessings follow you, as you fulfil these solemn duties. Farewell Herbert, my dear, my noble boy. A divine voice assures me, that my last prayers are answered in thee. God for ever bless, as I now bless thee,

REUBEN GLENROY."

Herbert had been summoned from the university in accordance with the prophetic words of the letter, to the dying bed of his father, scarcely in time to witness, for the first time, the most affecting and grand of all earthly scenes, the transit of an immortal soul. The recollection of the last glance his parent had turned on him, so solemn and confiding, came back upon him with a sublimity and power almost supernatural. He remained long moveless and silent, his eyes rivetted on the contents of the paper, then, placing it in his bosom, he knelt down on the spot where he had perused it, and offered up his self-sacrificing vow to that Being whose omnipresence his spirit felt and acknowledged. "God of the widow—Father of the fatherless," continued he, "do thou bless or curse me, as I am true or false to this vow." He rose, and it seemed to him, that new energies or capacities were born with him—that he had gained the experience of years, in the moral discipline of that hour. When he returned to the university, his fellow students perceived that a "change had come over his spirit," and waited impatiently for the revival of that hilarity, which was the charm of their convivial meetings. But they waited in vain. His cheerfulness was gradually restored, but he henceforth lost all relish for the mere follies of youth. The bold wrestler, the untiring racer, the hero of the gymnasium, became the deep and indefatigable student, the successful competitor for the highest literary honours.

It is necessary here to record one circumstance, which happened a short time before his graduation. Since his return to college, his intercourse with Charles Montford, which had never been very endearing, partook of inevitable coolness and restraint. Conscious of the obligations which his father had laid him under to the elder Montford, Herbert was too proud to pay any additional court to one whose character he despised. Montford, on his part, began to dislike Herbert, for the superior influence he had acquired, notwithstanding his own superior wealth.

There was a pale, sickly youth in their class, a charity scholar, second only to Herbert in literary rank. This pale son of penury, was the object of Herbert's especial kindness and even respect; and was proportionally scorned and neglected by the purse-proud Montford. He had not only to contend with the ills of poverty, but the feebleness of hereditary disease; and often when Herbert saw the anxious blush on his sallow cheek, over the uncompleted task, he would assist him in its accomplishment, even at the hazard of slighting his own. In the gymnastic exercises, Herbert always managed to get near his feeble friend, to guard him from the rough sports of his more athletic companions. Once, as they were assembled on the large common, where they were accustomed to cultivate the rudiments of their constitution, while they gave relaxation to their minds, the protegée of Herbert chanced most unintentionally to exasperate the pride of Montford to such a pitch that he gave him a most cowardly blow. Herbert placed himself before his insulted friend, glowing with generous indignation.

"Dare not, Montford," he cried, "dare not to lift your hand a second time. Strike me if you will, but this young man shall be sacred from your insults."

At this honest rebuke, most of the students burst out in an applauding huzza.

"Glenroy for ever! He's the lad for my money! That's your sort. Huzza for Glenroy!"

Shouts like these grated most discordantly on Montford's ear; while the hats which they tossed in the air, came down on his head and shoulders like so many black crows, and he almost fancied he could hear their hideous cawing.

"Glenroy," muttered Montford, shaking his clenched fist at him, as he darted from the play ground, "remember you shall pay for this."

Herbert thought of his father's letter, but he could not repent. He had been true to his integrity, and he felt that he had forfeited no blessing. Covered with collegiate honours, he was graduated the following autumn, and immediately commenced the study of that profession, which, though proverbially dry at the outset, leads to the most magnificent results. I mean the study of divinity; a profession in which man may exercise the noblest faculties of the heart and intellect. He remained a resident graduate, till his probationary studies were ended, when he returned to his native valley, to the mother and sisters bequeathed to his care, as a legacy so dear.

Margaret, the elder of the two, was now in the morn of womanhood, with the rose of England blooming on her cheek, and its spirit of intelligent independance enthroned on her brow. With the full approbation of her mother, she had solicited the office of assistant instructess, in an academy recently established at Hexham, and engaged with all her heart and soul, in what Miss Willoughby deemed the *vulgar employment,* "of teaching the young idea how to shoot. For this purpose, she had cultivated the fine powers of her vigorous mind from earliest dawn to latest eve; for this, after she was freed from the restraints of a boarding school, she had been the assiduous pupil of her brother, during his vacations and visits, and enriched her memory with scholastic lore. She knew not the incumbrance that weighed down their small estate, and there was no absolute necessity for her exertions; but Margaret Glenroy had very exalted ideas of the purposes of her being, and, though she might be enabled to ennoble the character of her sex, as it came under her influence and example, while the mould was yet soft and impressible. This conviction was not the result of vanity, but a proper estimate of her own powers. She knew that much had been given, and felt that much would be required; and, moreover, she had that love of independence, which is the birth-right of the daughters of England.

One thing, too, sweetened the task. Her younger sister was her pupil—the *spoiled child* whom Griselda Willoughby so pitied and condemned. But there was one strange inconsistency. Most of those scourges of society, spoiled children, appear in the form of domestic tyrants, selfish, petulant, and sour. Whereas, Constance Glenroy, wore that of a houshould cherub, kind, placid and sweet. She was, moreover, of that age, when she would not exactly like to be called a child, nor was she ready to assume the honours of womanhood; but this doubtful period, generally so awkward in most young misses, was so engaging in her, one could not look on her without wishing that she might remain just as she was, a half unfolded flower, fearing lest each leaf that opened to the sun, might loose something of its purity or bloom. I have compared her to a flower, but she resembled more some fair exotic of the green-house, than the healthy blossoms of her native fields. She had that fragile delicacy of figure and complexion, which reminds one of early decay, and the extreme redundancy of her flaxen hair, which had not yet known the discipline of art, with the pale blue of her soft downcast eyes, confirmed this impression of constitutional debility. She had discovered early indications of uncommon genius, which, though not unduly cultivated, was evidently the dawn of a bright intellectnal day. Thus fair, gentle, gifted, and an orphan, the youngest too, is it strange that she was the most beloved of all?—the most tenderly cherished and caressed?

I have dwelt, perhaps too long, on this family, and have yet spoken but transiently of the mother, for her character may be read in her children's, where a mother's virtues may be traced almost as clearly as the summer clouds on the transparent waters of the river.

     *   *   *   *   *   *   *

Lovell, the treacherous friend, we have said fled from the country, with a burning monitor within his bosom, which, while it rendered life miserable, made the bare thought of death intolerable. He returned to Italy, and freed the sister of his wife from the charge of his child, now seven years old, and buried himself in the retirement of one of the cantons of Switzerland, where he devoted his life to the improvement and education of the only momento that was time him of happier days.

In the course of time he accompanied his son, now fast approaching towards manhood, in a tour through the continent of Europe, and assisted him in acquiring that information, so essential to in intercourse with the world. But the slow fire of mental disquietude was gradually consuming the feeble taper of life; and to the inconceivable distress of his attached child, he yielded up his spirit into the hands of his Creator, at an obscure village in the north of France. Shortly before he expired, he narrated to his son the story of his misery, and besought him to avoid the crime which embittered his last hours, and warned him of the danger which might arise in any meeting with the son of his injured friend.

Gilbert Lovell continued his travels through the north of Europe for two years after he lost his parent: when, tired " of the abject servitude of submissive poverty, and the haughty tyranny of pampered wealth," and anxious to see a country, where he was induced to believe the feelings of the man were suffered to grow in all their native greatness, he changed his name, and, accompanied by a faithful servant, set sail for England.

It was a singular coincidence that, on his arrival in London, he should take lodgings at the same house, where Margaret Glenroy was paying a short visit during the vacation.

It was also singular that Gilbert Lovell should so far forget himself as to fall in love, at first sight, with the fair Margaret; but it would have been contrary to all rules, had the case been otherwise—To be brief; he followed her to Allendale, and, with a species of deception (which all novel readers will consider pardonable) concealed his real name until he had ascertained the state of her feelings towards him—when the secret was revealed. To Margaret the shock was great; but love triumphed, in the short, but violent contest that followed this unexpected and alarming enunciation—and Gilbert Lovell, in one sense of the word, was made the happiest of men.

CHAPTER VII.

" There is a dangerous silence in that hour,
A stillness, which leaves room for the full soul
To open all itself, without the power
Of calling wholly back its self controul;
The silver light, which, hallowing tree and tower,
Sheds beauty and deep softness o'er the whole,
Breathes also to the heart, and o'er it throws
A loving languor, which is not repose."—BYRON.

It was on a lovely evening, when Margaret Glenroy proceeded from her mother's house, to meet her lover in the Murderer's Glen. The moon shone out in all her melancholy splendour, creating that mellow light over the " vast expanse of waters," which saddens while it softens, and persuades even the most thoughtless to think upon another and a nobler state of being.

The air was soft, and the bright moon shed her clear light on the distant mountains. The road wound along the side of the river, which possessed all the characteristic variety of a Scottish stream—now gliding silently along, or seeming to stand motionless in the crystal depth of some shaded pool—now chafing and gurgling with lulling sound, over its pebbbly bed, while its steep banks presented no less changing features. In some places they were covered with wood, the formal poplar's pale hue, and the fringed larch's tender green mingling with the red leaf of the oak, and the brown foliage of the sycamore. In others, grey rocks peeped from amidst the lichens and creeping plants which covered them as with a garment of many colours, and the wild rose decked them with its transient blossoms.

Farther on, the banks became less precipitous, and gradually sunk into a gentle slope, covered with smooth green turf, and sprinkled with trees of noble size. On the opposite side of the river, a line of sycamore trees, that grew almost at the water's edge, threw a dark shadow upon the bank. Through these, at intervals, the bright moon-light fell upon the earth, and upon the quiet stream.

Margaret soon gained the bank of the river, she crossed the rustic bridge, and there, in the deep shade of the rocks and trees, she felt secure, at least from discovery, if not from danger. A few steps more and she reached the glen, where she was to meet her lover.

At another time she would have been charmed with the romantic loveliness and grandeur of the scene—Rocks, trees, and river, all gleamed in the pale pellucid light—not a leaf was stirring, and the solemn stillness was only broken by the rushing of the river, and the whooping of the owls. But to enjoy the tranquillity of nature, requires that there should be some sympathy between the mind and scene; and Margaret's feelings were but little in unison with the calm, the holy majesty of moonlight. Scarely daring to breathe, every instant seemed an age, till she beheld her lover advance with a quick but agitated step; and in the next instant she was locked in the embrace of one whose affection she valued above all earthly possessions.

When that short interval had passed away, in which neither Margaret nor Gilbert Lovell could utter speech; during which the lady leant her head upon her lover's bosom, in that fond familiarity which plighted faith is allowed to justifyi r the most modest maiden,—sobbing the while in the intensity of her emotions,— she then, at last, as she slowly regained her self-possession, said, in a soft and melancholy voice,—

" I am a foolish girl, Gilbert. I can boast like a blustering coward, when there is nothing to fear; and yet I weep, like a true woman, at the first trial of my courage."

" Ah, my dear Margaret, you are a brave girl," replied Lovel, as he held both of her hands and looked fondly into her face.

Gilbert Lovell was now in the possession of the vigour of early manhood; his his form would be called noble, for, united to the greatest possible symmetry, there were evident marks of powerful muscular force, aad a certain dignity of tread which plainly—showed the gentleman. The expression of his features, as the moon shone brightly upon them, was serious—perhaps melancholy : his complexion was unusually dark ; but it was evident that it was not naturally so, for when he moved his hat trom his head, a profusion of very handsome hair curled over and preserved the original fairness of a high, broad forehead. A hazel eye sparkled under the shade of a dark lash, and indicated an adventurous spirit.

He was wrapt in a large military cloak, which not only served apparently for the purposes of concealment, but also by the skilful adjustment of its folds, adapted every turn of the figure, served to display the robust form of the wearer.

After numberless little sayings and doings, which it would be preposterous to relate, they proceeded farther up the glen, and Margaret observed the servant of Lovell at the farther end, who, upon perceiving them advance, retired behind the trees—out of sight, but within call.

The Murderer's Glen was a narrow opening in the midst of the surrounding forest, and but for the unevenness of the earth, and the thick and knotted clusters of trees that joined their giant branches overhead, it might have appeared to a stranger no more that a large cavern cut through the verdant shade. By advancing through the trees, the foliage was found to thicken around ; a wild luxuriance of wood, briar, and bramble, choked up all access from the sides of the glen ; the grass rose high and rank, and intermingled with weeds of a redundant growth, while the trees embraced each other in inextricable union, forming themselves into an impassable barrier. To this peculiarity, which cast a mystery about the spot, and to the deepness of the shadow around, shedding, as it were, a dull green twilight, even in broad day, upon the scene, as well as to the wild gigantic trees that grew there, whose forms seemed witchlike, tempest-ridden, and distorted, the place owed doubtless some of its awe and many of its legends. In truth, there was a barren verdure, a thriving desolation about it, a prophetic silence, that might well inspire, if not dread, at least the sentiment of a deep melancholy. Besides this, there were some grey moss-grown stones, of more than ordinary size, piled in a heap to mark the spot where some horrid murder had been perpetrated. The tale of horror and bloodshed had rendered the spot deserted, and thus it frequently became the retreat of such as needed shelter ; and, indeed, it was well fitted to be so in many respects.

" Gilbert," said Margaret Glenroy, in an anxious and fearful tone, while her lover gazed upon her with an intensity of feeling which exhibited his fine countenance to the greatest advantage, "you have done wrong, very wrong; indeed, I fear that your precipitancy in coming here, will be the cause of the sudden destruction of our short-lived happiness. You said that you would delay your departure from London for some length of time."

" Ah! my dearest Margaret," replied the youth, fondly pressing the little han that trembled in his own, "why will you yield to gloomy anticipations ? we are happy now ; then let us not destroy the present by an unnecessary dread of the future. But what is your meaning, when you express the fear that my precipitancy will ruin us ? There surely can have been no unlooked-for accident ? My letters have not been seen—

" No, no," replied Margaret, "but I'm fearful lest my absence at this time may create suspicion, and lead to an investigation. Should my brother by any ccident————"

" But, my charming Margaret," interrupted the lover, " what can your brother suspect? My name is known to no one in this country but my servant, and I would almost as willingly confide in him as in you."

"Ah! Gilbert," replied Margaret, "you know little of Herbert's character. Behind all the appearance of frivolity and gaity, he conceals a deep and penetrating mind, and though seemingly indifferent to every thing around him, he is a close observer of all those little circumstances by which one gains an insight into the real thoughts and feelings of others, much more readily than by ayn attention to the more important events of life. If he noticed my absence, and the appearance of mystery which my meeting with you will occasion if questioned, Heaven knows what will be the consequence! Oh! Gilbert, let me beseech you to leave Allendale immediately; I know not what I fear, and yet I tremble when I think of what may befall you."

"Then, my dearest love, let me either anticipate or avert my fate, by at once throwing aside all concealment. Years have passed away since the occurence of that unhappy circumstance which has raised an apparently insurmountable barrier between us; the excitement occasioned by it must have subsided even in the bosoms of those most interested. Were I boldly to declare my name and family———"

"Oh! think not of it," screamed the terrified girl, unconsciously clinging to the arm of her lover, as if to detain him. "I can see now, my father smiling in the very agonies of death, as he cautioned his children to shun the society of the descendants of Richard Lovell.—Think you I long to embrace your lifeless corpse, or to weep over the body of a murdered brother!"

"Margaret, hear me!" said Gilbert, in a solemn tone, as he partly disengaged himself from her embrace; "in the presence of the eternal God, who knows the secret workings of my soul, I swear never to raise my hand against the brother of her I love—whatever may be the provocation: no—never. Your father, it is true, was deeply injured by mine; was not the death of my parent in all the pangs of remorse, sufficient to atone for his crime, but must his son perish, while a mysterious Providence has linked the fate of that son with your's? The love I bear you cannot cease to prevade every thought and feeling of my soul, until thought and feeling are no more. I think we were born for each other's happiness. and therefore let us not hesitate to secure it; make me your husband. Then should your brother think of revenging your father's injuries, it must be effected by your happiness or misery; he will be forced to forgive the husband of his sister, though he would not hesitate to destroy her lover. Then fly with me now, the means are in readiness; and should your family still prove vindictive I then will have the right to protect you. Margaret, why do you tremble? Look on me; you behold one whose every thought is of you, and whose only desire it will be to anticipate the slightest wish that can be formed within that gentle bosom. Love knows no duty but its object. You are the first and only being of my affection; to you my truth is confided. You do not fear me, that you gaze so widly? speak and relieve me from suspense; this state of things cannot last long the crisis is approaching and our only hope for happiness is to anticipate it."

"Gilbert," repiled Margaret Glenroy, laying her hand upon his arm, and speaking in a tone which plainly showed she was struggling to suppress her feelings "you ought to know me too well, to suppose that I tremble for myself; it was for you. I blush not to acknowledge that my very existence is so connected with yours, that it would require but one blow to destroy both; it is true we never can be united under the present circumstances, with the approbation of my friends; but, think you, were you to call me wife, that we could be happier? The same cause for disquietude would still exist; its power increased, its extent enlarged, were I to fly with you, and then announce the name of the man whom I had selected to be my husband: to my brother it would be an additional incitement to revenge, to think that his hereditary enemy had, as it were, ravished his sister from his protection—therefore, (observing that her lover was about to interrupt her,) speak no more of that. Since you are here, and purpose staying some time, I have a plan to propose; the execution of which is not difficult, and the success of which depends entirely upon yourself; I should have communicated it to you before, but I feared to trust it upon your paper."

"Name it, for the love of Heaven!

"Your real name is known only in France, and that to only a few, who perhaps forgot you as soon as you left them. Our intercourse in London was suppposed by none to be any thing more than ordinary; and I imagine that no one will recollect, or take the trouble to inquire, the reason why you left."

"But where does all this lead?"

"Gilbert," replied Margaret, with an expression of countenance which, gilded by the mellow light of the moon, would have touched to the soul a less interested person than a lover, "this is my only hope. Oh! crush it not; for, with it you will destroy a heart that will never cease to love, though your own hand should sever the cord by which it feebly and convulsively clings to life, and to you; you will not, you cannot allow pride to bar the entrance to it: forget that your name ever was Lovell, and appear as my suitor in the character you now profess to be: fortune will favour us, and the struggle, though a continued one, cannot be violent."

There was a pause during which she gazed upon her lover with a feeling little short of agony, as covering his face with his hands, he seemed affected by the most powerful and conflicting emotions. The contest however, soon was over; and with a countenance calm and determined, and with a voice sorrowfull, yet steady Gilbert Lovell broke through the silence.

"The name of my family is dear to me as life; duplicity is that which my soul abhors; I have done violence to every feeling of honour, by the concealment I have already practised; I envy my very servant the peace of mind always attendant upon honesty; I fear even to look my fellow man in the face, lest my countenance should betray that I am guilty of perpetual falsehood: but all this I will overcome; I will hear a parent whose memory I reverence, branded as a coward and a villain— and yet my eye shall never glance the quicker; my heart shall never throb the faster; I will listen to the voices of my children as they call down curses on the head of their father—and yet my bosom shall heave no sigh, my grief shall shed no tear; I will see the woman I adore shudder and turn pale, as savage revenge will whet its knife to bury it in the heart of her husband—and yet, my breast shall harbour no rash thought—my spirit shall forget that I am a man. Margaret! tomorrow shall blot out the remembrance of my ancestors; and I will be known to you, and to the world, as Gilbert Stanhope." After a few moments delay he again continued,—"In this glen, we will vow never by any chance of fortune or time; never by any fate of heaven or earth, to be separated. Whatever ensues of happiness or sorrow, we at least will be true, and all that influences others shall touch not us. Death only shall divide us. Fortune is mine to make us happy; we will be so; say, will you vow for ever?" He fixed his gaze upon her as if to divine how far this speech had worked with her.

"Here will I vow," cried the lovely girl; "all other hopes, prospects, and happiness laid aside, I am yours for ever. To my first affection I will be faithful, in spite of brother, friends, or kindred. What they shall say will be lost upon me; all, everything, but your good, shall be forgotten." "Well, Margaret," responded he, "it is well; and may the accursed ills reported of this spot, fall tenfold on us, if we forget this oath. and may they be wreaked on all those rather who thwart our affection; indeed, be any and all misfortunes their doom; for nothing can touch us, we shall keep our vow so sacredly. Therefore, whoever would break away our friendship, forcing our hearts into some other feeling, let them never know the sweets of lover's confidence or lover's truth, nor lover's fond affection; but if they have a choice let it be blighted in its early prime, or crossed by some mischance —so that they live, if they still live, both single: or die, if they should die, of blighted hope, and of a broken heart, and thus upon your lips I seal my oath."

All reply was prevented, for a rustling was heard among the trees, and Gilbert's servant advanced, and stated that he thought some person was concealed in the glen; here was a short convulsive embrace, and Gilbert was left alone.

He was about leaving the glen, when his attention was arrested by some motion behind the pile of stones which we have before observed marked the spot where some murder had been committed : the suspicion crossed his mind that there might have been a listener to their conference, and he determined to satisfy himself. Accordingly, he placed himself behind a tree and remained quiet and attentive. Presently, the figure of a man emerged from behind the stones, and proceeded silently and cautiously towards the entrance of the glen ; he was tall and well

formed, and, in his dress, had something the appearance of a sailor ; a large hat completely shaded his features.   To spring from his retreat, and to grasp him by the throat, was with Gilbert the work of a moment ; but the force with which he fell, threw both upon the ground, and the stranger by a dexterous turn of his body, loosed the hold upon him, and darted with great rapidity from the glen.   Gilbert, as soon as he regained his feet, pursued ; but the man outran him with the greatest ease, and soon was out of sight.

What could be thought of this ? That they had been watched, perhaps over-

No. 5.

heard, he was almost certain; otherwise why should the man have fled with such precipitation; concealment evidently was his object; and he had partially succeeded, for his face had not been seen.   Again, he might have been there with a very different intention; and, upon being suddenly and unexpectedly seized by a powerful man, whose presence he had just discovered, it was very natural that he should attempt an escape by flight.   An idea now crossed the mind of Gilbert, which in spite of himself made him tremble: it might have been the brother of Margaret;—this circumstance conspired to increase the gloom that clouded his mind, as he slowly returned to the village inn.

His heart was heavy and tortured with anxiety, as he seated himself in his chamber, in order to arrange his plans for the future; and though the arrival of Walter, his servant, informing him of the safe return of Margaret to her house without interruption or mishap, dissipated a large portion of his care, still his brain was so excited by a multitude of divers thoughts, so harrassed by mournful reflections and gloomy anticipatins, that day dawned before he sank into a feverish slumber.

Margaret, upon arriving at her home, retired to her room; she grew sick at heart as she was forced to look forward to an endless succession of torturing fears and anxieties, the bare thought of which made her tremble, while the certainty of their approch unnerved when it should have inspired her with confidence.   She now wished that Gilbert had not acquiesced so readily in her plan—that some difficulty had been started, or some objection made to it.

"Oh! fatal necessity for dissimulation," she exclaimed, as she sat alone in her chamber; "in every breath of the wind I shall find cause for alarm; in every, even the most trifling coincidence, I shall see that which will not fail to affect me with paralyzing terror and affright, and this to continue, not for a day, an hour, or a year, but throughout life!"   She covered her face with her hands, and wept.

"My respected mother! you little think of the misery that hovers over your child, who may, and Heaven knows how shortly, be doomed to see the man she loves separated from her hopes for ever.   Oh! if such wretchedness must be my fate, let me bury my afflictions in my bosom!   Oh! never may my mother know the secret of my love!"

CHAPTER VIII.

> Why she is fair, and fairer than that word
> Of wondrous virtues.
> Yet not the smoothness of her iv'ry skin,
> Not the carnation of her downy cheek,
> Nor the rich lustre beaming from her eyes;
> No, nor the tempting ripeness of her lips,
> That like a ruby casket open to display
> Her pearly teeth————
> 'Tis not her outward brightness claims my love,
> But the rich treasures of her angel-mind;
> Her virtues do enthral my heart, and make
> Me love her.   ANON.

IT was one of those gentle evenings in May, when the heart insensibly accords with the balmy temperature of the air, and is open to the sweetness of rural beauty and the influence of time and place, that Susan with her friend Edith Trevanion, accompanied by her father and mother, were returning homeward from a ramble which they had been taking on the road to Hexham.   In a neighbouring field a trilling skylark was mounting in the air, his notes doubling and redoubling —then fading, as he ascended into the calm and balmy atmosphere, till he himself was no longer than an atom, and at last totally disappeared.

Susan was following him with her ear, and was endeavouring to catch his little form with her eye; she had proceeded some length in advance of her companions when a sharp cry of terror aroused her from her contemplations. A pair of horses appeared approaching at full speed, dragging the fragments of a broken curricle, their manes streaming in the air, their heads stretched forward, with open mouth and dilated nostril, the half loosened traces flying about their feet, dashing first to one side of the road, then to the other, ungovernable, desperate, and abandoned to all the madness of fright. Each bound threatened the extinction of some human life, or that the affrighted creatures themselves would be dashed to pieces.

Susan had darted forward from the road to avoid them; but in her speed, overlooking an obstruction in her path, she stumbled and fell to the ground, where she lay motionless and insensible, till Edith arrived to her assistance. She quickly succeeded in raising the inanimate form of her friend, imagining that she had merely been stunned by the fall; but after a lapse of two or three minutes, perceiving no sings of returning consciousness, she began to grow seriously alarmed, and looking eagerly round in quest of help, hastily motioned her parents to advance. The fiery and furious animals were plunging with headlong speed towards them. Cries of " Stop them! stop them! save the ladies!" rung on the air; but as is generally the case in such emergencies, there were found many more to suggest this counsel, than to execute it. Their destruction appeared inevitable, and that stir and shudder with which men look on a bloody and terrible accident, broke from the crowd which followed in the distance after the horses, when Herbert Glenroy sprang over the bank from the field, and grasped unsuccessfully at the reins of the fugitive beasts, but dragged the two females from beneath their hoofs. Attention to them would have been more undivided, but for the catastrophe of one of those animals, from whose fury they were saved. Starting aside from the grasp of Herbert, the finer of the two leaped forward with an almost supernatural effort, and the shaft of the curricle entered into his body directly through the ample chest, as a sword plunged and buried to the hilt in a human bosom. The noble creature snorted painfully, expressive of agony and fear, and bleeding, sweating, foaming, trembling, and panting, came heavily to the ground.

A rush of people now closed in upon them. The dying horse was at once disentangled from his harness, the life-tide poured in a dark red flood, crimsoning the earth, and with each gush the pain of the poor animal appeared more insupportable while the vapour curled from his reeling flanks. He struggled and snorted and strove to rise and resume his flight, and his bloodshot eyes turned gleaming upon the faces of the spectators, as if soliciting aid, or at least compassion. But presently his breast heaved with a feeble motion. Weaker and yet more weak, grew his convulsive shudders, and his vain attempts to regain his feet, till drenched, quivering and gory—foam on his lips—terror and despair in his eyes, he stretched himself upon the ground, in the last throes of that dark crisis, that must come alike to man and beast.

His fleet limbs stiffened, his asthmatic breathing were silent, his broad and majestic chest moved no more; the damp lips curled from the large ivory teeth, the eyes started— started—and grew fixed and glassy, and that mighty form, which but a moment before had carried terror through the crowd, lay now transmuted to a senseless clod. A silence, as if a human soul had passed away, remained on the circle of passionate spectators. Just at that moment, however, a splendid equipage came up, and a young man, who had been acting as coachman, violently pulled in the reins, leaped from his seat, and respectfully proffered his aid in the cause of humanity. At the same time, two ladies, who were in the barouche pressed to the window, and were kindly assiduous in tendering restoratives.

At length, Susan, aroused probably rather by the pain which she suffered, than by the stimulants that had been applied, opened by her eyes, and ejaculating, in a tone of acute anguish, " Oh, Heaven! my arm!" sunk again on Edith's shoulder.

Mrs. Trevanion, whose speed had outstripped her husband, now joined them, and, her attention being directed by Susan's exclamation to the seat of complaint, she discovered with a cry of horror, that the left arm was broken.

" Do not be frightened, my dear mother," said Edith, struggling to appear calm with a view to allay in another the emotion in which she could but participate herself, " we must consider what is best to be done."

" Let her be conveyed to the nearest habitation, and I will immediately proceed to obtain surgical aid," cried Herbert Glenroy, as he gazed on Edith Trevanion, who was still supporting her friend ; and as he left them to seek Doctor Rovington, he thought her the exact counterpart of his model of female excellence, his sister Magaret.———" If ever I love," said he mentally, " the enslaver of my heart must resemble Edith Trevanion."

" Merciful father ! no time must be lost, or the bone may protrude,'" cried Mrs. Trevanion in agony.

" I think that she had much better be taken home at once," suggested Edith ; " we are not a mile from our home."

" But how shall we carry, her, Edith ?'' asked her mother, distressed almost to tears.

" We will put her into the carriage this instant,'" exclaimed the youth, who had been driving the vehicle, laying his hand on the lock of the door as he spoke. General Trevanion.by this time had reached the spot ; and after a brief recapitulation of the circumstances of the case, he reluctantly accepted the offer of the mode of conveyance nearest at hand ; and Susan, without farther delay, was lifted into the vehicle, followed by Mrs. Trevanion ; and the gallant charioteer resuming his office, drove off to the residence of the General, while Edith and her father hastened home on foot.

There is nothing new or remarkable in the event I have described. Every newspaper may speak of an overturned carriage, broken limbs, or more fatal accidents ; but this casualty, so common in itself, was ordained to have an enduring influence on the destiny of so many individuals. It was a link in that apparently unconnected but unbroken chain of events, with which an Almighty hand has girdled zone to zone and age to age. It is vain, and worse than vain, to talk of this or that lucky adventure, or unfortunate mischance. The same power that watches over the fate of empires, marks the falling of the dying sparrow. The same heavenly munificence that fed the glory of Solomon, clothed the lily of the field in its surpassing robes.

There is no incident, however trivial or chance-directed it may seem to the passing observer, but it may have the most interesting, wonderful and awful dependencies ; and though many a rural village may boast of more hair-breadth adventures than those that befel the Pirate's Daughter, yet I question if any of their simple annals contain a record more interesting than that which remains in consequence of the memory of some of the inhabitants of Allendale.

When Doctor Rovington arrived, he pronounced Susan to be in no danger whatever, as the fracture was perfectly simple, and she was free from fever ; and moreover, gave it as his opinion, that if his patient was kept perfectly quiet, and there was nothing done that could retard her recovery, there was no doubt of a speedy cure. Edith listened to this intelligence with heartfelt delight, and readily engaged that the injunctions should be solemnly observed.

The next morning, a servant in livery came to the house, with the kindest inquiries after Miss Adams' health, from Lady Helen Maxwell.

" There, General," cried Mrs. Trevanion, in a tone of triumph, as she handed the card over to her husband, " perhaps Susan's breaking her arm may be the luckiest accident that could possibly have happened ; Lady Maxwell, indeed, I am sure her ladyship is very polite."

" Not at all so ; it is nothing more than an act of common humanity, and what any one would have done under similar circumstances. I should have thought her ladyship very unfeeling if she had not sent to make the inquiry."

" Lord, General, that is always your way, you attach so little merit to people's good works ; I believe we must be all saints to please you. I do not know what you may think, but I say that it presents a very fine opening to us ; for if her ladyship should honour us with a call, I must of course, return the visit ; so it appears that we shall have acquaintance and society, though we take no trouble to form them for ourselves."

Trevanion frowned and replied—" You know that it is my will and choice that we live thus in private ; I might have had fifty carriages at my door on this occasion, if I had pleased."

"Ah, well I declare that it is very lucky."

" Time will prove," added the General drily, and rising up quitted the room.

On the following day, Lady Helen Maxwell came herself accompanied by her daughter, where they were met by Edith only, whose feelings of gratitude overcoming the reserve and diffidence that usually distinguished her manners towards strangers, she received her visitors with much warmth and cordiality.

Lady Maxwell said a thousand fine things, and in the course of conversation, her ladyship made it understood, that she was a widow, possessed of a very considerable property, nearly the whole of which, at her decease, devolved to her eldest son ; leaving his brother William and sister Matilda by no means proportionably provided for.

Lady Maxwell, after making a long stay, invited Edith to take a drive in the carriage, and afterwards join them at a family dinner ; and when Edith excused herself on the plea of Susan's indisposition her ladyship requested permission to leave Matilda to share in the tender offices of nurse ; an offer which Edith politely but positively declined ; and after an interchange of various civil speeches, they parted, mutually pleased with each other.

Lady Maxwell was a woman of the world ; formed to dazzle and triumph over the heart of man ; proud and selfish, unless where her interest was concerned, when she could render herself remarkably fascinating and conciliatory. She had trodden the flowery path of an admired belle, had early married her late husband, Lord Maxwell ; they loved each other well enough to be perfectly happy when together, or when apart. The blooming girl had scarcely changed as the beautiful wife, and the still glowing and graceful mother, till time—the destroyer of other's charms, but shedding only a deeper richness upon her's—matured her into the stately and magnificent woman.

Matilda, her only daughter, rose by the side of her mother, lovelier but not so gay, and winning all hearts with a less striking but far deeper power. Men hesitated upon which to bestow their worship. So sometimes the summer day lingers, drawing all eyes to the uncrimsoned west, even while the moon has long filled with her holier radiance the ascending Heaven. The singularity of this association could not escape the notice of the yet ambitious woman, and Lady Maxwell regarded Matilda with a curiously mixed feeling, wavering between the fondness of the mother, and the rivalry of the belle. There was perhaps a certain conscious magnanimity in the delight with which she gazed upon her daughter's expanding charms, fond as she herself was of admiration and accustomed to be its centre.

But yet, though they charmed alike, they could scarcely interfere with each other. The one was sure to overcome, when she desired to do so, by the long practised energies of her highly gifted nature ; the other always won love without wishing, and even without knowing it. The daughter valued not what she had never striven to obtain, and beheld with pleasure the triumphs of her queenly mother, who, in her turn, yielded the path with a sigh and a smile to the more unpretending excellencies of Matilda.

The object which her ladyship had in view on the present occasion, was the advancement of a favourite nephew, who was in the army ; a young man of small fortune, and indifferent conduct ; and Lady Maxwell calculated, that the recommendation of General Trevanion might probably procure for him that promotion, to which his own deserts never could entitle him ; and this was the sole motive of her ladyship's affability and courtesy to persons, who, however respectable, were certainly in a very inferior rank of life to herself.

Mrs. Trevanion, and the general, who by her persuasion accompanied her, made an early return of the visit; and was received by Lady Maxwell with great affability.

Glanmore Abbey, the name of the old seat, a building sufficiently ancient, as both history and appearance attested, to claim that reverence we feel for antiquity, from the romantic associations connected with it, lay contiguous to a sweetly, sequestered lake, to which the verdant lawn on which it stood gently inclined, the only place of any extent on the margin of the water. Backed by dark o'rtopping woods, that on either sides extended some way beyond it on the lawn, and where many a gnarled oak, and aged elm, proclaimed their ancient date; the building, half shrouded in the foliage, had still that air of monastic seclusion about it, that at once reminded the spectator of its original destination. Here for many generations the family resided, and, in succession, had been masters of the place; it had remained in their possession, without undergoing any other change or alteration, through a reverential feeling perhaps, than what time alone had effected, such as served only to heighten the deep interest it was calculated to inspire; for as he at whose magic power the rapt soul was made to thrill, who knew better than the heart itself he worked upon its depth of feeling, has observed—

> "There is given
> Unto the things of earth which time hath bent,
> A spirit's feeling; and where he hath leant
> His hand, but broke his scythe : there is a power
> And magic in the ruined battlement,
> For which the palace of the present hour
> Must yield its pomp, and wait till ages are its dower."

The varied hills and ivy-clad rocks,' intermingled with jutting trees, that at the bottom of the lawn appeared just to have parted, to permit it to advance between, gradually assumed a bolder character as they swept round the lake, till towards the opposite side, they rose and roughened into those tremendous fells, that strike the imagination with such awe, and which just here, that is, directly facing the abbey, retiring a little from the edge of the water, afforded a small space, on which stood the ruined castle of De Clifford, a picturesque object, with its tufts of long streaming grass and weeds, and wild shrubs, pendant from its rifted walls, especially when crimsoned by the setting sun; the battlemented towers, and projected turrets, wore a warm hue that beautifully contrasted with its grey portals, while the wild passes and deep indentures of the mountains were revealed by the bright effulgence.

Midway between it and the abbey, was a small island, that from its dark verdure, the shadows caused by its unequal surface, rising in different places into high turfy banks, o'erspread with foliage, the wildly-tangled trees and thickets with which it was nearly covered, looking exceedingly inviting. Here in days of yore, where all was calculated to dispose the mind to meditation, where neither sound was heard, nor sight was seen, that could disturb or draw back to the world that was renounced, the lonely anchorite had his cell. The old hermitage still remained, externally retaining all the vestiges of remote antiquity, ivy and its congenerous plants clasping the rough stones that formed it, and filling up every opening in them, but internally altered, so as to render it a pleasant resort; and here entertainments were often given.

For miles round the Maxwells were known, and the stranger who should have expressed ignorance of their origin, fortune, or name, would have been instantly set down by the more knowing and rustic throng, conversant in all and the minutest of these facts, as one, in truth, who knew nothing amongst, and must never hope for consideration from them again.

The day was spent by Lady Maxwell and her two visitors, accompanied by her beautiful daughter, in rambling about the extensive and beautifully diversified grounds of the abbey, than which nothing possibly could be more enchanting, especially at this delicious season, when all was

> "Half prankt with spring, with summer half imbrown'd."

Not a spot, not a turn, that did not present some new beauty to the eye.

> " The landscape glancing swift
> Athwart imagination's vivid eye !
> Or by the vocal woods and waters lulled,
> Indulge, in lonely musing, in the dream
> Confused of careless solitude, where mix
> Ten thousand wandering images of things."

Here sequestered seats, o'erwrought with woodbine, invited you to contemplation ; there a romantic cottage caught your eye, where an aged couple, that reminded you of Baucis and Philemon, had always refreshments from the abbey ready to present in a rustic parlour, screened from the meridian sun by fragrant and embowering shrubs ; here, on a soft green knoll, stood a temple dedicated to Flora, the descending ground, or velvet carpet, spread or strewed all over with her gifts,

> " With daffodils
> That come before the swallow does, and take
> The winds of March with beauty : violets dim,
> But sweeter than the lids of Juno's eyes,
> Or Cytherea's breath ; pale primroses,
> That die unmarried, ere they can behold
> Bright Phœbus in his strength ;
> Gold oxlips, and
> The crown imperial ; lilies of all kinds
> The fleur-de-lis being one."

intermingled with roses and lavender, and all that was lovely and rare, sweet in the sense, and grateful to the eye. There another, more secluded, to Hygeia, to gratitude for the pellucid bath afforded by a gush of water from the side of a low deeply-indented rock, all lined and overrun with creeping plants, and enclasping the damp-stones, while a thick wood behind served to render the spot still more sequestred, and, by its gloom, united to the noise of the spray, to inspire a pleasing melancholy.

Here a hermitage, couched under the shadow of a steep shelving bank, only wanted an Edwin to render it a meet refuge for a sorrowing Angelina ; and there the moss-clad fragment of a ruin recalled the days of other years, while the rural sounds that in every direction met the ear from the hill, the dale, the sheltered homestead, served, from the associations connected with them, to render the effect of the scenery still more delightful, by giving to the mind those images of tranquil happiness that have so soothing an effect on it.

During the ramble, the conversation naturally turned upon the accident which had been the means of introducing the general and his wife to Lady Maxwell."

" Do you know," said her ladyship to the general, " to whom the carriage belonged ?"

" Yes," replied Trevanion, " to a gentleman who has lately taken the house laying between mine and Mrs. Glenroy's ; he appears quite a stranger about here, as I have often met him rambling about the country ; he is well informed and of polished manners, and it appears from the gossip of the servants, that he is a man of some fortune."

" His name ?" said Matilda.

" Is Gilbert Stanhope," returned the general ; " but what his family connectio n are, I know not, for he is particularly reserved in his conversations upon tha head."

" Stanhope," said Lady Maxwell to herself several times ; " I surely know the name. Matilda, dear, we must endeavour to learn more about him, for his acquaintance will be an acquisition to us in the country, where there are not so many *gentlemen* as in London."

" They continued their ramble, conversing upon the topic which had been started by Lady Maxwell, till they reached the chapel belonging to the abbey.

This splendid relic of other days, with its pinnacles and perforated shrines, had originally formed part of the building, but the cloister that connected it with the main body of the edifice had long been destroyed, and the intervening space filled up with yews, and pines, and cypress, forming altogether what might be termed a funeral grove, above which it rose on a gently ascending hillock, studded with old tombs and grave-stones, many nearly lost in the high grass and weeds in which they were embedded.

It was the burial-place of the Maxwells ; here many a warrior slept, "and dreamt of war no more." It was also still used as a private chapel ; many of its embellishments remained, and its look of high antiquity, with the air of solemn ancient gloom that pervaded it, partially darkened as were the stained windows by the thick foliage of the trees that clustered near them, failed not to touch the feelings the moment it was entered. The thickness of the mantling ivy rendered it almost an aviary ; here the owl held unmolested its ancient solitary reign ; and here nought was seen, nought was heard, but what was calculated to awaken reflections that all should encourage.

General Trevanion stood in deep meditation, looking upon the tombs and wild flowers budding there, and in mournful mood he thus broke forth—

"Nature is of beautiful and God-like creation, and is the evident divinity of the skies, living in the might and loveliness of all around, and breathing through us in our own thoughts : but human nature is of the earth—the corrupted deity of the world—a glory shadowed by the likeness in which it comes, as lightning clothed with tempest. The soul, the spirit-born of native heaven sighs for some brighter region ; the body, sprung from the clod of flesh, yearns for its primal rest. Well, be it so ! and may we be forgiven. Alas! we are innocent; we are children of dust." And here the speaker ceased, and pondered another instant, then turning to Lady Maxwell, who had now joined him, continued—"A green and peaceful scene this, all verdure and all beauty ; yet, if we could rip open these tombs, explore their hidden treasures, the wreck of something that has loved and been beloved, the sight would fright us from our humanity. And yet, again, the revealed horrors of the grave, with all its ruin, would speak much less of woe, than would one glimpse taken of the living heard when it has known this life, or rather lived a life out of some forty years. What say you, my lady ?"

"Say, why I say we had better return to the abbey ; the evening is advancing, and the chill air will not be so pleasant for us, as a warm room," replied Lady Maxwell.

They now returned to the abbey, and after partaking of tea, General Trevanion and his wife took their departure, Mrs. Trevanion declaring she had never spent so comfortable an afternoon.

CHAPTER IX.

"Oh! many a shaft at random sent,
Finds mark the archer little meant."—SCOTT.

"If in originals such things appear,
Why should we bar them in the copy here."—CHURCHILL.

DOCTOR ROVINGTON had informed Miss Willoughby of the accident which had happened to Susan ; and never having spoken to her or her friend Edith Trevanion, Miss Griselda determined to make it an opportunity for introducing herself at the general's, for, although living so near, she had never formed an acquaintance with the gentle Edith, nor would she now had not Doctor Rovington spoken so much of her exceeding beauty. Accordingly, having made up her mind, she at once proceeded to the general's, accompanied by her cousin Alice.

"Is Miss Trevanion within ?" she inquired of the servant who opened the door, and showed them into the parlour.

"I'm not certain, ma'am, but I'll see," and she immediately left the parlour.

"Stop!" cried Miss Willoughby, but she was too swift for her voice. "How provoking," she exclaimed, "she's gone before I could give her our cards. It will be so awkward and countrified to introduce ourselves. I wish we had waited for Doctor Rovington; but I was afraid some one would get the start of me, and I always like to be the first in everything." And she looked as she uttered the last sentence, just like the daughter of Sir Reginald Willoughby.

"I do not think with you," said the sentimental Alice, "on the contrary, it wil be much more graceful to introduce each other to Miss Trevanion, than merely to give and receive a simple 'How do you do?' Do let your scarf fall a little farther off your shoulders, Griselda, and tell me, are my ringlets discomposed?"

Miss Willoughby suffered her blue scarf to fall a little farther from her shoulders, which, however, broadly displayed, had neve been compared to the statue's 'that enchants the world,' and Alice passed her white fingers over her sunny locks, as they heard the sound of approaching footsteps in the passage.

"Have you often seen her?" asked Alice of her cousin.

"Not to take much notice of her," replied Miss Willoughby.

"Then I think it proper that you should introduce me first, you know, as I have so recently come down here, and am therefore the greatest stranger," whispered Alice, when the door opened, and the maid servant again made her appearance.

"Miss Edith sends her compliments, and says she will wait upon you directly."

"How is her friend?" asked Miss Willoughby. "Is her arm very painful?"

"Yes, miss, her arm is mighty bad indeed," replied the maid. "She has not slept all night long, but she"s a deal easier this morning; Miss Edith has not had any sleep either, as she's been up with Miss Susan."

We know not how many questions the curiosity of Miss Willoughby would have urged her to ask of the garrulous maid, had they not been interrupted by the entrance of Edith herself, at whose presence the servant retired, like the shadow of night before the morning star.

"She is not so *very* handsome after all," thought Griselda, at the first glance, "not half so beautiful as cousin Alice—I wonder where Doctor Rovington's taste can be."

"She's not half so beautiful as I *feared*," said Alice to herself," her eyes are as heavy as lead, and she is pale even to sallowness. I am surprised at Doctor Rovinton's taste;" and her own image floated in rosy brightness before her self-approving fancy.

It is indeed true, that Edith Trevanion could not have appeared before the criticising cousins at a moment more unpropitious to her personal attractions. Watching over the bed of sickness is a sad enemy of brilliancy and bloom, and had they been kind enough to have recollected the words of the servant, that she had passed a weary night by the side of a suffering friend, with the depressing consciousness of being a stranger to them, they need not have wondered at the heaviness of her eyes, or the pallidness of her cheeks. We have read of features which only looked more angelic, through such "disastrous twilight" but we have never seen the face, however fair and lovely, that was not marred by the influence of suffering or sorrow. Even in her brightest hours Edith was far from possessing that radiance of complexion and faultlessness of feature, which is considered necessary to the perfection of beauty. But having once seen, you could not, if you would, forget her. Like the summer cloud, that now floats white through the morning mist, is now tinged with crimson by the setting sun, her cheek was colourless or glowing, as sensibility paled, or enthusiasm warmed, its surface.

As she was completely *en dishabille*, in a loose muslin wrapper, it was impossible to judge of the outlines of her figure, but she had one hereditary beauty, which remained unaffected by the vicissitudes of feeling, and which did not escape the scrutiny of her visitors, hands of such marvellous delicacy, so exquisitely refined, that Miss Willoughby was constrained to say, in speaking of her afterwards, "that it was a sin to have such a pair of hands, for they ought only to belong to nobility."

The conversation for awhile turned was cold and formal, consisting of commonplace remarks on the accident that had occurred—its disagreeable consequences—the hope that her friend would soon recover from the effects of the accident, and a polite but doubtful motion of the head of the other.

At length Griselda, after venturing far enough on the ice to see whether it would bear, became more loquacious and condescending, and Alice resumed her artificial warmth of manner. She had arrived at the conviction that the fair Edith was not likely to dazzle the imagination of Herbert Glenroy, and determined, in consequence, to find in her a congenial soul, a friend, to quote her own favourite expression, to whom she could open the deep foldings of her heart. But Edith seemed not to reciprocate her purpose; she expressed a becoming sense of the many attentions they proffered, and felt inclined to treat them as her mother had always done, with coldness, for she liked not the proud city upstarts; there was a slight shade of haughtiness in her manners, which, in spite of Griselda's self-complacency and want of tact, she felt uncomfortably.

"Our residence here," said Miss Willoughby, "has been but for a very few years. Born and educated in the metropolis, it was with almost unconquerable reluctance I accompanied my father into the country—I feared I should die with *ennui*, and that I should find no society in which it would be even proper to mingle. But there are really some very genteel families here! and as to the rest, you are not obliged to be so very particular in the country as in the city. One can afford to be condescending you know, and then there is so *much* pleasure in imparting *pleasure!*" She turned up her eyes as she concluded, with, with such ineffable complacency, it would have been barbarous to have doubted her possession of that last mentioned secret, more precious than the gold transmuting art.

"I care little to mix in society," said Edith, "I find sufficient in that of my mother and friend, who is now more than ever dependent on me for her happiness."

"Oh! my dear Miss Trevanion," exclaimed Alice, taking her hand with the most affectionate warmth, "we cannot suffer you to immure yourself in this manner. Permit *me* to divide at times, these interesting cares. I long to enjoy your companionship in some of the sweet shades of the valley, some of those lovely scenes, which seem all pure from the world's pollution, where the soul can unbosom itself to its congenial soul, and friendship may be free from the cold and artificial restraints of fashionable life.'"

"What a beautiful simpleton," thought Edith. "You are extremely kind," she uttered.

"You must let me have the pleasure," interrupted Griselda, "of introducing you to some of our most distinguished friends. Lady Maxwell—but unfortunately you cannot at present leave your friend, but when she is quite recovered, I shall claim the privilege of presenting you to her. You will be delighted with Lady Maxwell and her charming daughter."

"Pardon me," said Alice, "I do not think Miss Trevanion will be particularly delighted with Lady Maxwell; she is rather too proud for my taste, and I flatter myself I have discovered a congeniality of sentiment in the speaking eyes of Miss Trevanion."

The door opened as she spoke, and the servant again entered.

"Miss Edith," said the servant, "if the ladies will please to excuse you, Miss Adams wants to speak to you a moment."

"My absence will hardly require an apology," cried Edith, rising, "the summons of a friend, situated like mine, is indeed imperative."

She curtsied a graceful adieu, but Griselda, whose curiosity had received an irresistible impulse, suddenly exclaimed—

"Your friend, Miss Adams! Ah! who is she?" and her looks seemed to ask more than her words. "Has she a father, or is she without relations that she stays here so long?"

A dazzling sun-flash from Edith's eyes shot like a meteor across Miss Willoughby's face. The very brow of the young girl became crimson.

"Have you called upon me, madam!" she haughtily cried, "to insult Miss by your insinuations?"

The door closed upon her petrified auditors before they found breath to speak their shame and mortification.

"Gracious heavens, Griselda!" ejaculated Alice Cameron, in real and unaffected agitation, "what have you done? How could you be so coarse, so unfeeling as to make such a remark? You have exposed us both to everlasting disgrace."

"You may spare your philippic, Miss Alice," replied Griselda, wonderfully recovering her self-possession. "I do not pretend to your exquisite refinement. I have said nothing but what I was justified in saying, and her flying into such a pass on shows plainly enough that there is something suspicious about Miss Adams, and the sooner we find it out the better."

A philosopher might have judged from the violence of her defence that the accusing spirit was busy within; and it is very certain, in spite of her asseverations to the contrary, she did feel as if she had been gathering nettles. She was one of those who carelessly trample on the flowers of human feeling, then marvel to see them fading under so light a tread. She had no moral perception of those finer shades which constitute the beauty of sensibility, her own character being composed of broad and glaring stripes which knew no softening tint, nor was she conscious that any was required to form a harmonious whole.

Alice, notwithstanding the flimsy veil of artificial refinement in which she had involved herself, was really possessed of a good deal of native softness and delicacy, and had her education been directed by a judicious friend, and her mind received a proper bias, she might have been as interesting as she was fair. But unfortunately left to herself, her unpruned imagination luxuriated on romances, till she fancied herself one of the heroines of whom she read; and when she looked in the mirror, and saw reflected a face and form which seemed formed in the " prodigality of nature," it is not surprising she should associate herself with those who are always described with radiant eyes, rich waving locks, alabaster necks, and rose-leaf cheeks like her own. She now sighed for a hero of corresponding perfections, and as young Glenroy was the handsomest man she had ever seen, she had exalted him to that envied rank, though she thought him cold as—

> " The consecrated snow
> That lies in Dian's temple."

With her every interview was a *scene*—every incident an *event;* and she related to Sir Reginald the scene she had just witnessed with a pathos that was truly affecting. She adjured him most eloquently to go over immediately to apologise for his daughter, who, to show her superiority to blame, had seated herself at the piano, and began to thump out a favourite tune, while her cousin related her rudeness and its result.

Sir Reginald started out of his chair as if a hornet had stung him.

" Griselda," exclaimed he, banging down his gold-headed cane on the carpet with alarming emphasis, " Griselda, will you stop that thumping. You who have who have been brought up in the first city in the world, to behave as if you had passed your life in a pound. How came you to ask such a question?"

" Because, papa, I could not help it." She knew her father was really angry by his calling things by their right names—that is, her music, *thumping*, for he had a most overweening estimate of his daughter's talents. She tried to shelter herself under an air of playful simplicity, and again repeated—

" Indeed, my dear papa, I could not have helped speaking, if I had lost the gift of speech by it, which, you know, would be a grievous punishment to me. But I'm sure it isn't worth minding, they are *nobodies* after all."

" But they are somebodies," said Sir Reginald, raising his voice. " Is a man of the General's rank in the army to be treated with disrespect because he chooses to live secluded. Griselda, I am ashamed of you, that a daughter of mine should have behaved so unfeelingly. The rawest country girl in the land might have known better; our character for hospitality is ruined."

Sir Reginald had talked himself into such a glow that he was obliged to take out his silk handkerchief to wipe the labouring moisture from his brows. If Shakspeare had seen his daughter under the operation of this speech, he would certainly have compared the love-sick Viola to Griselda, rather than Patience on a monument, for she looked as if attacked by all the coloured melancholies that ever existed. Had she known the surmises that had glanced into Dr. Rovington's mind, but which he hid in his own honest bosom, she would have derived no small consolation. It was not the pain she had imparted to another, but the mortification she had inflicted on herself that so ruefully depressed the corners of her mouth, and quickened the motions of her heavy orbs.

" What can I do?" at last sighed Griselda, the words thumping, and raw country girl ringing in her smarting ears; " I'll write her a note of apology."

"And I too," said Alice, flying to her desk, delighted with an opportuny of displaying her talents at note-writing, an art in which romantic young ladies particularly excel."

"I'll go and apologise to her myself," said Sir Reginald ; and whistling to his shaggy eared dog, his cane was soon planted in the grass of the side walk.

I do not believe Sir Reginald Willoughby ever walked the street that people did not come to the window to look at him. Country people love to look out from the windows, and he was just such a figure as one likes to see walking, and one which dearly loves to be gazed upon. His dress was a three-cornered hat, placed on his full bottomed wig, a black coat, the fashion of which my readers may ascertain by referring to any of Hogarth's inimitable prints representing the "Rake's Progress," black unmentionables, with rich silver buckles, black silk stockings and shoes, not to mention the gold-headed cane. The *tout ensemble* was exceedingly imposing and ancestral-like. But the dress was nothing to the air which dignified it. His step was always measured to a slow march, and his shoes creaked as he walked, greatly to the admiration of the children, who gazed on his cane, as he lifted it almost perpendicularly in the air, then brought it down in a back-slanting direction, with as much awe as if it were the sceptre of Jupiter. He generally had something to say to one and all, for he was so fond of distinction that the homage of these future great men was no despicable incense.

"How are you, my little curly pate?" he would say to a little boy. "You've been curling dandelions on your head, I see," at the same time patting the sun-bleached locks of the urchin. Or, "that's a fine fellow, you'll be Lord Mayor of London by and bye," in return to the wide-scraping bow. "Does your father turn you out in the clover-field that you look so fat and rosy?" By such cheap, ready coin, gold when it comes from the heart's treasury, but dross when it issues from flattery's mint, did Sir Reginald Willoughby gain the veneration of the plebian throng.

On this occasion he walked with noticeable rapidity, nor stopped to put a single frizzled pate, though he met the whole bowing and curtseying gang.

"Tell Miss Trevanion," said he to the maid who opened the door, "that Sir Reginald Willoughby presents his most respectful compliments, and wishes to have the pleasure of seeing her for a few moments."

"Yes, sir, I will ;" and off flew the servant.

In a moment she came down stairs.

"Miss Trevanion says, sir, her friend is so unwell, she can't leave her."

"Go back and tell her I won't detain her a moment; that I have something of importance to communicate." A piece of silver slipped in the willing hand wonderfully accelerated the steps of the messenger.

She again descended bearing her young lady's refusal to see Sir Reginald.

"Is the general at home ?"

"No, sir, he has gone as far as Hexham, and will not return till late."

"Well," said Sir Reginald, "I will call another time, when I hope Miss Adams will be relieved from the worst effects of her accident. Present her my best respects, and beg her to command my services whenever she may feel the want of a friend. Good morning."

While Edith sat watching her sick friend, two notes were handed in addressed to her, both written on gilt-edged, rose-coloured paper, and one folded almost as inextricably as the Gordian knot. Edith opened them, though conscious from whence they came, and what must be their purport. The one she opened first was as follows :

"Miss Willoughby presents her most respectful compliments to Miss Trevanion, and regrets *extremely* the apparent inexplicable rudeness of her conduct this morning. Miss W, professes herself perfectly innocent of the slightest intention of wounding or insulting the feelings of Miss T. Miss W. hopes, that Miss T. will soon give her an opportunity of exercising towards her the hospitality of Hexham Hall, and that she will not remember another moment, what Miss W. fears, she *herself* can never forget."

The inextricable billet-doux ran thus:

" Will my dear Miss Trevanion permit one who is almost a *stranger* to call her by that sweetly endearing appellation? Will she permit her to hope that the *clouds* that *darkened* this *morning's* interview will *soon* be dispersed by the *rays* of *mutual* confidence and *affection*? Ah! my sweet friend, you see I cannot be restrained by the *cold* formalities of *ceremony*. *Friendship*, as well as *love*, like the electric spark, flashes with instantaneous radiance from heart to heart, and forms a direct and ethereal communication between congenial spirits. Never may the chill breath of suspicion blight the fair unfolding wreath, which I trust will henceforth entwine around the fair daughter of the north and her true and devoted

ALICE CAMERON."

A brief but polite acceptance of these characteristic apologies, was in due form dispatched to Hexham Hall; and thus was at last apparently healed the " imminent and deadly breach."

CHAPTER X.

" See where the winding vale its lavish stores
Irriguous spreads. See how the lily drinks
The latent rill, scarce oozing through the grass
Of growth luxuriant; or the humid bank
In fair profusion decks. Long let us walk
Where the breeze blows from yon extended field
Of blossomed trees. Arabia cannot boast
A fuller gale of joy. than, liberal, thence
Breathes through the sense and takes the ravished soul.
Nor is the mead unworthy of thy foot,
Full of fresh verdure, and unnumbered flowers,
The negligence of nature, wide and wild;
Where undisguised by mimic art she spreads
Unbounded beauty to the roving eye."—THOMSON.

IT seemed to Edith that she heard an invitation like this distinctly breathed into her ear, by the spirit of nature, as she stood looking from a window of the chamber in which she had for several days closely imprisoned herself, and gazing on a scene which nature's Druid bard has almost literally described, in the above inimitable lines. Her mouth was attuned, at this moment, to the rich harmonies of the season, for Susan had sunk into a sweet and refreshing slumber, and Doctor Rovington had just assured her, that his patient was better, very much better.

The lapse of a few days had partially healed the bruise her feelings had received from the rough trampling of Miss Willoughby, and they were now alive to the sweet influences that rose from the bosom of the earth, and descended simultaneously from the blue and benignant sky.

A path wound so temptingly just below the window, and she knew her mother would watch her sleeping friend, she could not resist the impulse; and putting on her shawl and bonnet, she was soon bounding along the path, with something of the step of a wild mountain girl. The change from a confined apartment to the unbounded atmosphere, from the paraphernalia of a sick chamber to the magnificent garniture of summer fields, was sufficient to give elasticity to spirits less mercurial than hers. She had the candour to confess to herself, that she had never witnessed anything so lovely, as the prospect that stretched around her. It was the season when the trees were in full blossom; when every rustic orchard resembled an imperial flower-garden; when every gale was redolent with excessive sweetness; and the path of the wanderer was literally strewed with blossoms, fair as if scattered by the fingers of Hope.

Edith directed her steps towards the ruins of an ancient castle, many of whose apartments were still nearly entire, though of the far greater number little but the walls remained, of which, in many places, huge massses strewed the ground. She seated herself, not from fatigue, but from pure admiration of a seat which the pastoral divinities must have made for the express accommodation of such un-purposed beings as herself. It was formed of the trunk of an apple-tree, which for a while forgetting its upright growth, had stretched lazily on its grassy bed, like many a human soul, that losing sight of its heavenly tendency, is grovelling supinely in the dust; but as the same soul, touched by divine impulse, springs upward toward its native heaven, the repentant tree had suddenly lifted its luxu-riant boughs, and the blossoming sprays now hung in beautiful wreaths, striving to cover the early degeneracy of the parent trunk.

Here Edith seated herself, happy in the mere consciousness of existence—happy in being the inhabitant of so fair a world. She forgot all the painful recollections of the past, and all the trembling apprehensions of the future. The soothing sound of the waters, as they flowed with soft, gurgling murmurs over their pebbly channels; the cool rustling of the leaves, as the west wind stole whisperingly and lovingly through the branches, which again bent wistfully over the stream, to whisper the secrets of nature to the passing wave, all served to lull the beholder into a state of delicious repose and self-abandonment.

"How often," she mentally exclaimed, as she looked around on its mouldering battlements and ivy-covered towers, "How often have the sounds of revelry, the shout of mirth, and the festive dance, re-echoed within those walls? The sons and daughters of prosperity once trod these spacious apartments, now desolated by the relentless hand of time; they are now forgotten! succeeding generations have ran the same gay career, and followed them to the same land of oblivion: the very structure, which for ages bade defiance to the rage of many a wintry storm, is now hastening to decay: the bird of night has chosen it for her dreary abode; the cold wind whistles through its broken arches, and dreary desolation reigns around; all, then, on earth, is born to fade!" She remained for some time buried in thought, and then again resumed her meditations: "How vain would it be to hope for permanent happiness in a world where all is doomed to suffer change! A few revolving years, and I must bid adieu to all its varying scenes: of what then will it avail, whether my journey through it was marked with joy or sorrow? The most essential point will then be, whether the prosperous days of unclouded felicity were cherished with becoming sentiments of gratitude and humility; and whether, in the hour of adversity, the afflicting dispensations of Providence were received with submission, and supported with fortitude."

On a sudden the sound of a human voice burst distinctly on her ear. She, however, fancied it might be only the effect of imagination; but a moment con-vinced her it was no delusion, as a loud hysteric laugh was again repeated, so close to her, that she started upon her feet as if she had received an electrical shock. She cast a hurried glance around, and beheld, at some distance, what appeared to resemble the figure of a man, resting against a projection of rock, whose deep shadow, thrown across the steep and uneven path, almost left it doubtful whether the object she contemplated was, in reality, what she conjectured it to be, or merely a phantom of her own creation. Certain it was she heard the voice of a human being; and that not raised in passion, but expressive of something she could have found no language to define; again it vibrated on her ear and shook her frame with agitation. Convinced that it proceeded from the gloomy spot on which her eye was still intently fixed, she felt the enervating chill of increased terror and superstition creep through every vein; each whisper of the breeze, as it agitated the surrounding foliage, or swept in low and sullen murmurs round the dilapidated turrets of the castle, increased the sensation of horror with which she was oppressed; she would have fled the spot, but actually felt as if rivetted to the earth on which she stood: besides, to regain the road, it was either requisite to penetrate into the thick recesses of a neighbouring wood, through whose intricate windings it would have been impossible to have found her way, or to have passed the precise place where this appalling object stood. With another shout, which was again repeated by the echoes of the rocks, and which again shook every nerve of the almost subdued Edith, this formidable figure darted from his retreat, and rapidly pursued his way, in a straight direction, towards the place she occupied.

It now first occurred to her that it would be most prudent to take refuge in the castle, and, with a fervent petition that the Almighty would protect her, she hastily crept through an aperture in the wall behind her which was nearly covered with weeds, but through which she had often passed to explore the interior, although, during the first moments of alarm, this seasonable retreat was unthought of.

Here, safe from observation, she watched the approach of the singular figure, whose appearance was not at all calculated to diminish her surprise or alarm. It was that of a man, whose tall emaciated form was fantastically attired in rich but obsolete and faded garments ; " whose hair was matted and his beard unshorn," and from whose wandering eyes a spirit, evidently dethroned, looked fiercely but mournfully forth.

He paused, surveyed the gloomy pile before him, then raising his eyes to Heaven, he exclaimed : " No, no! nature has no discords ; and here she reigns as pure and tranquil as when she came from the hands of her Creator. But the trail of the serpent swept over the blossoms of Eden, and its poisonous coil is under every wild flower that blushes in this second paradise of earth. Oh! I could tell a tale —such a tale as would make your blood curdle in your veins!" He gradually elevated his voice, and approached nearer as he spoke to the hiding place of the trembling Edith, who slowly retreated, with her eyes fixed as steadfastly upon him as the fascinated bird's upon the rattle-snake.

Edith shuddered, as the idea occurred to her, that the wretched being before her was some unfortunate lunatic, who had escaped from his keeper ; yet the sight of him created an interest more lively than mere compassion could have inspired, more overwhelming than the fear which had so lately oppressed her heart, and which now began, in some measure, to subside.

There is not a more affecting sight in nature than the wreck of an immortal mind. A whole kingdom laid waste, is less an object of desolation ; and all this sad ruin is visible at one glance, in that little orbit, the eye so well designated,
" The spirit's throne of light."

Edith shrunk from the presence of insanity, with a different emotion from that which agitates the young and unseared heart, when compelled to look upon a spectacle so humbling to human pride. The unfortunate stranger lifted his hat from his sallow forehead and bowed till his black, gipsy locks almost touched the ground, while Edith, rendered respectful by fear, curtsied as low, though not more gracefully : his bow, as well as his whole demeanour, being eloquent of better days.

" Stay," continued he, following her with earnest gesticulations ; " I have sworn to tell the story of my wrongs, to every ear that can listen, to every heart that can feel.—I have told it to the listening groves, and the groves have told it again to the babbling stream, and did ye not hear it as ye sat gazing there."

" Yes, yes!" she replied, thinking it expedient to fall in with his wild fancies still gradually moving though unconsciously, in a different direction from that in which she came : " yes, and from my soul I pity thee."

" Aye, aye! pity!" ejaculated he, " that costs nothing, and is easily given—I had a son once,—a noble youth—he was drowned and I pitied him—I believe I drove him to it—he went mad, I believe I was the cause of that—people say I'm mad, but I don't believe them—no, no"—and the man shook his head. " I had a home once, a noble mansion—I have none now." He cast a horrid glance around ; his eyes already emitted a beam of painful radiance, or an expression of despondent feeling, so mournful, that those of the gentle Edith filled with tears, and her audible sigh reached his ear. He darted forward, seized her hand with impetuosity, and, in agitated accents, exclaimed :—

" Ah! you also sigh! If you have lost a child, if you have lost a child, if you regret the premature destruction of all hopes of bliss, I, even I, will sympathize with you ; our tears, our sighs, shall blend together ; we will kneel on the sacred spot of earth, where, in the sleep of death, the objects of our love repose ; together

together we will pluck the flowers of each succeeding season to decorate their urns, and, bending o'er their graves, recal those cherished scenes of past felicity, those fleeting hours of joy, alas! for ever fled."

His frame shook with convulsive agitation, every particle of colour forsook his lips, and as he raised his fine dark eye to the vault of Heaven, its late alarming wildness was tempered by the tear of retrospection:—he raised the snowy hand

of Edith, and, as he respectfully pressed it to his lips, in a tone of the deepe melancholy, he again addressed her:—

"He is gone," said he, "for ever gone; no lamentations can now recal him; at least they tell me so; yet still I fondly imagine his gentle spirit wanders near, and marks the wanderings of his father."

At that instant a dark cloud obscured the bright rays of the sun; its appearance excited in the maniac some ide soothing to his distempered mind; the aation of his feelings subsided; an air   mild resignation overspread his

No. 7.

countenance; he extended one hand towards the beauteous orb which had attracted his attention, and with a voice of dignified serenity, exclaimed :—

"Just so, lady, has the dark shadow of death obscured the bright object of my earliest affection, the enlivening beam which irradiated my path of life ; (and he clasped his hands with impassioned fervour,) "yet the gloom will soon be dispersed ; it is but a passing cloud ; in those fair regions above, where all is peace and tranquillity, we shall meet again ; the radiance of eternal day will shine on our re-union ; the voice of the Omnipotent, the Omnipotent Judge of all, will dispense universal happiness around ; and those who have on earth bent beneath His afflicting dispensations, and bowed with resignation to His bereaving providence, may expect a rich reward. But is it not strange," he continued, "that I have never been able to ascertain where my much-lamented son was interred ? It is in vain that I have endured the utmost extremes of heat and cold, and that years have been devoted to this one object : the most remote climates have been explored, the proud summits of the loftiest mountains ascended, and the unfathomable depths of the wide-extended ocean traversed. I have travelled on the wings of the midnight tempest ; enthroned in clouds, i have wandered through fields of celestial radiance, among those innumerable gems, which we so often admire as they roll through boundless space, and which are indeed centres of systems wonderful and extensive as our own. You can form no idea of the splendour with which I have, at times, found myself surrounded in these aerial excursions ; of the bright beings by whom I have been attended, or of the persuasive arguments they have used to reconcile me to the apparent rigour of my destiny ; yet even they cannot give me the information I require, and nothing but disappointment and vexation has hitherto attended my researches." Then hastily turning round, and fixing on the amazed Edith the keen glance of inquiry, he added, "but perhaps you can inform me where the ashes of my poor boy repose."

Edith was perfectly at a loss in what manner to answer this strange, this incoherent speech ; she in fact felt a degree of terror she was unwilling to indulge, she therefore turned from him, and was about quitting the place when he again prevented her.

"Stay," he said, "I have not told you all my wrongs—look upon this lofty mansion," he raised his arm, and pointed to the noble ruin of the castle ; "here it stands in its pillared pride, the noblest model of architecture the world ever witnessed, where Gothic majesty, Corinthian beauty, and Doric simplicity were once harmoniously blended. In me you behold the legitimate master of all this fair domain. I planted it—I reared it—and I said to myself, the sons of genius and the daughters of beauty shall come and repose under the vines I have planted, and the great and honoured shall recline beneath the shadows I have spread. But the worm was at the root of my gourd, and its broad leaves withered in an hour. Yes ! the spoiler came—the cold-blooded villain who now dwells here, came and drove me like a beast from my home, demolished the statues I had reared ; set up my own image—yes, the image of me, who was formed after the similitude of my Creator, for the birds of heaven to lacerate with their bills, and the winds to buffet and deface. Oh, ye righteous Powers !" continued he, lifting up one emaciated hand to heaven, "send down a bolt, red with uncommon wrath, upon this lawless violator of all human rights."

There was an air of wild ruined grandeur about his person—an elevation in his language—a connectedness in his story, in spite of its apparent incongruities, that impressed Edith with an interest and awe that almost absorbed her personal apprehensions.

"You have indeed been most deeply injured," cried she, in a voice so soothing, it might have charmed the demon of insanity ; "but we are commanded to forgive, as we hope to be forgiven our transgressions." .

"I never wronged a human being," interrupted he, wildly. "I never trampled on the ant beneath my feet—but, like the persecuted Son of Man, I have not where to lay my head."

Here the unhappy maniac wrung his hands and wept bitterly.

" Unfortunate being," exclaimed Edith, her voice choked with painful sympathy ; "may He who looks forth from above, and knows our slightest actions, heal thy wounded spirit and bid thee live !"

Soothed by a voice so kind and sweet, touched by such visible sympathy from one so young and apparently high-bred, the softened maniac drew nearer and again attempted to take that fair hand, which seemed so formed to bind up with its soft touch the wounds of human suffering and woe. Recoiling with ill-disguised repugnance she darted from the place, and looked anxiously around for some means of eluding her strange companion. " Thank Heaven," almost escaped her lips, when she saw amid the ruins a gentleman and a young female seated on a rustic bench both intently reading from the same book. At another moment she might have hesitated to disturb them—" for both were young and one was fair"—and the arm of the young man was passed fondly round the waist of the fair girl, whose uncovered flaxen ringlets played softly against his bending cheek; but, situated as she now was, she would not suffer false delicacy to prevail over her judgment, and pressing forward, she stood directly before them, before either of them seemed conscious of her approach. The young man rose abruptly with a look of respectful surprise, for Edith, breathless from previous agitation and present embarrassment, was unable to word her claims upon protection, however eloquently her looks might ask it. If Edith had appeared under a partial eclipse when she presented herself before the severe scrutiny of the jealous cousins, she now amply vindicated the praises of the admiring doctor. Pure air, exercise, and excited sensibility, three of the best cosmetics in the world, had lighted up her eyes with their intense radiance, and mantled her cheek with a bloom more beautiful than all the budding roses of Christendom. Her bonnet was entirely thrown back, and though it certainly was not intentionally done, she might have been pardoned for the act, so soft and burnished were the dark chestnut folded locks, which were thus revealed.

Before the young man had seen half the "blushing apparition" that flitted over her face, he was made conscious of the cause of her alarm, by the appearance of the poor maniac, and assuring her he was perfectly harmless, he entreated her to be seated by his sister, whom she now recognized as Constance Glenroy : a kind and friendly greeting passed between them. and anxious inquiries after the health of Susan were made by Constance; while Herbert Glenroy whispered in the ear of the maniac, who, after turning and bowing with the same courtly respect his gypsy locks to the ground, retreated with rapid and noiseless steps through an opposite path.

" I regret, Miss Trevanion," said Herbert, " you should have suffered so much alarm from one of the most inoffensive of human beings. The wildness of his person, the startling energy of his language, and the peculiar character of his madness, justify, however, all thee motion he has excited. I knew him when he was a boy, in his brighter days, and I never look upon the ruin without sighing for the lamp that once burnt within the gates of the temple. To all who are acquainted with his history, he is an object of the deepest commiseration rather than of terror."

" He told me," said Edith, " the history of his wrongs, and he must indeed have a pitiless heart who could not commiserate a being so deeply injured and oppressed."

" Alas ! poor fellow," answered Herbert, " his own ambition has been his worst oppressor."

" You do not know, dear Edith," said Constance, " all the secrets of these groves. Many is the wild flower bouquet he has gathered for Margaret and myself, in gratitude for our listening sympathy."

" You excite my interest to know his real history," said Edith. " He says he has no home to shelter him——no spot wherein to lay his head." " It is not that there are no kind hearts to welcome him—no hospitable hearths to give him kindly warmth," replied Herbert. " But he scorns a meaner habitation than the one he fancies he has erected, and which he deludes himself has been lawlessly wrested from his possession. Of all the forms of madness which I have ever witnessed, I recollect none so touching as his ;—such a deep-rooted conviction of unmerited injuries, so eloquently supported and affectingly described. For hours he will sit and gaze upon these ruins, and his eyes will drop tears as fast as the myrrh tree its medicinal gum. But if I do not tax your patience too far, I will relate all I know of his earliest life."

"You will find me an interested auditor," said Edith, "but I protest against your standing in that respectful attitude before the throne, of which I have so abruptly dispossessed you. I would not be an usurper, nor exclude from his kingdom the legitimate sovereign."

She moved as she spoke and vacated the seat by Constance, which Herbert resumed with a gallant bow, saying (how could he do otherwise?) "I should be greater than Cæsar, were I to refuse to share the honour of a throne like this."

There was an irresistible charm in the frankness of Edith. It lifted her above all petty affectation, and like the bland summer atmosphere, seemed to open and expand all hearts within the reach of its influence. What would Miss Willoughby have said had she beheld her movement, and heard its accompanying speech? She would have elevated her hands and eyes, and exclaimed, " Did you ever hear of such confidence? To ask a young gentleman to take a seat by her side, to whom she had never been introduced? She who was so cold and distant to us! But we are only ladies."

Herbert Glenroy related the following particulars respecting the maniac, to which Edith attentively listened.

CHAPTER XI.

In a retired spot, about a quarter of a mile beyond the beautiful and picturesque village of————, stood as mall villa, the property and residence of Captain Evelyn, under whose immediate superintendence the edifice had been constructed ; and the embellishments of its external aspect, together with the expensive and costly fittings of the interior, marked the mind and character of the owner.

In the same regiment of which Evelyn was the captain, there was a young lieutenant of the name of Beverley, to whom Evelyn had, in the course of military service, become most sincerely attached. Beverley was the youngest son of a highly respectable family, who entertained an expectation that in forming an advantageous matrimonial connexion, his handsome person and insinuating manners might compensate for his deficiency of fortune. But Beverley, early in life, frustrated their ambitious hopes, by marrying a beautiful German peasant, of whom he had become enamoured while employed on foreign duty ; an act which had so much exasperated his haughty relations, that when he returned to England, they universally refused to acknowledge him, and he retired on half-pay, with his wife, into Yorkshire, where they resided in contented poverty, for eight years ; till, on the death of Mrs. Beverley, her husband, by the advice of Captain Evelyn, whose friendship had never deserted him, came up to London, in order to make one more application to his offended family, hoping that since the cause of their estrangement existed no longer, they might become reconciled to him, or at least, be induced to afford that protection to his child, of which he felt that she would, at the decease of her only surviving parent, stand so much in need. Even the independent-spirited Evelyn, who made it his boast that he had never stooped to solicit a favour on his own account, ardently advocated the cause of suffering merit, and addressed a long letter, possessing more of energy than grace in its composition, to the imperious adversaries of his injured friend. The blunt though forcible appeal was made in vain ; and Beverley, with more pride than prudence, declared, that he had rather see his child starving, than condescend to farther supplication. This mortification and disappointment, together with the loss of a beloved wife, so preyed upon his spirits, as to produce a low, nervous fever, which brought him to the grave : having first bequeathed his daughter to the friendly care of Evelyn.

As Beverley had been compelled to live up to the full extent of his narrow income, the property that he left at his death was found to be barely sufficient for the defrayment of his funeral expenses.

Evelyn, having seen the endeared companion of many a social hour, the friend of his younger days, decently interred, evinced his regard for Beverley's memory, by taking his daughter to his own home ; resolved to treat her in every respect the same as if she had been his own daughter.

At the age of fourteen, Katherine Beverley received every attention and consolation under the hospitable roof of Captain Evelyn. Her grief was at first deep, and a settled dejection overspread her beautiful countenance ; but a few months restored her to tranquility by convincing her, that though the author of her existence, the beloved protector of her early years, had been called from a life chequered with many trials, and could no longer bestow on her the smile of approbation, or accost her with the endearing accents of parental love, she was yet left in possession of those blessings to which thousands not less deserving than herself were perfect strangers. As she grew towards woman's estate, she became, from her excessive beauty and artless demeanour, the admiration of all that beheld her. She was indeed a lovely creature ; her fair flaxen hair, her soft, sweet, dark blue eyes, her delicate complexion, her light and fragile frame, gave her altogether the appearance of a creature not designed for this world ; while her disposition was as affectionate, as flexible, as docile, as generous, and as modest, as the exquisite symmetry of her outward form might have led the spectator to expect.

She soon became the constant companion of the Captain's only son, who would leave his boyish sports to attend her evening rambles, and followed with avidity every study, every pursuit, he thought agreeable to her. Each revolving year, while it matured their persons, enlightened their understandings and expanded their hearts, strengthened the affection each bore the other ; and so absolute became the ascendancy Katharine gained over Charles Evelyn, that he appeared to live but in her presence, and if at any time he was deprived of her society for a few short weeks, he mourned her absence as though the separation had been for years.

Captain Evelyn saw and sanctioned their love, he possessed sufficient to give his son an easy and independent fortune, sufficient to procure for them the elegancies of life. A sweet sequestered cottage, situated in a retired spot, and surrounded with everything beautiful in nature, was purchased for the occasion ; the most exquisite taste was displayed in its embellishments ; and the future appeared decked in all the bright colours of permanent felicity ; each loved retirement, while, blest with the gifts of fortune, health, and the society of each other, unalloyed bliss appeared their future lot ; the day was at length fixed and all was revelry and joy.

In the mean time a neighbouring castle, whose ivied towers and lofty battlements, were plainly visible from this sequestered spot, and which had long been fitting up for the reception of an English family, was completed, and Sir John Waldegrave, his only daughter, and a large establishment, came down to reside in it for the season. Soon after their arrival a splendid entertainment was given, to which all the surrounding gentry were invited ; the lovers were of the party, and unconscious of the impending storm ready to burst over their devoted heads, spent a happy evening and returned home, delighted with the hospitality and condescension of their host.

Sir John Waldegrave was possessed of an immense fortune ; had married young, been unfortunate in his choice, and on becoming a widower had resolutely determined never again to alter his condition ; firm to his purpose, he continued insensible to the beauty, wealth, or accomplishments of the fair votaries of fashion by whom he was constantly surrounded, and devoted his whole time to his daughter.

Having no heir to inherit either his title or estates, he wished to bestow his daughter, to whom at his death the latter must devolve, on some virtuous and distinguished character who would neither waste them by extravagance nor squander them at the gaming table, or on the turf. He felt pursuaded (however erroneous such an opinion might be, since virtue was never yet confined to one particular station of life) that such a being could not exist in the gay circles of fashion, he therefore determined upon commencing his researches in the country, far from the baneful influence of the metropolis, far from the contaminating example of the great.

The fete had been given expressly for the purpose of assembling all the young people in the vicinity of his domain, and while apparently engaged in promoting the comfort and amusement of his guests, true to his purpose, each individual underwent the strictest scrutiny.

The unconscious Charles, emulous to please the beloved object of his choice, anxious to appear to advantage in the eyes of her who was all the world to him, shone superior to the rest, his fine manly countenance beamed with candour and intelligence, his bright expressive eyes shot the fire of genius, and every action might have graced nobility. The flattering, the universal attention he met with from every party, especially from the mothers of young and blooming girls, at once, in the opinion of the baronet, stamped his value, and he exulted in the happy destiny which promised so soon to crown his sanguine wishes with success.

Miss Waldegrave was the gayest of the gay ; very little of the *hauteur* of high life was perceptible in her deportment; her motto appeared to be " present enjoyment ;" and her affability on this eventful evening created her an interest in the hearts of many of the sons and daughters of the surrounding gentry; they adored that genuine cheerfulness, that disposition to receive and bestow pleasure, which assimilated so strongly with their own character ; her person was showy, her dress was fashionable and expensive, her accomplishments rather brilliant than solid ; she possessed that confidence in herself which ever enabled her to display every accquirement, however trifling, to the best advantage ; and she was by nature endowed by that happy facility of expression, that eloquence which embellished every subject she discoursed on. She entered into conversation with many of the party, and appeared particularly pleased with Miss Beverley, whose manners and appearance, however, presented a striking contrast to the gay Maud Waldegrave ; who laughed, and joked, but certainly appeared less the lady than Katherine ; it is true neither her modest unassuming manners, or the rumour of her approaching nuptials, had escaped the observation of Sir John Waldegrave, but as his own had been an alliance of interest, he was a stranger to the power of real love, and considered it only as the offspring of romance, or, as he sometimes laughingly observed, the " Poet's toy." He was therefore ill able to appreciate the value of the sacrifice he required.

Judging by the examples which are daily occurring at court, he thought it impossible that Charles Evelyn should refuse the advantageous proposals he intended making, should another interview, and the enquiries he intended setting on foot, confirm the opinion he had already formed of his respectability. Maud, he was well aware, would raise no obstacle to his plans, as the smallest wish of his had ever been a law to her ; nor was he less willing to contribute towards those she formed ; the most perfect harmony had invariably subsisted between them: nor was the project now in contemplation at all calculated, with a girl of Maud's disposition, to diminish it; and having ever considered vanity as the peculiar characteristic of the female sex, he supposed a more brilliant conquest would be a sufficient compensation for the disappointment he was going to inflict on Katherine Beverley ; he accordingly intended promoting an intimacy between her and his daughter, as he doubted not that, among the gay throng who would frequent the castle, many would be found eager to supply the place of the devoted Charles.

Having thus deluded himself, and found a cover for his injustice, he sought the earliest opportunity of waiting on Captain Evelyn. He made known his wishes and received a willing ear. Delighted with the honour conferred on his son, dazzled by the glittering prospects arising before him, and fired by his natural ambition, which, till now, had laid dormant for want only of a stimulus, Captain Evelyn eagerly gave that promise which sealed the doom of the unfortunate lovers, and a day was spent at the castle as a preliminary step to an explanation with his son.

Maud, informed of her father's wishes respecting his visitors, was all smiles and animation; she treated Charles Evelyn with the most distinguished attention, and certainly took infinite pains to ingratiate herself with the sweet Katherine Beverley, whose future happiness Sir John Waldegrave was industriously endeavouring to undermine, and, never suspecting that any obstacle could arise to frustrate his plans, Maud congratulated herself on the election her father had made, having frequently declared a handsome husband was the summit of her wishes. She was gay, sprightly, and votatile, the very counterpart of what Charles once was; the exact companion he probably would have chosen, had he never felt the influence of Katherine's softened manners. On his return home, his father was warm in his encomiums on Maud Waldegrave, and expatiated on the magnificence and hospitality which reigned at the castle, declaring he had never, till now, been sensible of the real value of wealth.

On the following morning, having summoned his ill-fated son to the library, he made him fully acquainted with what he termed the disinterested proposals of Sir John, and after enumerating the benefits likely to result from a union with his lovely daughter, he expressly forbade him, under pain of his displeasure, to encourage any future intercourse with Miss Beverley, as he could not, in conscience, any longer sanction an attachment which would so materially interfere with his future advance in life. He then with the utmost indifference proposed settling the affair with Katherine, and advising her to accept an invitation she had long had from an aunt in the country. "It will," he continued, "remove her from the scene of disappointment, which, I doubt not, her good sense will soon convince her is unavoidable; and, indeed, such is the disinterested generosity of her nature, that I am convinced she will rejoice in your elevation rather than wish to be the barrier to it."

Charles Evelyn stood riveted to the spot for some time, incapable of reply. He saw all his dreams of future bliss for ever blighted, and found himself on the point of being bereft of what he valued more than life itself; at length, with a look of mingled agony and surprise, he exclaimed, "My dear father, you cannot— no—you cannot be in earnest; what on earth could compensate for the loss of Miss Beverley's affection? Deprived of her beloved society I feel that I should cease to exist." His agitation increased as he continued; "Sir John cannot be aware that my faith is plighted to another, that every sentiment of my heart acknowledges the superiority of that lovely being, whose destiny in a few days will be blended with mine."

"Hold! sir," cried his disconcerted parent, "this is trifling, this is romantic folly, the mere chimera of a heated imagination; think you, your immaculate Katherine would, if offered to her acceptance, reject a splendid alliance out of consideration to your feelings, or from any mistaken idea of propriety? No, believe me, Charles, women are as fickle as the wind; I have found them so, and love, as the baronet observes, is but the offspring of fancy, and has no existence in the heart; respect and esteem are different things, and may be felt for every deserving object. Why cannot you cherish the same sentiments for Miss Waldegrave that you have professed to feel for Katherine? she is equally worthy of your attention, and will be a much more desirable bride."

"No, never, never," exclaimed Charles with impetuosity, "can I relinquish those prospects which have constituted the happiness of my life; it would be an insult to Miss Waldegrave to offer her a hand while the affections are unalterably fixed upon another, nor am I capable of repaying the acknowledged preference of my beloved Katherine with an action so replete with every thing repugnant to the feelings of a man of honour. Sir John must be made acquainted with my present engagement, and of the impossibility of its being superseded by any other claim."

"My determination is fixed," retorted his father; "the baronet is aware of these circumstances, but he thinks them of no importance ; he is pleased to express his conviction of your principles being such as would induce him to place with confidence his lovely Maud under your legal protection ; he wishes to see her married, and the distinguished honour he has conferred on you, to whom the alliance offers rank and splendour, surely merits some sacrifice."

The wretched victim of his ambition expostulated, but in vain, and the misguided father at length in a frenzy of passion, exclaimed———

"Degenerate being!———do I live to behold a son of mine reject the noble descendant of an illustrious house, and brave the just displeasure of the author of his existence, because a romantic passion has subverted his reason ; but, mark me, Charles, no more objections if you value my affections ; as my curse, my eternal curse, will attend a deviation from that duty I require as a parent at your hands: I have set my mind on this union and any further opposition on your part will assuredly call down my everlasting denunciation."

He then hastened to Katherine, ere the angry flush of disappointment had subsided, and, however conscience might intrude, he endeavoured to silence its unerring dictates by pursuading himself that the laws of nature entitled him to an implicit obedience from the being who had derived his existence from him.

He found Katherine in the library, she stood looking from a window, listening attentively to the warblings of a favourite bird ; on his entrance she advanced to meet him, and without appearing to notice the cloud that hovered on his brow, cheerfully tendered the salutations of the morning. He answered her with hesitation, for he was revolving in his mind the best method of introducing the subject next his heart; at length he took her hand———

"My dear Katherine, I must now solicit your candid attention; you will be surprised at the intelligence I am going to communicate, and should I unwillingly inflict the pang of disappointment on your susceptible feelings, I trust your good sense and just idea of propriety will enable you to bear the unavoidable event with becoming resignation."

This exordium, combined with the unusual circumstance of Captain Evelyn having absented himself from breakfast, together with the agitation that still marked his countenance, and the private interview he had just had with his son, prepared Katherine to hear something dreadful, but of what nature she could not possibly divine. Unused since the death of her father to affliction, Captain Evelyn forsaw, in whatever shape it assailed her, the probability of its making a lasting impression ; he felt he had an arduous task to perform ; but the glorious result, the gratification of that ambition he had long in secret cherished, at once superseded every returning feeling of equity and paternal affection ; and averting his eyes from her pallid cheek and quivering lip, with one desperate effort at self-possession, he proceeded to inform her of Sir John Waldegrave's proposals, concluding with observing—"Charles and I have discussed the matter between us ; and with that readiness to obey my wishes which he has ever manifested, he has consented to abide by my decision ; he leaves everything to my arrangement, being thoroughly convinced that I must be the best judge. I am a father; you cannot therefore wonder, nor do I scruple to acknowledge, that I shall feel pleasure, infinite pleasure, in seeing him adorn that station he is so well calculated to fill."

He met with no interruption from the object before him, he therefore proceeded to entreat that she would not, by any opposition which could ultimately produce no alterations in his sentiments, destroy the brightening prospects of a family who had protected her for so many years, at the same time hinting at the propriety of accepting the invitation of her aunt.

Katherine had sufficiently conquered her feelings to be enabled to listen to him with the profoundest attention ; one truant tear had died on the burning surface of a cheek now crimsoned with the glowing tints of justly awakened resentment, but no sigh escaped her bosom ; no tremulous expostulation murmured on her lips ; she broke not the silence she had imposed on herself till the captain proposed the visit to her aunt, when, with a look of dignity that he had never before seen her assume, and a glance that penetrated his very soul, she coolly said,

"Do you, then, fear the effect of my presence may have on your son? Do you fear I shall exert the little remaining influence I may possess to tempt him from his duty?—or are you actuated by a nobler motive?—you, perhaps, commiserate

my feelings, and wish to spare me the humiliating prospect of a rival's triumph—if so, allow me to observe, I should support it with a firmness that might surprise you both, as my only source of regret would arise from having trusted in vows which the paltry glare of grandeur could so easily dissolve, from having been the dupe of his duplicity. The first maxim my ever-to-be-lamented father strove to inculcate in my youthful mind was, to sacrifice my dearest interests where the happiness o another was at stake ; I shall now glory in fulfilling what would have been his injunction had he lived to be the arbiter of my fate ;—that Charles's union may be

No. 8,

happy is my sincerest wish ; that his future peace may never be disturbed by past events, or by a recurrence to his broken vows, shall be my constant prayer.''

She then left Captain Evelyn totally at a loss to decide whether her conduct was the result of insensibility or true greatness of mind ; tears and reproaches he had been prepared to encounter, but her calm dispassionate renunciation of her claims at once staggered and confounded him : that he was ambitious admitted not a doubt, but, had he given the subject mature deliberation, it is most probable nature would have triumphed :—but as the mountain torrent, when swollen with repeated rains, oversteps the boundaries assigned by nature, rushes impetuous over the plain, and bears down all that impedes its progress, so, led away by the impulse of the moment, and heedless of the misery he was going to inflict, he resolved to persevere, without reflecting that ruin and devastation might mark his course. But by whatever motive Katherine might be actuated, he dreaded her remaining in the house, as, without the greatest circumspection on his part, an explanation would unavoidably take place between her and his son ; which, while it branded him with infamy, would probably frustrate all his plans.

How greatly was he relieved when a chaise, which she had ordered immediately on her quitting the apartment, drove to the door ; he saw her quietly seated in it with sensations almost bordering on delight, as more than half his obstacles appeared removed.

Katherine had ever appeared timid in the extreme ; she yet possessed spirit, which, when once roused, nothing could subdue ; she felt indignant at Charles, led by his father to suppose his concurrence had been obtained with little difficulty— told that he considered the demands of duty more binding than those of love,—she rejoiced at, rather than regretted, her newly-acquired freedom : but, had she known a father's threatened curse had not yet power to extort compliance, how different would have been her feelings.

As the carriage wound along the glen, her eye rested on the lovely spot that was soon to have been her residence and the seat of that felicity she had so long anticipated ; a confused combination of feelings swelled at her heart—feelings she could now indulge, unrestrained by the intrusive eye of curiosity or the humiliating glance of pity ; but the theory of Katherine Beverley was invaribly reduced to practice, and the sentiments she had avowed in the presence of Captain Evelyn, though at the time the impulse of the moment, were yet the guide of her future conduct ; and the only appearance of weakness she betrayed on this distressing event was, when about to envelope the beautiful resemblance of her lover in the packet that was in all probability to exclude it for ever from her sight. She certainly gazed upon each unconscious feature with a sensation of intense agony ; a few tears fell on the sparkling gems that surrounded it, and a deep and audible sigh testified her regret that a form so fair should enshrine a heart so false ; but ere she quitted her chamber every mark of distress was banished from her countenance. It may be supposed she was devoid of feeling, but that was not the case : the children of adversity had often witnessed the tear of sensibility shed for them, she had considered Charles as the first of created beings, her affection for him was founded on the basis of virtue and esteem, the decided preference her heart had accorded him had never been disguised, but its duration could not in Katherine's well-organised mind, exceed that hour which presented him to her view as the degraded being who could sacrifice the long-cherished wishes of his heart at the shrine of ambition : her love had been strong, but her reason was stronger, and however she might inwardly regret the degeneracy of him whom she had considered so perfect, she resolutely determined that no murmur should escape her lips, and no gloomy discontent disturb the domestic felicity of those among whom she must in future reside. She had hastily enclosed all her lover's letters and presents, with a few lines from herself, and delivered them to the servant for her young master.

It is probable, that to a person possessing a knowledge of the world, a doubt might have arisen respecting the veracity of the captain ; but Katherine was artless herself ; she felt the most profound respect for her guardian ; she never knew him deviate from the paths of truth and rectitude, and depended as implicitly on him as she had ever done on Charles ; no suspicion, then, intruded itself on her mind : she actually believed the case to be as it had been represented to her, and while she supposed father and son alike swayed by interested motives, they both sunk in her estimation in proportion as they had hitherto been exalted.

The servant, faithful to her trust, carefully concealed the packet, and determined to deliver it to none but Charles. Accordingly, when the captain was quietly seated at his solitary dinner, without, however, much appetite to enjoy the delicacies that smoked before him, she hastened to his son's apartment, and gently tapping at the door, put it into his hand, informing him that her young mistress was on the road to her aunt's ; and, without waiting his reply, hastily left the room.

Charles opened the packet with impetuosity ; and totally unacquainted with the particulars of his father's interview with Katherine, an electric shock could not have produced a greater effect than the knowledge that she was really gone ; gone, too, under an impression of his inconstancy—gone, with the professed intention of forgetting him ! Unacquainted with the alarming denunciation that awaited him, should he refuse to comply with the heart-rending mandate, her parting note harrowed up his soul, convulsive agitation shook his frame, and every limb trembled with emotion as his eager eye traced the following lines :—

"CHARLES EVELYN—

"It is not my intention to reproach you ; no, I leave the abode of so many years, desirous only of obliterating from my heart the remembrance of one whose image was once indelibly engraven there, desirous of forgetting what were once my prospects, though still anxious that yours may ever remain unclouded ; nor do I wish to distress you by a repetition of those protestations in which I once fondly confided. I have enclosed your miniature ; to retain it would now be criminal, as I must learn to consider its original as the form only in which I had enshrined the creature of my own imagination ; the delusion now no longer exists ; experience has convinced me how fallacious was my dependance on human excellence. As you have resigned your claims, I urge not mine, but hasten to conclude with the fervent hope that the brilliant prospects ambition is now opening to your view may be as replete with happiness as the more humble ones you once professed to anticipate with so much pleasure might have been ; and that your happiness may be permanent will ever be the sincere prayer of

"KATHERINE BEVERLEY.'

In an agony of grief he sought not to restrain, he frantically exclaimed, "My destiny then is fixed ; suspected of an action I would die rather than commit, stamped with the character of a villain, and denied the privilege of exculpating myself to the dearest object of my love, can a father's curse inflict greater anguish than I now endure?"

Reflection increased rather than mitigated his despair :—accustomed, from infancy, to pay strict obedience to his father's will, he had never, till now, disputed his authority ; but when he saw all that rendered life desirable torn from his eager grasp—when on the point of being made indissolubly his, when he compared the bright visions of the preceding day with those of the present, when he cast his eyes towards the adjoining glen, of which his window commanded a prospect, and contemplated the preparations that were going on, the improvements which his Katherine had planned—great was the conflict. The workmen were pursuing their tasks with alacrity, exulting in the approaching festival, unconscious of the sad reverse a single day had produced. Almost maddened at the sight he threw himself on the couch, then rose again, and hastily closed the shutters of his apartment, in the vain hope that darkness might ease his tortured heart : towards evening his father entered his chamber : he was desirous of ascertaining whether his son was better reconciled to the proposal he had made him in the morning. Charles started from his recumbent posture, but the obscurity of the room prevented the deep anguish that was imprinted on every feature from being visible.

"I am come," said his father, "to inform you of the result of my conversation with Miss Beverley. I can assure you, Charles, she did not raise a single objection; she appeared to think me perfectly right; and, with that prudence I ever gave her credit for, immediately quitted the house, that her presence might not be the means of your incurring my displeasure."

"She is gone!" exclaimed Charles, starting from his seat, " and evidently thinks me the most degraded being in existence! Oh! if you can feel one spark of pity, remove the stigma your representations have cast on my character; suffer her not to believe me the sordid wretch you must have pictured me."

"Suffer me to ask," resumed his father haughtily, "from whom you have received your information; who told you, sir, that I had pictured you a sordid wretch, or that Katherine Beverley considered you the most degraded being in existence? Answer me; did the artful, insinuating girl, for whom you thus oppose my wishes, seek an explanation with you before she left the house?—No prevarication—have you, or have you not, seen her?"

Here he paused, for passion impeded further utterance. After several ineffectual struggles for anything like composure, Charles replied, "No, sir; Miss Beverley sought no explanation, nor could she wish it, as, superior to every mean and selfish action herself, she can in future cherish no sentiment but contempt for a person who is capable of dissolving an honourable engagement with the mercenary hope of gaining a few unnecessary thousands, which, so purchased, could only be productive of misery, nay, even infamy, to the possessor."

Captain Evelyn considered these keen reproaches as levelled at himself, though in fact Charles was only endeavouring to point out the light in which his own conduct was, in all probability, viewed by Katherine. His father, however, absolutely stormed with rage, bestowed the most disgraceful epithets on the unconscious and unoffending Katherine, and after having levelled at his son a volley of abuse, he rushed from the apartment and retired to his own for the night, a prey to every evil passion that could deform his breast.

The displeasure of his father sunk deep into the heart of Charles, while, persuaded that the vengeance of Heaven was the never—failing consequence of a parent's curse persuaded, too, that no argument would be sufficient to prevail on the lovely injured Katherine to brave its dread result—reason's empire shook, and ere the morning sun had again illuminated the eastern sky, the once animated, intelligent Charles Evelyn, was a wretched maniac: the glorious luminary of day rose with its accustomed splendour, but it rose the harbinger of woe; it shone from a cloudless sky, but the intellectual powers of Charles were set in the shades of night.

From dreams of future grandeur, spacious palaces, and sumptuous revenues, the father was awakened to a sense of his misfortune by the frantic ravings of his son! those alone, who like him have been the cause of so fatal a catastrophe can form any just conception of the agonizing feeling he endured, when he beheld that son who would have been the solace of his declining years, whose talents were the admiration of all who knew him, stopped in the prime of his life, in the beginning of a career his virtues might have rendered brilliant, doomed to worse than death, to years of lingering misery and woe. With desperation in his eye he surveyed the wreck before him, struggling to disengage himself from the grasp of the domestics, whom the bustle had brought to the apartment, and who, seeing the deplorable state he was reduced to, had secured him to prevent his injuring himself or others. He retained an indistinct idea of his misfortune, but his disturbed imagination suggested to him that relentless death had deprived him of Katherine, not the imperious mandate of a father: with frenzied accents he exclaimed, "Hold me not—death has robbed me of her—the grave is cold, but not so cold as the heart of Charles Evelyn.—You weep," continued he, turning his wandering eyes towards the varying countenance of his father—"I cannot weep: I know you pitied her; Heaven bless you for it! I know you wished to save her, yet who would not? for she was loveliness itself, I would have died to have saved her."

At this appeal his father uttered a deep groan, and unable longer to sustain the conflicting emotions that tortured his heart, sunk senseless on the ground. As if actuated by some secret impulse Charles became more calm: he gazed mournfully at him and then at the attendants;—"Is this death?" said he. "How silent!—my Katherine, too, is silent. If you see her," he continued, addressing the inanimate form of his father, "if you see her in the world to which you go, tell her, I will never cease to love her; tell her I will deck her grave with flowers, tell her I will soon lie down to rest upon the turf that covers her."

Tears of pity fell from the eyes of all the attendants, some of whom had lived in the family many a long year, though to the heart of each the object of their commiseration was endeared by the constant urbanity of his manners, and the benevolence of his disposition. The father was at length conveyed to bed, where he long continued in a state of insensibility, and Charles suffered himself to be led to his apartment. Medical assistance was procured, the most skilful of the faculty were called in, but all that could be done was without effect; it was not a transient delirium that opiates could remove: the most distressing ideas pervaded his imagination; death, with all its gloomy appendages, appeared to flit before his eyes; he talked of nothing but the grave and his beloved Katherine, and expressed no other wish than to share the cold vault in which his distempered fancy had placed her. Every endeavour to remove these painful impressions proved abortive, and they could only look forward to some remote period, and fearfully cherish the hope, that time and judicious treatment might, eventually, remove the malady they so much deplored: to have told him Miss Beverley lived, would not, it was apprehended, at present have produced the desired effect, and to know that she existed without a possibility of being united to her, would only have excited greater irritation; it was therefore deemed most expedient to suffer him to mourn her loss, as time, if it did not restore him to all he once was, might blunt the edge of his distress, and render him more tranquil.

Yet his was comparative happiness when compared with what Captain Evelyn endured; had the afflictive Providence been the result of any thing but his own imprudence, he could have borne it with resignation; but the reflection that he could now make no atonement, embittered every moment of his life. As his son, however, appeared most calm when with him, he devoted his whole time and attention to him, watched every turn of his complaint, and, with the most anxious solicitude, strove to anticipate his smallest wishes.

Charles Evelyn appeared to have gained strength of body in proportion to the decay of his mental powers; he climbed the steepest acclivities, and wandered for hours in the most intricate windings of the forest, appearently insensible to fatigue. The most gloomy and unfrequented spots appeared most congenial to his feelings, and the name of Katherine Beverley dwelt almost incessantly on his lips. His father, attended by a strong robust man whom he had engaged to take charge of him, generally followed him in his rambles; and was often, from inability to ascend some of the rocky crags which his son appeared to feel particular pleasure in gaining, obliged to seat himself on some projecting stone till fatigue compelled him to return.

But who can describe the agonized feelings of the father as his eye rested on the figure of Charles, now standing on the summit of some lofty pinnacle of rock, near the impetuous fall of some mountain stream; now leaping from point to point, or descending, at the hazard of his life, its rude projecting side. He at times became, from the influence the fear these rambles excited, almost bereft of reason; yet the least check to this distressing impulse of his son was invariably succeeded by a fit of phrensy too terrible to be often hazarded.

Charles Evelyn had for some time been much better, and his father one evening strolled out with him alone. His endeavours to amuse him were for a period successful, and his son proposed sitting down on a bank by the river side; the air was unusually mild; the moon in all her splendour was just emerging from a cloud, whose silvery edge formed a striking contrast to the clear azure of the glowing firmament; the river, from the late heavy rains, was much swollen; nothing disturbed the stillness of the scene but its waters dashing over some fragments of rocks at their feet, while the moonbeams glittered on its agitated surface. The grotesque forms of the surrounding rocks, the dark shade of the neighbouring woods, was a scene so truly picturesque, so much in unison with the melancholy feelings of the father, that, lost in contemplation, he sat unconscious of the lateness of the hour, till roused by his son clasping his hands, and exclaimed, with more sanity than he had yet shown, "What a heavenly night."

His father turned hastily round; a ray of hope shot across his half broken heart; but it was a delusive hope, resembling the lightning's transient blaze, which serves only to show more plainly the surrounding darkness. Charles gazed wistfully on the rolling wave beneath him, "She is there, father," said he, pointing at the water, " see how her eye rests on me."

His father grew alarmed, and, tenderly taking his hand, said, in a voice trembling with emotion, "My dear Charles, we had better return home."

"For pity's sake detain me not," cried Charles with returning wildness; " Katherine, my first love, I come, I come—" when breaking from the convulsive grasp of his agonized father, he leaped into the foaming torrent. Captain Evelyn raised his hands and eyes to heaven. "My God," said he, "forgive me; and if I cannot save him, suffer me at least to share his fate;" then, regardless of the danger that attended that hazardous attempt, with one desperate plunge he followed him: but vain were all his efforts; the impetuous torrent rolled on with increasing violence; it bore the object of his search far away, while the dashing spray impeded his progress; he contended, but in vain, till, completely exhausted, life apparently forsook him.

The waves had borne him near the shore, when a cottager, who had seen the transaction, hastened immediately to the spot, determined if possible to rescue him. Accustomed from infancy to brave the tempestuous scene, it had no terrors for him, and he soon succeeded in drawing the senseless body to the shore; while his feeling heart lamented his not having reached the spot time enough to have saved his life: he however left him to the care of his wife, with strict injunctions to try every means likely to restore animation, while he went in search of the other body. After much fruitless exertion he found a hat, and was preparing to return home, when his attention was arrested by several voices: supposing them to proceed from persons in quest of the captain, he waited their approach, and, in the unsophisticated language of true feeling, gave them a distinct account of the fatal occurrence.

The hat was the son's, not a doubt remained of his having perished, in mournful silence they followed the cottager to his humble abode.

The woman had been indefatigible in her exertions, and signs of returning life appeared to crown her labours; everything that could minister to the comfort of Captain Evelyn was speedily procured from the house, but when all around congratulated him on his rescue from a watery grave, he declared with a groan, that a life like his, which must hereafter be marked with wretchedness and remorse, was not worth preserving; that it was his wish to have perished, since the only remaining tie that bound him to the earth was now broken. He however expressed his sense of the cottager's kindness in the warmest terms, and promised to seize the first opportunity of returning him something more durable than thanks.

"Think not, my brave friend," said he, "though existence has become hateful to me, that I am equally indifferent to my preserver, or that your intrepidity will be requited only with discontented murmers."

On the following day Captain Evelyn was removed home, but the sight of each surrounding object so reminded him of his lost son, that Sir John Waldegrave insisted on his being conveyed to the castle, where every endeavour humanity could devise, or hospitality suggest, was used to lighten his affliction: but the remorse that incessantly haunted him, united with the fatigue he had lately undergone in attending the unhappy victim of his imprudence, had so completely weakened his frame, that he long languished on a bed of sickness, a prey to unavailing regret.

Upon his recovery, he left the country for the metropolis, hoping that a change of scene would remove from his mind much of the unfortunate circumstances which through his ambition he had occasioned. Here he mixed amongst fashionable society; still the death of his unfortunate son haunted his imagination, and in a fit of desperation, he sought a change in the excitement of the gaming table; from small sums, he became induced to venture much larger ones, and in one night he lost a large sum of money. Hoping to retrieve his losses he again visited the gaming house, but his bad fortune still visited him, and after playing deeply and rather desperately, he rose in the morning from the table, a ruined man. His property was sold to pay his debts—he became a brain-stricken wanderer, and fled from the companionship of man, to hold fellowship with the beasts of the field and the fowls of the air.

Katherine Beverley shut herself up in her aunt's cottage, and there pined her life away. Her constitution, naturally delicate, gave way under the pressure of outraged feeling; and, long before the winter gave place to spring, she was carried to her grave.

   *   *   *   *

Edith thanked the narrator for a story which she believed had no parallel in the annals of man for its affecting interest, then rose with a remorseful twinge of conscience, for having a moment forgotten her friend. Her companions rose to accompany her.

"I look like some stray bird on the wing," said Constance Glenroy, shading back her unbonneted locks; "but I make my home in these shades, and think as little of arraying myself to wander here, as the cattle that are grazing round us. I think I had better stay here, Herbert, until you return, lest they take me up as a runaway, and bind me with my own flaxen withes."

"Nay, rather both remain," cried Edith, "even should my persecutor re-appear, he is now disarmed of all his terrors. Besides, my path is quite familiar to me; I did not think to meet you here, when I was tempted through the beauty of the scene to come hither, the banks of the river looked so temptingly lovely, and I thought I might ramble with impunity through a path so sheltered, unmolested by sylvan nymphs, with whom my fancy peopled this Arcadian scene."

"Do not suffer the meeting to intimidate you from future excursions," replied Glenroy, "for I pledge myself by all the vows of chivalry, to be your sworn champion, in every peril that may threaten from shore to stream, and to rival La Mancha himself in bravery and devotion."

"I thought the days of chivalry were no more," she answered; "but I may call upon you to redeem your pledge. Constance shall be witness of the vow, and it shall be recorded in the archives of knighthood." She turned to the fair girl as she spoke and extended her hand in token of farewell. "I trust," she added, "we shall soon meet again."

"Indeed, I hope it will not be long," replied Constance, blushing at her own ardour, and returning the cordial pressure with all the warmth of friendship.

"Farewell, Sir Knight" added Edith. "Nay, follow me not, or my displeasure shall blight the fair flowers of chivalry in their bud." Perceiving that he persevered in his intention, she repeated in a tone which left no doubt of her sincerity, and of her resolution to be believed, "I came unattended, Sir, and I wish to return alone."

Herbert immediately drew back, and answered her parting curtsey with a most respectful bow. Edith did not look back to see if she was pursued; but she walked with true rustic rapidity, till she found herself again by the side of Susan, whom she found still wrapped in the sweet, restoring arms of slumber.

CHAPTER XII.

Oh, leave me to my sorrow,
    For my heart is oppressed to-day ;
Oh, leave me, and to-morrow
    Dark shades may pass away.
There's a time when all that grieves us
    Is felt with a deeper gloom;
There's a time when hope deceives us,
    And we dream of bright days to come.   HAYNES BAYLY.

SUSAN's health now mended rapidly, and she became uneasy at the long silence of her father. She had returned to Miss Glenroy's upon her recovery, and assisted her in the school, when at last she received a letter from him, which ran as follows:—

"My dear child, for so I may call you for the last time—Susan, you will say, after reading this letter, that I have never loved you, for if I feel what I express, why do I abandon you? The hand of fate separates us for ever, but the God who rules over us all, and now reads the agony of my heart, knows how dear you are to me. How I have lived since I left you I cannot reveal, but I have enclosed a sum sufficient to pay the expenses incurred with Miss Glenroy, together with a note for a hundred pounds for yourself. This is all I can do for you, and alas! it must be the last time I address you. For your future support I should recommend you to proceed to London and procure a situation as governess in a family. I can never claim you. I am unworthy to call you my child, and I could not bear that your innocent heart should know what a wretch you call father."

With a sickening heart Susan read the letter, and in the agony of the moment she thought that happiness was henceforth to be a stranger to her. She sought Edith, and confided to her her altered circumstances. She told her she should follow the advice of her father, and seek employment in London. Edith requested her not to leave Allendale until she had procured a situation, in which her father might possibly assist her. General Trevanion, upon being informed by his daughter of the circumstance, wrote immediately to London to an old and valued friend, and in a short time received an answer, stating that a governess was wanted by an acquaintance of his, to educate a daughter, and if the young lady would come immediately to London, it would be procured for her.

We shall pass over the parting of the friends, and the journey to the metropolis. The novelty of her situation so wholly occupied her thoughts ;—a thousand nameless but overwhelming sensations made every gift of nature at that moment a mere burden ; and gladly would she have compounded for rejection, unseen and uncatechised.

Lady Melton was, however, at home when Susan called ; she was immediately ushered into a drawing-room, and her appearance seemed no less to impress the lady than the footman, who employed himself in removing two lazy lap-dogs from the arm chair on the vacant side of the fire. Upon Susan delivering the letter, which she had received from General Trevanion's friend, Lady Melton instantaneously dismissed the man; and guiding Susan, by a haughty glance of the eye, to a seat, she began to examine the note, while Susan surveyed her dress. That of the city ladies she had often heard ridiculed ; but it was only now that she could know with what reason. Laden with expensive fineries, Lady Melton gave a lamentable proof of want of taste. She had been dressing for a dinner; and the dress she wore was loaded with French trimmings enough for three !—while her head, of an enormous height, was frosted, alike by art and nature, and adorned with flowers:—her whole figure forming, from its rotundity, an absolute conical mountain, the lower part covered with roses, and the summit with snow. Having perused the note, she did not hesitate to turn in silence towards Susan, of whose outside she took as exact a survey as ever she had done of hers; then, rudely addressing her, said,—

"You are the person mentioned in this here letter—are you, miss?—what's your name?"

Susan bowed.

"Pray, was you ever out in the world before?" continued Lady Melton.

"Never, madam."

"Then what do you purtend to larn young ladies?"

"To speak and write English and French," replied Susan, "all kinds of elegant work; embroidery, and tambour. I know something too of drawing, and have been thought a little skilled in music."

"Pray, miss, do you live with your parents?"

"No, madam, I have none in England. My mother I lost in my infancy, and my father is at sea."

No. 9.

" Hum !" cried Lady Melton, as Susan wept, with inexpressible humiliation ; " a great loss ! a monstrous loss, indeed ! How old may you be, miss ?"

" Just twenty, madam," answered Susan.

" And what terms do you ax ?"

" Forty pounds a-year, madam, and a chamber to myself; with such consideration in the family as my education, and, I hope, my conduct, will entitle me to."

Lady Melton considered for a short time, and then exclaimed,—" these here terms, miss, are prodigious high ! My darghter is quite accomplished—completely edicated; but she is too young to come out yet. She was six years at a great boarding school, within a stone's throw of our country house; and her governess says she talks French better than herself. You will have nothing in a manner to teach : indeed, you will be more my companion, as well as hers. I should hardly think of such a useless kind of person, but to be in the fashion; for every body has a French governess now, I think. Can you do plain work neatly ?"

" I never made that a study," replied Susan.

" Ah ! I thought as much," exclaimed Lady Melton; " its fifty times more useful, miss, though, than all your imbrydery and tom bores ! We always make all our linen at home ; and you must lend a helping hand—besides working my things and Tommy's waistcoats."

" I shall never object becoming useful to your ladyship, in any proper manner," replied Susan.

" So you had need, miss. What's your name ?—Forty pounds a-year keeps many a poor parson and his family : not that I should begrudge it, had you been a French woman born. Lady Gingerly, my next-door neighbour, has got a real French governess for her daughter, who can't speak a word of English, and they only gives her forty guineas. However, you seem a genteel, comfortable kind of body ; so, for once, I will be a little extravagant. As to a chamber to yourself, I have not a spare one in my house ; but, you will sleep with my daughter, and always dine and sup with the family, as well as go with us to the villa every Saturday."

Lady Melton having thus concluded this original harangue, rang the bell, and ordered her daughter to appear. But, alas ! very different was her address from that her mother had spoken of. The accomplished, completely educated, boarding school miss, was as raw and unpolished as if she had now only begun her career in one. She had, unluckily, just reached that size and age which makes an overgrown girl, or an unfinished woman, and was dressed in a manner that showed every disadvantage in the worst point of view, flat heels, a short frock, and a cap, with bells made of ribbon hanging to her shoulders.

Susan addressed her politely in French. She coloured, and fidgetted with her feet, as if she had St. Vitus's dance ; but not one word passed her lips in answer.

This irritated her lady-mother ; and, at her command, the poor girl at length uttered a few words of a most unintelligible jargon. She seemed, however, humble and tearful.

Sir Timothy Melton was a banker of reputation and fortune, and his lady was many years his housekeeper, previous to her marriage ; she was the mother of both a son and this daughter, ere Sir Timothy repented of his sins, and married. But, alas ! if he once repented the sin, he had never ceased to repent the atonement ; for his wife was a high spirited, insolent woman, though neither unsociable, nor an unkind mistress.

Sir Timothy was a snug, sober cit ; content to endure all his wife's lectures, so that she would only permit him to sit down to supper in his velvet nightcap, and smoke a pipe in the parlour after it. He had amassed an immense property ; and would, perhaps, manage a spendthrift son better, but that his mother reigned over the strong box, as well as over her spouse, and supplied all the young man's extravagance.

Susan had been a week in possession of her new dignity, and had already begun to entertain the unlucky idea, that it was not so easy to be happy, as, in the vanity of her heart, she would fain have imagined. She found Mr. Thomas Melton to be the principle of action in the whole family : he had attained years of maturity—not discretion, and, in his own way of thinking, he was a perfect fine gentleman. Although, as far from handsome as amiable, he expected all to think him both ; execrated all business ; and, if he committed any rudeness to Susan, disdained an apology. He was continually followed by a kindred race of puppies, who snatched at every thing in the shape of eatables they came nigh ; and one nearly inflicted a severe bite upon Susan, in attempting to snatch a piece of bread from her hand, and then, as if she had not been sufficiently frightened and hurt, the gallant master of the dog squeezed her hand till she could hardly avoid screaming out, and then, throwing his arms around her, kissed her no less rudely ; laughing and saying, he liked "to take the bloom from the plum."

Mr. Thomas Melton was, however, his mother's idol ; and a thousand such impertinences she considered only as a proof of his spirit and *ton* ; nor had she an idea that a young woman, in a subordinate situation, is not born to amuse and conform to the will of all who are above her. For this youth, Susan had to sing, whether she was inclined to it or not ; with him, she must dance, if he chose it, and, in the opinion of his mother, she had no right to raise an objection to any wish he might form.

Lady Melton made herself a slave to the wretched coxcomb's humours ; and, so far was he from being thankful for her weak and boundless indulgence, that he gave himself a thousand sulky air, if she prevented his wishes as to money. She often stroked his ugly cheek, with an air of tender humility, and presented to him the bank notes which she scolded his father out of. To all her entreaties that he would not ruin his constitution by drinking, her dear Tommy would only reply with an insolent nod, and her health in a bumper.

The daughter with whom Susan passed most of her time, she found to be the most supportable being among them ; yet her ideas of pleasure reached no further than pampering canary birds, and filling her pockets with stolen fruit, while her sense of pain was confined to a scolding from the gardener or a frown from her mother.

The family, at the end of a week, started for the villa, as Lady Melton always called her country house. After filling the boot with provisions, and the seats with best clothes, that they might, as Susan fancied, feed as well as appear like christians, according to her ladyship's phrase, the summons for entering the coach arrived. Sir Timothy and his lady, Miss, and our heroine opposite ; as well as a fat housekeeper, two birdcages, one lap-dog, three bandboxes, my lady's cane and parasol, together with Sir Timothy's best hat and fishing tackle. Thus stowed, they had not much room to spare.

After a charming dusty drive, they were set down, as the evening closed, at a house large enough, and substantially but well furnished. On the following morning Susan was summoned by Sir Timothy to visit the flat roof on the top of the house. While the family were descanting on the various beauties which the view of Richmond presented, and the beautiful windings of the Thames, Susan cast an eye on the home prospect. The mansion stood in a court-yard, close by the great road, which at once amused them with an eternal rotation of carriages and as eternal clouds of dust. The garden lay chiefly on one side, and was a curious olio of the ancient and modern. Toward the road it was bordered by arches of yew trees, with which dust was so incorporated that the possibility of resuming even their own dingy green was a thing out of all hope. Within these triumphal arches lay a well cropped field, which the owners were pleased to call a shrubbery, bordered with expensive exotics in fancy earthen pots, and a serpentine walk, of sulky contrivance, for only one person could walk in it at a time.

To the kitchen garden they were led by two more magnificent arches, though composed of no other than the mournful materials of which the long range in the front were formed.

Two stone vases marked the gate, where Lady Melton, with grief, informed Susan, once grew two swans, that by her account Leda would have admired ; but that a ruthless gardener, knowing how much she valued them, one day in her absence, and on purpose to plague her, cut them off, in the bloom, as one may say, of their days.

The chamber appropriated to Susan's use opened into a closet which, by a flight of steps, communicated with a retired part of the garden. The afternoon was a lovely one, and upon retiring after dinner, she repaired thither.

As she was slowly pacing a shady path, absorbed in the reflections her change of circumstances had inspired, she was startled on a sudden by beholding young Melton at her side.

Perceiving her emotion, " I fear I have alarmed you?" he cried, smiling.

" No," answered Susan, recovering herself, "only surprised me a little, as I supposed you had joined some of your friends at Richmond."

" What!" exclaimed he, in a tone of tender reproach, "after hearing you avow your intention of staying within doors during the remainder of the day!"

Susan, thinking these merely words, of course only smiled.

After a little conversation, he continued, " There is a beautiful and romantic spot, a little distance from this, which I think you would be highly delighted with. Will you permit me to be your guide to it?"

Susan objected, but he would not take a denial, and she reluctantly accompanied him.

They accordingly quitted the garden by means of a wicket gate at its extremity, and sweeping round some noble plantations, entered upon a shelving path, bounded on each side by high shrubby banks, in many places overtopped by clustering elders and hollies. The balmy sweetness which the wild plants and flowers that bespread these banks gave to the air—the melodious carolling of the birds that filled the woods—and the incessant humming of the busy insects that swarmed the adjacent shades, rendered this walk delightful. After proceeding some distance, the banks suddenly cleared away on one side, and disclosed to view the river, on the banks of which stood a beautiful fancy cottage, shaded in the rear by a complete grove of lilac, inclosed within a green paling, which added much to the rustic appearance of the place. The banks of the river were clothed with the finest verdure, and tufted with shrubs, interspersed with knots of flowers, myrtles, geraniums, and all such exotics as during the heat of summer can bear the open air.

Susan was too much charmed to resist the importunities of Mr. Melton to take a nearer view of the cottage, and on gaining the door he threw it open, and admitted his fair companion into a spacious room, but fitted up with a simplicity that made it perfectly accord with the exterior of the building.

Susan was in raptures with all she saw, and Melton professed himself equally delighted at having been the means of affording her so much pleasure. While she was looking about her he slipped away, but shortly returned with a basket of strawberries, which he had procured from an old gardener, who occupied the back part of the cottage, in order to take care of it.

Melton having induced Susan to accompany him thus far, considered the present tempting moment the best for revealing his sentiments, and he began by degrees to betray them. At first Susan treated as a jest what he said to her ; but by degrees the increasing warmth of his language, his still more impassioned glances, and some liberties he attempted to take, made her drop her rallying manner, and she determined on leaving him immediately ; but on making an effort to quit the seat in the inner room, with a kind of gentle violence he detained her.

" Mr. Melton," cried Susan, as she struggled to free herself from him, " I—I insist (almost panting with anger and alarm) on your instantly releasing me. Do not, by persevering in this audacious conduct, make me repent having formed a better opinion of you than you deserve."

" If I have been so fortunate," returned he, in a most insidious tone, but still preventing her quitting her seat, " to inspire you with a good opinion, surely my only yielding to the feelings inspired by your resistless charms—to the impulse of adoration, of admiration, cannot—or rather ought not, to rob me of it; come, my adorable girl, do not look upon me with such an indignant aspect—believe me, you could not find a more grateful admirer than I shall be."

"This language, sir, is as unbecoming your situation, as it is insulting to me."

"And why unbecoming? nothing can be unbecoming that is not unnatural; and surely it cannot be reckoned unnatural for a young fellow like me to speak of love to a beautiful woman."

"Let me go—let me go," exclaimed Susan, struggling with him; "or, if you wish me to forgive your conduct, wish me to believe you not lost to every feeling of honour and humanity, leave me. That you have strangely misconceived my character, I must suppose, or you would never have insulted me in the manner you have done; but this is no extenuation of your conduct, since out of respect to the situation which I hold in your family, I should have been treated very differently. Unhand me this moment, sir, or you will oblige me to expose your conduct, by calling to the servants."

"My angel, to prevent your fatiguing yourself with such an exertion, know that the good dame and her husband are gone out into the town, so that neither obtrusive eye, nor listening ear, need we dread."

As he spoke, he attempted again to strain her to his breast.

"Listen to me, Mr. Melton," cried Susan, endeavouring to check the terror his conduct inspired, emphatically laying one hand on his arm, and with the other parringing off the efforts he made to kiss her.

"My lovely girl, think no more of it—"

"Wretch!" exclaimed Susan, bursting from his grasp, and escaping from the room, almost maddened at the thoughts of the irreparable injury her character might sustain, if it was known that she had remained so long in company with him, in such a secluded spot.

Melton pursued her till she gained the wicket leading to the garden, when he paused, fearing he might be observed.

On reaching her chamber, which, owing to her swiftness, she did without further molestation from him, her first impulse was to seek Sir Timothy immediately, for the purpose of informing him of the conduct of his son; but when she came to reflect on the consequences that might ensue from such a measure, she relinquished it altogether, for the present, but determined if such conduct was again repeated to acquaint Sir Timothy.

With mingled horror and astonishment she revolved his conduct, the vile and ungenerous advantage he had taken of her confidence in his honour to inveigle her into solitude. That he was a hardened libertine she could not doubt; and who knows, thought she, that he may not again take an opportunity of insulting me.

Solely engrossed by the recent incidents, she thought not of retiring to rest, but seated herself at an open window. In another frame of mind, and the scene without would have communicated the most delicious feelings to her bosom; as it was, she could not gaze upon the starry heavens, or the full-orbed moon rising majestically, and extending her silver beams athwart the landscape, inhale the dewy freshness of the odorous shrubs and flowers; or listen to the soft sighing of the night breeze amidst the foliage, without a sensation of pleasure—but pleasure, 'tis true, of a melancholy nature; and rendered still more so by the solemn silence of the hour, the monotonous noise of distant waters, and, at intervals, the hollow bark of the watchful house-dog, the sentinel of the farmer.

CHAPTER XIII.

Under how hard a fate are women born!
Priz'd to their ruin, or expos'd to scorn;
If we want beauty, we of love despair,
And are besieged, like frontier towns, if fair.   WALL.

THE following day, they returned in the same vehicle and manner to the city, but part of their baggage was exchanged for the more fragrant one of myrtles, flowers, and the last fruits of autumn.

This mode of life, though uniform and uninteresting, was rendered only inconvenient to Susan, by the insolent and overbearing kind of gallantry displayed by Mr. Melton, and which, as she knew not how to remedy, she felt it would render her ridiculous to complain of.

His continual visits to the apartment of his sister became so troublesome and inconvenient, that she at last complained to Sir Timothy and his lady, for she found that she must either be kissed and hugged by him, or abandon her situation. Lady Melton refused to chide him; and his sister's company only licensed that intrusion which solitude would have saved her from.

She again complained to Sir Timothy, and they had a few days of quietness. He seemed to comprehend her cause of displeasure; for he gave her a paternal shake of the hand; said that he was glad his daughter had such a good girl to keep her company, and that he should always love her for her candour. Indeed she had hitherto been a favourite with the old gentleman.

The family she found ranked with the mere talkers; and the very few ideas they had, were spent on the most frivolous subjects. The approaching ball, on the Lord Mayor's day, had engrossed them for the last month, in anticipation; and Susan expected the succeeding one would be lost in recapitulation. Her pupil was, after endless discussions, admitted to make her *entree* there; and Lady Melton, who thought hardly any article of apparel rich or expensive enough for herself, had been so amazingly saving as to her daughter, that Susan began to find her pride interested in getting some finery added to her apparel. At this juncture the mantua-maker most happily dropt the secret, that Miss Gingerly, the daughter of their neighbour, had a most expensive and costly dress ordered. Lady Melton's economy gave way to her insolence, and she forthwith bought one of the same kind for her daughter, whose heart fluttered for the first time with the hope of eclipsing her neighbour, Miss Gingerly. Her god-mother had sent her a suit of rich lace, and a pair of pearl earrings. She thought, talked, and dreamt, only of my Lord Mayor's ball. A dancing-master came daily, to refresh the memory of Mr. Melton and his sister. Nor was my lady less intent on rivaling all the mammas. Good Sir Timothy twisted his velvet night-cap; smiled on the shoes of one, and then on the necklace of the other; asking only to be quiet, if that favour might by his lady be permitted him.

The eternal jaunts abroad, and consultations at home, produced by this meditated exhibition, seemed rather to fatigue than enliven the spirits of our heroine; for she, alas! found nothing on earth so infectious as folly. Reduced, by people and plans of this kind, to contemplate rather the weakness than the strength of the human mind, we yield insensibly to the very failings we despise. They are but false philosophers who do not turn to us the bright and illuminated side of human nature. Could we begin our career in life with all that knowledge which we pass our best years in acquiring, I am afraid it would only eclipse the brilliancy of youth, without substituting the discretion of age, and deprive us at once of the capacity of either charming or being charmed. It is admitted, amongst naturalists, that the optic nerves of an infant are very imperfect, and gain strength from every following day. It is plain that the mind has the same dimness: nor need we doubt, but that the Omniscient Being, who ordained both, knew what was best for us: to attempt to become wiser than he meant to make us, may in his sight be a crime, and to ourselves is certainly a misfortune.

At length, however slowly, the long wished-for day arrived; and the splendid dress, with all all its fine trimmings, greeted the transported eyes of Miss Melton, who never yet had called a fashionable dress her own. How often was this spread out, surveyed, admired, tried on! and how anxiously did she inquire of each by-stander, if it became her! All this and ten times more had been gone through; when, at length, powdered, adorned, and self-satisfied, Lady and Miss Melton were conveyed to the ball in the new painted carriage, in which Sir Timothy returned from the dinner; for that worthy man now seemed to prefer his cap, slippers, and the newspaper, to every other human good—if he might.

Susan was weary beyond expression with only seeing all this attiring and magnificence, and sat down for some hours to read and recover herself. When she was summoned to supper, Sir Timothy alone was in the parlour, and, as he was a man of few words, their meal was almost a Carthusian one. Leaving him to his news and his meditations, Susan quickly adjourned to her own room, which happened to be an addition to the house, and over some of the offices. Taking up a book she resolved to read till Miss Melton returned ; but, almost in spite of her own intentions, drop into a gentle slumber. A slight motion in an adjoining closet, the door of which stood a-jar, reached her suddenly : she sat transfixed, as it were, but, accusing herself of cowardice, she sprang up, and taking the candle hummed a tune to deceive herself with, and valiantly threw open the half closed door; but her tune was changed into something like a scream, when forth darted Mr. Melton, who, seizing her, entreated that she would not be alarmed.

"Villain ! monster !" exclaimed she, as, almost breathless with terror and indignation, she struggled to burst from his grasp, "are you then lost to every feeling of shame and honour ?"

"To all but love," cried he with the languishment of an Adonis, straining her still more closely to his bosom.

Unable to disengage herself from him, and two well apprised of the remote situation of her chamber to hope the exertion of her voice would obtain her any assistance, terror now completely overpowered her. The dropping of her head upon his shoulder, and the cold dampness of her lips, against which he audaciously pressed, apprized Melton of the state to which he had reduced her : he bore her to the window, where by degrees the air revived her.

"Leave me, sir," she exclaimed upon recovering, and at the same time attempting to break from him, "leave me and by so doing, you will give the best proof of the honour of your intentions ; if you refuse I shall not scruple to alarm the family."

During this speech, he gradually lost his air of mildness and submission, he assumed that knowing and harsh character natural to his course of features ; smiled upon her several times in an almost insupportable manner, and grasping both her hands, as if he thought them as large and hard as his own, exclaimed :—

"Upon my soul, when I consider you are but a girl, you queen it rarely ! But dost take me for a fool, love? Couldst thou in thy conscience think I meant matrimony? absolute, serious matimony ? Lord help thee, child ! these are words of course ; and girls take ours for the performance of articles. I see you have been reading Pamela, and mean to figure away in the same character ; but faith, my dear ! you will not find Mrs. B s. more plenty than such damsels at fifteen. Alarm the family, indeed ! Have more discretion : that is the whole virtue of the best of you. The family in the first place are far enough out of your reach : in the next, were they at the door, what good would that do you ? I came here, it is true, by means best known to myself ; but though I own this to you, I would deny it to all the rest of the world, unless you use me more handsomely. Come ! —virtue or reputation, choose between them ;—you would have too great an advantage of your sex, were I to permit you to keep them both."

The perverted understanding, impudence, and hardness of heart, shown in this speech, incensed her beyond all prudence." "Monster !" she cried, " be the consequence what it will, I am determined to expose you."

She struggled in vain to disengage her hands from his huge strong ones; and, turning anxiously towards the bell, perceived, with a terrible shock, that the tassels were tied up higher than her head.

"Come, come, my dear little girl?" cried he, with an insolent kind of softness: "I love you too well, you see, to put it in your power to expose yourself: sit down and let us talk this over at our leisure. Though I will not marry you, that is the only thing you may not persuade me to do. I roll in wealth; and you shall have every wish that the vainest woman can form gratified. My father has riches enough——"

"To cover his son's defects ?" retorted Susan contemptuously ;—"you err in your calculation: the Indies could not do it."

"By Heavens!" cried he, "I will kiss you for that, you dear little sarcastical angel! I love your person, but a girl of wit I adore."

Hopeless of preventing his keeping his word, she gave a shriek that might have been heard at the Mansion-house; when, in a moment, both of them distinguished Sir Timothy coughing and in motion in one of the counting-houses, which most luckily was under her room. Young Melton, who, no doubt, thought his father was in bed in a distant part of the house, let her go through mere surprise; nor had he presence of mind enough to quit the chamber, though he had ample time; and Susan, unable to utter a syllable, waved him to the door, not unwilling to escape that *eclaircissement*, in which innocence is too often the sufferer.

Expecting Miss Melton, she had, most happily for her own character, left the door unbolted: Sir Timothy presently threw it wide open, and made his *entree*, lighted up by two servants armed; when, casting his eyes upon his son, who rested against one of the pillars of the bed, he looked around for the object of Susan's fear; but finding only his son, he seemed almost petrified with astonishment. Susan no sooner saw herself protected, than, overcome with terror, she sank into a chair, and gave way to a flood of tears.

"What," at last stammered the worthy old gentleman, "what, Tommy, am I to think of this affair? what have you been about?"

Tommy, however, was by no means prepared to answer his father; who, therefore, addressed the same question to Susan, and she was attempting to recover recollection and speech, when a thundering rap at the street door announced the return of the ball party. The little composure Susan had regained, vanished at this unlucky sound, which seemed hardly to have a less disagreeable effect on the nerves of the two gentlemen—the one wished himself in a horse-pond, and the other snug again in his counting-house.

The servants who had lighted up Sir Timothy, involuntary led their lady the same way. "Why, what's the meaning of this? Why must I go to my daughter's room?" cried she; when, bouncing in, she cast her eyes upon the three statues, and almost added one to the number. "How," at last she exclaimed, "came you here, Sir Timothy?" Then, turning to her son, "And pray, most polite sir, how came you here? What might be the reason of your leaving me, and your sister, to shift for ourselves at such a bustling ball? What! have you all three lost the use of your tongues? Sir Timothy! I say—you I will have an answer from. Leave fiddling with your spectacles, and let me understand what all this means."

The poor knight knew the tone, and obeyed. "Why, lovey," cried he, "I cannot tell you what I don't know myself. I only went to look over the cash book, in the office below, and, all of a sudden, Miss gave such a squall, that I thought there was a thief in the room, or the house was on fire: so, when I had waked the men, we all came up in a hurry, and found not a soul here, but our Tom."

Lady Melton, guessing all perhaps, but certainly a part of the truth, and only anxious to screen her worthless son from his father's anger, turned towards Susan with a contemptuous severity:—

"Pray, Miss, do you usually admit young gentlemen into your bed chamber? I am sorry to find you do, by my son's being here." "How Mr. Melton came here, he must inform you himself, Madam," returned Susan: "if with my knowledge, I should not have called on Sir Timothy for protection. I need hardly add (I am so new to insult) that this is the first I ever met with from a lady."

"Insult truly!" she exclaimed in accents of fury: "why if I did insult you, have you not given me cause? Let me tell you, miss, when a gentleman takes these here liberties, it generally proceeds from the forwardness of the girls: and I don't know how you should teach my daughter to behave, when, as one may say, you don't know how to do it yourself—are you not now carrying on a shameful——!"

"Hold, madam! hold!" cried Susan, with still greater vivacity, "for your own sake as well as mine, I caution you to silence, for be assured I am neither so destitute of spirit, or of friends, as to allow my character to be attacked with impunity.

By thus defending your son in the greatest breach of decorum and hospitality, you reflect much more on your own character, than mine. His present impertinence proceeds from my having scorned his odious gallantry, while sheltered under the name of honour. I can appeal to himself, if such was not, half an hour ago, his language."

Susan turned impatiently towards the base wretch, in the persuasion, that, however bad his heart, he was taken too much by surprise to maintain any assertion to

her disadvantage, when she found, to her infinite vexation, that, during their altercation, he had contrived to steal away.

"Lord help us!" cried Lady Melton, with provoking vulgar irony: 'you girls are all mighty glad to get off by pleading promises! So our Tommy promised you, did he?"

"Nay," interrupted Sir Timothy, "if the lad promised you, my dear, I must needs say—"

No. 10.

"Fiddlesticks, you must needs say !" exclaimed his virulent rib ; "and what, in the mightiness of your wisdom, did you mean to say?"

"Allow me one word, Sir Timothy," cried Susan, " your ladyship will admit I have right to speak,—I equally despised Mr. Melton's promises and himself. His troublesome gallantry was all that I thought I could have to encounter disagreeable in the family, for little did I imagine that your ladyship would countenance your son in an insult, which, if any other man offered to his sister, you would so highly resent.''

"True, miss," returned Lady Melton haughtily : "but there is a great difference in the persons. (There is, indeed, thought Susan.) Girls like you, who are to work for their living, ought to keep their betters at a distance ; and then it is easy enough to be virtuous."

Susan could hardly, on recollecting her ladyship's own history, which she had heard from the housekeeper, avoid smiling in her face. Alas ! how theory and practice may differ. However, she governed her looks, and only coldly replied,

"True, madam ; but that very dependance gives women, when ill-treated, a double claim to pity and protection."

"Lovey, let me speak," cried the knight : "positively I will speak this once. You may see, with half an eye, that Tom has been all along in love with miss. The boy is old enough to marry and settle ; and e'en let him please himself, as his father did before him. She is a fine young woman, and, faith, she speaks like an oracle. Such a sightly smart girl will keep the spark in good order ; and we sha'nt have the devil to pay, every two months, with some grandee's kept mistress. A fig for birth ; we never care for that on this side Temple Bar ; and I have money enough not to mind her having none. When folks marry, good nature and good sense is the principal."

Lady Melton had suffered her spouse to proceed in Susan's praise, not as approving it, but because speechless through surprise and rage : she now recovered utterance, and starting up, her face crimson with passion, and her two little gray eyes flashing fire, she exclaimed ;—

"Are you tipsy, bewitched, or mad ? or is the devil himself in that foolish head of yours, Sir Timothy, to-night ?" Marry her ! consent that your only son, with one hundred thousand pounds, should marry a little fortin-hunting, pitiful, seaman's daughter ! If a boy of mine had so little spirit he should have as little money ! Marry him to her indeed !''

" 'Tis quite unnecessary, madam," replied Susan with a look of ineffable scorn, " to trouble yourself about it, you needn't be under any alarm about his marrying me, for I never would have such a low, mean-spirited wretch ; and after what has just passed, I intend leaving your house to-morrow, so that I may not subject myself to any fresh insult."

"Oh yes, you mean to leave me, to be sure," cried Lady Melton sneeringly, "but come, Sir Timothy," laying hold of his arm, " you have been here long enough—in the morning we can talk it over again."

Susan, upon being left alone, sat for some time meditating upon her future plans : she determined in the morning to write to Edith, giving her the whole particulars, and asking advice from her father and Mrs. Glenroy. She then threw herself upon the bed without undressing, just as day-light was beginning to dawn through the window-shutters; but though fatigued in the extreme, the discomposure of her mind was too great to allow of her enjoying much rest, and at an earlier hour than usual she arose, with the intention of writing the letter to her friends.

CHAPTER XIV.

Oh, they were happy together—no word
Of unkindness between them was there ever heard ;
He seemed in her eyes to interpret her thought,
And all that she wished for come ere it was sought.
How gay was the laugh of their innocent mirth !
Oh, they were happy ! too happy for earth !   HAYNES BAYLY.

THE accidental meeting between Edith Trevanion and Constance Glenroy renewed the friendship which existed between them while at school, and was the commencement of an intercourse productive of the purest social enjoyment, and of both enjoyment and utility. It brought forth not only blossoms but fruit.

She had promised, at the earnest solicitations of Margaret and Constance Glenroy, to join a fishing party, which had been some time in agitation ; when a boat was to be launched, with due ceremony on the bosom of a lake, a few miles from Allendale. Had she felt no disposition to join a festive scene, she would have found it difficult to have resisted pleaders so eloquent and interesting. She had always admired the high-spirited and independent Margaret, but she loved the sweet and spirited Constance. Perhaps she did not love her less, for being the sister instead of the betrothed of her own gallant champion. Edith's heart was not made of those inflammable materials, which kindle into unhealthy radiance at the first sight of youth, beauty, and genius—it was covered with the asbestos shield of moral delicacy, and the flame of unbidden passion could not penetrate it. But she was human ; and it is perfectly natural that she should feel more pleasure in the society of such a being as Herbert Glenroy, with the conviction that he was free and unshackled as herself, than if she believed his rich treasures of intellect and feeling were already appropriated by another. The circumstances of her first meeting with him had a kind of romantic charm over their future intercourse. The playful vow of knighthood invested him at once with the privileges of an earlier acquaintance, and whenever an opportunity occurred of displaying the chivalrous character he had assumed, he supported it with such gentlemanly grace and spirit, such a freedom from all coxcombry and affectation, she scarcely wished to see him in any other. Yet, when she beheld him the idol of his own household, the devoted son, the affectionate brother, merging every selfish consideration in the all-governing principle of filial and paternal affection, she felt that he appeared in a far more endearing light. Without one shade of pedantry, his conversation constantly displayed the resources of a mind richly endowed by nature, and polished by assiduous cultivation.

" Do you not sometimes feel the hours drag heavily and wearily along," asked Edith of Margaret, as they walked together through the shaded path that led to the house ; " do you not find such constant confinement a bondage to the freeborn spirit? and yet your's always seems as elastic and bright as if the particles of time in your glass were golden sparks instead of sandy grains."

" It is a very old adage," replied Margaret, " that employment gives wings to time ; and it is an opinion as ancient, that the consciousness of duty gilds the plumage of these wings with the hues of the rainbow. I have proved the truth of both these aphorisms. Constant occupation excludes the troublesome intrusions of *ennui*, and the hopes of acquitting myself in such a manner as to meet the approbation of my great taskmaster's eye, gives me strength to fulfil the most arduous duties."

" I should deceive you," resumed Margaret, after a thoughtful pause, " if I led you to believe that I assumed these duties from an abstract love of them. Our father's death deprived us of affluence, and threw us upon the protection of a young and only brother. The extreme delicacy of my sister's constitution renders her entirely unfit to meet the peltings of life's storms. We have never known privations yet, but should any misfortune befal us, I shrink from the thought of ever being a burthen to the noblest, most disinterested, and affectionate brother, two orphan sisters were ever blest with. Better, far better, to become accustomed to the yoke, while the feelings possess the pliability of youth, and the spirit, unstiffened by pride, bows readily to meet its destination."

"How deeply you make me feel my own inefficiency," said Edith, touched by this unexpected confidence, and still more by the spontaneous tribute to fraternal worth. "I believe I might be capable of making great sacrifices for those I love; but were I called upon to lay daily, hourly offerings on the altar of principle and duty, I fear I should be incapable of the exertion; or were I to make the effort, the sacrifice would be rejected, because it came from a cold and unwilling heart."

"Oh! do not exalt me to the honours of martyrdom," replied Margaret, "my path is not filled with brambles, and there is many a sweet blossom by the way-side."

Just as she spoke, in literal fulfilment of her words, a fragrant nosegay was proffered to her acceptance, by one of her young pupils, who had been lingering in her path to catch an opportunity of presenting the sweet-scented gift. Margaret received it with a smile of gratitude while another bashful little rustic pressed forward with a similar boon.

"A few minutes back I was inclined to pity you," said Edith, "now I am half disposed to envy you. I begin to have new ideas of happiness."

They had now reached the gate, and Constance was seen running down the steps to meet them, like a fairy spirit of gladness.

Edith had often, while under the tuition of Margaret, admired the simple elegance with which every thing was arranged—the true unstudied gentility which reigned in the household. There was no costly furniture, no laboured display, but an air of taste pervaded the mansion. No ornaments are so common as flowers in a pastoral dwelling, and certainly none are so easily obtained; and the vases on Mrs. Glenroy's mantel-piece were always filled with the fairest of the valley, wreathed together with so much grace, it was not difficult to detect whose fingers plucked and placed them there. Constance was certainly a most lawless plunderer of Flora's sweets, and disliked to see a short awkward stem so much, that she was guilty of the murder of many a promising bud, in search of the unfolding blossom. Some think this a flagrant outrage upon Nature's rights, and will carefully pluck a full-blown rose, unrelieved by the green of bud or leaf, rather than squander the bounties of Providence. But whenever you see a lady with such a bouquet, you may be assured she is neither a painter nor a poet.

One of Margaret's first cares was to preserve her nosegay from withering. For this purpose she put it in the midst of Constance's flowers, without perceiving how much she discomposed her beautiful arrangement.

"Oh! pray, Margaret," said Constance, whose poetical eye was immediately pained by the want of harmony, "do put it in the central vase, where I've clustered the largest blossoms. It looks so stiff and coarse by the side of those fair queen lilies."

"Am I not right?" continued she, appealing to her brother, who had just entered the room. "What does this look like here?"

"Why, it reminds me," answered Herbert, taking possession of the insulted nosegay, "of Norval's description of the moon, 'round as my shield,' and it certainly presents a most imposing battery of sweets. But if you call me as an umpire, I must acknowledge that Margaret has violated the strict rules of taste in introducing it among this slender painted populace."

"If I were to decide," said Edith, "I should say it was fairer than all the green lilies in the universe. It was the offering of gratitude and affection, unpolished by one selfish and worldly motive, and it must therefore have imperishable charms. I was never so conscious of the feeling of envy as when I saw your sister receive this fragrant gift."

"Thus offered, and thus presented," cried Herbert, restoring it to its original station, "let all the lilies and roses of the valley do homage to its loveliness. See Constance, how they bow their scented heads towards it, as if instinct with moral veneration for its worth. Do you not blush for its injustice?" Constance did blush, and busied herself most industriously about the vases, to hide the tears that were gathering in her eyes. The warmth of Edith's expression rebuked the folly of her remarks, and she could not endure the idea of being thought unfeeling and ungrateful. Edith saw the emotion, and twisting some of the wild flowers together, she playfully wreathed them in the pale golden locks of Constance, and bade her look in the mirror to see if she ever wore a coronet so fair.

This was a trivial subject, but Mrs. Glenroy felt there was more to admire in the simple sentence that Edith uttered, and the simple act that followed it, than all her external fascinations of grace and beauty. Such is the transcendant charm of goodness.

All the best feelings of Edith's nature were called into exercise in this domestic circle. What Margaret had told her with respect to their unportioned condition, and her own motives for exertion, sanctified it in her eyes. She thought she could perceive an occasional shade of anxiety on Glenroy's brow, which sometimes deepened to sadness, but was again succeeded by such beaming cheerfulness, it might be, after all, an illusion of her own imagination. When she saw, however, the perfect confidence which subsisted in this family, their cloudless union and unrestrained affection, and thought of the mystery that shadowed her friend Susan, she felt how poor a compensation were the bounties of fortune for the injured privileges of nature.

Edith would have returned at twilight, but so many temptations were held out to induce her to remain a *little longer*, she found them irresistible. "Do not go so soon," said Margaret; "if there is anything about us that approaches to the agreeable, it is discoverable in a moonlight evening, when we cluster on this terrace. It has quite an inspiring influence upon me, and makes me forget all the dull lessons of the day, learned and conned by rote."

"Oh! stay with us a little longer," cried Constance, with caressing importunity. "I will go myself and ask forgiveness of your father, and tell him we held you in bondage. You do not know how sweet the moonbeams play through the lattice-work, and dance and sport as if it were nature's holiday. Already they begin their evening pastime. See how softly the shadows flit yonder!"

She drew Edith gently into the piazza as she spoke, repeating,—

"Oh! come, then, to our fairy bower."

Edith was about to confess herself a willing prisoner, when Glenroy, of whose near presence she was not aware, drew forward, and leaning over the balustrade of the terrace, continued,—

"Our holiest time is the moon-light hour,
And never was moon-light so sweet as this."

How fortunate it is that the bounties of nature are inexhaustible, and that the mild satellite of our planet still shines with the same pure, virgin brightness as she did in the morning of her creation. It has been said that authors are passionately fond of describing those nights, when the fair bride of the sun walks through the blue chambers of heaven, attended by the sparkling *coquetry* of the summer skies; but it should be remembered that almost every interesting event occurs in such hours. There is nothing tempting abroad in a dark, rainy, gusty evening; and since Adam and Eve sang their twilight hymn of adoration in the groves of Eden to the moment that Herbert Glenroy finished this exquisite quotation, the moon has thus been the undrained fountain of all inspiration, romance, poetry, music, and love.

"Angels and ministers of grace defend us!" exclaimed Glenroy, looking from the terrace; "see who comes to remind us that we are denizens of earth—not the privileged children of romance."

"I am sure the beautiful Miss Cameron is the very genius of romance," said Edith, while she almost groaned in spirit at the sight of Griselda Willoughby, with the fair sentimentalist, walking up the garden, escorted by the agreeable Dr. Rovington. Margaret cast a rueful look at Constance, and Constance looked as if she could have cried, if it would have done any good.

"We were so happy," whispered she to Edith, "and Miss Willoughby always says something to make everybody feel uncomfortable."

Another figure, which was not at first perceptible, as the path only accommodated three at once, emerged from behind the trio as they entered the piazza. But it would be unworthy to introduce this personage at the end of a chapter. It is much more proper she should dignify the commencement of a new one.

CHAPTER XV.

> Toil not up the sandy steep,
>   Thorns and scorns await thee there—
> Slave of wealth and fashion, keep
>   Where thy lowly sisters are.   *   *   *
>
> The rank is but a guinea stamp,
> The man's the gowd for a' that.   BURNS.

MISS TABITHA SHANKS, according to her own genealogy, was a collateral descendant of the ancient and honourable family of Sir Jacob Shanks, whose ancestral tomb rises in a romantic little vale in Cumberland. It was supposed, however, that this was a dream of her own imagination, and that all the affinity she could possibly claim was her name, being really descended from an honest, but untitled family, whose claims even to *gentility* were somewhat disputed. Her parents were good, industrious, unpretending sort of people, who knew no wish beyond the limits of their farm, and no anxiety but for their two daughters. The eldest married a young farmer, and was settled most comfortably in a snug little nook near Allendale ; and when the elder Shanks' were gathered to their fathers, they opened their hearts and doors to the orphan Tabitha. But Tabitha was incapable of appreciating their honest, downright affections. She had imbibed— heavens know how—some very patrician notions, and despised her sister's grovelling ideas of happiness. She had always manifested something of this aspiring humour, and her father had often sung to her, when she held the milk-pail so daintily, and washed the dishes with the tip ends of her fingers, "Ah! Tabitha, your top-knot must come down,

> " To a linsey-woollen gown
> And you shall marry a farmer."

How Tabitha first contrived to edge herself into the circle, which was denominated the *gentry* by her relations, we do not recollect ; but after she had once entered the golden ring, the power of man or woman could not get her out again. She was a perfect Machiavel in her line ; she managed to obtain invitations to this and that place, and under such circumstances she was obliged to make a *visitation* instead of a visit. She was for awhile at the summit of her ambition ; for she had installed herself in the household of a Mrs. Heathwood by one of the best manœuvres in the world. This lady, whose literary genius seemed to flow from the fountains of benevolence, and would gladly have fertilized the whole valley with the waters of Helicon, kept a select library for the express accommodation of those whose minds were richer than their purses, and thirsted for knowledge they had not the means of acquiring. Tabitha heard of this rare bounty, and suddenly felt an intellectual famine whose craving could not be appeased from any other source. She started for Mrs. Heathwood's at the commencement of an equinoctial storm, and Mrs. Heathwood was too kind to suffer her to walk several dreary miles in the drizzling rain and chilling east wind; besides, she was gratified by her literary taste, and recommended a most judicious course of reading and instruction. Mrs. Heathwood paid dear for her hospitality. The sun-beams came back, dazzlingly bright, but Tabitha still adhered to her as firmly as a piece of melted sealing-wax; and she would probably have stuck there till another equinoctial storm if her ambition had not taken another vault, and she immediately set her wits to work to climb the Alpine height *on* which she gazed. After the arrival of the Willoughby family, Tabitha began to lose her relish for the society of the elegant and refined Mrs. Heathwood, and she was really worn with fatigue, from loitering so long on the stilts of gentility and literature. She had penetration enough to perceive that, notwithstanding the wealth and the many advantages of Miss Willoughby, that she had a natural vulgarity, a coarseness of the grain which no artificial polish could conceal. She also discovered that she was very accessible to flattery; and with this sweet and gracious unction she oiled the path to her favour and her home. Hexham Hall possessed one attraction strong as magnetism to Miss Shanks. Sir Reginald was not only an elaborately fine-looking man for his age, but a widower with *muckle gold,*

"And mailen plenish'd fairly;"

and as Tabitha was already on the shady side of youth with still unappropriated charms, she did not think maturity of years the least objection to her well-digested plan of a future establishment. Napoleon, when he saw his banner waving near the pyramids of Egypt, felt not a prouder throb than that which swelled the heart of this indefatigable home-seeker when she found herself a fixture in Hexham Hall. And to do her justice she did not eat the bread of idleness. She insisted upon hemming Sir Reginald's cravats and bandanas, always jumped to pick up his cane if it chanced to fall, flew to ring the bell if he wanted a servant, and even arrived at the envied privilege of tying up his queue. She worked ruffles and mended gloves for Griselda; was sure to ask her to play whenever the gentlemen lounged in, and was equally sure, when the ladies called. to bring in accidentally, "As Mr. Glenroy was saying to you, last evening, Miss Willoughby;" or as "Dr. Rovington was telling you this morning;" and similar allusions to all the beaux of the country.

Griselda would willingly have paid a salary to any one for a service like this; for she had been obliged to be the herald of all the attentions she received before the valuable acquisition of Tabitha; she therefore offered her a sinecure, and made her the heiress of her cast-off finery. Griselda found the presence of Miss Shanks very desirable on another account; she thought she might serve as a foil for the jewels of her own loveliness, for Griselda, like Desdemona in gazing on her Moorish lover, saw her visage, in her own mind, and it was attractive in her own eyes. The person of Tabitha Shanks was too remarkable to pass unnoticed. She was somewhat tall, but her waist and neck were so uncommonly short they gave her the appearance of being eked below. Her features, tolerably well formed in themselves, seemed all drawn towards the centre of her face by the chemical attraction of aggregation; and her mouth, following this principle, approached so inconveniently near her nose it was a matter of speculation how she could smell. Her eyes, of a pale stone colour, obeyed the same general law, and turned in a slanting direction towards the nasal organ, which had likewise an obliquity towards its point. Tabitha, however, really possessed two or three attributes of female beauty which she valued accordingly. She had very redundant hair, which had a natural frizzle (*she* called it a *wave*), which she took particular care to arrange in such a manner as to show the *contour* of her ear, of which she was particularly vain. But what she considered her murdering point of beauty was her foot, which almost rivalled Babel's, in Kotzebue's novel of "William and Jeanette." It must have been her foot, after all, which first suggested her dreams of gentility, having heard, probably, that it was evidence of a *born lady* to have a taper termination to the body. Never did she suffer this charm to be in the back-ground. It was her greatest misfortune that she could not step forward both feet at the same time

but in sitting she managed to display them both most gracefully.   She always
placed one of the limbs to which this attraction appended over the other, and
turning the point downward, in the second position, kept up a little trembling,
tilting motion-like zephyr among the young leaves of the forest.

It was Miss Tabitha Shanks who emerged from the shadow of her patroness
and formed the fourth of the party that broke in so unexpectedly on the moon-
lighted group.

After a few words of congratulation had passed between them, Alice Cameron
turned to Glenroy, resolving to divert the attention of the company, and rivet
it upon herself: and asked him what influence such a heavenly night had upon his
feelings.

"I cannot exactly define," he answered; "but I think I can always pray more
fervently."

"And you, my sweet friend," added she, appealing to Edith, "does your spirit
hold nearer communion with the burning stars, or hover more tenderly round
those you love on earth?"

"It would require a deeper metaphysician than myself," she replied, "to explain
the full influence of such an hour as this; but-I have always felt in the stilly
brightness of the evening, as if I had capacities of the soul—deeper sensibilities of
the heart—keener susceptibilities both of pleasure and pain.   I have often prayed
that I might *die* gazing on the moon, as it is the most beautiful image of the
Creator's mercy."

"And I," exclaimed Alice, clasping together her white hands, which she had
ungloved for the occasion, and fixing her soft brown eyes, first on the moon, and
then on Robert Glenroy, "I too would die in such an hour; but my last fading
glance would turn from yon glorious planet, to rest on that round which woman's
faithful heart for ever fondly moves—the star of earthly love."

There was something so direct in this speech, and in the melting glance that
applied it, that Edith was perfectly shocked, and had the grace to blush most
intensely at such a violation of her sex's delicacy.   It is true that her modest sense
of propriety was deeply wounded; but it may be questioned if she would have felt
quite as much shocked if the fair Alice had perpetrated her romance on Doctor
Rovington.   She could not help glancing at Glenroy, to see if the lambent lightning
played on an impassive surface; but he had conveniently recollected that his temple
locks were discomposed, and his hand, as it passed over his brows, completely
shaded the stars of Alice's earthly love.

"I declare," suddenly uttered Doctor Rovington, "I declare, Miss Shanks, they
have slighted us most shamefully—nobody has asked us how *we* are affected by
these sweet trembling rays.   Tell me, Miss Tabitha," added he, applying his
fingers to her pulse in the true professional style, "how do you *feel* this celestial
evening?"

"Ah! doctor," simpered she, "you always will be witty.   But why don't you
ask Miss Willoughby?   I'm sure she will have something interesting to say, she
has so much imagination."

"I—don't bring my name forward, if you please, Miss Shanks," said Griselda,
in high displeasure at being left so much in the background.   "I can have nothing
to say on such a common-place and hackneyed subject.   I only know that fools
and maniacs babble and rave to the moon, and that dogs and wolves bay at it."

"Alas!" sighed the doctor, "how little we know of each other; I always thought
it most of all propitious to a meek and heavenly spirit."

A compliment, even in jest, was a never-failing renovator of the spirits of
Griselda, and she condescended to be amiable the remainder of the evening. Alice
managed to monopolize the conversation of Glenroy, and Margaret and Constance
sat on either side of Edith, finding in that privilege something of an indemnification for interrupted happiness.   Constance was seated on a little foot-stool, and
when Edith was speaking, she would look up in her face with such admiring attention, while her fair ringlets, reclining on her lap, gave her an expression of almost
infantine loveliness.   Edith's heart yearned towards her with a sister's fondness;

yet there was a melancholy mixed with this tenderness, for there was something about this sweet young creature that foretold an early doom—a kind of shadowy brightness, like the halo of the moon, beautiful in itself, but the precursor of a day of darkness. As she sat in the attitude of childish gracefulness, the chaplet of wild flowers loosened and fell, shedding their fading sweets in Edith's lap.

"See," said Constance, lifting the drooping wreath, "with what ephemeral honours you have crowned me. I do not know that I am superstitious, but I have often thought, when looking on a young, pale, lifeless flower, I read, as from nature's oracles, a prophecy of my early fate."

"Do not speak so sadly," said Edith, though she felt in her own heart a low echo to the prediction. "The only lesson you should learn from these, is that which Waller's lovely rose was commissioned to breathe to youthful loveliness—— to die,

"That she the fate of all might see,
That are so wondrous sweet and fair,"

Often and mournfully did this passing scene hereafter recur to the memory of Edith.

There was nothing worthy of record in the homeward walk of the party, but the flirtation of the doctor with Miss Shanks, to the great annoyance of Miss Willoughby, who hung upon his other arm. There had been a life-giving shower in the morning, leaving here and there a silver pool by the way-side. Whenever they approached these sparkling transparencies, the doctor would exclaim, with fervent anxiety—

"Oh! Miss Shanks, take care of your feet—it would be a sacrilege to soil such a sole as your's with the slime of this lower world." And Miss Shanks would slant and point her toes more inveterately than ever, till at last, whether by accident or design, in jumping her over one of the largest pools, he loosened his sustaining hold, and the Chinese beauty stuck, fast as a pond lily, in the mud.

"Oh! my stars," cried Miss Shanks. "What shall I do? I've ruined my new kids—and I scarcely ever can get a pair of shoes small enough to fit me in the whole town. Doctor how could you be so cruel as to let me go?"

"I beg a thousand pardons," said the doctor, kindly asssisting her out; "I am the most unfortunate being in the u niverse. But upon my word it was no my fault; your feet are too delicate to support your frame, and you cannot in consequence, keep a proper equilibrium. Here is Miss Willoughby, to whom nature has been more bountiful in that respect, found no difficulty in reaching terra firma."

Miss Shanks would have stood in a mill pond all night for the sake of such a compliment, and skipped with added agility till they ascended the marble flagstones of Hexham Hall.

"How exquisitely beautiful is Miss Cameron," said Edith to Glenroy, almost unconsciously thinking aloud, after they had left the spoiled child of romance at Sir Reginald's gate; "I do not think I ever saw a face so faultlessly lovely—with such perfect regularity of features—such purity and brilliancy of complexion combined."

"She is indeed resplendently beautiful," replied Glenroy, "and if outward loveliness were all, the sons of men might fall down and worship at her feet. But for my part, I deprecate a faultless monster even in beauty. The icicle gem is not more cold in its wintry splendour, than a mere dazzling union of red and white, and an eye sparkling with sole animal brightness is the same to me. I love to linger on the face which the shades of feeling and the sun-beams of intellect alternately darken and illumine, the cheek where the warm blood comes and goes, as one of our most eloquent has expressed, 'with tidings from the heart.'"

Edith was not vain, but she could not but be conscious of her characteristic attractions, and she knew that every emotion of her heart sent a glowing herald to her cheek. There was a depth of feeling too in Glenroy's voice, very different from the gay tones in which he had pledged and supported his chivalrous vow of allegiance, which deepened as he continued—

"But it is not for one like me, sworn brother to necessity, to lap myself in golden dreams, in the bowers of fancy, when the straight though perhaps thorny path of duty lies besore me. Young as I am, I must make myself an anchorite in heart, nor think of gathering another blossom, save those which nature may have scattered near my hermitage. "Tell me," added he, with a sudden flash of animation, as if struck with a conviction of the singularity of his manner, "what poetical eremite shall I make my model? He who, far in an unknown wild, passed his smileless days in prayer and praise? He, the solitary and plantive mourner of man's unavailing glory, or the benign soother of human suffering—the gentle hermit of the dale?"

"Were you to ask me," answered Edith, infinitely relieved by the change he had given to the conversation, "were you to ask me which was the most interesting in poetry, I might hesitate what selection to make, but as a moral exampler, conscience clearly directs my choice to the active reliever of the sorrows of man. It would be madness to imitate the devout sceptic of the wisdom of providence, for you may not, like him, find a descended angel crossing your path to dissipate your doubts and vindicate the dispensations of heaven."

"Most true," he replied; "and were I to follow the example of the gentle moralist, it is not likely that a fair spirit in woman's form would enter my solitary cell, and cheer it with the light of constancy and love."

Leaving Edith at her own door, we shall again return to Susan, and commence a fresh chapter.

CHAPTER XVI.

The silver-crested moon pours on the
Swelling tide her placid light; the helmsman
Cheerly sings, while on the polar star, in
Steadfast gaze, his eye is fixed. Then home, and
Perils past, employ the thoughts of all the busy crew.
One hapless wretch avoids the noisy throng,
And sad and lonely sits apart, and chides
The prosp'rous gale; and as the land recedes from sight,
Drops tears of anguish in the rolling waves.

SUSAN having written the letter to her friends proceeded in the evening to the post-office. She had had an interview in the morning with Lady Melton, who refused to let her leave under a month, saying she considered a month's notice was requisite, in order that she might have time to provide her daughter with another governess.

Absorbed in thought, she proceeded through one of the innumerable alleys on Cornhill, to the post office; she heeded not surrounding objects, till she was about emerging into Lombard-street, when raising her head, she beheld two men of mean appearance following her steps beneath the shadow of the houses. Struck with alarm, fear instantly lent her wings, but notwithstanding her speed she was quickly overtaken by them, and seized by a strong arm, a thick covering was thrown over her head, and she was lifted from the earth by some one, who, in spite of her struggles, ran with her in his arms with incredible swiftness, and as it seemed to her terrified imagination, to a considerable distance. Her senses forsook her at the moment, and, on regaining them she found herself seated in a carriage by the side of one of the ruffians; for a few minutes she felt wild and confused, as if awaking from a frightful dream; then, coming entirely to herself, she looked from the carriage to see where she was; they were proceeding at a rapid rate through a narrow street which she knew not.

Having in vain, for some time, demanded by whom and for what purpose she was placed in the carriage, she was told by the man if she valued at all her life, to refrain from asking questions, which at that time would avail her nothing.

"Whither are you taking me?" at length burst from her, after they had proceeded for some time in silence. "O! tell me what is the meaning of this outrage?"

"All in good time you'll know," was the reply.

"Now, now, I implore you," cried Susan; "but perhaps," with a sudden change of voice, "you have mistaken me for some other person. Yes, yes, it must be so," she added, with a kind of joyful quickness.

"Are you sure of it," said the ruffian.

"I think it must be so," returned Susan.

"Don't make too sure of it, my lass."

"Tell me my name then," resumed Susan, "and that will put the matter out f doubt?

"I fancy I sha'nt be far from the mark if I say 'tis Adams."

The shock Susan felt at finding she was wrong in her conjecture, for a few minutes deprived her of the power of utterance ; on regaining it, she exerted all her eloquence, to try and prevail on the ruffian to release her.

Her supplications, however, might as well have been addressed to an ear of marble, brutal laughter being all they excited.

Still, however, Susan continued to weep, and to implore ; at all events, if he would not release her, to let her know by whom he had been employed to carry her off.

"It's useless," replied the man, "questioning me on the subject, you will know in time, so you may keep your tongue quiet, I dare say you will find a use for it by and by."

Susan again assailed the ruffian with tears and entreaties, but to as little purpose as she had before done ; and at last in absolute despair of succeeding with him, ceased her importunities.

They continued to travel at a rapid rate, through the streets, crossed London Bridge, and took the direction towards the river's bank ; after proceeding for some time, the carriage stopped. Susan was lifted out by the man and carried to the edge of the water ; here a boat was stationed, into which in spite of her resistance, she was forced, and six stout men rowed with all their might towards a vessel which lay in the river. The boat urged on its way, cut quickly through the water and soon reached the side of the ship, which with her sails set, and her anchor weighed, only waited their arrival. Several times Susan attempted to throw herself into the river, but the wary seamen held her down in the boat, and succeeded in placing her safe on the deck of the vessel, where the captain waited to receive her. In extreme agony, Susan inquired of him by whose instigation she was brought on board his ship, and whither he intended to carry her ?

With much politeness the captain lamented not having time to answer her interrogations ; then calling to his mate, from among a group of seamen who had gathered unperceived around, and were eyeing her with licentious gaze, he ordered him to conduct her below ; he then turned away to a distant part of the ship.

The glances of lawless passion are more significant than language ; and, thrilled at once with the instinctive dread of her sex, Susan followed the mate to the cabin. Some of the crew stared at her and smiled as she passed, but all were too busy to attend to her distress, or her questions respecting their destination.

The crew consisted of about one hundred men, and was composed of Englishmen, Frenchmen, and other continential adventurers, together with a few negroes, and nothing could be more startling than the banditti-like appearance they presented. Although the respective countries were at variance, the subjects of each had shaken hands that they might assist each other in violating the laws. The quiet and surbordination of a king's ship was not to be expected here :—loud obstreperous mirth, occasional quarrelling, as one party by accident, or intention, wounded the national pride of the other ; French, English, and Spanish, spoken alternately or at the same moment—created a degree of confusion, which proved that the reins of government were held lightly by the captain in matters of small importance, but, although there was a general freedom of manner, and independence of address, still his authority was acknowledged, and his orders implicity obeyed. It was a ship's company which pulled every way, as the saying is, when there was nothing to demand union ; but, let difficulty or danger appear, and all their squabbling was forgotten, or reserved for a more seasonable opportunity ; then they all pulled together, those of each nation vying in taking the lead and setting the example to each other.

The garb and accoutrements of this lawless gang were as picturesque and various as their faces. The Negroes were nearly destitute of clothing, except cotton trowsers, or their native " longooties," which in the freedom of their present condition many of them had chosen to assume. Some few in addition had shawls bound round their loins ; while their shaggy curls of raven black hair were confined by kerchiefs of orange, or crimson silk, in a style at once fantastic and becoming. The dress of the Europeans, if more complete, was not less regular; for they had appropriated most costly articles to a use for which they were never intended, in a way which most grotesquely contrasted with their rough appearance of those parts of their ordinary habits which they still retained.

Such was the crew of the vessel, in which Susan found herself. The major part of them were so young, that the downy promise of a beard was hardly visible on their chins; but a ferocity shone in their restless eyes which showed that they were old in crime. This haggard wildness in those of riper years was much subdued; and in its stead there reigned a sullen, cold, remorseless frown, ill according with the cunning leer which strove to hide it.

The vessel slowly dropped down the river, and had passed Greenwich some distance, the lights began to sparkle in the windows of the distant city; and here and there, the lofty sails of vessels half becalmed, stole slowly up over the glittering bosom of the deep, like spectral illusions from an unknown world.

Presently the "signal gun" of evening roared from Tilbury Fort; its sullen smoke rose in mid air, and vanished; at the same moment the roll of drums, and a clear deep symphony of martial music from the garrison, marked the curfew hour;—and with dying echoes lingered on the water, rose in a mild and broken melody.

The breeze freshened, and the ship flew threw the water, dashing the white spray from her bows into the air. Longer than a large brigantine, strongly timbered, singularly buoyant, with ample breadth of beam, and a mould with curves graceful as the swelling outlines of a female form, the Tiger had a fit-out of a yacht; and was so contrived and formed, as to be worked either as a xebec, or as a lugger; her compliment of sails, spars, and rigging for either, being beyond the common allowance. In fine, she was one of that "overtrimmed" sort of craft that look too knowing to be honest; and though they have no gun in sight, have often a convenient ballast of cannon-balls and a tank for powder, as well as for water. Rakish as she was, we will not promise all this for the Tiger; yet still she had enough—she was built for the game of death, when the ocean takes the odds, and had qualities that would bear her out, in the roughest and the worst.

Confused and full of terror, Susan suffered the mate to conduct her to the cabin, which she found handsomely furnished, and seemingly prepared for her reception. The mate placed before her various refreshments, but he either was ignorant, or pretended to be so, of all that related to her, and of the ship's destination.

The door being closed upon her, she was left to weep and tremble alone, and picture the evils to which, in her defenceless state, she was exposed. A thousand times she invoked the name of her father; and driven to desperation, she would have thrown herself from the winds of the cabin, but precaution had fastened them; and while she wept and wrung her hands, the increasing motion of the ship convinced her they were under weigh. In pacing the cabin, a small door half-open discovered a narrow but elegant bed; her fatigues required repose, and having secured the door, without taking off any of her attire, she threw her wearied limbs on the bed, where in a short time, in spite of terror and sorrow, sleep closed her eyes, and lulled her senses in a happy though transient forgetfulness of her condition.

The vessel was now lugger-rigged, and with studding sails boomed out so far that she seemed like a drifting cloud; and from the way in which she clawed on the wind, and stood carefully aloof of every sail she passed, it might very safely be surmised, that there was a better reason than caprice for her "prudence:"—in other words, her conduct was suspicious.

The wind fell light after midnight, and at dawn of day the lugger was gliding through the smooth water, at the rate of three or four miles an hour, shrouded in a thick fog. The sun rose, but his rays had not power to pierce through the fog; and, shorn of his beams, he had more of the appearance of an overgrown moon, or was, as the mate quaintly observed, "like a man disguised in woman's attire."

A change now took place in the weather. Large heavy masses of dark clouds were coming rapidly up with the wind, while every now and then some small cloud was detached from the main body, but was soon scattered and dispersed by the force of the blast, which was rapidly rising. The long heavy swell of the sea had assumed the appearance of arching waves, rolling thunderly on, and breaking and reforming every moment.

"I say, Dick," began the captain to the mate, who was holding the tiller, and anxiously watching the signs of the weather, "I dont like this—here's a pretty storm brewing. 'Tis coming on so fast, that I'm afraid we'll have to run to the south'ard, and that, I guess, is right into the teeth of the sharks, and be hanged to them !"

"I cant say as how I like it at all," replied Dick, "'specially as them ere gulls are making such furious sail to the land; if them land-lubber. But as for the matter of running to the south, why, I think it would be better to run her right ashore, and take our chance ; we may perhaps cheat Davy that way, but, by the other, 'tis all up with us.—Belay, there, with you pipe, you young offspring of the fallen angel !" roared out old Dick to an embryo free-trader, who was whistling most unconcernedly on the forecastle, " or I'll make this rope and your behind better acquainted. I wonder you haven't hoisted in more ballast in the article of sense since you've been to sea, than to whistle in a storm. A pretty sort of a place you sarved your time in, you son of a female dog, not to know better than that. I'll accelerate your collective mass with more velocity if I come behind you."

"Will you though," muttered the boy, moving slowly away.

"Dont answer me, you juvenile progeny of a marine dresser of wittles," responded old Dick ; " move off there, or I'll come and make you."

Old Dick, the mate, had acquired that cognomen by a habit of always carrying about with him a small edition of Johnson's Dictionary, in the study of which he used to employ every leisure moment, not for the purpose of improving himself in orthography—for which he evinced the most sovereign contempt, even in the most simple words—but for that of exercising his memory in the acquisition of a stock of the most inflated and sonorous words he could find. Great was his ingenuity in substituting the most jaw-breaking and high-sounding terms for the more common and inelegant, but plain-spoken language of his messmates, and his application of them was often ludicrous in the extreme. I will give one or two instances of the ridiculous results of his dictionary mania. Instead of using, when in a passion with any of his shipmates, the common and blackguard epithet, which, for the benefit of ear polite, I will translate, " son of a female dog," he substituted " offspring of a canine quadruped ;" and instead of a still more injurious term of reproach, which I will not mention in plain English, he adopted, " you spurious progeny of a meretricious female." Dick was a clever man of letters in his own estimation, whatever he might be in that of others. He had no enemies, however, though his shipmates enjoyed many a hearty laugh at his peculiarities, and his age disarmed animosity. His beloved Dictionary was his inseparable companion ; his watch below was employed in poring over its well-thumbed leaves, and, in his watch on deck, he availed himself of every opportunity of astonishing his hearers with his euphony.

"Ahoy, there—aft !" sung out a voice from the bow, where the lugger's look-out was stationed. " A sail rising seaward on the starboard bow ! She's coming up right afore the wind, under reefed topsails and jib."

"I'm blowed, if I don't like this about as much as a stripped marine does a drummer !" exclaimed the captain. " Who the devil can she be ? Ahoy, there—aft ! What is it now, lad ?"

" The strange sail's hoisted her main double-reefed, and has veered a point more to the nor'ard."

"This is no joke now, captain," replied old Dick. "Take the glass, and see what you can make of her."

"By Heaven, Dick, her hull's rising; she's a king's ship as I am alive. Who the devil can she be? Strike my tops; but she sees us now, and here she comes with a vengeance. We must clap on more sail—our spars will bear it; but it is very unpleasant to have this here nest of sharks flung in our way, when we'd made so sure of having the coast clear. All hands, ahoy! Let out another reef in the main, and hoist the foresail. Are you ready there, foremen?"

"Ay, ay!"

"Away with it then. That's right, my lads. She's walking a little faster now, Dick. Are we dropping her at all?"

"No, no!" sung out Dick.

"Then our only expedient will be to risk more canvass, though, by-the-by, we must fall a point off the wind for that purpose."

This was immediately done; and soon the bending and overloaded masts of the Tiger bore a cloud of sail, which, if it promised safety in one sense, was now itself most critical, as the overstrained spars and half-buried hull began to testify.

The gale freshened; and, as the frantic horse of Mazeppa bore his bound and naked rider over the waste, staggering forward with convulsive bounds so the overpacked lugger floundered through the surging waters, gunnell down at every lurch, but still scudding onward with a wild impetuous speed, her head submerged in jets of boiling foam, and her nearly started rigging quivering and creeking as she passed.

On the offing, in the meanwhile, still loomed the cutter, winning her way, as it seemed, without an effort; and, as both vessels were now moving at nearly the same velocity, she seemed even stationary in the distance.

"She's let out another reef in her main, and hoisted the gaff with a single one," suddenly exclaimed the mate.

"We must fight them, Dick; and if we've any luck, we may send one of her masts by the board; but she's too old, I think, to have any hope in her yawing. Clear the deck there, and out with the tompions; we may perhaps make our sixes rattle in a way she'll like about as much as nine-water-grog on a banyan-day. Knock the head out of that cask, and lash it to the main; there'll be enough of fighting-water in it. Are you all ready now, every soul of ye?"

"Ay, ay?"

"Then listen, my lads, while I speechify a bit. You see we've but three chances —first, run and so get clear off; second, fight and beat them; third, blow ourselves and them to the devil together. We'll try them all in turn; and now lie in, every mother's son of ye, and let not a gun be fired till I give the word."

The cutter was by this time within a mile of the smugglers, and had now altered her course, so that in a short time she would have run across the lugger's bows, and brought her whole broadside to bear on her. But Captain Harrop was too old a hand to be caught in that way; and putting the tiller a little to starboard, the Tiger, in a moment, was running parallel with her foe.

"Ha, ha, old boy!" muttered the smuggler; "too deep for you this tack I imagine. He's beginning to speak now, Dick, and seriously too."

A cloud of smoke rushed from the cutter's side, and a whole broadside of her shot passed harmlessly over the smuggler, owing to her falling, luckily, in the critical moment, into the trough of the sea, while her antagonist was at the same moment, raised on the crest of the wave.

"See, Dick, he's tired of this, and, by all my hopes, here he comes, right afore the wind! Bring her a point more to the wind, Dick, and we'll rake her. Steady, my lads, steady; for God's sake wait till I sing out!"

The cutter was now within pistol-shot of the lugger, never suspecting she could have any metal weight enough to harm her, and was just rounding to bring another broadside to bear, when Captain Harrop, springing forward, sang out—

"Away there, ye Tigers, up with the ports, and give it them cheerily, my lads!"

The ports were up, the guns run out, and fired by the eager and anticipating smugglers, almost before the words were out of theirCaptain's mouth. The cutter shook to her very kelson, under the unexpected volley. Down came her foremast, her rigging was almost cut to pieces, and in a moment she lay nearly a wreck upon the waters, tossing ungovernably. The smugglers, taking advantage of her helpless state, soon shot far ahead of her, but not before Harrop sung out,—" All hands, ahoy, there, and clear your pipes, and give us the Tiger's song ; 'twill serve as grog, by way of a relish to their supper. You three musicians there, are ye all ready to make sail on it ?"

" Ay, ay," answered three of the men, who, from their having rather good voices, with tolerable ears, had obtained that sobriquet from their companions.

" Heave away, then ;" and instantly, with clear but strong voices, they struck up the following rude strain,—

> Here's to the lads that plough the deep,
>   Where winds and waters roar,
> Who spread the sail when others sleep,
>   And ply the midnight oar ;
> Brave souls that fear not rock nor shoal,
>   And wind and tide despise,
> Who drain the flask, and quaff the bowl,
>   Despite the King's excise.
>
> In vain they prowl from cliff to cliff,
>   And watch for evermore,
> The gallant smuggler's bonny skiff
>   Comes safe and sound to shore.
> For never did the broadest keel
>   That drew a watery line,
> His dark and secret path reveal
>   Across old Ocean's brine.

It sounded far from disagreeable, especially when they commenced the second verse, when the voices of the whole willing crew gave it a cast peculiar to their own wild kind of life ; and the lashing of the waves against her sides, and the whistling of the wind through her cordage, formed a not inappropriate accompaniment.

The song was finished : her sails were double-reefed, her hatches closed, and all made snug to meet the storm, which by this time had almost risen to a hurricane.

The cutter had not been left a mile astern, before the mate perceived a large vessel bearing down towards them.

" We can't carry on much longer," said old Dick, " for there's a cruizer, if I mistake not. A gun here is the same to the cruizer, as a splash in the water is to the ground sharks at Antigua ;—up they all come to see what's to be had. I thought we should not be allowed to continny our perry-grimashums in sollytoode. We shall have a lot of them above the horizon before the horb of day has sunk."

" Avast heaving with that fine lingo of your'n ;" exclaimed the boatswain, " it puts a plain-sailing man's pipe out ; it's as bad as old double Dutch coiled against the sun. It warn't for nothen they gev you the name of Old Dick ; for blow me if Old Nick himself could understand you, when once you begins to talk dix'nary."

" And what do you know about it, you hignorant disciple ?" said old Dick, sharply ; " 'tisn't all men are blessed alike with larning. When I speaks to a juvenile like you, its for your hedicashion—hedifeckashun, I mean—and if you doesn't understand me, it ill-beseems you to wag your hunruly member at me."

" Well, well, old boy," said the boatswain, " take a sure turn with that 'till I pipes belay. Half your jabber is like the wind to me—I hears a noise, but I doesn't know what it is all about ; I thinks you're learned in what the long-shore chaps calls the hunknown tongues. I b'lieve if the old gentleman himself, what made all them words in the dix'nary, was to hear you, he wouldn't know his own children."

Captain Harrop soon made out the strange sail to be a frigate, coming down upon them under a press of sail, attracted, as old Dick had observed, by the firing of the guns. What made their chance of escape more uncertain was, that she was evidently making signals for the lugger to lie to : this was disregarded, when a boat was seen lowerin from the frigate. The seamen seated themselves regularly on the thwarts, and the strokesman, after reeving the main-sheet through the fair

leader abaft, sat with it in his hand in such a position on the after-thwart, that though his face was turned to windward, his eye would occasionally meet that of his commander. As the light boat lay down to the wind, and became steady in her course towards the chase, the crew had time to look around them. The lieutenant having ascertained that each man had his cutlas beside him, he proceeded to examine the priming of his pistols, which he finally placed in his waist belt, and wrapped himself in a cloak which had been spread for him in the

No. 12.

stern sheets abaft. Taking advantage of the first heavy swell, he rose in the boat to catch a glimpse of the lugger, which he discovered broad on the lee bow. Having directed the attention of the bowmen to her position, both resumed their seats, and the lieutenant shaped his course so as to board her on the quarter.

Not a word as yet had escaped the lips of any of his men, who sat cowering in a bending attitude, with elevated shoulders and arms crossed, fearful of changing the position of a limb, lest it should occasion any alteration in the boat's trim. Thus aided by every effort of art, and impelled by the breeze, the boat soon gained rapidly on the chase ; which, perceiving that the boat from the frigate was evidently in pursuit of her, bore round-up, making all the sail she could carry before the wind. The bowman just then looking under the foot of the lug, pronounced her to be a large lugger, which he had before seen on the station, under similar suspicious circumstances. The lieutenant, putting up the helm, instantly edged into her wake, and followed precisely her track.

A short period, however, sufficed to show that the lugger, from the quantity of sail she was enabled to carry, had decidedly the advantage ; and the wind continuing to blow hard, she rapidly distanced her pursuer.

The crew of the lugger, who had been all merriment at the successful termination of the late combat, (for there was not one of the crew scarcely wounded) now walked the deck, or looked over the bulwark with serious and foreboding aspects ; the foreigners particularly began to lament their fate, and already considered their voyage and anticipated profits at an end.

Captain Harrop, on noticing their discontent, ordered the men aft, and thus addressed them,—

" My boys, I have been in a much worse scrape than this before now, and have escaped it ; and I still think that if you obey my orders, and behave with coolness and determination we shall we ather it now. If the crew of yon boat should board us , we must fight while we have a drop of blood left ; if we are taken, my lads, you know what our fate will be." Here Captain Harrop made a significant motion with the fore-finger of his right hand, casting at the same time a glance to the end of the fore-top-sail-yard of the Tiger, which left no doubt of his meaning.

He then proceeded to explain to his crew the manœuvre that he intended to practise, and upon which their only chance of escape would depend ; the men returned to their stations, if not contented, at least with increased confidence in their Captain, and strong hopes of success.

In half-an-hour she was hull down ; the haze of evening growing every moment thicker, she became imperceptible to the view of the boat's crew. The men now involuntarily turned their eyes, which had hitherto been strained on the chase, to the stern of the boat ; the appeal was unnecessary—the lieutenant was already occupied in council with the coxswain ; his trusty favourite hesitated not to dissuade him, in terms respectful, yet decisive, from continuing so unequal a chase, more particularly as there was no chance, in the dark, of communicating by signal, either with their own vessel or any cruizer which might be off the station.

A heavy swell had now set in from the same point in which the wind had continued all day. The sun had set with every indication of stormy weather ; a pale yellow streak of light, partly reflected on the east, formed the only contrast to the general murky gloom of the horizon ; across which the gull and other sea fowl, hastily fled the approach of the gale, already indicated by the swift drifting of the scud, which overtook them in their flight, and suddenly enveloped all in darkness without the intervention of twilight.

They had got so far to leeward, that to return with the boat was impossible. The sail had already been lowered, the mast struck, and the boat brought head to wind ; when the crew, shipping their oars, bent their broad shoulders to pull her through the heavy sea, which flung itself in sheets of spray over the bows, and drenched every man on board. It was soon found that oars were unavailing to contend against the force of a sea like this, in which it was scarcely possible so small and delicate a bark should live much longer. The waves were rolling from the main in aggravated violence, and the united strength of the men could barely keep her head to wind ; who, perceiving there was no longer the slightest prospect of making any progress, or the wind moderating, sullenly contented themselves with hanging on their oars.

Apprehension soon put an end to all subordination. Remonstrances on the impossibility of successfully persevering in their present course, were now muttered by every seaman, except the coxswain, whose features betrayed, notwithstanding, no less anxiety than the rest. A heavy sea, which struck the larboard bow, making, in consequence of its being impossible to keep the boat's head on, a rapid accumulation of water every minute, soon decided the reluctant lieutenant—though at the obvious hazard of her destruction—to run the boat ashore in the first situation which might offer a chance of saving the lives of his brave companions.

"Lay in your oars, my lads," cried he; "step the short mast—close reef the storm lug ; we must run all hazards, and beach her under canvass."

. Whilst executing this order the bowman sung out, " A sail close a-board, sir ; if she don't keep her luff, she'll run us right down."

" Luff, luff !" cried aloud every man in the boat. The lugger's course, however, remained unaltered ; there could now be no doubt, her object was to run over the boat, by taking her right abeam.

Destruction appeared inevitable in their helpless condition. A shriek of despair, mingled with execrations, succeeded as she neared the boat, when the lieutenant rose in the boat, levelled the pistol at the steersman, and fired : the hand which grasped the tiller relaxed its hold, and old Dick his life. The lugger instantly broached-to, passing to windward of the boat.

"Our oars, my lads," said the lieutenant ; "we'll board the villains."

" Ay, ay, sir," exclaimed several voices, with an alacrity which might be taken for the surest earnest of meditated vengeance. The oars were again manned, the boat in the meantime pitching bows under, and shipping green seas fore and aft. Before she had got way on her, two of the weather oars snapped short in the rowlocks, and her intention to board being suspected by the smuggler, she had no sooner paid off, so as to get the wind again abaft the beam, than Captain Harrop determined upon a desperate manœuvre to escape. He had a gallant and staunch ship under him—she had not yet sprung a spar, nor split a sail—and his men—he could not see them captured. He therefore set his fore-top-sail and close reefed the main-top-sail, which urged his ship through the water with great velocity.

The lieutenant saw the plan, and attempted to make sail ; but all would not do, and he saw that his only chance for safety was, if possible, to elude the shock at the very moment of the expected concussion.

> Nearer, still nearer, their shouts are heard ;
> They are chasing a ship with the speed of a bird ;
> The furrow is deep, in the waters they sever,
> And the ship they pursue will go down for ever!
>
> On came the prison of souls to view,
> Enveloped in clouds of a fiery hue :
> Her bellying sails gave way to the blast,
> And bent the lithe topsail and stately mast,
> While in strong relief on the lurid glow,
> Was painted each spar of the " mariners' foe."
> On—fearfully on !—the warm blood froze,
> As the shriek of undying thirst arose—
> An instant—she passed ! and the trough of the sea
> Received the trim form of the daring and free.

The lugger came down upon them with terrific precision. " Hard to port !" shouted the lieutenant to the helmsman.

" Hard to port !" echoed the smuggler to his. One tremendous crash—one wild frantic shriek of despair—and all was hushed in death.

CHAPTER XVII.

Oh! for a soft and gentle wind,
I heard a fair one cry,
But give to me the roaring breeze,
And wild waves beating high.
And wild waves beating high, my boys,
The good ship tight and free,—
The world of waters is our home,
And merry men are we.   ALLAN CUNNINGHAM.

Through the haze of the night a bright flash now appearing,
"Oh, oh!" cried Will Watch, "the Philistines bear down,
Bear a hand, my tight lads, ere we think about sheering,
One broadside pour in, should we swim, boys, or drown."   WILL WATCH.

CAPTAIN HARROP now considered he had escaped all danger, but upon looking through his telescope he still perceived the frigate bearing down upon them in the distance.

She hove-to, to attempt to save some of the drowning men. All eyes from the lugger were turned with a fearful interest on the frigate, as her heavy sails were swung to the tops; the yards manned, while the courses were bent with a celerity which showed the ardour and high discipline of her crew.

Instantaneously the fore-sail shot aloft; the spanker shivered in the gale,—they bellied with its surging pressure; and, all at once, the gallant fabric again began to stem the rolling tides of ocean!

The noise of the firing on board the lugger awoke Susan in the morning, and recalled her to the recollection of her sad mysterious situation; and, with tearful eyes, she surveyed the narrow limits of her prison—for such to her it appeared, the door of the cabin being locked on the outside; from the windows she beheld only sea and sky, and by the rapidity with which the ship cut through the waves, she judged that the wind was favourable to its course, and that they were then many leagues from England.

Upon first awaking, she pressed her fingers upon her eyelids, and looked again. "I must dream!" said she, in a low, silvery voice. "Edith, oh Edith!" and she looked up, when the firing of a gun make her start. "What?—No!—I still dream," she cried, placing her hands over her eyes, as though endeavouring to collect her thoughts. "Oh God! what a dream! what a fearful dream I have had!" and again she removed her hands, and gazed wildly round the cabin.

She now heard distinctly the sound of rushing waters, and was conscious of motion. "Father, father! where am I?" she shrieked wildly; "this vessel— the dashing waves! Ha! who is it that calls? Oh God! oh God! I know it all—all!" she shrieked, as the deep mellow voice of Captain Harrop, addressing her from the inner cabin, fell upon her ear; and the wretched girl buried her face in her hands, and shed burning tears.

"Ha, that voice again! miserable Susan! utterly lost—lost!" she exclaimed. Suddenly her eye rested upon a knife lying upon t floo.

"My God, forgive me; but thus I can save my honour!" and she seized upon the weapon.

In a moment the door was thrown open, but ere the smuggler could enter, the weapon was grasped in the hand of the maiden; her eyes were uplifted, full of sublime and holy devotion. "Forgive me, merciful Father!" she uttered, with wild and affecting energy; and the glittering knife was descending into her breathing bosom, when the smuggler sprang forward, and seized upon her uplifted arm.

"Nay, lady, life is sweet even in wretchedness;" and Harrop wrenched the knife from her hand, and flung it through the door-way.

"Oh that I may find it so!" she exclaimed, while her beautiful and excited features expressed the intensest mortification at her disappointment; her dark eye kindled with anger, while her colourless lip showed maidenly apprehension. For a moment she stood in the attitude in which she had been arrested, with these several passions agitating her bosom; but the last overcame all other feelings; and with clasped fingers, and the uplifted eye of a Madonna, she said, imploringly, and with touching eloquence,—'I implore you by your mother—by your hope of heaven—by your fear of hell! See, I kneel to you! Oh, sir, I know I am in your hands; but as you hope for mercy, inform me why I am brought on board your ship, and who is the enemy who has so basely contrived to get possession of my person?"

"How is it possible so lovely a creature can have an enemy?" replied Harrop; "whoever beholds you, madam, must be your slave."

"I ask not for compliment," said Susan, rising from her suppliant posture, "but a sincere reply to my question."

"Plainly and sincerely then," resumed the captain, "you have no enemy, but an ardent adorer, whom mighty love has prompted, like—like some one of whom I've heard, who carried off a beautiful damsel, while two other foo—zounds," said the captain, checking himself in the middle of the word fools, "while two others fought for her."

In happier circumstances, Susan would have laughed at such bombast, but now her heart was depressed with sorrow, and her vivacity was subdued by dismay.

"Does love delight in acts of baseness, cruelty, and oppression?" said she; "Why did not this adorer boldly, openly, and honourably solicit my approbation? why have I been forcibly placed on board this ship—why placed in the charge of ruffians?—If these, sir, are the actions of love, I beseech you, tell me what worse could the most inveterate hate inflict upon me."

Captain Harrop shrugged his shoulders, placed his hand on his breast, and protested he had no hand in the ill-treatment she had received; but while on board his vessel, she had nothing similar to apprehend, for he would do all possible to render her comfortable.

"I thank you, sir," resumed Susan, "for this assurance; the terror of violence being removed, I shall be the better able to support the misfortunes in which I am plunged; but I beseech you, sir, inform me by whose authority you act, and whither you are conveying me?"

"Pardon me, madam," said Harrop; "I am not at liberty to satisfy you on these points; but rest satisfied your questions will shortly be answered—your adorer will himself explain his intentions; he will, I am certain, deplore the terrors you have unavoidably suffered, and will compensate your afflictions by the tenderest solicitude and attention to your future wishes. Hark, lady, my presence is required on deck," he suddenly exclaimed as the report of a gun was heard; "I will send you an attendant, the daughter of my mate, who will attend to your slightest wish."

As soon as he had quitted the cabin, the girl made her appearance. Susan rejoiced to see a female, though but a child; the countenance of her attendant pleased her, and she hoped to learn from her innocence, what the art of the captain concealed. But Fanny had not been on board many hours before herself —she was going with her father to the south of France, where he intended staying, as he was about leaving his present dangerous employment, after this one trip. This was all the girl knew; and Susan, ceasing to question her, burst into tears.

Her spirit was entirely so wrapped in its own dark fears, that even the voice of kindness remained for a while unheeded; but now, when unwillingly convinced that every chance of reaching her friends at Allendale was hopeless, she sank upon the bed, and wept bitterly. The first indication of returning serenity was when the meek-eyed girl, raising her pale countenance in the mute eloquence of heart-felt devotion, appeared to breathe a prayer; and then, after a turn or so across the cabin, with her clasped hands pressing on her bosom, as if to restrain the unwonted wildness of its throbs, she paused before her companion, who, in a voice of gentleness, inquired if she was ill, and if she could do aught to relieve her.

"I am not ill, Fanny, but I am most deeply afflicted," said Susan; "Heaven alone can relieve me."

"I will pray for you, lady," returned the girl; "my poor mother often cried, when she thought father was risking his life on the stormy sea, and she taught me to pray for his safety—lady, I will do so for thine."

Susan sank on her knees—"We will pray now," said she, "for I have much need of heavenly support and consolation."

Fanny lifted up her hands, and her lips breathed the prayer of an unsophisticated heart. Susan felt the efficacy of prayer, for she rose from her knees, comforted and full of hope.

Several hours had elapsed, and still the chase continued with that awful sameness, that equipoise of fear and hope, which keeps the mind on the tenter-hooks of suspense till the very heart aches with defeated expectation.

"We shall have one of those violent storms common in these seas, anon!"—Well let it come! though it wrap us in the gloom of hell, it were now welcome."

"I think the frigate nears us," said the boatswain.

"I think so too," replied Harrop, who had just withdrawn his eye from the glass:—"Tiller," he said to the boatswain, "have all sail made on the lugger; stretch out every rag she's got; make every thread tell. Set stun-sails both sides alow and aloft, see to it?"

The additional sails rose on either side of those before standing, as if by magic. Men moved quickly in all directions, yet each obedient of his own officer, and each engaged in obeying a particular order, as if but one had been given, and he the only one to execute it. The masts were soon white with broad fields of canvass, stretching far out on either side of the vessel; and the increased ripple around the bow, and the gurgle heard about the rudder, indicated that she felt the new impulse, and was moving with increased velocity, rapidly cleaving her way through the water; the boiling masses bursting in sparkling foam beneath her bows, the spars aloft were heard to crack, and complain in every direction, under the heavy pressure of the low and lofty canvass, which proudly towered on each mast like a pyramid, despite of the gathering gale. The studding sail-booms were topping upwards, and threatening each minute, as they bent to the breeze, to snap short in their confining irons. By the additional weight of their outer wings, the top-sail yards thus extended, notwithstanding the support afforded by their taughtened lifts, and well-bowsed burtens, were bowing in the slings, and drooping their extremities; whilst the towering topmast was observed, not without some ominous foreboding, yielding to the blast, or moving to and fro with the "send of the ship," like a supple ash tree on the mountain top, contending with the storm.

"Our light spars cannot bear this tearing service much longer," observed the boatswain, looking to the crowd of straining canvass overhead, with a solicitude which showed he was nearly as anxious about the fate of the Tiger as his captain was to escape from the frigate. "Don't you think, sir, we're pressing her a little too much? The sticks, you see, sir, are beginning to complain! If anything should start we're lost beyond all hope'."

"But half an hour, Tiller, and the threatening storm will puzzle the frigate rather too much to leave her time to think of us."

"It's a desperate alternative, replied Tiller.

"Yet, let it come; and it is but right to remember that we must have encountered the weather if we had never seen the frigate. If we have time to make all snug the Tiger has nothing to fear from the roughest sea that ever swept a deck; if not, our hope must be that the extra stays will save the lower masts."

"Ah! the wind is leaving us; there flaps the fore-topsail against the mast," suddenly exclaimed the boatswain, as the wind began to lull. "She does not now move two knots through the water," he added, glancing over the side; " we shall have it dead calm in a few minutes.   Hark, it thunders !"

" Take in the lower stun-sails, Tiller, and stand by to hand in all the light canvass ! we shall have it soon!" and Captain Harrop continued giving the necessary orders, till in a short time the vessel was stripped to her two topsails, spanker, and jib.

The peal redoubled ; and, as it echoed through the firmament, the clouds that had enshrouded the moon were suddenly detached, as if attracted towards the water, where they formed a moving fog-bank, enlarging rapidly and gathering windward.

The several orders had been executed ; and the Tiger lay rocking, with scarcely any progressive motion, on the sluggish surges, which all at once began to heave and swell as if lifted by some vast and mysterious power beneath. She was nearly divested of her canvass ; yet still beautiful in her nakedness, showing to advantage the graceful symmetry of her tapering spars, and the exquisite shape and proportions of her hull. Like a sea bird seated on the water, she yielded to every undulation of the heaving billows with a grace that seemed the instinct of life.

In the meantime a dull vague dimness suffused itself around ; and imperceptibly the vapoury bank in the distance swallowed up the intervening space, until the offing seemed diminished to a span with a curtain of black and moving mist, beyond which flashes of lightning began to gleam with momentary radiance ; and a deep moaning sound was heard, like the winds howling in caverns under-sea. Gradually it grew louder, and at the same time the dark cloud cast itself across the skies towards the zenith, its edges streaming in advance, like hair blown out by the wind. The gloom increased, until it wrapt all things in its blackness, except one lurid spot, where the moon still faintly shone as an omen of disaster. The pursuing frigate still came on, darkly dim, like a moving shadow sailing in the air.

It is an awful suspense to watch the storm approach, while every moment brings it nigher ; to wait for the shock which you can only abide ; and the bravest holds his breath " for a time," when the furious tempest strikes the poor ship, and sends her reeling beneath the wave to emerge again covered with foam, and trembling through all her timbers.

Deeper and more awful grew the moan of the storm as it swept down the sea. Louder and louder it came, and now was distinctly heard the roar of the agitated waves, tossed by the shrieking winds, and between the sky and the sea, which seemed to meet within reach of the hand, glared a line of white foam, seeming, to the imagination, the glittering and gnashing teeth of the mad tempest.

With all the promptitude of high resolve, Captain Harrop had taken care that his vessel should be prepared (as far as might be) to encounter the crash of elements expected to ensue. The lugger was now under bare poles, and left to the mercy of the hurricane. The roar of the coming tempest was now deafening, and the vessel began to pitch wildly, yet there was no sensible agitation of the air.

" After all," said Harrop, " the storm may pass away,—and yet 'tis strange that we have no rain ; the clouds are actually down upon us, and floating upon the bosom of the deep."

Even while he spoke, the whole atmosphere seemed changed into a mass of flame, the hurricane raged furiously, the thunder roared, the lightning flashed, and the ocean boiled around the good ship like a hell. The tempest had burst upon them, as if a cloud, swelling with wind and rain, had broken over the vessel. Instantly all who were on their feet were prostrated. Howling and shrieking through the rigging, accompanied by a crashing and splintering that appalled every soul on board with the present sense of danger, it swept over them with terrific fury. Borne down by its weight, the vessel careered till she almost lay on her beam's end, while the mad surges leaped over her bulwarks, and threatened to annihilate the whole gallant fabric. The darkness became illumined by a wild strange light from the foaming sea, and every object was distinctly seen by its supernatural glare,—for several seconds flash followed flash, spreading a glare of intolerable light over the whole horizon, and revealing the relative situation of the vessels.

The frigate having before taken in sail, had been lying-to in utter uncertainty what course to steer, but that point being thus ascertained, the next flash showed her bearing down upon the lugger.

Again the distant thunder growled; and elated with their approaching triumph, the crew of the frigate cheered loudly, and laboured with redoubled zeal. The vessel was driven with the force of the tempest with inconceivable velocity; the waves seemed to lift her hull, and hurl her onward like a feather. The lightning grew more fiercely rapid, and still as she neared, the exulting shouts grew louder; then all at once they ceased, and presently arose a long deep wail, and yells of agony and fear.

A thunderbolt, bright and dazzling as the sword of heaven, had struck the frigate mid-ships, and passing aft, had filled her with wreck, and all-consuming fire! In a short period the ship must have presented, even to a far distant spectator, a most awful and imposing spectacle. The fire had got total possession of her, and rose like a bright pyre against the black sky, surmounting in vivid bursts the very top-gallant truck, whilst hurrying along each slender spar, or searching the involutions of each pitchy rope, the subtle flame was seen coiling and winding its way through the rigging like a snake of living fire.

Happily the greater part of the crew were forward—for the others, but few escaped with life; and of them, some unfortunate wretches, scorched, blackened, and shrieking with agony, were crawling from the open ports.

Obedient to her helm, the fiery fabric broached instantly to, throwing up her blazing bow to the wind; then rising for a moment on the summit of a topping wave, she fell over to leeward down the steep descent,—gave a heavy lurch, the effects of which were heard through all her groaning timbers. The shock thus given to the lofty mast, now bereft of all support, combined with its ponderous weight, snapped short above the cap, and pitched it, all flaming, amid the hissing foam of the sea.

Vast volumes of smoke, with roaring, dazzling sheets of flame, and showers of sparks, now burst through the stern windows, the ports and scuppers, until the decks yawned open, and all was one dread and glowing pit of floating fire. The destruction of the gallant vessel was inevitable; and as the boats had been washed overboard by the tempest, the crew seemed altogether without a refuge;—presently, however, it was evident that they were attempting to construct a raft—when suddenly, a loud explosion was heard, the magazine had taken fire, and many hundred gallant souls were launched into eternity.

"The frigate has blown up, captain," said Tiller; "and thanks be to Heaven, we are safe from their clutches!"

At that instant there came a second blast of the tempest, and a large sea breaking over the vessel, swept Tiller into the water, and bore several of the men into the sea, who in the next moment were lost in the darkness astern.

We must now return again to Susan, who, from the rough motion of the ship, imagined that the wind had increased considerably. "A storm is approaching," said she, as a flash of lightning at that moment darted through the window—"All hope then is at an end, and father and friends are lost to me for ever!—Well, be it so! I am content to perish, for who knows what might have befallen me had I landed on a foreign coast?—the brutal wretch who has forced me here might—"

The unfinished sentence died on her lips, for sickness assailed her, and as her eyes turned upwards, she beheld the dark and lurid appearance of the sky, indicating a fierce and heavy tempest. A serenity, astonishing even to herself, took possession of her mind. Existing circumstances had effected this resignation to what she conceived inevitable destruction: in happier moments, the very idea of being at sea, beating about at the mercy of the wild winds and waves, would have filled her with consternation; but now she listened to the loud thunder, and beheld the boiling waves with a calm and steady eye—"Perhaps," said she, "this storm is the means employed by Providence for my deliverance from brutal violence. If so, welcome death! Father Edith, we are fated to meet no more! but my last breath will sigh your names—my last prayer will be for you!—But, alas, while I perish through the guilt of others, I shall appear criminal in your sight; for who will vindicate the fame of the unfortunate Susan? who will convince you that she was carried off by violence?"

The harsh voices of the mariners mingled with the roaring wind, which every moment seemed to increase in fury, and convinced her that something terrible had happened on deck; but too sick to quit the cabin, and unable to keep her seat, she clung to the window, and continued to watch the heaving billows, foaming and swelling into mountains.

     'Now frantic horror treads the deck,
     And views the ocean's agitated rage;

No. 13.

> While round the fated ship loud breakers roar,
> And through the yawning sides the billows dash,
> Till the despairing crew, by madness led,
> Plunge in the deep.'

Certain it is, the boisterous wind and heaving waves, which every instant seemed to strain and crack the labouring vessel, were heard and beheld by Susan without dismay; for dreadfully sick, and every moment expecting to sink, she patiently resigned herself to the destruction she believed inevitable. In the midst of the wild uproar of the elements, the horror of which was every moment increased by thunder and lightning, she was astounded by a hollow burst of sound, which she imagined were guns fired as signals of distress; but was, in fact, the explosion of the frigate. Hopeless of human aid, her soul lifted itself up in prayer to Him whose power directs the tempest.

> 'Didst thou not mark the vessel reel,
> With quivering planks and groaning keel,
>   At the last billow's shock?
> For look on sea, or look on land,
> Or yon dark sky, on ev'ry hand,
>   Despair and death are near.'

While kneeling, and offering up her prayer to Heaven, the cabin door opened and young Melton entered, exclaiming :—

"It's all over with us, we are lost! Miserable man that I am! what business had I venture to sea?—What devil possessed me to trust my life to a few planks for the sake of a woman?"

Susan, in dreadful alarm at a voice so well remembered and so justly detested, shrieked with surprise when she saw before her the author of all her misfortune, who, until the present moment, had kept from her sight, and had not intended to appear before her till they had got some distance at sea."

"Why do I see you here, sir, at such a time?" said she, as the mystery of her fate was now clearly explained; "wretch! detestable monster!—I now behold the ruffian at whose instigation, and by whose villanous contrivances, I have been brought on board the ship. But hope not to triumph—for surely as you have exulted in the success of your diabolical schemes, so surely will vengeance overtake you."

Melton was a coward by nature, and the intemperate life he led had not contributed to strengthen his nerves; he trembled and turned pale, as if the retribution she denounced was that moment falling on his head.

"We must all go to the bottom," he exclaimed, as fear showed itself visibly in his face, "we have sprung a leak, and though all the sailors are labouring at the pump, the water gains upon us every moment. Oh, that I were but on land again! miserable sinner that I am; but that will never be—our rudder is torn away, and every sail is gone—we must perish—we must sink!"

"If such is your opinion," replied Susan, "all our thoughts should be given to Heaven: repent your offences, for you have many to repent, and prepare yourself to meet the death you have brought not only on yourself, but me; prepare yourself to meet the terrible account that will, in that world to which we are hastening, be demanded of you for all your wicked actions."

Terror, if not repentance, smote the heart and shook the frame of Melton; he attempted to kneel, but a sudden lurch of the ship threw him on his face, and he lay groaning and deploring his miserable lost condition.

A loud and horrible crash on deck made Susan start from her recumbent posture; and, resolved to learn the extent of their danger, she was making her way to the cabin door, when Melton, raising his head, cast on her a rueful look, and in the most abject terms entreated that she would not leave him alone to the horrors of his own afflicted conscience.

"Miserable wretch!" said Susan, "all the society in the world would be unavailing to save you! The fiat of destruction is gone forth—take advantage of this, perhaps your last moment—probe well your corrupted heart, and endeavour to make your peace with offended Heaven."

Near the cabin door she encountered Fanny, who was lying on a chest and weeping bitterly. Susan in her agitation would have passed her; but the girl caught her robe. "Do not go upon deck, lady," said she, "the mast has fallen— the men are working hard to save us all—I thought to have seen my father, but the Captain tells me he is dead." Here the girl buried her face in her hands and sobbed violently.

The heart of Susan was full of her own father; but she had no words of consolation to offer the poor girl. "Let us go on deck, Fanny," said she, "no one can tell what Providence designs for us—we may all be saved."

"No, no," resumed Fanny; "the ship is sinking—we shall be all drowned." Susan took the hand of the girl, and after much trouble, from the violent rolling of the ship, reached the deck, where the tremendous roar of the winds and waves, mingled with the prayers and execrations of the despairing crew, was horrible beyond all that fancy had conceived.

> ' The labouring hull already seems half filled
> With waters, through a hundred leaks distilled,
> As in a dropsy, wallowing with her freight,
> Half drowned she lies, a dead inactive weight;
> Thus, drenched by every wave, her riven deck,
> Stripp'd and defenceless floats, a naked wreck.'

Some of the sailors lay exhausted on the deck, the water rushing over them; others were making fruitless efforts to repair the pump, which was rendered useless; the captain, pale as a corpse, was endeavouring to cut away a broken mast. On seeing Susan, he entreated her to go below, but on declaring herself unable to return to the cabin, he besought her to pray for them.

"The guilt of others," said he, "has brought you to this terrible end;—you may hope for happiness hereafter; but for me, and that wretched man, whose gold at this moment I would give worlds I had never touched, we are so full of guilt, we dare not pray for ourselves."

Susan held out her hand to him—he pressed it respectfully to his lips. "May we all meet in Heaven!" said Susan; "and Heaven be my witness at this awful moment, I sincerely pardon all who have injured me!"

Day at length broke upon them, what a day! scarcely to be distinguished from the night. There was no sun to cheer and invigorate, and the dark storm raged with unabated fury. The crew of the Tiger had been for several hours hard at work at the pumps, which they had managed to repair; but their incessant exertions scarcely sufficed to keep the water under, and now they began to flag with despair. The foremast had gone by the board, and they were obliged to cut away its companion, so that nothing but the hull of the vessel remained.

> ' And many a leak was gaping fast,
> And the pale steersman stood aghast
> And gave the conflict o'er.'

Over this poor relic of a vessel, lately so beautiful, the waves continued to dash with remorseless violence, insomuch that the stout heart of the Captain, who had remained upon deck during the whole night, and had been thoroughly drenched for the last twelve hours, could endure it no longer. He disappeared through the companion, flung off his clothes, and in a few minutes was asleep in his cot.

The storm had considerably abated towards the evening, the rain had ceased, and the thunder passed away, but the wind continued to impel the labouring hull of the Tiger at a rapid rate through the water. The captain had contrived to stop the leak, either by inserting the foresail into it from the outside, or by some other ingenious device, with which his long experience had made him acquainted.

The crew were now released from the pumps, but firmly impressed with the conviction that the storm, and their consequent peril, were entirely owing to their having on board young Melton; and nothing but their instructive fear of the superiority and determined spirit of Harrup had kept them from using violence towards the object of their hate. Exhausted by the fatigues they had undertaken, they departed to their respective cots, while the Tiger continued to drive through the water.

The second morning came; the heavens were still dark and gloomy, and the vessel continued drifting with the gale. As the morning mist rolled back into the distance, Melton appeared upon deck, stern, gloomy, and wrapt in the contemplation of his own private thoughts.

Louder than the " Al Allah " of the charging Turks, wilder than the war-scream of the savage Mohawk, was the yell of the seamen, when he was noticed by them. With one impulse they rushed in a body towards the poop of the vessel, and before the ill-fated wretch was aware of their design, he was in the power of the infuriated crew. Only one man attempted his rescue—it was the captain. He sprang across the deck, and felled with a blow of his fist the most forward of the assailants; but in a moment he was surrounded and held fast. It was now all over with Melton; he was hurried to the ship's side, and, without a moment allowed for preparation, with all his many crimes unatoned for and unrepented of, he was hurled, struggling, screaming, and blaspheming, into the sullen depths of the insatiable sea. For a long time he struggled with the billows and death; but at last his arms were thrown wildly, for a moment, into the air, and, with a bubbling groan, he sunk down into the fathomless abyss.

The ship continued to drive before the wind, and the scene on board the wreck was now awful in the extreme: every sea that broke over her swept away new victims, and those who were left clinging to life with the energy of despair, shuddered as they missed their companions, in the anticipation of their own approaching doom. At first they stood together in a group, gazing gloomily upon one another; but as the roar of the tempest became louder and louder, and the conviction of inevitable destruction became stronger, they dispersed to various parts of the ship. Some went aside, and seemed engaged in earnest prayer; some hung down their heads, and, seated upon the deck, appeared sunk in dejection; while some went below, broke open the store-room, and drank madly of the spirits which they found: then rushing furiously on deck, they raged like emancipated demons. They shouted, yelled, and laughed in hideous glee. But they could not drive away the knowledge that their end was at hand; and, in a moment, the thought would flash across their minds, blasting their maniacal revelry like the breath of a simoom. They then would stand still in the midst of their furious mirth, and weep and wail, and beat their breasts in agony; while some would throw themselves upon the deck, and writhe and roll about in the height of despair.

The ship began to settle faster and faster, and rolled uneasily in the angry waves that now boiled around her. Her race was nearly run; the prolonged suspense was intolerable. A pen of fire could not paint the agony that scared the souls of many of the wretched sailors; their fortitude had been wrought up to the highest pitch, and now it entirely gave way. Some gave vent to their anguish in loud and dismal yells, some stood with open mouth and fixed eyes, gazing upon the hell of waters before them, whilst cold drops of sweat started from the face and brows. The bravest and coolest could only breathe by gasps; and the bitterness of death, though in different degrees, was in the hearts of all.

Night now added darkness to the fury of the tempest, and Susan, kneeling at the shattered stern, with Fanny, who had thrown herself at her feet, prayed devoutly for her enemies, that their offences might be expiated by the horrible death they were about to meet. At that instant a loud and piercing shriek of despair burst from the men, and a tremendous wave struck the stern of the vessel with such violence, that Susan was thrown from the place on which she knelt against the yawning timbers, where her head received so violent a blow that she remained for some time stunned: when she again recovered sense, she found her knees encircled by the arms of Fanny, and the part on which they lay separated entirely from the vessel, of which not a single vestige now appeared :—

————'Each sent to his account
Unknell'd, uncoffin'd, and unknown,
With all his imperfections on his head.'

With only a few frail planks beneath them, they were now driven by the boisterous wind and billows that seemed boiling round them, and rising to a terrific height, threatening, as they broke, to overwhelm them.

The clothes of Susan clung to her shivering limbs, and her long dark hair hung from her uncovered head, dropping with rain, that now fell in torrents from the dark sky. The dismal hours of the night passed in this dreadful state, during which the gentle Fanny comforted Susan with the hope that they should soon meet in heaven.

Tho prayers of Susan were fervently breathed, as well for the perished crew of the Tiger as for herself and those dear friends whom she supposed she should meet no more.

The long wished-for dawn at length arrived, and brought calmer weather, but no other consolation. As far as the eye could reach they beheld nothing but the broad expanse of sky and water, and were totally ignorant of which way to direct their course. In this desperate situation, Susan did not cease to implore the assistance of Divine Providence,—the only refuge and support of the unfortunate.

In this miserable manner the day passed away, and night came : a full moon was stealing up the sky, throwing first a yellow ghastly glare, and then, as she mounted higher, a silvery glory over the scene. As the night lapsed on, the clouds gathered over the sky, and the moon was occasionally hidden, now and then to dart down a snowy beam through the driving rack, giving a wild and spectral character to the whole scene, which was before sufficiently awful. There were indications of a renewal of the storm ; pale sheets of lightning ever and anon whitened along the sky, and the thunder rolled.

Fanny had been some time silent, and Susan was about to thank Heaven that the innocent girl had by sudden death escaped further suffering, when a deep-drawn sigh convinced her that the companion of her horrible fortune still lived.

The moon continued to rise, the clouds to darken, the lightning to grow brighter, and after a time the storm again burst over her ; the artillery of heaven was at last heard, pealing and crashing, and adding its elemental music to the boom of the waters. What horrible loveliness now sat upon the scene! Now the descending torrents of rain were veiled in impenetrable darkness—in a blackness of death and chaos ; and anon the red bolt of heaven, bursting from the cloud, glared around with ghastly splendour.

Exhausted with fatigue, the enfeebled maiden was every moment losing the little strength she had left ; till sleep irresistibly weighed down her eyelids, and her last thought, as she sunk into forgetfulness, was the hope that her eyes might open on another and a better world.

CHAPTER XVII.

What Shakspere said of lovers, might apply
To all the world—' 'Tis well they do not see
The pretty follies that themselves commit.'
Could we but turn upon ourselves the eyes
With which we look on others, life would pass
In one perpetual blush and smile.
The smile, how bitter !—for 'tis scorn's worst task
To scorn ourselves ; and yet we could not choose
But mock our actions, all we say or do,
If we but saw them as we others see.
Life's best repose is blindness to itself.   L. E. L.

NOT possessing a prompter's whistle, we must use, as a substitute, to change the scene, the boatswain's call, and, at his shrill pipe, shift the scene again to Allendale.

The day at last arrived, when the boat was to be launched ; and never was day lovelier, or sky more blue. It did indeed seem as if the green of the earth and the blue of the heaven vied with each other in brilliancy and depth of hue ; and, some time after the hour appointed, a considerable cavalcade moved from the lawn of Sir Reignald Willoughby's mansion.

Doctor Rovington was chosen the honoured knight of Miss Willoughby and Alice Cameron, not to mention Miss Tabitha Shanks, the inseparable one of all parties of pleasure, who fastened to him *gratis* on this occasion. Constance was the companion of Herbert Glenroy and Edith, while Margaret was accompanied by Gilbert Stanhope.

The road that led to the lake was almost as smooth as a floor, and offered a pleasing variety of up hill and down. The rain which had fallen the day previous had hardened the dust, while it brightened the green of the way-side, and the wheels of the gay party kept as regular music, as they rolled along, as a military band.

At length the smooth beaten road was left, and a diverging path entered through the green and less frequented woods. This resembled a kingly avenue, so amply and richly wreathed were the high branches that arched over head, forming a waving canopy, that intercepted the full rays of the sun, but permitted the blue heaven to peep through here and there, like the bright eyes of beauty, behind a curtain's velvet folds. Glimpses of the river, winding at a distance, like a silver ribbon, were occasionally caught, and the soft, hazy outline of the far-off hills, scarcely distinguishable from the sky on which it was defined.

"There it is," exclaimed Constance, with delighted eagerness, "there is the beautiful lake, and the naiad with its awning fluttering in the breeze."

Edith looked in the direction of the sweet enthusiast's glance, and beheld the fair, translucent mirror, giving back the images it reflected so dazzlingly clear, one might almost imagine it was the concave arch of heaven itself that they beheld.

Around this circling bed of rippling crystal, nature had planted a hedge of luxuriant shrubs, leaving an inviting opening through which the barge displayed her beautiful form. The entrance of this bower was interdicted to Edith till their return from the lake, and she pledged herself not to indulge her curiosity till the proper time, professing it an unfathomable mystery, though various nicely covered baskets, transported thither from the different vehicles, sufficiently explained to what purpose it was dedicated. She was aware of the general rules of pic-nic parties, but as she was the stranger guest, she accepted the compliment as it was intended, and did not offer her contribution to the rural feast.

"Now you have entered Nature's drawing-room," said Glenroy, following the glances of animated pleasure which Edith cast on every side of this really enchanting spot. "Here are her curtains so tastefully festooned and looped—and there is her looking-glass, in which the fairest maiden in the land might array herself for conquest."

"Come," cried Doctor Rovington, leading the way to the water's side, "who shall have the honour of first setting foot on the untracked barge? Miss Shanks"—Miss Shanks lifted one fairy slipper with the grace of a lapwing, but her flight was suddenly arrested by the mortifying conclusion of the Doctor's speech :—"I beg a thousand pardons—I mean Miss Trevanion. Let me have the honour of thus consecrating the virgin planks. Mr. Glenroy will console himself with Miss Willoughby's hand."

Glenroy felt half disposed to push the Doctor head foremost into the lake, but the good humoured "devil" that lurked in his eye, laughed to scorn all impotent attempts at anger against him. One by one the company entered this floating *omnium gatherum,* those only being left behind who were selected to fit and decorate the bower. Constance was one of the chosen handmaids, for no one could wreathe a garland so gracefully, or ornament cake or fruit so tastefully. Her very touch seemed to impart a charm, as if she had received a fairy gift. "Remember," said she to Edith, as the boat pushed off from the shore, "you are to be the queen of our bower, and I shall try to dress it fairer than it ever looked before."

If there is one thing in this world soothing, romantic yet exciting, it is the gentle, feathery, undulating motion of a light pleasure boat, on the bosom of waters clear, deep, and transparent—when the soft heaving waves keep time with the dipping oar ; when the bland summer gale flutters round the awning above, and softly parts the forehead locks of those who sit beneath ; and when the spirit of quiet gladness, like the wings of the brooding dove, settles gently on the heart. Edith gave herself up to the sweet influences around her. The enchantment of novelty was added to every other charm, and gazing silently down in the clear depths of the water, she almost wished she might lead a floating life, situated just as she was at that moment. The fairy voyage of her imagination was checked by a sudden shoal, which manifested itself in the form of Miss Willoughby's tongue.

"Does your father," said she to Edith, "still intend going to Scarboro' this summer ? I fear, after you leave us, you will never favour us with a visit."

"Ah ! my charming friend," said Alice Cameron, "how shall we live without you ?" Never was anything more devoutly wished in her own heart than Edith's absence.

"Do not speak of Miss Trevanion's leaving us, at such an hour as this," cried the Doctor : "you are the most cruel of created beings. You might as well talk of blotting out the day-star from the skies. Glenroy, what shall *we* do? Shall we make us a willow bower on these banks, hang up our harps on the branches, and mourn together?"

"I think I should prefer a solitary retreat," answered Glenroy in a husky tone of voice ; his face, even to his temples, suffusing with deep crimson.

"Won't you have my fan, Miss Trevanion?'" asked Griselda, with a sarcastic emphasis, stretching out the showy feathers. "You look oppressively warm ; but perhaps it is only a reflected glow.'"

"You are *oppressively* kind, Miss Willoughby," replied Edith, putting back the proffered civility, or rather impertinence, with an impatient gesture—most fervently wishing her on the very summit of Mont Blanc. Leaning over the edge of the boat, she sought to evade the scrutiny of her tormentor, and it was well she did. . Agitated by the sudden emotion Glenroy had manifested at the mention of her departure, struck by the consciousness of the pang that had shot through her own heart at the thought, and deeply mortified by the confusion she had herself betrayed, tears which would not be repressed rushed to her eyes, and even fell into the wave over which they floated. Glenroy could not help perceiving this, as he sat by her side and was gazing intently on the current, so slightly ruffled, and attributing her agitation to sensibility, wounded by being brought so rudely into observation, he moved so as completely to screen her from the invidious eyes she shunned. He was no coxcomb, though possessed of the most dangerous gifts a young man can be endowed with—extraordinary manly beauty, set off by the most graceful and attractive manners—just that due proportion of dignity and gallantry which constitutes the fascination of a gentlemanly character. It would be going beyond the truth to say that he was not conscious of the bounty of nature, for the bright eyes of beauty had told him too many flattering tales to suffer him to remain in ignorance of the fact. Whenever he appeared in the glittering ring,

‘ On him each lady’s look was bent ;’

but, like the glacier in the sunbeam, his heart had hitherto shone, but never warmed beneath the rays. It was guarded by the sacred shield of filial and peternal love, and, believing it impenetrable to every assault, he yielded himself freely to the gratification which every man who is not made of stone must feel, in being the constant object of undisguised admiration. The deep self-sacrificing vow he had made over the posthumous letter of his father was synonymous with that of lasting celibacy, and never until this moment had he felt the bondage of poverty—the weight of the chains that fettered him. Had he no widowed mother, no orphan sisters, clinging to him for protection and support, with such a rich inheritance of genius and talents, he might have marked out his own brilliant destiny ; but for their sake he kept down the eagle soarings of ambition, and limited himself to the sphere of his native valley.

When he first saw Edith he admired her as a graceful, spirited, and highly intellectual young female, introduced to him in a novel and interesting manner. When he again met her in his own domestic circle, adorned with all those gentle and womanly graces which rendered his own sisters so inexpressibly dear to him, embellished by a still higher polish of refinement, participating most cordially and unaffectedly in all their household enjoyments, admiration deepened into the warmest, most delighted interest. Unconscious that he was nurturing a sentiment which would hereafter be the murderer of his peace, he gave himself up unresistingly to the charm of her society, with a freedom which she, in the true yet modest frankness of her nature, never wished to check. When the Doctor, in his honest drollery, appealed to him so abruptly on the subject of her departure, he felt, for the first time, a moral conviction that she was interwoven with the very life-chords of his existence, and her own unconquerable emotion, which Miss Willoughby’s remark alone could hardly justify, admitted of a construction, which, had he been free to act, he would have welcomed as the wandering Peri the glimpse of that paradise from which she was banished, but which now pierced him with a pang of strange self-upbraiding. While these with other blending thoughts were revolving in his mind, he sat with folded arms, watching the downcast face of Edith, to which sensibility now lent a thousand mutable charms, forgetting in the singular fascination of the moment that the singeing lightnings of envy and jealousy were darting around them.

Most fortunately, and perchance most kindly, Doctor Rovington requested Miss Willoughby to favour them with one of her delightful songs—a request which she was never known to refuse. She selected the following one, and suffered her voice to swell to its topmost note over the astonished waves.——

The dews are falling fast, and the day is off the sky,
And the western clouds, like shadows, have assumed a deeper dye;
The flocks have sought the fold, there is silence on the lea,—
Then Alice, sweetest Alice, why come you not to me?

I look around o’er heath and hill, but no one is in sight,
I hear the village clock announce the coming hour of night,
Gloom gathers fast around, the wind blows chilly o’er the lea,—
Then Alice, sweetest Alice, why come you not to me?

You know, you feel, how well I love, you see it in my eyes,
You hear it in my faltering voice, you breathe it my sighs,
You tell it by my nightly stroll along this silent lea,,—
Then Alice, dearest Alice, why come you not to me?

Doth sorrow—that despotic lord of all beneath the sky—
Hang out his raven banner in thy dim and darken'd eye?
'Doth illness weigh thy gentle heart?—then come not o'er this lea—
Or creep into my bosom, love; its warmth shall shelter thee.

If I thought I e'er must see the hour when we should meet no more,
When death should pale that pretty face I've kiss'd so oft before,
The world—the laughing world—that now is sunniness and glee,
When thou are gone, sweet Alice, would be a blank to me.

For dearer than her first-born to the mother's beating breast,
When with looks of perfect happiness she watches o'er its rest,
And dearer than their native home to exiles on the sea,
'Mid the uproar of the mighty waves—art thou, sweet girl, to me.

Then come, my love; beneath yon elms your presence I await.
Already—hark! the village clock has struck the hour of eight;
Already—but me thinks I hear light footsteps o'er the lea,
And yonder gleams a fairy, fairy form—she comes, she comes to me.

Alice Cameron was next entreated, and after repeating her " pretty oath by yea and nay, she could not, she would not, durst not sing," she consented, and, setting aside the demi-semi-quavers of affectation, sang the sweetly pathetic song of ' The Bride" with a great deal of taste and melody :—

They brought me to another land,
Across the ocean wide,
To dwell with strangers and to be
A young and happy bride.
They call'd me beautiful and fair ;
But yet I know mine eye
Hath lost the brightness that it had,
Beneath my own sweet sky.

They wreath'd into my shining hair
The jewels of their race ;
I could but weep to see how ill
They suited with my face,
Alas ! upon my alter'd brow
Their garlands flash in vain ;
My cheek is now too pale to take
The tint of joy again.

I tread the fairy halls at night,
And all have smiles for me ;
I meet with thrilling looks that make
Me dream of home and thee.
How beautiful are all things here ;
How wonderful and bright :
The very stars appear to shed
A softer, newer light.

But yet I feel my heart would give
Them all for one sweet flower,
Pluck'd from the valley where my feet
First trod in childhood's hour ;
Where I beheld the ocean flow
So proudly by the shore,
And saw the moonlight stream upon—
What I shall see no more.

I loved upon the dark green rock
To take my lonely seat,
And watch the heaving billows throw
The sea-weeds at my feet ;
To meet the summer wind, and hear
Its murmurs in the trees ;
And think thy voice was whispering me,
With every passing breeze.

Yet sometimes in my dreams I view
High ruins, lone and dark ;
And sometimes I am on the sea,
Within my own lov'd bark ;
And softly then we float along,
Beneath the twilight star—
Once more I see the sky I love,
My own dear home afar.

Once more I twine around my brow
The little flowers so pale,
Once more I think my mother's voice
Comes sighing on the gale ;

And then there is a wild sweet joy,
That thrills me in my dreams;
Flinging its radiance on my heart
Like sunset's golden beams.

Margaret Glenroy was never guilty of a note of music in her life, though Constance was an unwearied nightingale; and when Edith declined the invitation extended to her, the Doctor thanked her from the bottom of his heart, assuring her, if he once heard her dulcet strains, it would give him an everlasting distaste for all earthly sounds. There was an all-pervading, irresistible influence in the Doctor's humour, which gradually communicated itself to those around and about him; and when the boat approached the shore, the friends who hailed them from the banks could not perceive that a cloud had flitted over them—the shadow had gone.

"See, Mrs. Heathwood is returned," exclaimed Margaret, springing from the boat, and accosting a lady who advanced from a group that surrounded her, to welcome the eager hand extended towards her.

"Is it possible this is Mrs. Heathwood?" thought Edith, who had never before seen her, not having been allowed by her father to visit any of the surrounding gentry, and who, from one of those unaccountable caprices of the imagination, had represented her, to herself, as a blue-looking, stiff, withered lady, dressed with severe precision and an utter disregard to external attraction. She had never heard her person described, though the Glenroys had often spoken in the most exalted terms of her great intellectual endowments. Instead of the blue, cold visage she had depicted, she saw a mild, delicate face, lighted up with an expression as winning as it was intelligent, a figure of uncommonly fine proportions, and a dress in which the elegance, though not the extravagance, of fashion was conspicuous. Griselda Willoughby seized Edith's hand and presented her to Mrs. Heathwood as a most particular friend, whom she had been extremely desirous to introduce to her acquaintance; and as much as Edith deprecated the appellation of Miss Willoughby's friend, she felt her heart spontaneously rising to meet the gentle warmth of Mrs. Heathwood's smile and glance. This lady had returned the day previous from a visit to the metropolis, and hearing of the party determined to meet her friends in this unexpected manner. She did not now welcome Edith as a stranger, for the enthusiastic Constance had often described her to Mrs. Heathwood as the most beautiful and loveable of created beings, only a little "lower than the angels;" and it is no small compliment to Edith, that in spite of the disadvantage of Constance's hyperbole, Mrs. Heathwood looked with delight, surpassing her anticipations, on the fair union of intellect and feeling embodied in the youthful form before her. She was a romantic woman. Her romance had outlived the glow of youth, and there was nothing that she so much loved as to watch in the character of others the development of those traits which it yielded. Constance had long been one of her cherished favourites, and one glance convinced her that she had found another in the interesting Edith.

They were now summoned to the bower, where a rural collation was served up in a manner which would have done honour to the divinities of the grove.

"Tell me truly, Gilbert," said Margaret to her lover, as they walked to the bower, somewhat apart from the others of the party, "tell me if you do not think our own dear village an earthly paradise? Can there be a sweeter spot than my childhood's home, so calm, so quiet, so rich in nature's gifts, that it is not to be wondered at that my gentle sister and myself have never cherished in our breasts a thought beyond it, or a wish to leave it?"

"My beloved enthusiast! my charming Margaret!" exclaimed Gilbert Stanhope, as he pressed her soft hand within his own; "how many blessed and happy hours will thy light and buoyant spirits give to those around thee, while the unruffled temper that has never felt the chill of discontent, will strew thy path with thornless flowers, whose glowing tints resemble thine own sunny thoughts."

"But you have not answered the question," cried Margaret earnestly,—"Do you not think as I do, that there is a calm contentment seems to reign around this spot, which, while it adds to its beauty, impresses the beholders with the gratifying and delightful idea, that tranquil happiness dwells within the walls of each lowly cottage ?"

"There can be little doubt of it, dearest Margaret," replied Gilbert; "and you, my dearest, derive much pleasure, I am certain, from the delightful occupation of administering to the wants of those who stand in need of assistance."

They had now approached the bower, where a table, covered with a snow-white cloth, extended the whole length of the arbour, and this spotless lawn was embroidered with every variety of cake, and every fruit the season offered. The cakes were chiefly frosted and ornamented with party-coloured sugar plums, arranged so as to form hearts, diamonds, and true love knots; and the top of each variegated loaf was decorated with clusters of flowers, gathered round central sprigs of box or cedar, that stood as perpendicular and prim as Miss Tabitha Shanks. As each young lady, who participated in the party, contributed to the feast, the spirit of emulation produced every kind of embellishment which female ingenuity could invent, or manly gallantry could admire.

The dishes which contained the fruit were edged with a fringe of broad curling green leaves, interspersed with wild flowers, making a charming union of the gifts of Flora and Pomona. The gentlemen furnished wine refreshments, and a band of music, stationed behind the bower, now struck up a most inspiring air, which rolling in the forest gale, from the instruments of the invisible musicians, had as electrifying an effect as if each verdant spray were transformed to an Eolian lyre.

"Enchanting," cried Edith; "this realises my dreams of Arcadia."

"I am not surprised," said Mrs. Heathwood, sympathising in Edith's unaffected rapture, "I am not surprised at the vividness of your expression. A few summers back, on a similar occasion, I came hither, accompanied by a friend of mine, a foreigner, a man whose imagination seldom gains the ascendancy over his reason, for he is of the most melancholy temperament. He declared that though he had travelled through many lands, and seen much that was admirable in nature and art, he had never beheld a spot more perfectly lovely; and that the young party assembled on the green, in the bright holiday of the heart, reminded him of those *fetes champetres*, celebrated by the peasant youth near the vine-hills of France."

"Speaking of vine-hills, said Doctor Rovington, "by a natural transition, we turn to the juice of the grape. Let us fill our glasses with the sparkling fluid, and drink to the bonny lasses of Allendale."

While he was uttering this gallant speech, he poured out a liquid, clear and bright as Champagne, which Miss Shanks, "careful soul," had deposited by Sir Reginald Willoughby's particular request, with the sweet things collected by Griselda and Alice. "Be sure," said Sir Reginald, while the notes of preparation were echoing around him, "be sure, Miss Shanks, to put up two bottles of my best Maderia to drink my health, as I cannot share your festivity."

Miss Shanks, ever on the alert to follow Sir Reginald's bidding, had placed two bottles in the basket, from which Doctor Rovington now filled "high the wine cup," and proffering one first to the fair hand of Edith, passed them on to the other guests. At the first sip, every face assumed that indescribable expression, which the taste of an unripe orange imparts, the visible essence of acidity encroaching on the curve lines of grace and beauty.

"Gracious heavens, Miss Shanks!" exclaimed Griselda, the pupils of her eyes vanishing upwards in the horror of the moment, "what have you done? you have put vinegar instead of Maderia. Papa will die of mortification."

Poor Miss Shanks stood the image of Lot's wife, only with this difference, that she looked as if turned into a bottle of vinegar, rather than a pillar of salt. Bursts of laughter echoed on every side, till the very woods became vocal.

"Never mind, Miss Shanks," said the Doctor; "it was a perfectly natural mistake,—a true exemplification of the principle of affinity. Allow me to pledge you in a glass of congenial pungency."

"Nay, Doctor, you are unmerciful," interposed Mrs. Heathwood; "if I were not obliged to return, I would take Miss Shanks under the shadow of my protecting wing."

Mrs. Heathwood, whose health would not permit her to be exposed to the evening air, now rose to depart, and as she made her parting adieus, she lingered to express to Edith her earnest wish to be made acquainted with her parents, and to receive them as guests of her own household. She spoke of her husband's absence, her own loneliness, the retirement in which she lived, and urged it as a personal favour to herself, rather than to them.

Edith's heart bounded at this invitation, and she promised to use her influence with her father, and inform him of Mrs. Heathwood's morning visit.

"You must beware of this fascinating young girl," said Mrs. Heathwood to Glenroy, as he assisted her into the carriage. "She captivated my heart at the first glance, and I am resolved not to rest till I have secured her to myself. Still, after warning you of the danger, I bid you welcome to brave it, under my own roof."

"Your caution is kind, Madam," replied Glenroy, with an acknowledging bow; "but it may come too late. The moth, after being accustomed to the torch's glare, draws nearer and nearer to the blaze that is to consume him."

"I wonder what Mrs. Heathwood said to Glenroy, as she drove off," whispered Griselda Willoughby to Alice Cameron. "See, he looks as if he had the scarlet fever."

"I don't care if he has," answered Alice pettishly, for once speaking an unadorned sentence. "I only wish I were at home, for it is the dullest party I ever attended in my life."

This did not seem to be the general opinion, for the voice of hilarity rung merrily around them. The old legitimate Maderia had been produced from other baskets, and the Doctor was distributing his toasts as "plenty as blackberries," and as brilliant as the jewels of Jamshid. Every pause of mirth was filled by the invisible band, and in spite of the assertion of the jealous Alice, it was the most exhilarating scene that can possibly be imagined or described. A proposition was made to take another sail before they returned, which most of the ladies declined, but the Doctor, whose spirits had received an irresistible impetus, declared he would not be refused, and vaulting over the seat, alighted at the feet of Miss Shanks, and begged her companionship to the boat. She had never yet summoned fortitude enough to refuse a gentleman's hand, offered in any manner; and notwithstanding a little lurking displeasure at his remark about the vinegar, she consented with alacrity, and ambled by his side, till she was once more seated in the boat. Two young men seized the oars, and calling out "an elopement," pushed merrily off from the shore. The Doctor, highly delighted with the movement, sprang up on one of the seats, and extending his arms towards the banks, ejaculated,—

"Onward we move—applauding Cupid's guide,
Jove bears Europa o'er the conscious tide."

"Beware," cried Glenroy, in a loud warning voice, "the boat leaks on that side—she will lose her balance. Bear down with the opposite oar."

Miss Shanks, alarmed at the earnestness of his tone, and at the danger he indicated, imprudently jumped upon her feet, thus increasing the peril she was seeking to shun. The boat, which was defective in construction, and top-heavy from the profusion of its awning, gave a sudden and frightful rock on that side which contained the devoted pair; they lost their equilibrium simultaneously, and sunk into the bubbling waters, while the loud laugh of thoughtless mirth was converted into the wild shriek of agony. It was scarcely a moment before the waves again parted and closed around the form of Glenroy, who plunged in impulsively to their rescue, and was immediately followed by Gilbert Stanhope, who swam towards the Doctor. It was dismaying to hear the cries of Margaret and Constance when they saw the perilous situation of their brother and Gilbert; and Edith looked as if every drop of blood had forsaken her face to freeze round her heart. Alice fell into a deep swoon, though she did not look half so pale as Edith; but this scene of consternation was not of long continuance, for Glenroy soon appeared emerging from the waves, bearing the dripping form of Miss Shanks, followed by Gilbert Stanhope, supporting the Doctor, who had for a short time buffetted the waters most lustily for his own deliverance, but would inevitably have sunk had not Stanhope arrived in time to assist him.

Poor Miss Shanks, however, lay lifeless as a blighted dandelion, in the arms of Glenroy, who, compassionately bent on her restoration, did not pauze to gaze on the pale lips and blanched cheeks his danger had made, but directed his steps towards the low but comfortable cottage of Farmer Grundy, which peeped modestly through the trees, and was always resorted to in any particular emergency. The Doctor followed with Gilbert, " wet as drowned rats," and Rovington looked pierced with real remorse at the consequences of his levity; but he could not forbear saying as he approached Miss Willoughby, " that he felt penitence gnawing at the bottom of his heart."

It would be tedious to recapitulate the process of resuscitation, rapid as it was, under the superintendence of the kind and hospitable Mrs. Grundy, whose blankets were unrolled, and whose hearth was lighted up with life-restoring warmth as if by magic.

Her benevolent cares were speedily rewarded, and Miss Shanks once more unsealed " the eyelids of the morn," and drank gratefully of the warm penny-royal tea, which Mrs. Grundy insisted upon her taking, to keep the cold air out of her stomach. The good woman was deeply afflicted at the obstinacy of Glenroy, who had left the cottage, after depositing his precious charge on a counterpane as white as Dandie Dinmont's, without drying his saturated garments. He had merely shaken the loose moisture from his coat, " like dewdrops from the lion's mane," and suffered Margaret to absorb with her handkerchief the dampness off his heavy locks; though Mrs. Grundy kept all the while repeating, " It would be a thousand pities if such a nice young man should catch his death-cold keeping on his wet clothes. If he would only drink some *yarb* tea, it would be better than nothing." She found the Doctor and Gilbert more docile, who consented to go into another apartment and assume some of Farmer Grundy's best clothes, while she arrayed Miss Shanks in her own Sunday attire. The resuscitated spinster knew there was no alternative, and with passive agony beheld herself mantled in robes, which recalled but too vividly the scenes of her childhood, and that kind but plebeian parent who was happily now unconscious of her daughter's vain ambition. The scant calico frock, with short full waist, and narrow tight sleeves, formed a ludicrous contrast with the full falling skirt, and large fashionable sleeves, which hung dripping by the fire. The nice starched linen half-handkerchief superseded the almost evaporated Zelia; and oh! misery of miseries! the thick clumsy loose calf skin shoes, which Goody Grundy thought the perfection of gentility, took place of the tight little prunella slippers, which lay entombed in the bosom of the lake. In vain did the careful hostess entreat " her just to slip on a cap to keep her ears from ringing, for it was a desperate bad thing to have a cold in the head."

Miss Shanks was inexorable, and sat with imperturbable gravity, amidst peals of congratulating laughter. But even *her* rueful countenance relaxed when the Doctor and Stanhope made their appearance from the inner apartment. Rovington was dressed from top to toe in a suit of fustian home-spun, ornamented with a profusion of shining yellow buttons, the waistcoat of surprising length, with immense pockets, stout new cow-hide shoes, and a large shirt collar sticking out on each side of his face, which though it looked as if it were washed in " fairy well water," was the boasted product of Goody's own loom. Farmer Grundy was a large, iron-framed man, and his garments hung in cool easy folds on the limbs of the disciple of Esculapius, who, having again and again reiterated his gratitude to Mrs Grundy, and his remorse to Miss Shanks, for having been the cause of such a. unlucky accident. Gilbert Stanhope was dressed in one of the farmer's best smock frocks, and had a shirt collar, similar to the Doctor's, sticking out, a pair s leathern unmentionables, with blue stockings and stout heavy shoes to match. He cut as ridiculous a figure as the Doctor and Miss Shanks. Glenroy now drew near the cottage, and his astonishment at the merry cachinations within was soon merged in admiration of the extraordinary figures which presented themselves to his view. The good-natured dame joined heartily in the mirth; though she said, "she thought it became a body to be serious after such a powerful deliverance, and it ought to set them thinking on their latter end, and on the vanities of time." As they were about to leave with many benedictions, she stopped them at the door, with a most embarrassing qustieon, dictated by the spirit of a true woman's inquisitiveness.

"You have not told me who this sweet young lady is," said she, putting her spectacles down over her eyes, as she looked smiling at Edith. "I know who the rest are pretty well. Ah! I guess I can tell," added she, nodding her head significantly at Glenroy; "I think I can tell. Its the old general's daughter, who lives so secluded from his neighbours, and the young squire's sweetheart."

Edith looked upon Doctor Rovington as her guardian angel, when, by taking the hand of Miss Shanks, with a bow of ludicrous depth, he led the way, covering her confusion in the renewed mirth excited by so ridiculous an union. Notwithstanding his sorrow at his former folly, he could not resist the temptation of showing off Miss Shanks in her new costume, displaying at the same time his own acquired graces. Edith insisted upon an immediate departure, for she trembled for the consequences of Rovington's exposure, though, not wishing to allege the true reason, she pleaded indisposition. As they approached the bower, pursuing the path which led to the carriages, the band commenced a quick spirited dancing tune, to which the Doctor's feet immediately kept admirable time, whirling Miss Shanks round, like a feather in the wind. He was always remarked for his active grace in the ball-room, and he now cut the pigeon's wing with the cowhide shoes, his broad fustian coat waving to and fro, with all the finished elegance of a votary of Terpischore.

"Come, Doctor," said Glenroy, who was already mounted for departure, "I believe you would jest and frolic under the 'ribs of death.' If you do not follow directly I shall offer myself as attendant to Miss Willoughby's carriage also."

This proposition was welcomed by the young ladies, and the Doctor, recollecting what was due to those he had volunteered to protect, dismissed the character of buffoon, and was the polite and attentive gentleman during their homeward ride.

"Margaret," said Herbert Glenroy to his sister, the following morning at the breakfast-table, "will you walk with me in the garden? I have something to say to you—it's a beautiful morning," said he, as they walked towards the summer-house.

"Very," replied Margaret, endeavouring to appear composed, not knowing what her brother had to communicate to her.

"I like your Mr. Stanhope very much," continued Herbert, after a short pause, "you seemed quite pleased with him yesterday."

"Why do you say 'your' Mr. Stanhope, Herbert?" asked Margaret in a suppressed tone.

"Upon my word, a very pretty question for you to ask! Oh, there is no necessity for looking so innocent; do you think I have not heard of certain transactions? you may as well confess."

"Confess what?" said Margaret, struggling hard to conceal her agitation.

"You are the lady, I believe, that aunt Denby, while you were in London, held up as a model for prudence and caution. I am disposed to think that perhaps her opinion might undergo a little change, did she know all that I do. You never saw Mr. Stanhope before you met him here, I suppose?"

"Nonsense, Herbert," replied Margaret, not much relieved; "you have often heard from aunt Denby about his politeness and attention to me while in London."

"It is a little singular that his engagements should bring him down here directly you left London."

"Nay, brother, how can I account for his coming down, unless on a mere visit of curiosity and pleasure ;" said Margaret, beginning to be terribly alarmed : "it was natural for him to prefer seeking the company of one who was not a perfect stranger to him in the country ; besides, as I understand, he has lived wholly abroad until now."

"Certainly ; and you reason so feelingly on the subject, that you would compel the most obstinate cur in the world to agree with you. Don't look so frightened ; I am only about to advise, not scold you ; it is my right, as elder brother, you know. There is no man that I have met with (excuse my plainness) whom I would rather call brother-in-law than this same Mr. Stanhope ; the first moment I saw him, I felt such an unaccountable prepossession in his favour that I actually was disposed to run out into the road and ask for the honour of his acquaintance. I see you are beginning to smile now—but, notwithstanding all this good feeling towards him as regards myself, as soon as I found you were a party concerned, I blew it to the winds, and thought of nothing but your honour and happiness ; and, on this account, am induced to say that a little prudence would not be in any manner out of place."

"But, Herbert," said Margaret, now completely relieved on the most important point, and attempting a playful smile, "what is your authority for all these intelligent surmises and assumptions ?"

"Trifling don't become you well, my dear Margaret," replied her brother, affectionately taking her hand ; " but do you really think that the glow of pleasure which diffused itself over his fine countenance, when he found you were to be his companion yesterday, was entirely the effect of his foreign politeness, or any other equally powerful cause ? or that the sudden and evident, though instantly subdued, expression of—shall I say—delight, that lighted up the face of a certain lady about the same time, as she cast an inquiring glance at her brother, was nothing more than simple ordinary acquiescence ? But my intention was to speak of the mystery in which Mr. Stanhope is enveloped. He is a gentleman, or I am very much mistaken ; his fortune must be ample, but no one knows, beyond hearsay, from what part of the world he comes, or what is his real object in visiting this country ; he is acquainted with no one, nor does he seem anxious either to seek or to avoid intercourse with any. I noticed, yesterday—though it might have been but fancy—an appearance of care about his manner and countenance, which induced me to suppose that he might be absent unwillingly from his native land. At any rate, it is a singular if not a suspicious circumstance, that he should be altogether without letters. I can never consent, (in a tone which was playful, but which showed that the meaning was serious) unless he authorizes me to write to his friends, and learn his character and standing from those who know him best. You may tell him so, Margaret."

"Upon my word, Herbert," said Margaret, making a violent attempt to put on an appearance of gaiety, "you are proceeding at a most rapid rate ; you have laid an humble admirer at my feet, and actually marked out the course he is to pursue, while perhaps he may be dreaming of a charmer in some far distant land, and entertaining the lowest possible opinion of all the rest of the sex, on her account."

At this moment the servant entered the garden, to announce a stranger ; this broke up the conference, and Herbert hastened to receive him. He immediately recognised his old college class-mate, Charles Montford.

CHAPTER XVIII.

And yet it is a wasted heart;
　　It is a wasted mind
That seeks not in the inner world
　　Its happiness to find.

For happiness is like the bird
　　That broods above its nest,
And finds beneath its folded wings,
　　Life's dearest, and its best.

A little space is all that hope
　　Or love can ever take ;
The love that in the circle spreads,
　　The sooner it will break.—L. E. L.

I said to Penury's meagre train,
     Come on ! your threats I brave :
My last poor life-drop you may drain,
     And crush me to the grave;
Yet still the spirit that endures,
     Shall mock your ~~force~~ the while,
And meet each cold, cold grasp of yours
     With bitter smile.——ANON.

A PROPHETIC chill ran through the veins of Glenroy, as he met the cold eye of the companion of his boyhood, and the foiled competitor of his collegiate honours. He remembered the uncancelled debt his father had disclosed ; and as he could not impute this visit to the cordial reminiscences of earlier friendship, he conjectured he came to demand the money in his father's name.

"I suppose you have heard of my father's death?" said Montford, after some desultory and constrained conversation.

"I was not aware of your misfortune," answered Glenroy, in spite of his utmost efforts, visibly agitated. "I did not know your father, but I recollect to have heard mine often speak of him in terms of the warmest affection."

"Is this the son of Mr. Montford, whom your father so much loved, Herbert?" asked Mrs. Glenroy, turning towards the young man a look of sad and heartfelt interest. "He was the man, whom of all others Mr. Glenroy honoured and trusted."

"My father sometimes bought the devotion of his friends at too dear a price," said the unfeeling son. Herbert knit his brows over his kindling eyes, but as he looked on the mild, pallid countenance of his mother, to which resignation to the heaviest of all earthly woes had lent a religious and holy charm, then turned to the lovely faces of his sisters, fair with youth and hope, in the midst of their now happy home, and thought of the blow that might now be impending over them, indignation yielded to anguish of spirit."

"My father died on his homeward passage from India," continued Montford. Since his death I have been involved in all the intricacies of business. Something of this kind has brought me to Allendale, and as I am exceedingly pressed for time, I shall be obliged to hasten the moment of my departure. Mr. Glenroy, would you favour me with a private interview?"

Mrs. Glenroy and her daughters immediately rose, but they saw, with infinite apprehension, that Herbert's cheek was pale and his brow contracted, and though they were happily unconscious of the cause of his emotion, they closed the door with trembling hearts.

"Now, sir," said Herbert, rising with more pride of manner than he had any intention of assuming, "now, sir, we are alone."

Montford deliberately drew forth his pocket-book, and presented a paper to Glenroy.

"This paper," said he, "fully explains the purport of my visit. Your father may not have left a record of the transaction, but the signature of mine cannot be disputed."

"I have no intention of disputing it, Mr. Montford," answered Herbert; "thank Heaven! I have other testimony than yours. My father has left an undying record, which has never left the memory of his son. Even when the hand of death was on him, he penned this letter, and every injunction here written shall be most religiously fulfilled."

That morning Herbert had been reading his father's letter, that he might find, in its sacred character, strength to resist the fascinations that were gradually winding around the disarmed and slumbering giant. He had placed it in his bosom, and now drawing it forth, gave it into the hands of Montford.

Had one spark of noble or generous feeling warmed the heart of this mercenary young man, it would have been elicited by the strong and affecting appeal of an expiring father to a young and unportioned son. But the rich flowers of the tropics will sooner bloom in the regions of polar ice, than the warm and generous affections in a soul given up to the chilling dominion of avarice. And more than avarice impelled Montford to the cold-blooded act he meditated. He hated Glenroy, He envied him for his immeasurable superiority, and cherished, with vindictive malice, the recollection of the scene on the college green, when he had been forced to yield to the boldness of moral worth.

"Your father believed me mercenary," said Montford, coolly folding up the letter. "Be it so.—Justice is often stigmatized by this opprobrious epithet, But he forgot one very important item in his statement. The money loaned was not my father's and he had no right to pledge himself that it should not be demanded. It was mine—taken from the inheritance bequeathed to me by my maternal grandmother, over which my father was appointed guardian. His own property was only sufficient for the support of his own family. If he proved faithless to the trust reposed in him, the weakness is not hereditary, as the conduct of his son shall prove."

"Had I the means of cancelling this debt, Mr. Montford," cried Glenroy, endeavouring to hold down the throbbings of his indignant heart, "I never should have submitted to the humiliation of this moment. From the moment I read that letter, boy as I was, the hope of freeing myself from this bondage, has stimulated all my exertions, has indeed been the predominant principle of my existence. My father left no fortune but this estate, which only serves as a support to his widow and orphan family. I have just entered on the career of manhood, and have as yet earned nothing but a good name. No ! I have not earned it—it was my sole inheritance, and it will be the glory of my life to preserve it untarnished."

"This is all very fine, Mr. Glenroy," replied Montford, "but I did not come to hear high-sounding words. So renowned a knight should know that 'deeds, not words,' is the motto of chivalry. It is in vain to plead inability on your part, for comfort and luxury reign in your household ; and wherever Herbert Glenroy has appeared, in the city as well as the country, he is quoted as the 'glass of fashion, and the model of taste.'"

"Whatever be your power over me," cried Herbert, his lip curling with irrepressible scorn. "I will not brook insult from you or any living man. I have told you our situation. Do what you will—I never will degrade my father's name and fame, by stooping to solicit favours from a man whom——" He paused, and bit his lip till the blood came.

"Whom you despise," added Montford, with exasperating coolness. "Well, be it so—I know all the strength and depth of your contempt. I feel it through the whole of my collegiate career. In the paths of literature and ambition you constantly crossed me—insidiously winding yourself into the affections of all around you, by the assumption of heroic and chivalrous sentiments which never penetrated your heart. Remember you not, when you lifted your hand against me, in defence of that drivelling boy, I told you a day of reckoning would come? It is now arrived, and I feel as little disposed to offer favours as you do to solicit them."

"Not for myself would I stoop, even to royalty, sir," replied Glenroy, in a choking voice ; "and I heed your insinuations as little as t.. whistling blast. But in remembrance of a vow which has been attested by Om potence itself, to sacrifice everything, even the pride of manhood, on the altar of filial love, I will make one appeal in behalf of the mother that bore me, and the sisters I have sworn to cherish as my heart's blood. Were the blow you threaten to fall on me alone, I would welcome all that the vindictive passions of man can inflict. I have hands that can toil, and a heart that can endure ; but to see my mother driven from the home hallowed by the recollections of domestic love, my young sisters despoiled of their inheritance—rather than witness such a scene, I will humble my proud spirit, and throw myself on your mercy. In the strength of my youth, I will labour day and night. I will moisten the soil with the sweat of my brow, and transmit to you, from week to week, from month to month, the fruit of my industry. I ask but this reprieve. Let my mother remain in ignorance of this transaction— let her know not that she is destitute in her declining years."

"You exaggerate your difficulties, Mr. Glenroy," replied Montford; "your sisters are too pretty to remain a burden on your hands. There is no danger of their being in want of lovers, and as to your mother—"

"Forbear," interrupted Glenroy, in a commanding tone. "The name of my mother and sisters shall be sacred from your insulting levity. It is well you are under the protection of my roof. No servile dread of future consequences shall deter me from asserting my own dignity and their claims to the respect of every true and honourable man."

"As to your last proposition," continued Montford, disregarding the interruption, though his dull eye perceptibly quailed beneath the flashing glance of Glenroy, "I do not see that my taking immediate possession of the estate will render it unavailing. Your real property will not cover a debt of five thousand pounds, and you may rest assured that in this instance I shall go to the full extent of the law."

"Go then," said Glenroy, "I recal the humbling appeal I addressed to a heart of stone. I would rather live on the dregs of poverty for countless years, than be indebted for one hour to the scornful pity of the callous mercenary. Begin this moment, if you will. We are ready."

Montford rose, and taking his hat moved leisurely towards the door,

"I have business to transact for a day or two in the adjoining town," said he. "You can be making what arrangements you think proper in the meantime. Upon my return I shall make no delay. A family in London, who wish to leave the city during the summer months, will receive permission to take lodgings here, on your departure."

A haughty bow was the only answer, and Montford left the house with as much gratification in his selfish heart, as successful malice is capable of feeling. He passed the vines and plants, redolent of summer, that decorated the piazza; he looked into the garden, that lay quiet and fair in the shades of evening, and as he closed the gate and cast back one glance upon the dwelling—so admirable for its simplicity—he exulted in the thought that the proud Glenroy would, in a few days, be an outcast from the home of his fathers, and his family be doomed to eat the bread of dependence.

"Yes!" muttered he to himself, "let him labour at the plough. Let him gather in the harvest another has planted. I should like to see his dainty hands hardened by daily toil, and his ambrosial locks moistened by the sweat that drops from the labourer's brow. He dared to despise me when a boy, he spurns me as a man; but he has learned by this time, that King Log has turned into King Serpent, and can sting the frogs that jumped croaking on his back."

While Montford pursued his path, indulging in reflections like these, Glenroy was endeavouring to arm himself with fortitude to break to his mother a knowledge of her destiny.

"How can I do it?" cried he; "if my father could not summon resolution for the task, how can I?" All the bitterness of his lot pressed upon him with overwhelming force, and throwing himself on the sofa, he leaned his face on the arm, and let it not be a stigma on his manhood, if the covering of it became moistened with his burning tears. He heard a soft step enter the apartment, but he moved not. A moment more, a gentle arm was thrown around him, and the mild voice that had soothed the sorrows of his childhood was breathing in his ear.

"Herbert, my son, what means this emotion? You alarm, you terrify me. Good heavens! what calamity can threaten, when my children are around me?"

Glenroy lifted his head, and turning his bloodshot eyes upon his mother, saw that she was as pale as ashes. One horrible apprehension entered her mind, and clasping him almost wildly in her arms, she exclaimed,—"If sorrow comes to me through you, Herbert, let me sink into my grave at once. Oh! if it is as I fear, open your father's grave and lay me by his side. I could not meet a blow like that."

"Dearest mother, you rave, what is it you fear? Is it I who would premeditate death-blow to strike at your heart? Have I merited this?"

"Forgive me, my son! I heard loud and angry tones—the unexpected coming of that young man—your strange emotion—the horrible idea flashed into my mind, and I knew not what I uttered. Relieve my dread. Tell me what evil impends, and if it does not approach in the form of my children, I can bow to meet it."

"I have, indeed, been insulted, mother; and had not your image stood with rebuking sadness before me, all that you dread might be impending; but—let Margaret and Constance come in. Let us gather together before the storm begins to pelt, and shield each other from the pitiless blast."

His sisters came and stood with white lips by his side; and Mrs. Glenroy lifted a silent prayer that whatever cup of bitterness was prepared for her, she might drink it with unmurmuring lips. Herbert then unfolded his father's letter, and having explained the solemn circumstances of its reception, proceeded to read it, in a faltering voice, interrupted by the deep sobs of his auditors. It seemed as if the cerements of the tomb had been broken, and as if the departed husband and father once more entered the bosom of his family, to reveal the mystery that he had veiled during life.

There was no comment made: they understood at once the extent of their calamity, and they saw it was irremediable. Mrs. Glenroy covered her face, that the anguish of her heart might not be visible to her children; Margaret knelt by her side, as if to shelter her in the hour of extremity; while Constance, incapable of self-control, threw her arms around her brother's neck and wept unrestrainedly. Herbert kissed the fair young brow that drooped in agony on his bosom, and he felt as if every selfish wish and purpose were annihilated within him.

"Weep not, my fair sisters," cried he, "we will not always be in darkness. I have an arm of strength and a heart of youth; and affection has wrought miracles when its power has been tested in the hour of adversity. Be comforted, my mother; we will find another home, where you shall still be happy in your children's smiles. The world may call us poor, but we are still rich in unborn wealth."

"What!" cried Constance, desparingly, "must we leave our beautiful cottage, the vines we have planted, the flowers we have reared, and go—we know not whither—the objects of pity and scorn? Oh! it will break my heart."

"Constance," said Margaret, rising from her knees, and taking the hand of her sister in both of her own, "think of our mother, and imitate her resignation. Not one murmur has breathed from her lips, and shall her children selfishly repine? Think of our brother; on him the burden of the tempest falls; but he will not tremble at the blast, if like the bruised reed we patiently bow till it passes over us. I can work, I can toil; I'll do it cheerfully, gladly, and feel no degradation. If the world scorn us, why let it—I will only rise prouder beneath its contumely."

While the noble girl gave utterance to these sentiments, her pale cheek rekindled, and her eye sparkled with its wonted fire; but Constance continued to weep in silence, completely overwhelmed by the suddenness of the shock.

Mrs. Glenroy at length gathered composure to converse with her children upon their future prospects, and to consult with her son, in what manner to meet the emergency they could not avoid.

During this scene of domestic sorrow at the Glenroys, a very different one was passing in the chamber of Griselda Willoughby.

A number of guests happened that evening to colleet in Sir Reginald's drawing-room, some conversing with him on his favourite topics, some uttering pleasing nonsense to the beautiful Alice, and others paying court to the rich heiress. Miss Shanks found herself completely overlooked, and, never feeling contented in a state of insignificance, thought, as it was such a clear bright evening, she would just run down to Mrs. Glenroy's and tell them Miss Trevanion had gone to Mrs. Heathwood's, for it was her greatest ambition to be the first to communicate news of every description. She had an admirable excuse for going to inquire after the health of Herbert: after his dangerous exposure in her behalf, it was proper she should make some manifestation of her gratitude. She tripped along, light as a grasshopper, under the trees of the side walk, till she arrived at the gate, which she opened so softly, one would have believed a ghost was entering. She always had that stealthy, cat-like way of approaching a door, as if her feet were shod with cotton, and she had an inveterate habit of standing awhile, if it were ajar,— whether to collect her own ideas or those of others, she never divulged. As she stole up the steps of the piazza, she heard voices in an elevated tone in the front room, whose windows were opened to admit the bland breath of the summer's day. She paused to ascertain if they were the voices of strangers, and distinctly heard the words of Glenroy, in the commencement of his conversation with Montford. Irresistible curiosity and unutterable astonishment, rooted her to the spot. She almost stopped breathing, lest she should lose a syllable of the secret of which she was becoming the favoured mistress. She lingered till she had swallowed the last bitter morsel that fell from their tongues, when the movement of chairs awakening her alarm, she flitted away, noiselessly as a mote on the moon-beam. When she re-entered Sir Reginald's drawing-room, there was no evidence of her absence having been observed; but to her infinite joy she saw Griselda disengaged, her particular entertainer having just made his parting bow. Panting to unburden herself of the mighty secret, she made a whispering request to Griselda to accompany her to the upper piazza, as she had something of the utmost importance to communicate. Griselda, hoping that some despairing lover had commissioned Miss Shanks to supplicate for her compassion, did not hesitate to comply with her request, and followed her to the south-west corner of the upper piazza, being the spot most remote from the drawing-room.

"Well, Miss Shanks," interrogated Griselda, "what is your important communication? You breathe as if you had the asthma, and look as if you had seen a ghost.'

"I never could have believed it, if I had not heard it with my own ears," cried she, holding out both palms.

"Believed what?" said her impatient auditor.

"What will become of them? What will Miss Trevanion say?"

After winding up Miss Willoughby's curiosity on the tenter-hooks of agony, she at last revealed all she had overheard between Glenroy and Montford, interspersing the narration with some embellishing episodes of her own.

Griselda caught up Miss Shanks's words as eagerly as the famishing Israelites the heaven-sent manna of the wilderness. The Glenroys ruined beyond redemption!

A sudden thought, the lightning of invention, flashed into her brain, and brightening after its entrance, almost set her wits into a blaze. She saw a way opened before her, by which she could effectually triumph over her atrociously beautiful cousin, and the still more fascinating Edith. In spite of her wealth and boasted pretensions, she still hung like an ungathered rose on the stalk, at the imminent danger of one day withering there. Of all the gentlemen she had ever seen, she had most admired young Glenroy, but his impenetrable coldness had chilled her condescensions, and prevented her from showing herself as amiable as she was disposed. She had seen with great complacency that her fair cousin was lavishing her romance on a most ungrateful object; but her quick eye perceived the spell which the fair Edith had thrown around the heart which had resisted all other attractions. She perceived, too, that Edith participated in the ardent sentiments she inspired. To triumph over all her rivals, to appropriate to herself the prize so many had sought to win—this was the glorious design that now quickened every pulsation of her being.

"My wealth," thought she, "is my own. I am accountable to no one for its disposal. Papa is as rich as a Jew, and when he dies I shall inherit all his property. The fortune I received from my aunt would furnish me with an ample marriage dowry, and cancel the debt of the Glenroys likewise. It will be no derogation from the delicacy of my sex, if, under such circumstances, I should offer myself and fortune to Glenroy, and redeem his family from misery. He will look upon me as a guardian angel, and forget his present foolish fancy for Miss

Trevanion. The world will never know the part I've taken, and I shall have the honour of making a conquest, of which any lady in the land might be vain."

While these cogitations were working in her mind, she walked up and down the piazza, almost unconscious of the presence of Miss Shanks, who, beginning to be tired of her silence, was stealing down the steps, to watch her opportunity of re-galing the ears of Alice with the same tale.

"Stop, Miss Shanks," said Griselda, "you must promise me one thing before you leave me. Never mention to a human being what you have overheard to-day."

"Never mention it!" gasped out the petrified Miss Shanks, who had already planned a thousand visits on the morrow, to accomplish the benevolent purpose; "why not?"

"Because it would be very unkind : the affair may be hushed up after all, and nothing which is threatened take place. I dare say Mr. Glenroy will make some compromise with him when he returns, and it would be a shame to publish the ruin of the family prematurely. If you would not wish to forfeit my favour ever-lastingly, Miss Shanks, you must comply with my positive request."

Miss Shanks was aghast with astonishment at such unwonted sentiments from Miss Willoughby's lips. She gazed at her to see if she was not talking in her sleep, but Griselda's eyes had a kind of ominous brightness, and shone through the gloom of evening, something like a cat's in a cellar.

"You may mark my word," continued Griselda, observing a doubtful shrug of Miss Shanks's shoulders, "if you slight my injunctions, you are no longer a guest of my father's, and the world shall learn from me the obscurity of your origin."

"Miss Shanks tottered at the bare idea of falling from the height up which she had so painfully toiled, and promised, with servile submission, to obey to the letter the wishes of her invaluable friend.

That night, long after the bright eyes of Alice Cameron had been closed in slumber, Griselda tossed on her restless pillow, deliberating in what manner to execute her magnanimous design. She must see Glenroy alone—but how to solicit an audience unknown to her family and his? How keep her purpose secret from the prying eyes of Miss Shanks? But woman's invention never failed her in the hour of need, and, after once "screwing her courage to the sticking-place," she did not long hesitate upon the best method of accomplishing her plan. Yet, in spite of all the opiates she applied to her delicacy, and that innate sense of propriety, of which none in woman's form is utterly destitute, she sometimes trembled at the boldness of the undertaking. The possibility of a refusal occasionally damped the ardour of her anticipated triumph.

"But no," she repeated again and again to herself, on her wakeful couch, "he cannot, he dare not do it. I will meet him with a loving heart in one hand, and needed gold in the other, and ere another sun goes down, I shall see him in sub-missive gratitude at my feet."

With this delightful vision swimming before her, she at last fell asleep by the side of her unconscious cousin.

CHAPTER XIX.

——'Tis mine to tell their tale of grief,
Their constant peril, and their scant relief;
Their days of hunger, and their nights of pain ;
Their manly courage, e'en when deemed in vain ;
The sapping famine, rendering scarce a son
Known to his mother in the skeleton ;
The ills that lessened still their little store,
And starved e'en hunger till he wrung no more ;
The varying frowns and favours of the deep,
That now almost engulfs, then leaves to creep,

With crazy oar and shattered strength, along
The tide, that yields reluctant to the strong;
Th' incessant fever of that arid thirst
Which welcomes, as a well, the clouds that burst
Above their naked bones, and feels delight
In the cold drenching of the stormy night;
And from the outstretched canvas gladly wrings
A drop to moisten life's all-gasping springs;
The savage foe escaped; to seek again
More hospitable shelter from the main;
The ghastly spectres which were doomed at last
To tell as true a tale of dangers past,
As ever the dark annals of the deep
Disclosed for man to dread, or woman weep.

ANON.

"LADY, dear lady! hark! I hear a gun!" was the joyful exclamation uttered by Fanny, which awoke our heroine.

This joyful intelligence infused new life into Susan, who was almost exhausted; she listened, but no sound met her ear, except the hoarse roaring of the waves that broke against their frail bark. The rain had ceased, and the wind had sunk, but yet no hope of deliverance appeared, and the almost frenzied imagination of Susan beheld the horrors of famine at no great distance. Silent and despairing, she gazed on the wide expanse of water, on which the faint light of morning was gleaming; and while she prayed for death as the pangs of famine assailed them, she heard a gun, and the sound appeared at no great distance. Clinging to the edge of the planks that supported them like a raft, she gazed anxiously around, and fancied she beheld a ship; but as yet the light was not sufficient to distinguish objects clearly, and what she took for a ship might only be a hanging cloud, or perhaps, a rock projecting from the sea.

At length Fanny clapped her hands, and shrieked with all her might,—"It is a good right ship, lady, we shall be taken on board, we shall be saved!"

A salutary gush of tears prevented Susan from fainting; for the hope that they might be delivered, was attended with emotions that almost overcame her weak and agitated spirits. The light of morning now permitted her to see a large vessel, apparently in the same direction with themselves; but, convinced that their voices could not be heard at so great a distance, she tore off a part of her dress, and waved it above her head, till fatigue obliged her to resign it to Fanny, who, in joyful accents, said,—"They come, lady—I see them—I see a great many get into the boat; they come, they come."

She then clapped her hands with wild demonstrations of joy. Susan beheld the boat approaching, and she with difficulty restrained her own shrieks. Again she waved the signal of distress above her head, and had the transport to behold it was answered by the men in the boat which was standing towards them.

"Heaven is merciful!" said Susan; "our prayers are heard; deliverance is at hand. Blessed men! they come like angels to our assistance."

The boat was now within hearing, and, joined by Fanny, she cried for help with all her strength. Soon the voices of men, which an hour before she had despaired of hearing again, met her ear, and to increase her transport, she distinguished the language of England. Her tears and her cries were now the strong emotions of joy, bursting from an overcharged heart, which had been so many dreadful hours sunk in horror and despair.

The boat in a few moments was close beside them, and she could hear the exclamations of wonder and pity uttered by the sailors, to see two helpless females in such a situation of peril and terror, sufficient to appal the hardy mariner accustomed to buffet the ocean in the midst of storms and dangers. With a wild shriek of rapture, such as no pen can describe, nor any heart conceive, except those who have been snatched at a moment big with destruction from the jaws of death, Susan threw herself into the arms of the officer in the boat, who, at the imminent risk of his own life, had climbed the shattered part of the stern on which she and her little companion had been borne, and which now appeared separating in every joint. Being safely placed in the boat, the strength which had hitherto supported her gave way, and she fainted.

Fanny became alarmed, and fancied that Susan was dead; she began to weep bitterly. The officer who commanded the boat compassionately soothed her agonies, and having wetted the pale lips of Susan with brandy, she opened her eyes,

and expressed her gratitude to her preservers, who in their turns evinced the utmost astonishment as they surveyed the disjointed planks which had been her deliverance from a watery grave; but perceiving that she was too much exhausted to reply to their inquiries respecting the ill-fated vessel from which she had been separated by the fury of the tempest, they humanely forbore to question her, and with all the speed that the still swollen and rough sea would permit, they made for their own ship, the deck of which was crowded to behold beings who had been so fortunately rescued.

Susan and her little attendant were immediately carried down to the cabin, when an exclamation of, " Merciful Providence! my child!" made her unclose her heavy

No. 16.

eyes to meet a most unexpected sight—her father was bending over her with looks of compassion and surprise. But too weak to support the sudden transitio from extreme misery to excessive joy, she sunk again into insensibility, and was borne to a bed, and every assistance given to restore her wasted strength and harassed spirits.

The following day Susan, having in part recovered from her fatigues, was able to relate what she suffered since the commencement of the storm; she also informed her father of all that had occurred to her since he left her at Allendale; which we shall pass over, the reader being already acquainted with the adventures of Susan up to the present time.

During the remaining hours of daylight the vessel stood steadily on her course, without shifting a sail; and as the rigging required no immediate attention, the men were lounging on the deck in listless inactivity. Here and there cards, or dice, gave an apology to idleness, but in the estimation of the greater number sleep was evident felicity, as their sonorous nostrils gave ample evidence.

They were a desperate band, with hard looks, and the aspects of men accustomed to crime and inured to danger. Every man was armed with pistols and cutlasses, upon the hilt of which, as they slept, walked, or conversed, their hands mechanically rested; while racks of these weapons, with the addition of boarding pikes and muskets, were ranged about the masts and bulwarks, and other convenient places, ready for their grasp in the moment of battle. Order and discipline prevailed throughout the wild company, and save the buccaneer-like character and build of the vessel, it differed not materially in its internal arrangements from a king's ship.

Malcolm Graham, whose bold spirit kept these inferior and scarcely less free fierce beings in subjection, walked the deck with a determined tread, now bending his eyes in thought, now lifting them, flashing with excitement, towards the sea, and rapid scanning its wide circle.

The wind fell, and there was not breath enough to toss a curl on a maiden's brow. The surface of the ocean was undimpled, and sleepily rolled its polished waves along. The vessel rose and fell upon the swell with a swan-like motion. Every spar and line of rigging was painted upon the water with the accuracy of reality.

The hull, which was about ninety feet long, would have challenged the unanimous admiration of those who could appreciate the merits of her build, had she been anchored in any of the most frequented harbours or docks in the universe. So beautiful were her proportions, that she might almost have been considered a created being, ordained to be received upon the bosom of the ocean, and fashioned, by the Divine architect, to add to the number and beauty of his creation; she was constructed with great breadth of beam, and flush from stem to stern; like her spars, she was painted black, with the exception of a narrow ribbon of white paint drawn around her just below the gunwale. From her unusual breath amid-ships the eye would be deceived in estimating her tonnage too large; but the extreme sharpness of her bows more than qualified this unusual width, and while it contradicted her apparent burden, promised unusual speed.

Two large boats were lashed in the centre, and a smaller one hung on each quarter. Directly amid-ships, and just before the mainmast, was mounted upon a revolving carriage a thirty-two long brass pounder, so arranged that in bad weather it could be lowered down and housed while in the frame-work: around it were several thirty-two pound shot. Besides this frowning emblem of war, on either side of the vessel, and half run out of the ports, which were thrown open for free circulation of air, were six guns of different calibre and metal, some of them being of brass, and originally intended for the field, the others of iron, carrying eighteen and twenty-four pound shot.

The arms of Spain were impressed on one, while the lily of France, the lion of Great Britain, the eagle of Russia, and the crown of Portugal were stamped in bold relief upon the remainder. Their carriages were made of heavy African oak, painted green, and rigged with chains and cordage to keep them in their places. Her build proved the skill of the architect; and nothing had been sacrificed to, although everything had been directed by taste ; and her neatness and arrangements, showed that in the person of her commander, there was united, to the strictest discipline, the practical knowledge of a thorough seaman.

Graham after taking a longer survey than usual of the horizon, and turning away with an exclamation of disappointment, was addressed by a tall hard-featured man, whose long, matted hair descended to his broad shoulders, and who had been silently pacing the leeward side of the deck.

"What's in the wind, captain ? You have loved your own thoughts since you have found your daughter so well, as to forget to speak."

"You are right, Jones," said Graham, smiling at the blunt address of the seamen. "Listen," he said, walking aft, followed by Jones, where they could speak without being overheard by the helmsman.

"Now harken to my plans !"

"I have half guessed them."

"What ?"

"Some vessel, ballasted with bars of gold, which you have heard of while ashore."

"Far better than that. I seek revenge. You are no stranger, Jones, to an amour pursued by me at Philadelphia some few years back."

"What !" exclaimed Jones, "looking rather surprised, "the lass I helped you to carry off, when we were intercepted by the Rattlesnake."

"The same."

"Well then," continued Jones, "I think I do recollect her ; bless her heart, it was through her intercession, at London, that I escaped being hung, when I was taken there in the Rattlesnake, and tried for piracy ; she pursuaded her husband, Captain Elliot, to write to the Admiralty in my favour, and my sentence was transportation, however I managed to escape that."

"Captain Elliot," said Graham, "is going to America as govenor of one of the provinces, accompanied by his wife. You know I have an old account to settle with him. His ship, I expect we shall fall in with shortly, as a vessel answering her description I understand sailed from London some weeks back."

"Shiver my topsails ; we will soon fall in with him if he's steering this way."

The ship continued steadily on her course, and in obedience to Graham's orders, some alterations were made in the working state of the ship, many of the supernumerary sails were taken in, and her head-gear having been rendered lighter, she was laid on a tack much nearer to the wind.

The air had indeed freshened, but it was still as gentle as the breathings of an infant's sleep ; and although there was no moon, yet the glorious stars shed a benign though weaker radiance. It was, in sooth, one of those balmy nights, when the spirit of man seems conscious of a kindred with the silent harmonies of external nature, and the heart grows warm, in the delicious yearnings of its own sympathies.

Attracted by the tranquillity of the hour, Susan was pensively leaning over the taffrail, listening attentively to a group of seamen who were seated on the deck at a short distance from her ; like children round a nurse gifted with mystic lore and fairy legend, in the hope of being amused with a tale from a seaman, whose talents at description, and adroitness in nautical metaphor, where not to be equalled by any on board the ship. He was an old sea dog, and a clever fellow, he had seen all sorts of service, and knew all sorts of stories.

"Come, spin us a yarn, Joe, my boy," cried one of the seamen.

"Come, Starboard," said another—"come, tip us a twist—one of your thorough bred starers, you know."

"Well ! well !" says Joe, who was never at a loss for a yarn,—"will's the word, so here goes for a real true story——one, my boys, that I can swear to, for its partly my own life."

The seamen bent forward, eager to listen, and after the usual preliminary of a fresh quid, he began spinning, as it is termed by sailors, the following

YARN.

"I shall begin, messmates, as early as I can recollect. My father was a sailor before me, and married my mother after he was discharged from a man of war; I was born within the following year; so that by the time he returned from his first trading voyage, my mother took me in tow, a yawl of a thing, and followed my father from Portsmouth to London, where he moored himself I think somewhere about Wapping, in a house, where other sailor's families lived.

"My father was a brave rattling lad, and whenever he came home off a voyage, we had—that is, my mother and me, shining times of it; for he liked to make his glittering money fly like the dust in a summer's day, saying blithely, when my mother thought him over extravagant, 'that it was more in the scattering than in the gathering that right seamen made their valuations.' She was a fair and gentle woman; and I thought, because she spoke the English, that she was surely come of something o'er the common—for the neighbours spoke a horrible lingo, I think they must have been all Irish; however that may be, I forget now where we come from, and she died before I was four years old; so it's no wonder. But I cannot forget her; she was the most of a lady, I think I ever seed—so sweet and so pleasant! sure am I, had she been acquainted with the queen, she would have been taken for a maid of honour, or else have had her fortune made. But she died, messmates, while I was a little boy, and my father was on the sea. I soon forgot my kind and loving parent; nor did I see my fine merry father any more, for the ship he was it, was lost in the Bay of Biscay on her homeward voyage, and he, with the captain and another man, were washed from the deck by the sea, and carried away by the waves.

"I was then left destitute, but was passed by the parish to an old grandmother in the country; she was a lone woman, and received me kindly, saying often,—that He who took pains to make the creature would surely provide for it—however, messmates, she brought me up, and an old soldier who lodged with her, and had lost one of his legs in his country's service, often persuaded me to be a soldier; he would sit by the hour together telling me of the battles he had fought; but it was no use, my father was a sailor so I determined to be one myself. I think I see the old soldier now, sitting by the fire, telling his tales to the pastor of the parish, who would often come in of an evening to listen to him, while I sat on my grandam's lap listening attentively—'Faith, but your honour's mighty condescending,' he would exclaim, 'to listen to the chattering of ould Teague. Fifty years have marched off under General Time since I first shouldered the firelock,' and the old man would shoulder his crutch, 'and I am now daily expecting the route, for my time is nearly expired, to assemble for the grand review before the searcher of all hearts.

'The brave poor soldier ne'er despise,
Nor treat him as a stranger;
For still he'll prove his country's stay,
In every hour of danger.'

"But he's dead now, messmates, and lays in a corner of the churchyard, below a time-shattered elm, beneath a turf raised mound. It was a lonely spot, and the villagers took delight in keeping it clear from weeds. A few wild flowers blossomed around, and some rustic hand had carved a rude memorial on a slab of wood, and upon it was written the simple elegy,—

A SOLDIER'S GRAVE.

"It was indeed a soldier's grave, and a sailor's tear was shed upon it.

"In course of time, my old grandam got me made a cabin boy with Captain Bowline, in the tobacco trade; and her house was my home till she died, in the winter after, and left me alone in the world.

"It's a heartsome thing for a friendless orphan to be a sailor-boy, for, if he behave himself, he makes friends of all on board, as is natural for those that are stowed together to discern a necessity to bear and forbear, so

"The ship she was my dwelling place,
And my home was on the sea."

" In the last year of my apprenticeship, I was belayed to Hamilton More and navigation ; and in the passage out that spring, the skipper taught me to take observations, and said I did so well, that the mate could not do better, which was then to me an omen that I should rise myself to be a captain. But it's well for us that a fog lies on the land a-head, and that hope jars us—true, it hides a brave country.

" We were coming home, after a long voyage, and had neared the Land's End, when we saw a man-of-war's boat on the look out, she came off to our vessel. I yet see her oars, as she came, glancing in the sun ; she had a midshipman, with a press-gang on board, and when she reached us, they sprang on deck. They were not, however, ravenous, for they only took three men, but they were the best of the crew ; I being an apprentice they could not meddle with me, but there was one Robin Buntin that they made a prize. Robin was a tightly lad, not a year married, and was full of the thoughts of seeing his wife ; but when he was pressed his heart filled full, and the tear was ready to fall from his eye when he went to the steerage to rowst up his kist. We were all very sorry for poor Robin, but said nothing for a time, as it was in those days the duty of a sailor to obey the call of his king and country.

" I mind as well as yesterday, that I was sitting on the windlass seeing the pressing, and saw the wee midshipman looking at me, with the tail of his eye, thrice he spoke my name to himself, while he looked at my indenture which he got from the captain, as if he was a bad un to read ; he was a sharp younker that, and knew well that an anchor was not a buoy.

" This middy, and the dumps that Robin Buntin was in, brought thoughts into my head, especially when he said to one of his men, that he wished he might nab me, and leave Buntin, who was so down in the mouth. When I heard this, and thought my time would soon be out, and that all the wide world and the sea to the bargain, was only the orphan's lodging, I stepped out and said to the middy, that if he would get leave from the captain, I would go for Robin.

" In a jiffy the barter was made, Robin was set free ; and blithe he was. I was taken into the man-of-war's boat, every one on board shaking hands with me at the gunnel—the very skipper was jovial, and said it was a sympton that I was ordained to be an admiral : it was the first day I felt what it is to be proud, and I thought he spoke like a prophecy, for it was the very thing my grannie had called me.

" Being taken to the ship, we were not long aboard till soon it was known fore and aft, in the sloop of war, how I had entered without the bounty ; all the officers came and spoke to me, even the captain was told the whole tot of the story, and he made me the very next day the captain of the fore-top, which gave the men under me great satisfaction, for all the crew were pleased to hear how I had come to save Robin, and for nothing.

" That was my first step for promotion, and everybody told me that I must get on, for I was then a steady and tight lad, and having the use of my limbs, was willing, brisk, and handy.

" Merriwile Terry, the midshipman, or, as they used to call him for shortness, Merry Terry—and a right good name it was, for he was as gay a lark as ever gave life to a mess-table—was one of the noblest middies that I ever knew. He was as full of rigs and jokes as a French man-of-war is of music, and they were quite as harmless, too ; for Merry never said anything to hurt a shipmate's feelings, and no one ever thought of getting angry at his fun. There was'nt a reefer in the whole fleet that didn't love him as a brother ; nor a boy that when there was hard duty to do, didn't favour him all he could ; for Merry had a delicate constitution, and couldn't stand the rough and tumble of the service as well as some. But he was no skulk, and blow high or blow low, Merry never shrank from his watch. When the relief was called at night, whether it was calm or storm, all sail or close top-sail and fore-sail, it made no difference, on deck he always was before the sound would be out of the bell. He didn't tumble up the hatchway either, as some of the reefers did, with their hands in their pockets and their bow-ports half shut, or fumbling at your button holes like a greenhorn at a gasket; but up he sprung, wide awake and rigged from clue to earing, as if all pressed to go ashore on liberty. As I said afore, everybody from stern to stern, liked Merry Terry, or for the matter of that from one end of the navy list to the other—all except one man. As for the sailors it would have done your heart good to see how they watched his eye when he had charge of the deck, as if they wanted to spell out his orders before he had time to speak'em. They would do more for a single look of Merry, than for all the curses and dams of the skipper, though backed by the boatswain's mate with the cat in his hand. It wasn't from any fear of him, you may be sure, for I don't believe Merry ever stopped a man's grog, or as much as gave him a cross word, in his life; but it was from pure love and respect. When he spoke to be sure, there something in his tone and manner that seemed to say he must be obeyed; and when he looked at a man, who had been cutting up rustics, though he didn't frown or swell, or try to look big, as I have seen some officers do, yet there was that in his eye that made the stoutest quail. It was just so among the reefers at the mess-table. If two of them was sky larking or quarrelling, or doing anything ungentlemanly, Merry would just look at them, and they would leave off at once and drop their heads like a dog-vane in a calm. I said everybody loved him; I remember once, when we were beating up the straits with a Levanter dead a-head, and blowing so heavy it almost took the very buttons off our jackets, that Merry somehow or other, happened to fall overboard. He had been standing on the taffrail, with his quadrant in his hand, trying to get a chance at a lunar, when all of a sudden the old hulk made a heavy lee-lurch, and away he went splash into the water. Though there was a sea running like so many mountains chasing each other, yet before you could say Jack Robinson, no less than four stout fellows were overboard after him. It liked to have gone hard with the whole five, for it was more than the stoutest swimmer could do to keep his head above water, and before we could clear away the stern boat, though we didn't stop to cast off the gripes, but cut and slashed away, they was almost out of sight to leeward.

"Old Tom Bowman, the quarter gunner, and Bill Williams, the captain of the forecastle, made out to reach Merry just as he was going down the last time; and though it was as much as their own lives were worth, they held him up till the boat came to his assistance. I well remember the joy of all hands when the boat pulled up under the stern, near enough for 'em to see that Merry was in it, and when they hooked on the tackles, I don't believe that ever a ship's crew ran away with the falls with as much good will, as ours did that evening running up the jolly boat that had saved Merry Terry.

"I was a long cruize that we were together, and Merry got to be as much of a man in size and appearance as any of us, before it was over, though he couldn't have been more than eighteen then. On their arrival in England, the most of the middies got their walking papers as soon as they could, and made sail each for his own home. Merry's connexions lived in Yorkshire, and it was that way he laid his course you may be sure.

"I remember very well the morning, when I had the cutter called away and manned for him; and, as we wrung each other's hand at the gang-way, neither of us had voice enough to say good-bye. My stomach felt all that day as empty as a midshipman's locker, and the ship seemed as lonesome to me as the old brig Nancy did once, when all hands died off of the yellow fever, and left me and the old tom cat the only living souls aboard of her.

"For about two years after Merriwale and me parted, I lost the run of my old shipmate. He continued ashore, but I soon got tired of being cooped up in the narrow streets, with no chance of seing more of the sky than chose to shine between the tops of the dingy houses. Happening to hear that some of my acquaintances were going aboard a ship, then fitting out at Plymouth, I applied for a berth myself, and was soon once more where I had a little sea-room, to ware and haul upon.

That was a short cruize, and by the time twenty months were up we were all home again, the crew discharged, and I with my hands in my pockets, spinning yarn, and having nothing in the world to do.

"The next ship I was ordered to was the Spitfire, she was lying in the Plymouth-roads, ready for sea. The first man I met, as I went up the accommodation ladder, was Merry Terry himself, who stood upon the gangway-sil to receive. I knew him at a glance, though he was a good deal altered ; and he knew me too, as soon as his eye rested on my face. Merry was by this time twenty years of age, or thereabouts, and a finer looking fellow never trod the quarter-deck. He had lately lost both his parents, and this had given a sort of sad expression to his countenance, that made him appear handsomer than ever. I soon found that he was the general favourite on board the ship, as indeed he always was, go where he would ; and it was expected that before we sailed, he would get his parchment from the Admiralty, and mount a swab. An elegant luff he would have made too, for if ever man knew how to work a ship, it was Merry Terry. When he had the deck, the old craft herself seemed to know it; and no matter what kind of weather we had, she was sure to behave as obedient as a side-boy. I have seen him put her in stays where there wasn't a breaker of water to spare, with rocks both a-head and a-starn, and the wind whizzing round and round, like a bee in a bucket of tar ; but when it was " helm's-a-lee," and Merry had the trumpet, there was no such thing as missing stays.

" I mind I told you a while ago, that everybody liked Merry Terry, except one man--that man was the skipper. Somehow or other, he hated him worse than a devil hates a marine. He used to ride him down like a main-tack, would row him on all occasions, and put him on all kinds of disagreeable duty. It was even thought he clapped a stopper on his promotion. The story among the reefers went, that Merry had come athwart the captain's hawse in some love affair, but whether that was so or not, was mere dead-reckoning, for Merry was as close as an oyster, and never spoke a disrespectful word of his commander. In return for all the abuse he received, he would only curl up his lip a little, and look at him dead in the eyes—but such a look as he would sometimes give him ! I would rather for my part, have been on short allowance of grog for a month. Well, things went on in this way for some weeks, till at last sailing orders were given out, and of course, there was no more going ashore for the middies. The boats were run up and stowed, the top-gallant mast struck, and storm stumps set up in their place ; all hands were called to unmoor, and we even hove short, so as to be ready to trip and be off, whenever word should come from the cabin to that effect. When all this was done, the captain sent up an order to have his gig lowered away and manned, and directly after came on deck himself, in a full rig of landsman's togs. Merry Terry stood in the gang-way, leaning over the hammock cloth, when he heard the boatswain's mate pipe away the gigs ; and, as the familiar sound struck his ear, I noticed that he started and turned pale. It was a glorious night—much such an evening as this, only later, about two or three bells in the first watch, I think. As the captain passed over the gangway, he gave a peculiar kind of look at Merry—something like what a monkey would at a marine after stealing his pipeclay—and then, turning round to the first luff, he said,—

" ' Remember, Mr. Orlop, that you are under sailing orders, and that no one must leave the ship on any pretence.' "

" As he spoke this, he turned another malicious glance at Merry out of the corner of his eye, and jumping into the stern-sheets of the gig, ordered the men to let fall and give way."

" As long as the sound of the oars in the rowlocks could be heard, Merry stood as still as a stock fish, his eye following the wake of the boat till it was lost in the haze of distance. When he could neither hear, nor see it any longer, he began to walk about as wild as the devil in a gale of wind ; and the reefers, who would have gladly done anything to soothe him, saw clear enough that it wasn't a matter for them to meddle with. In the midst of his agitation, a shore-boat came along-side, the waterman in which, handed a note up to the middy that went to the gang-way to receive it, and immediately shoved off again. The note, of course, was given to the officer on deck, according to man-of-war fashion, and he, being a stately pompous sort of a fellow, took his own time to send one of the side-boys for a lantern.   When the glim came up, he walked to the fife-rail, and looking at the superscription, discovered that the note was for Merry Terry.   The latter, on learning this, eagerly extended his hand for it, and tearing it open, rapidly devoured its contents : then, rushing to the gangway, he would have sprung into the shore-boat, which he hoped was still alongside ; but, during the officer of the deck's delay, it had already got far beyond hailing distance.   Three or four times Merry paced up and down the deck in violent agitation, his lip as white and quivering as a gib in the wind, and his eyes shining like the top-glim of a commodore's ship. All at once, he walked right up to the first luff, who was standing abaft leaning on the taffrail, and in a voice that seemed to come from the cable tier, it was so hoarse and deep, he said,—

" ' Mr. Orlop, I must go ashore to-night.' "

" ' You cannot, Mr. Terry, you heard the captain's orders.' "

" ' Damn the captain ! ' "

" (It was the first word I heard Merry swear, though he and I had been mess-mates going on five years.) "

" ' Mr. Terry, you forget yourself ! ' answered the first luff, in a mild yet firm tone."

" ' If you use such language, sir, you will force me to a disagreeable exercise of my duty.' "

" ' I mean no disrespect, to you, Mr. Orlop,' said Merry, partly recollecting himself ; ' but I am half distracted.   If you will lend me your ear, sir, in a more private part of the ship, I will relate to you what may perhaps change your notions of duty.' "

" Mr. Orlop was one of that class of officers who, to the knowledge and skill of an able seaman, added the feelings and address of a perfect gentleman.   He, as well as everybody else on board, had seen and felt indignant at the treatment Merry received at the captain's hands ; and some of the whispers respecting the cause had also reached him.   Perceiving that poor Merry was now uncommonly agitated, and, fearing that he might commit some indiscretion which would oblige him to exert unpleasant authority, he readily complied with his request, and led the way to his own state room."

" The conference, whatever was its nature, was of short duration ; but while it lasted, many a curious glance was cast towards the state-room door, and I'm most ashamed to own it, many a listening ear was inclined towards the bulk-head. There was little satisfaction got that way, howsomever, for nothing was heard but a low, humming sound, now and then broken by a muttered curse in Mr. Orlop's voice ; and terminated at last by a sudden exclamation of that gentleman, loud enough for the whole steerage, and birth-deck into the bargrin, to hear.

" Enough, Mr. Terry, enough !" cried he, " you shall have it—if it costs me my commission, you shall have it !   There is a point where obedience becomes a crime.   When discipline conflicts with the principles of honour, I will be the first to set an example of insubordination."

As he spoke thus, the door of the state-room was thrown violently open, and the two officers issued suddenly to view.   Tha cheek and lips of Merry were still pale and quivering, while the face of the other was flushed with a deep red.   They both ran rapidly up the companion-ladder, Mr. Orlop, at the same time, calling out to me,—

" Starboard," said he, " call the boatswain, and order him to get out the first cutter immediately.   Do you attend yourself, sir, on the birth-deck, and start up all the men !"

" The cutter was no sooner in the water than Merry Terry sprung down the side, and the crew after, who, though they wondered as much as all the rest of us, officers and men, how all this was going to end, yet seeing they would oblige their favourite by moving lively, shoved off, and had up their oars in the crossing of a royal."

" Mr. Terry," cried the first luff, " remember your word of honour that you will return to-night, provided you find or make all safe !"

" Upon my honour," answered Merry, laying his hand on his heart : then turning quickly to the men, " Give way!" and as long as we could hear him, he kept saying every now and then, " Give way, my hearties, give way—pull with will," and such like.

And they did give way too. They were a set of as stout oarsmen as ever manned a frigate's first cutter ; but they never showed themselves afore as they did that night. The boat fairly jumped out of the water every clip, and the foam that

she dashed from off her bows formed a long white streak in her wake, as bright and dazzling as the trail of a Congreve rocket. You may think it wasn't many minutes before they reached the shore, going at that rate as if the devil had sent 'em an end. Merry steered her, right head on, and never cried " rowed of all," till she struck the sandy beach with such force that she ran up high and dry, pitching the two bow oarsmen, who had got up to fend off, about half a cable's length from her. At the first grating of the keel upon the gravel, he leaped ashore, and, without stopping to say one word to the men, darted off like a wounded porpoise, running with all speed up the bank. For two or three minutes, the boat's crew

No. 17.

looked at each other with their eyes stretched wide open like a dying fish, as much as to say, ' What the devil's all this?' At length they began to consult together in a low grumbling tone, as they were afraid to hear themselves speak, and Bill Williams, who was coxswain of the cutter, was the first to offer a suggestion that met the approval of the rest."

" Only hark," said he ; " how his feet go, clatter, clatter, clatter, as fast as the flopping of a jib-sheet in the wind. I'm feared, my hearties, that Mr. Terry's runnin 'mongst the breakers, and if you'll stay by the boat, I'll give chase—and, if so needs be, lend him a lift."

The proposal of the honest coxswain was relished by all, and he accordingly set off in the same direction that his young officer had taken. But Bill Williams, although he could run about a ship's rigging like a monkey in mischief, was no match for Merry in a land-chace. His sea legs was'nt used to such business, and he went pitching and heaving a-head like a Dutch lugger afore the wind, and seemed, at every step, to be watching for the weather roll."

In the mean time, Merry linked it off like a Baltimore clipper going large. He had proceeded perhaps about a mile from the boat, along the road which he had struck into directly after leaving the beach, and instead of shortening sail, appeared to be crowding more and more canvass all the time, when, all of a sudden, he luffed up and hove to, on hearing the clatter of an approaching carriage. The noise of the wheels sounded nearer and nearer, as they came rattling along over the rough road, and it wasn't long before the quick trampling of the horses' feet, and the clicking of their shoes against the stones, indicated that they were near at hand. The place where Merry had paused was about midway of a steep hill, and if he had chosen a spot, it couldn't have been better suited to his purpose. The road, which had been rough and uneven from the first, was at this point broken into deep gullies by recent heavy rains, rendering, apart from the difficulty of the ascent, extreme caution necessary in passing with a vehicle. On one side, a steep wooded bank rose to a considerable height; and on the other, the surface of the ground gradually descended to the water, which was not quite excluded from view by a few scattering trees, that grew close to the roadside, and threw a deep shadow over it. Merry, gritting and grinding his teeth, crouched down, like a lion watching for his prey. The carriage had already gained the foot of the hill, and was slowly labouring up, when a deep gruff voice cried out to the driver from within, bidding him drive faster; at the sound of that voice, Merry's eyes fairly flashed fire. The black, with instinctive obedience, cracked his whip, and was about to make a more effectual application of it, when a figure suddenly sprang from the road side, and seizing the reins, commanded him to halt ! The command, however, was scarcely necessary. The jaded horses had reached a short level stage in the ascent, and not even the sound of the whip had elicited any indication that they intended shortly to leave it. Merry, with a sailor's quick eye, perceiving this favourable circumstance, in an instant was at the side of the carriage, within which a voice of a very different tone from that which lat issued thence, was earnestly beseeching succour.

" Help ! for Heaven's sake, help ! save me from a ruffian !" cried a female in imploring accents. The last words were scarcely articulated, and were uttered with a smothered sound, accompanied with a noise of struggling, as if the ruffian was endeavouring to hold the lady still, and so silence her cries by pressing his hand upon her mouth.

The incentive of this well-known voice seemed hardly wanting to add more fury to the rage of Merriville. Choking with mingled emotions, he called to the ruffian to hold off his hand, and, with an effort of desperate strength, tearing open the door, the fastening of which he did not understand, he seized the inmate by the collar and dragged him to the ground.

" Scoundrel !—ruffian !" he cried, " I have you in the toils, and dearly you shall rue this night's violence."

" Mr. Terry—I command—you shall suffer for this—a court martial——, and various similar broken ejaculations were uttered by the wretch, who violently struggled to get loose from the strong grasp in which he was held. Merriville, though not of a robust constitution, yet possessed much muscular strength. In the present contest every fibre received tenfold vigor from the energy of the feelings that raged within him, and made him an overmatch for the guilty being who writhed within his arms. The faces of both were inflamed and convulsed with mighty passions, though of a widely and obviously different character; for the rage of the one, though fierce as ten furies, had yet something noble and commanding in it, while that of the other seemed kindled by a demon. The captain (for it's useless to tell you it was he) struggled hard, but was evidently becoming exhausted. In the excess of his emotion, he had bitten his lip nearly in twain; and the blood which, in their tossing to and fro, had been smeared over the faces and clothes of both, gave additional wildness to their appearance.

The female, who by this time had recovered from the swoon into which she fell when the voice of Merriville first reached her ear, now screamed as she saw the blood with which he was so profusely stained, and, imagining him to be mortally wounded, she sprang from the carriage and tottered towards him across the road. A sudden move of the combatants, at the same moment, changed their position in such a way as to bring the back of Merriville towards the approaching figure, and, at this instant, his antagonist, having succeeded in releasing his arm from his grasp, hastily drew a pistol from his pocket, cocked, and fired it. The ball whizzed through the air, only slightly grazing the neck of the intended victim; but a piercing shriek from the lips of the female, heard above the loud report, announced that it had done more fatal execution in another quarter. As if by mutual consent both parties ceased from their struggle for a moment and rushed towards her. She staggered two or three steps forward, mumbled a few scarcely audible words, among which the name of Merriville was the only intelligible sound, and fell bleeding to the earth. In the meanwhile the horses, which had been scared by the near and loud report of the pistol, pranced suddenly round, and dashing down the hill, were soon lost to sight. Poor Merriville, with a groan of agony which he could not, which he did not seek to repress, bent over the form which lay stretched and pale before him, and raising it partly from the ground, gazed for a stupid moment in utter unconsciousness of all things else, upon the features of her still lovely face. The ball had passed directly through the heart, from which life had already bubbled out in a crimson tide, though a few darker drops continued to ooze from the livid orifice of the wound. Merriville whispered her name, but she answered not. In vain he leaned his ear to her lips, or bent his eyes upon them, till the hot tearless balls seemed bursting from their sockets—no sound, no motion, made reply. He laid his hand upon her heart—but its pulse was still. He looked into her eyes—but they returned not, as they were wont, an answering look; their light had gone out—the spirit had departed from its house of clay—she was dead, quite dead! As this fact impressed itself upon his brain, a maddening consciousness of the cause seemed slowly to return; his eyes rolled up till the balls were nearly hid, his face became of a livid darkness, and his teeth were clenched together, like those of one in mortal agony. Suddenly starting up, he turned quickly round, and with his arms extended, and his fingers curved like the talons of an eagle, he sprang wildly towards his guilty commander. The motion seemed to have been anticipated, for the wretch had prepared himself with a second pistol, which, as his antagonist approached, he deliberately aimed at him and fired. Whether the ball took effect or not, it did not defeat poor Merry's object. He darted like a hungry tiger on the wretch, and with both hands, seizing him round the throat, he dragged him down to the earth. In vain his victim struggled—the sinews of his antagonist seemed hardened into steel. He tried to shriek for aid, but the grasp round his neck choked his utterance, and his words died away in a rattling sound, like the gurgling in the throat of a drowning man. With a strength that seemed supernatural, Merriville raised him from the earth, and dragged him along the road. The struggling of the wretched man grew fainter and fainter, but still an occasional convulsive quivering of the limbs told that he yet lived. His face was almost black, his tongue lolled out of his mouth like a dog's, and his eyes, bloodshot and glassy, were protruded a full inch from their sockets. Blood had started from his nostrils in his mortal agony, and a thick wreath of mingled blood and foam stood upon his lips, which, wide distended, seemed stretched in a horrid laugh.

In silence and with a strength that seemed more than human, Merriville continued to drag his victim along, till he reached the boat. He had been met by Williams not far from the scene of the first part of the contest, but he appeared not to see him. Williams on his part was too much awed to speak. The firing of the pistols had prepared him for some fatal event; for he had a dim and dark suspicion of the object of Merriville's errand, inasmuch as he had been the bearer of several notes between him and his betrothed; and had heard also that his captain was a rejected suitor for the same hand. One glance at the group served to shew him the dreadful nature of the burden Merriville dragged along with him; he saw that his commander was already a corpse, and besides he was too much intimidated by the unnatural lustre of Merriville's eyes, by his pallid and unearthly hue, and by his still and terrible bearing, to interrupt the silence with a word. As they approached the boat, Williams waved his hand to the crew, who were anxiously waiting on the beach, and signified by an expressive nod, that they must not speak. Silently and sorrowfully they followed their young officer to the water's edge, entered after him the boat, and commenced rowing back to the ship. Poor Terry, still holding the body by the throat took his seat in the stern-sheets, and leaned his head down on the gunwale in such a way that his garments concealed his face. The face of the corpse, however, was exposed in the broad moonlight, and as the head hung partly over the seat, with its features distorted and bloody, its hair matted with clots of blood and earth, and its glassy eyeballs apparently staring at the men, a superstitious shudder crept over them, which with all their manhood they could scarcely repress.

"In this way and in silence, they drew near the ship. The sentinel hailed them; but no answer was returned. As they came to the gangway, the officer of the deck called Mr. Terry by name; but still no reply. He saw by the terror painted on the countenances of the crew, that something dreadful had occurred, and descended quickly into the boat, where the whole terrible truth was soon ascertained. They were both dead! By the discharge of the second pistol, Merry had been mortally wounded, and his life had oozed away while his hands were still clasped with desperate energy around the throat of his victim. Even after death his fingers did not loose their tenacity. The officer tried to unlock the death-grasp, but without effect! and the two bodies locked in an embrace, which, stronger than that of love, had outlasted life, were obliged to be hoisted up together."

*   *   *   *   *   *   *

Starboard had scarcely finished his narrative, and while his messmates were making their different comments on his story, the look out, from the main-top-gallant yard, sung out "Sail, oh!"

"Where-a-way?"

"Broad on the weather beam, sir; here, in range with that light cloud that is just lifting from the water."

"Can you make out her rig?" said Graham to Jones.

"Jones was silent, but his look was long, and more critical than that of his captain. When it had ended, he cast a cautious glance towards the crew, who were curiously regarding the stranger, that had now become sufficiently distinct by a change in the position of the cloud, and then answered in an under-tone,—

"It is a large English frigate, captain Graham."

Captain Graham again seized the glass, and, examining her, said with animation, "Her hull has lifted, and she shews a tier of ports. It is Elliot!" he cried with joyful surprise, then turning to his daughter who still remained on deck, he beckoned her to follow him to the cabin.

"I must leave you for a while, Susan," he said, "remain in your state room, and both you and your maid be careful to lie on the floor below the line of shot. God bless you, my child." He embraced her with the utmost parental affection, tenderly forced her to enter the state cabin, and closed the door.

Upon his return to the deck, order was given for "All hands to clear ship for action."

Instantly all was animation and intense anxiety on board. The guns were double shotted, the hammock nettings were stowed firmer and closer than usual, hand-grenades lined the decks, and every missile and weapon of offence or defence that could be pressed into service on so desperate an encounter as that anticipated, was brought forth and placed ready for use. All that skill and determination to conquer could devise was done ; and, under a steady but light wind on her larboard quarter, she fast neared the stranger, who was also observed to shorten sail and make other demonstrations of a hostile character.

CHAPTER XX.

Long, long has he baffled all vengeance and might,
He weathers the storm and he welcomes the fight ;
Let him show his broad flag, and where'er it may be
'Tis known and acknowledged the scourge of the sea.
'Tis the Rover ! the Rover ! he revels in fame,
That spreads like a pest round his vessel and name,
No threat can deter him, no chasing can catch,
For the Rover has never yet met with his match.

But a mettlesome ship is saluting him now,
With cross at her mizen, the jack at her prow ;
Her crew is of English, her ribs are of oak,
And her vollying guns pour their thunder and smoke.
They grapple like bull dogs, the cutlasses flash,
The Rover is bleeding from shot and from gash.
He has fought tlll his deck is as red as the flag
That now trails o'er the halyards a bullet torn rag.

ELIZA COOK.

THE two vessels continued to approach each other, until less space than a mile separated them, when Graham, who, with his trumpet in his hand, had taken his place in the main rigging, shouted,—

"Hoist the ensign and pitch a shot from the weather-bow across his fore-foot."

The flag instantly ascended to the peak, and unfolded his black field, the banner of death. At the same time a column of flame shot from her sides, and the vessel shook with the loud report of the gun.

The frigate was now within long gun shot range, when finding himself closing with his antagonist, faster than he could possibly complete his preparations for battle, he took in his studding sails, and came to the wind on a parallel line with the pirate. In this position, he remained for some minutes, until perfectly prepared to commence the mortal, and, as he seemed to anticipate, murderous conflict. His lower yards were already slung in chains—the booms were sent down : the lofty sails were furied ; and, in short, all the preparations then customary, appeared to be made with the usual promptitude and skill.

By the time the preparations were effected on board the frigate, she was within three cables' length of the pirate, and by the light of the moon, which now rose like a shield of pearl, and flung her pale, snowy light along the dark waves, and by her lights, the decks could be distinguished with the naked eye. The moon shone white on all, while its rays were reflected in quick flashes here and there, as if from steel : from amid the dark masses on the decks, conspicuous stood the commanders of each vessel, directing their several courses, and giving commands that were distinctly heard from one vessel to the other.   Graham's commanding figure, on the quarter deck near the helmsman, with a stern and hostile expression in his eyes, and the attitude of one impatient to mingle in the conflict, which he seemed to anticipate with vengeful triumph : the captain of the frigate, calm, cool, and commanding, his features glowing with the excitement of the occasion, and animated, as it seemed, with an honest ambition to punish a lawless buccaneer.

The pirates were at their respective guns, displaying anxiety to pour out their fire on the frigate, which they saw approaching through the port-holes.   Nothing could be more imposing, than the fearless eye, the high bearing, and efficient state of preparation displayed on board the pirate, whose men were all bare necked, bare armed, having tucked up their shirt sleeves to their shoulders, to prevent being incommoded from duty and without either jacket or waistcoat.   Each had tied a handkerchief extremely tight round the waist as a support for the trowsers, during possibly a long protracted exertion.   Above this was buckled a black leather belt, sustaining the cutlass.   The black silk kerchief was transferred from the neck, and now bound round the head, restrained within its folds, those long straggling curls depending from the temples, which most young sailors love to cherish with no little vanity, as ornaments the most becoming in the eyes of the fair.

"Now, Jones," said Graham, "we shall have a fine shot at her," and he proceeded to level the long gun—"let me single out their captain.   Ah ! there he stands before the mainmast ; a fine fellow he is too, and Elliot is by his side.   Now is our time," he added energetically.

As he spoke, he coolly placed the lighted rope to the touch-hole of the long gun, and as had been preconcerted, the guns, beginning abaft, were coolly fired in succession into the frigate's ports.   The effect produced by this deliberate and deadly discharge, appeared some moments to paralyse the efforts of the foe.   Terrible cries of men wounded and in pain followed close the deep-mouthed roar of the guns ; the volumes of smoke that shot half way towards the pirate, then rolled swiftly back upon her, and were blown to leeward, leaving a full view of the enemy. A shot from the gun which Graham fired had killed the captain, who lay in the arms of the men, while Elliott stood over him, giving order to the crew ; it then buried itself deep in the mainmast, which, with its chain of connected yards, snapped off even with the deck, and fell with a terrible crash and dire confusion, and ruin into the sea.

"Neatly done," said Graham, "we have thrown them into confusion."   He had scarcely spoken, when, amid a loud yell from the seamen of the frigate, who had recovered from the surprise of their rough salutation, and returned a heavy broadside : the balls came singing through the air, splintering and crashing the sides of the vessel, tearing up the decks, crippling the rigging, and creating terrible confusion, while shrieks of the wounded rose appalling from every part of the vessel.   Both vessels continued running off the wind at a few fathoms apart, maintaining for some time a galling fire in this effective position.   Fast and fierce from the muzzles of their guns burst the vivid flashes of fire.   The guns were fired as they were loaded, and dealt out death and destruction.

A scene of mutual slaughter ensued, indeed, on both sides ; it seemed as if their courage increased with the carnage.   The mangled and mutilated bodies of the dead were now seen thrust from the port-holes—staining with a crimson hue the bosom of the dismal deep.   The elements were even lulled by the thunder of the cannon ; the sea went down, and the wind abated : this seemed to facilitate their near approach.   Both vessels at the same moment steered closer together—they were nearly muzzle to muzzle.   Now came the work of death and destruction, the guns were fired with rapidity, but without aim, into each other's ports, a struggle of strength ensued even " at the cannon's mouth."   The pirates, gnashing their teeth, and with their eyes distorted and almost starting from their sockets, commenced fighting through the port-holes with their sponges and rammers, lunging fiercely in savage ambush with their boarding-spikes and sabres.

The moon still lighted up the scene of carnage ; there was peace and loveliness floating on her silvery beams; but the evil passions of men reigned, and their souls were closed to aught bright and heavenly.

"Pour in your fire, my lads!" shouted Graham, with the utmost coolness, to his crew; "aim wherever you can see the glitter of an eye."

The simultaneous discharge of pistols, muskets, and blunderbusses was like a volcanic explosion, while a body of the pirates, trusting to their dangerous cutlasses, pressed forward over the bows in dark swarms. From every part of her that offered any prospect of reaching the frigate they leaped, without waiting for the vessels to come together, with cries and execrations most appalling, into the main chains, or sprang for the bulwarks, catching recklessly by their hands at whatever offered. Some attempted to affect an entrance at the ports, but were hurled into the sea by those who repulsed them; some jumped overboard and swam to the side with their cutlasses between their teeth, and drew themselves up by the rigging of the mainmast which hung in the water, but ere they reached the deck, they were cut down by the English seamen, who severed their hands from their wrists, and, dripping with blood, they fell back again into the sea.

Thrice did the gallant Elliott sheath his sword in the breasts of as many of those lawless beings, and cast them back lifeless into the sea; and as a fourth, who had thrown himself from the rigging upon the deck, attempted a stroke at him with his sabre, he was thrust on one side by a powerful arm, and the voice of Graham was heard exclaiming,—

"Ha! Elliott, do we meet again? I have sought thee to enjoy this moment. Back, men, and let me deal with him."

"Then let thy wish and mine be now gratified," said Elliott, making a cut at him with his sabre. "Hurrah for King George!" he shouted, and his voice re-animated the crew; and so sudden and well-directed was the charge, that the pirates gave back in a body till they reached their own vessel, and not one of them who had succeeded in boarding the frigate, retained a foot-hold on her decks. Their first repulse checked for a moment the ardour of the boarders, and they waited for the word of command from Graham before they made the second attempt.

"Board her again, lads!" shouted Graham, leaping forward, and passing his cutlass through one of the British seamen. "Flesh your blades in their carcasses! —board! board!—follow me—press on, press on!"

Like a crew of savage Indians, yelling and shouting menaces of death, mingled with fiendish curses and oaths of diabolical vengeance for their slaughtered comrades, they obeyed the energetic and sanguinary orders of their chief. Some were headed by Jones, who, with a strange recklessness of life, precipitated himself from the hammock nettings with a cutlass in each hand, into the midst of a grove of sharp steel, amidst a shower of balls, that, while they took effect in the bodies of some of his followers, seemed to pass by him harmlessly, as if he bore a charmed life. More devils incarnate than human beings, the pirates followed their leader, and cast themselves from the bows, some jumping over the heads of their comrades and leaping on board: and all rushing, crowding, and falling upon the deck in every possible attitude, seemingly indifferent so that they gained the frigate's decks, in what manner they reached it. Such a torrent of desperate men was irresistible, and the conflict became most terrible and sanguinary. Elliot fought like a lion, thrice clearing a space around him in which he could sweep his cutlass, but seeing Graham rushing to the companion way, he placed his back against it, and met his fierce lunges with well-directed thrusts, turning aside their descending strokes with the skill of a swordsman. Every sweep of his blade was fatal, for he fought for one dear to his heart whose life and honour were at stake.

For some time the battle was waged with doubtful success, many fell and the narrow arena was soon slippery with blood. At one moment the pirates, who, after the first wild charge, had formed into a body, would be driven over the side, and at another they would press the defending party towards the stern. Graham, who was everywhere present, cheering them on with animating cries as often as they were beaten back towards their own vessel, was again opposed to Elliot face to face.

" Vengeance! Vengeance! Upon them! Cut them down!" he cried.   " Let not one remain alive! Vengeance!"

Loud and terrific was the cry of vengeance, followed by a rush of the pirates that was irresistible. The seamen were cut down scarcely ere they had risen to their feet, and sabred with hellish ferocity wherever they could be grappled with.

Glaring balls of fire sailed over the heads of the combatants, and fell among the throng in the rear, some of the grenades were kicked overboard ere they exploded, and the explosion of others was followed by a shock that shook the vessel to her keel. Some grappled each other in the death struggle, and rolled overboard, and their struggles hardly ceased, ere their bodies parted the waves to rise no more.

Elliot cast a glance behind him, and began to think of selling his life as dear as possible in the cabins. That glance was arrested by the white sails of a vessel, which had not before been perceived.

"Sail ho!" was shouted at the same time by the combatants, and Graham for moment arrested his arm.

" Ah!" he exclaimed, " there is no mistaking the cut of those sails, or the lofty rise of those spars! The stranger is the Rattlesnake, I know her well!"

One glance told Elliot that the pirate was right, another sufficed to show what was necessary.

",Hurrah! my brave friends," he shouted, "rally lads, rally, see Captain Effingham is bearing down upon us in the Rattlesnake."

" Retreat men, and cast loose the grapnel—cut it—away with it clear!" were the orders shouted by Graham in a voice that rose commanding and clear amid the roar of the combat.

In an incredibly short space of time, the frigate's decks were clear of the buccaneers. The sails of the vessel were trimmed, the ship was got in command, and before the vessels had been asunder ten minutes, the duty of the vessel was in its ordinary train. The yards were filled with nimble top men, and broad folds of canvass were flapping in the breeze, as the new sails were bent and set. Ropes were spliced, or supplied by new rigging, the spars were examined, and, in fine, all that watchfulness and sedulous care was observed which is so necessary to the safety of a ship. Every spar was secured, the pumps were sounded, and the vessel held on her way as steadily as if she had never fired nor received a single shot.

Three hours later, and all was silence on board the pirate. The labour of repairing the damages had ceased, and most of the living, with the dead, lay alike in common silence, but the deep stillness of the moment was suddenly broken by the loud appalling cry of " fire."

The dreadful fact was too soon apparent to every one on deck. The alarm which brings the blood in the swiftest current to a seaman's heart was now heard in the depths of the vessel. The advancing uproar, the smothered sounds below and the rush on deck with the awful summons in the open air, succeeded each other with the rapidity of lightning. Buckets were put in request, and the pumps worked into the hold by pipes, but still the fire gained ground, and defeated every effort to subdue its violence. The flames, however, soon convinced them that their only security would be to let in the water between the decks a foot deep, but clouds of smoke issuing from below, and the flames increasing, prevented this from being done. The hold of the ship was a fiery furnace, and the deck forward was getting too hot to be endured, and there were places even in which the beams had given symptoms of yielding.

The crew still courageously exerted themselves, feeling there was no escape if the vessel perished. Blankets, sails, and everything which offered, and which promised to be of use, were wetted and cast upon the flames. But the confined space, with the heat and smoke, rendered it impossible to penetrate to those parts of the vessel where the conflagration raged. One man ventured below, but the heat was so intense, he was obliged to return, and they were forced to dash water over him while there to prevent his being burned.

" The flames are getting to the cabin," the man whispered to Graham, when he returned.

"Our only chance then is the boats." Graham now ordered them to be got out, but the long boat was slung high up, and as they were about to put her over the side of the ship, the fire caught the mainmast, and she fell down on the guns, and staved in her side. Thus it became impossible to use her. The yawl was then hoisted out, and a party of the men immediately took possession of her, and

pushed off from the ship. The fate of those on board now seemed but too clear. To perish by fire or water was the inevitable doom of every one on board, and was so felt. Lamentations and bitter curses resounded through the ship, amid the cracking of the flames. The great principle of self-preservation acted upon all. Yards, spars, hen-coops, everything on which there was a hope of floating, were flung overboard. Many leaped into the waves; others swam to fragments of the vessel which floated around. The shrouds and yards of the vessel were covered with hesitating men, who could not yet determine on their mode of perishing.

While the fire had been raging within, another element without had aided to lessen hope for those who were abandoned. The wind had continued to rise, and during the time lost in useless exertion, the vessel had reeled to the larboard side. When hope was gone the helm had been deserted, and this had afforded a few minutes of preservation longer; for the flames on the starboard side raged from stem to stern.

Orders were instantly given to make a raft, and all of those on board gave themselves to the task, heart and hand. The danger was one that admitted of no ordinary or half conceived expedients; but, in such an emergency, it required all the readiness of their art, and even the greatness of that conception which is the property of genius.

A raft was soon constructed of the spars of the masts lashed firmly to gun carriages and empty casks. Susan and Fanny were lowered safely to the place prepared on it for them, they were followed by Graham, Starboard, and about a dozen seamen, and the raft immediately pushed off from the ship. Jones, on whom a great portion of active duty had fallen, and who had been wholly occupied in trying to save the ship, when all hope was over, had begun to contemplate the horrors of his own situation. Looking around him, he found Graham had deserted the deck, he saw him at some distance in the raft.

The floating masts and yards were covered with men, who were striving for a momentary existence. The guns now went off shotted, and destroyed many who were struggling in the waves. The conflagration had advanced with renewed fury, had reached the starboard gallery, and was seen blazing wofully within the window of the roundhouse and great cabin, and then the flames which had so long ravaged the depths of the vessel, now glared forth vividly in the open air.

Jones now stripped off his clothes, intending to slip down a yard, one end of which was in the sea, but it became so covered with fugitives, that he rolled over them into the water. A seaman, in a drowning state, caught hold of him. He dived, but in vain, to get free from the man's grasp; he plunged a second time, the man still holding firmly on, until the poor wretch having swallowed much water, found his strength fail him, and probably sensible that Jones was sinking a third time, he dreaded being carried down along with him, and loosened his grasp, which was no sooner done, than, to avoid a repetition, he dived again below the surface, and rose as far from the spot as possible.

This incident made him more cautious for the future; he even avoided the dead bodies, until he was forced to move them on one side with one hand, while he made way with the other, and his mind all the time impressed with the apprehension, that each of them was a person who would seize him and involve him in his own destruction.

At last his strength began to fail for want of respite, he fell in with part of the ensign staff, and put his arm through a loop in the rope to secure it. In this manner he swam some little time as well as he could, till perceiving a yard, he seized it by one hand, but observing that it scarcely supported a man who held on at the other end, he quickly abandoned so slight an aid, and one which seemed incapable of contributing in any degree to his preservation. He next fell in with the spritsail yard, which was covered with people, whom he feared to approach. Some were quite naked, others in their shirts; yet, in their own miserable situations, they seemed to feel pity for him.

The spectacle that was now exhibited on all sides was of the most heart-rending description, and sufficient to have dismayed the stoutest courage; the mainmast, which had the lower part consumed by the fire, fell overboard, killing many by its fall. It was soon after covered with seamen, and driven about by the waves. Jones now perceived two seamen buoyed up by a hencoop and some planks, he hailed them, and begged them to swim to him with the latter. They did so, accompanied by more of their comrades, and each taking a plank, which they used instead of oars, they contrived to paddle along upon the yard, until they gained those who had secured themselves upon the mainmast. So many changes of situation only presented to him new spectacles of horror; they were every moment exposed to death from the discharges of the cannon in the ship.

After all hope of deliverance had been so long deferred as to be beyond all expectation, Jones, to his great joy, observed the raft close at hand, and immediately requested to be allowed to participate in their fate. Graham told him if he could swim to the raft he would take him in, as he did not choose to undergo the risk, by approaching the mast, of being swamped by the rest of the seamen. Jones, summoning up all his courage, succeeded in reaching the raft; and two men, following his example, were seen and taken in.

The flames still continued to rage with unabated fury, and as the raft was endangered by being within half a league of her, she stood a little to windward. The fire soon after this reached the magazine, which immediately exploded. The air was filled with a sheet of streaming fire, while the ocean and the heavens glowed with one glare of intense and fiery red.

A deep, heavy detonation proceeded as it were from the bosom of the deep, which was followed by a thick, heavy cloud, and amidst the dreadful blackness nothing could be seen but pieces of burning timber thrown into the air, and threatening to overwhelm with destruction the number of miserable wretches still struggling in the agonies of death. The burning spars, the falling fragments, the blazing and scattered canvas and cordage; the glowing shot, and all the torn particles of the ship, were seen descending. Then followed the gurgling of water, as the ocean swallowed all that remained of the Rover, which had for some time been the terror of the seas. The fiery glow disappeared, and a gloom like that which succeeds the glare of lightning fell upon the ocean.

The sea for a considerable distance was covered with pieces of wreck, and intermingled with the mangled bodies of their unhappy shipmates who had perished, and some half consumed, who still retained enough of life to be sensible of the horrors which were overwhelming them.

CHAPTER XXI.

' How gay and brave they sailed from port! How many a kind heart threw
A last farewell to the parting ship, and her young and gallant crew!
Now in the desert sea she lies, a helpless silent thing,
Linked to the tale of blood and crime, of death and sorrowing!

W. B. CHORLEY.

' They ate up all they had, and drank their wine,
In spite of all remonstrances, and then
On what, in fact, next day were they to dine?
They hoped the wind would rise, these foolish men,
And carry them to shore—'
' And their baked lips, with many a bloody crack,
Sucked in the moisture which like nectar stream'd;
Their throats, were ovens their swoln tongues were black
As the rich man's in hell.'

"She's gone!" said Graham, "and those who have been called to their last dreadful account, have met their fates by a death, such as none but seamen can imagine. I have been at sea in all weathers, have weathered many a gale, and encountered hardships I never dreamt of; but this is the worst. I trust it will be the last;" then turning to Jones he said to him, "We are not in a condition for a long cruize, Jones; not one morsel of provisions have we with us!"

Jones proposed that they should approach the wreck, in the hope of picking up provisions or articles of use to them, as they were now exposed to the hazard of a death even more horrible than that which their companions had suffered. They found several barrels, which they expected might contain something to relieve their necessities, but what was their mortification on ascertaining that they were some of the casks which had been thrown overboard during the conflagration!

Before night set in, they fortunately discovered a keg of brandy, part of a cask of salt pork, a small cask of wine, some bags of biscuit, and a piece of linen with a small quantity of cordage, but they durst not venture to retain their present situation during the night, as they were endangered by the fragments of the wreck from which they could not disengage themselves.

They rowed as far as they could from the spot, and although it was night, began to get the raft into the best trim practicable for sailing.

None of the party had taken any food before they left the ship, and hunger beginning to oppress them, they mixed the biscuit with some of the brandy and sea water, and distributed it in small portions to each man; they then began to labour with the greatest assiduity, and everything which could be converted into use was employed; the piece of linen was thrown over a small spar which was lashed to an oar for a mast, and a plank served for a rudder. The equipment of the raft was soon completed, as well as circumstances would allow, notwithstanding the darkness of the night; but a great difficulty remained, for they were without charts or compass, and being many hundred leagues from land, they knew not which way to steer.

Susan and Fanny, with woman's faith in that divine Being who alone could avail them, and with woman's high mental fortitude in moments of protracted trial, had both known how to control the exhibition of their terrors, and had sought their support in the same appeal to a power superior to any on earth, fervently praying for His direction and guide.

At length a favourable breeze sprang up, and the survivors of that numerous crew were wafted from amidst the bodies of their miserable shipmates. The wind continued to freshen, and the sea began to swell; the only consolation now was the belief that they should discover a sail on the following morning. About midnight the weather became very stormy; and the waves broke over them in every direction. The heavens were obscured with thick clouds; and they struggled against death, holding themselves closely to the spars which were firmly bound together; tossed by the waves from one to the other, and sometimes precipitated into the sea; floating between life and death, mourning over their misfortunes, certain of perishing, yet contending for the remains of existence with that cruel element which menaced to swallow them up; such was their situation till daybreak

The next night came on, still the same! The boiling billows high and impetuous, and covered with white foam, commingled together in one vast whirlpool; and if at times the tempest lowered its voice of thunder, and murmured only through the hollows formed by the waves, it seemed to recover fresh force from that momentary repose. And then a shaking long whistling rent the air; and that was succeeded by a hoarse and rumbling din which appeared to emanate from the very entrails of the deep—and upon these conflicting noises would break short and plaintive sounds which resembled the cries of human agony.

And with every wave the raft experienced a new shock; and it spun round upon the uneven surface of that tremendous sea, for the helm and mast had been destroyed by the fury of the tempest, and they had no power to guide it. But, as the principles of its construction were such that it offered no resistance to the fury of the angry main, it could not sink: it merely succumbed beneath the force of every billow which broke over it; and, while it was submerged for a moment, its platform was completely swept by the raging torrents.

And for five days that terrible storm lasted. It was no longer the brave and daring crew of the once dreaded Rover, that now occupied the frail raft: it was a troop of ghastly and miserable objects! It was a number of beings without names—discoloured, cadaverous, their garments wet through, their long hair hanging over their shoulders, their eyes wild and glaring, their bleeding and cracked lips wreathed in hideous and mocking smiles—for during three days those emaciated creatures had experienced the horrors of famine! They were a prey to all the imperious nature of their wants—beyond the vital instinct all within them was as with the dead! Hunger gnawed their vitals, thirst burnt their throats: their wounds, red and painful, were rendered more galling by the salt of the ocean that dashed ove them. Rage was in their breasts, curses upon their tongues ; and still they clung to life—to that life with all its agony! Arrived at such a pitch, with them suicide was impossible ; for suicide is the effect of a reasoning faculty, and that faculty was lost to them.'

Moreover, suicide is but little in vogue where misery and privation abound. Suicide requires sumptuous and intoxicating repasts—perfumes and women— flowers and costly wines. Suicide must concentrate in one single joy all other pleasures known or dreamt of, and fill its jewelled cup with that essence of every bliss ; and then, having drained the goblet to the dregs, suicide must exclaim, "The bowl is empty, adieu!" Then only can existence disgust, because it has brimmed over on every side.

But in the midst of miseries most horrible—when scarcely a spark of life remains—oh! how that flickering light is cherished, watched, and cared for, as if it were the last ember of a fire which we would not wish altogether extin- guished. Thus, on board the raft, did those wretched beings cling to existence ; although, to support the wretched crew who survived, there was only a little biscuit and a small barrel of wine.

With one accord the unhappy creatures could have put an end to that horrible state of agony, But, no—they must live—live in tears, in hatred, in torture, and in crime. And what matter how they lived? They did live!

And amongst them no longer existed the distinctions of officers and subor- dinates. On that miserable raft were beings who were devoured with hunger, and who in order to eat, would attempt everything. Good luck to the strong : misery to the weak!

One man alone, however, appeared to be above the pinching wants which oppressed the others ; this was Graham. He was still the same—calm, un- moved, and cold. Standing near the stump of the broken oar, which had served for the mast, on which he leant with one hand, he tranquilly observed all that was passing around him.

At every shock occasioned by the waves, some bent their heads upon their breasts, others endeavoured to oppose the force of the billows with a feeble plank, and a few, lying on their backs in a species of lethargic indifference, with their glassy eyes wide open, gnawed a piece of rope or glove which hazard had thrown in their way. A sort of half-waking dream, a wandering of the imagination, seized some of them : they fancied they saw around a beautiful country, covered with the most delightful plantations ; others became wild with horror and threw themselves into the sea.

Some, whose legs wire caught between the planks of the raft and were nearly shattered in their concussions with the waves, laughed wildly, reckless of pain. Grief and hunger had made them mad. The greater portion standing, or huddled together in the centre of the raft, obeyed, like an inanimate mass, the oscillations of the frail platforms which saved them from eternity.

A remnant of subordination had hitherto left the officers in command of the little food which was yet on the raft. Jones supported himself upon the cask of wine, and watched Graham, who in his turn was gazing on his daughter.

Susan, seated upon the raft, with her head supported upon her emaciated arms, never took her eyes off her father. Fanny saw nothing—felt nothing—she was inert.

The tempest now seemed to redouble its violence, and the raft, floating upon the mighty waves, which hurled it up to heaven and then dashed it fifty feet into an abyss beneath, was sometimes almost perpendicular in that chaos of storm and danger. It was in vain that the officers endeavoured to give the men certain orders which would enable them to resist the shocks thus occasioned by the motion of the raft. They were not listened to.

At this terrible crisis, the sailors, fancying themselves to be in danger of death, and after a few words exchanged amongst them, advanced towards the placew her the rsuperiors were standing.

"We want wine!" cried one of the men, brandishing an axe; "we want wine that we may die in peace!"

Jones rose suddenly from the cask, and presenting a pistol at the head of the ringleader, exclaimed, "Wretch—it is our only resource. We must economise it to the utmost of our power."

"Ha! ha! ha!" cried the man, knocking down the muzzle of the pistol, "the powder is wet, it will do no harm to any here. Wine! wine!"

"Wine! wine!" shouted the sailors, "give us wine, or die!"

"You dare revolt!" exclaimed Graham, looking round for a cutlass.

"There are no longer any officers here!" was the reply of the men, "we are the stronger party—give us the wine!"

"Never!" exclaimed Graham.

"We will have it!" replied the sailor who had first spoken, advancing in a menacing way towards Jones.

Starboard rushed forward to protect him; but the man felled him with the axe; and Jones, in an attempt to avenge him, was also wounded. Then, covered with blood, and supported by Graham and two faithful sailors, he endeavoured to oppose the designs of the mutinous crew: but they were beaten back and forced to succumb.

In the midst of the infernal tumult, Fanny, carried by the crowd of mutinous sailors towards the edge of the raft, fell into the sea, and was borne away by the waves, vainly extending her hands to Susan for assistance. But Susan saw her disappear without being able to succour her; for she was compelled to hold by an iron ring in one of the planks, to prevent herself from sharing the same fate.

"Wine! wine!" shouted the seaman, with one hand upon the cask, and the other flourishing the toe of an old shoe over his head.

"Wine! wine!" responded the others, "let us drink our last stoup, and die drunk!"

And they rushed with one accord upon the cask which was immediately broken open and speedily emptied. The wine soon worked its baneful effects upon those brains which had been attenuated by want and privation; and amidst the howling of the tempest, and the roaring of the infuriate sea, they began to chaunt strange glees in hoarse voices; and their song resembled the hymn of a madman! By the reddish light of the portentous moon, some endeavoured to dance upon the raft: but they tottered at every step, and then, blinded by intoxication, they fell upon the spars, rolled here and there for some moments, and at length disappeared in the surrounding billows without uttering a single cry!

One of the sailors now suddenly espied Susan crouched up by the empty barrel and desperately clinging with one hand to the iron ring, while with the other she supported her once lovely head.

"There—drink," cried the man, who was thoroughly intoxicated: "drink—I say!"—and he placed the toe of the old shoe to the lips of the maiden.

Susan drank with avidity every drop that remained; and her countenance became flushed with a sudden glow.

"You begin to look pretty again," cried the sailor, "so for my trouble you may as well permit me"———And the inebriate wretch with his foul lips imprinted a kiss upon the mouth of Susan; and as she scarcely pushed him aside, exclaimed, "Oh! that wine as done me so much good! I am still thirsty: give me more—Oh! give me more!"

Two days after the tempest was entirely calmed. The sky was blue—the air pure—and the sun rose gorgeously from his palace in the eastern main.

The wine was all gone—the biscuit crushed under foot or spoilt by the salt water—and the miserable creatures upon the raft were fain to crunch hats, shoes, and ropes. Some had, in their inebriate madness, drank the salt water with avidity. Others put nails and little pieces of lead into their mouths, with the hope that the metallic moisture would abrogate a portion of their thirst. They talked about home, which they never expected to see again, and wives and children from whom they supposed themselves parted for ever. Grief, pain, and tribulation succeeded each other, hour after hour, as memory pictured past enjoyments, which they had thought little of at the time—and then there were agonizing cries and prayers for mercy every now and then bursting out, till their throats got swelled and parched.

At last, there were red eyes, and ravenous glares, and grinding of teeth, as they looked upon one another; the first mutineer sucked his own blood from his arm, and it made him laugh with such savage fierceness as rendered him more like a devil than a human being: and then he stared first at one and then at another with the eagerness of a famished tiger; but it spoke not, though it was plain enough to be seen what his thoughts were.

They all sat silently clutching their hands, and snatching their breath, as if each had something to communicate, but dared not clothe their thoughts in words—then there was an indistinct muttering of doing the best to save their lives, till it came to a question of what was best?

Then arose a quarrel between two sailors about leathern waist-band, which each wanted to possess, in the dispute the one was slain, and his body supplied food for the famished crew. But this execrable food only served to abridge the existence of those who partook of it.

With difficulty could two or three sailors, besides Graham, maintain themselves upon their feet. They kept their eyes intently fixed upon the horizon, and watched its vapoury boundary with the most painful anxiety.

" A sail! a sail!" was the feeble cry that suddenly issued from the lips of those wretched men.

Graham in particular watched the spot where the sail appeared with the utmost attention; for he himself began to entertain the most dire apprehensions. Up to this moment he had not felt the tortures of hunger, but his means of existence diminished; and he lost all hope of seeing the raft cast upon the African coast by the currents, for the wind had impelled it afar from land. It was therefore with an expression of joy that he exclaimed, " a sail! a sail!"

That magic word—" A sail!"—was echoed even by the lips of the dying. Glazing eyes recovered a gleam of lost fire—the wounded rose with difficulty—and every glance was directed towards the spot indicated by Graham. Others joined their hands together—many burst out into loud and wild shouts of laughter—and a few were so happy as to shed tears in profusion! For a moment grief was dumb—hunger appeased—and thirst quenched! Hope eradicated every sentiment of hatred; and all unkind feelings were banished by the thought that succour was at hand. And then those men, lately so fierce—so cruel—so terrible, rushed into each other's arms, shook each other's hands, and gave vent to the most unfeigned joy.

Jones and Starboard exchanged a significant glance, and indulged in a long and fervent embrace. And Susan, poor girl! sat dozing near the ring which it was not any longer necessary for her to hold, as the sea was now calm; but she heeded not the joyous shout, " A sail!"

And the sail gradually became more distinct; and at length a large frigate was discernible in the horizon, its white canvas reflecting the rays of the effulgent sun. Oh! how delicious was that moment—when all doubt disappeared—and when that sign of safety was welcomed by the enfeebled voices of the suffering crew! The sailors who had before mutinied and blasphemed, now felt a species of religious gratitude steal into their breasts: their lacerated hearts could not contain so exceeding a joy; and they experienced the necessity of pouring forth their souls in prayer and thanksgiving. Their burning eyes were moistened with tears:—it was a sublime picture, those men—pale—emaciated—and suffering— joining their hands together to thank God for so unexpected a relief! And the frigate drew nearer—and nearer towards the raft.

" We shall leave the raft in regular order," said Graham, mechanically resuming the reins of discipline.

" Yes—yes, captain!" cried the sailors with one joyous accord.

" My daughter first," continued Graham, " then the seamen—thirdly Jones— and lastly myself."

" You never will be able to climb on board without the help of the accommoda
tion ladder," said Graham to his daughter, with a smile.

" My dear father," returned Susan, " I know not what secret voice told me we
should not be separated yet awhile. And, in sooth, Heaven could not part us ; for
I implored its aid often enough for thee, my father—oh, I prayed for thy safety
night and day ! And Heaven never abandons those who pray with sincerity, as
His unlooked-for aid must prove to you."

" Heaven !" cried Graham at this moment i a tone of deep emotion and alarm ;
" What does that mean ?" he added, as he pointed out the frigate to a sailor who
was occupied in preparations for a speedy departure from the raft.

" She can't bear down upon us, sir," replied the man, " but at the tide will—
oh !—no—no."

And the man screamed like an infant disappointed in its desire to possess some
toy.

" Rage—hell—damnation !" ejaculated Graham suddenly, stamping his foot
with violence upon the planks beneath him.

" What is the matter ?" demanded Jones.

" She has not seen us," returned Graham, in a voice of thunder, his eyes flashing fire, and his teeth grinding against each other. " Ha ! ha ! my fine singers of
psalms—' Heaven never deserts those who pray—eh ?'" and the irony of that man
pierced like a dagger to every heart.

" Oh ! it is impossible !" cried Jones.

It was however too true. The frigate luffed, and was speedily out of sight. So
long as even the faintest outline of its sails was perceptible upon the horizon, the
occupants of the raft would not give up all hope : they could not—dared not—believe that destiny, or fate, or Heaven, could have prepared for them so atrocious a
mockery.

But when the vessel had entirely disappeared—when nothing but the sun
glanced upon the waters of the Mediterranean, calm and deserted—oh ! it was
then that the horrors of their situation were felt in all their acuteness—all their
poignancy. And, as is the case in all moral or physical re-actions, a state of
torpor—of feebleness, succeeded to that predicament of exaltation of joy.

This prostration of the nerves lasted some minutes, that length of time appeared
to be necessary for those wretched men to precipitate themselves from the eminence of sanguine hope to the depths of the darkest despair. When the horrors of
their situation were again felt in all their intenseness, when they once more saw
themselves face to face with the most awful of deaths—and when (the sky, the
sea, and the horizon being without a speck) these terrible convictions rushed to the
heart of each, cold and piercing like the bite of a dying man,—oh ! then what a
dread commingling of oaths and prayers, blasphemies and supplications, and cried
of rage and of death, ascended to that heaven which a few minutes before had been
so sincerely invoked by all. And then, also, those, who ere now had embraced
each other, felt the sentiments of hatred, and the pangs of hunger, more acutely
than before ; and the wretched mortals to avenge their miseries as it were upon each
other, rushed in wild tumult together, and fought with exasperation and frenzy.

Graham also uttered a terrible cry, which was wrung from him by an acute
pain, and fell senseless upon the raft. For one of the famished creatures was endeavouring to cut a morsel of flesh from his leg.

On the following morning, this access of frenzied rage had passed away, and hunger had once more stifled every other feeling. Jones and Starboard were lying
close to each other—their tottering reason seemed to be ready to abandon them—
everything appeared to turn round, as if they were under the influence of wine.

" Here we are," said the first mutineer, " starving, perishing, if we continue so a
few days more, where shall we be ? Wouldn't it be better for one—" and he
stopped for a minute or two, for all expected what was coming next and shuddered
for the very thought made them more eager for food. At length he said, " One
must die that the rest may live."—" Suppose we wait till to-morrow morning afore
we proceed any further," said Jones, " we've stood it thus far; surely we may
weather it out a few hours longer."

The mutineer said nothing, but watched his opportunity. He crawled towards Graham, who was lying on the raft, and appeared to be motionless, and was about dashing the hatchet on Graham's head, when he was pushed on one side by Jones. A terrible struggle ensued, and Graham recovered from his swoon.

"You wish to murder me," said Jones, in a feeble voice. "You see," he added, as he continued to wrestle with the seaman, "that this hatchet must decide between you and me. Now—murderer—and all for a mouthful of food. Ha! ha!" and he split his head in two.

The night soon put an end to that scene of horror; and on the following morning, Jones, awakening out of a heavy and deep sleep, fancied that he had been under the influence of the nightmare.

It was mid-day. The vertical sun darted his rays upon the placid waters of

No. 19.

the Mediterranean, on which the raft was almost motionless. The fragile rampart of barrels, casks, and netting had been broken, and the actual platform alone remained upon the ocean, which was now smooth and polished as a mirror. Here and there floated the remnants of garments, of cordage, and of planks, on which the sun shone gaily and gorgeously. The sailors who survived were all stretched upon the raft, their eyes brilliant, their lips red, their countenances flushed, animated, and resplendent. Only, instead of that soft and penetrating heat, which their external appearance seemed to indicate, they were bathed in a cold sweat, and their limbs were stiff and iced. Except this phenomenon and a nervous *tic*, which gave a singular and awful expression to every countenance, nothing bespoke the long torture to which they had been exposed; for some began to arrange their jackets, pull down their shirt sleeves, and tie their cravats, and exclaimed, —"The captain is going to commence the inspection; we must be decent and clean !"

Others fancied that they saw in the distance a city resplendent with gold, and marble, and verdure; and they said, "That is Tunis."

"We are arrived there," observed one. "My God! how lovely is that prospect. There are the domes, and the harbour, and the orange trees; and there are fair women, who beckon to us."

And thus they laboured under this delusion, took each other's arms to advance towards the city, and falling from the raft into the sea, they sunk to rise no more, save as disfigured and inanimate corses. The waters rippled for a moment, and the ocean became still and tranquil as before. Similar delusions continued with those who were left. Some commenced a gay waltz to celebrate their near approach to land: alas! the dance was commenced upon the raft and finished in the waters. Others fancied that they were in the cottages where they were born, surrounded by their wives and children, and all that was dear to them; and they melted into tears —and they blessed their offspring, and promised their wives to tempt the dangers of the ocean no more.

But all this was done with a smile upon their lips, or with tears in their eyes, as circumstances seemed to suggest; it was an allusion which was expressed by voices so convincing and so natural that a blind man would have taken those aberrations of fever for undoubted realities.

At the sight of this horrible drama, Graham was stupefied with silent horror. He and Jones were now the only two that retained their faculties unimpaired. And therefore was it with the most terrible emotion that they perceived Susan rise with an almost supernatural force from the place where she had hitherto remained seated. She was emaciated and haggard; but her eyes shone with supernatural lustre; her cheeks were suffused with a scarlet hue; and her lips were red as if they were dyed with gore.

She advanced towards Graham.

"Oh, father," she said, in a tender and touching tone of voice, "this is a punishment sent for your evil deeds."

"Oh! let me die," ejaculated Graham, in a tone of voice that pierced to the very hearts of those who heard him, madmen as they were.

"Who speaks of death?" cried Susan, gazing wildly around her, "Ah! see, he's coming," and she extended her arms to the ocean. "Now, father, I go before thee. Come, hasten!"

And the poor girl beckoned Graham to follow her. She hastened towards the edge of the raft, as if she would endeavour to walk upon the surface of the sea; she made one more step, and would have sank in the deep abyss of waters, when Graham rushed forward, and caught her in his arms.

CHAPTER XXII.

I felt my sorrow ere it came,
    As storms are felt on high,
Before a single cloud denotes
    Their presence in the sky.

The heart has omens deep and true,
    That ask no aid from words;
Like viewless music from the harp ;
    With none to wake its chords.

Strange, subtle are these mysteries,
    And link'd with unknown powers,
Marking mysterious links that bind
    The Spirit world to ours.—L. E. L.

Enough that we are parted, that there rolls
A flood of headlong fate between our souls,
Whose darkness severs me as wide from thee
As hell from heaven.—MOORE.

THE sun rose bright and cheering the morning after the eventful evening at the Glenroys, but its beams brought no healing to their saddened hearts. The breakfast was carried from the table untasted. Mrs. Glenroy looked several years older than she did the preceding morning; the renovating principle of gladness had fled, and the shadows of time settled on her brow. Constance was as colourless as a lily of the valley, and sat under the vine leaves she had trained, as desolate as Jonah, beneath his blighted gourd. Herbert made many unavailing efforts at cheerfulness, in which Margeret generously seconded him ; but the angel of peace had spread her wings, like the dove of the ark, to seek a green spot above the waters of grief.

"Here is a note for the squire," said a little boy, scraping before the door.

Believing it came from Montford, Herbert took it haughtily from the brown-faced messenger. He saw at once it was a lady's hand, written with studious care, and sealed with the device of the sunflower, turning to her 'god when he set,' her faithful and golden breast. Wondering at so unexpected attention he broke the symbolical wax, and read with increasing surprise the following lines:—

"If you recognise my handwriting, you will probably wonder at the circumstance of my addressing you, and you will even marvel still more at the singularity of my request. It is necessary that I should see you alone. I have something to communicate, which no other human being must know, and yet it is of everlasting importance to us both. Decide not harshly against the apparent boldness of my conduct, till you are acquainted with the motive, and if, after learning it, you do not appreciate it, I am entirely and altogether mistaken in my estimation of your character. If, in one hour from this time, you will walk to the turn of the river near the Murderer's Glen, you will meet with one who dares not commit her purpose to paper; yet she will glory in acknowledging it."

Herbert found no difficulty in recognising the handwriting of Griselda Willoughby, as she had often addressed notes to his sisters, since they became acquainted with each other.

He was bewildered as to the subject of their meeting, of such mysterious and everlasting importance to them both ; for his vanity never suggested to him a whisper of the truth. There was nothing of levity in the style of the note, and not doubting she really had some urgent motive, he did not hesitate to comply, pre-occupied as he was, and, turning to the messenger, asked if he waited a reply.

"No, not exactly an answer," said the boy, turning his hat on his thumbs; "I guess as how there's no need of that."

"Well, take that, and begone," said Glenroy, in a sterner tone than the child ever heard him utter before, at the same time throwing a piece of silver in his hat.

Harassed as his mind already was, the vague curiosity excited by so singular a summons added to the restless and feverish impatience of his spirit. Long before the appointed time, he walked to the place of assignation, and traversed with troubled steps the turf on which the fresh dew of morning still glittered, where it had been unkissed by the sunbeam. It was the very spot where he had so often seen the fair form of Edith Trevanion, and met the lightening smile, that now beamed on his memory with such lambent but fatal brightness. There was the very bank where he had sat by her side, wondering what sweet vision had alighted there, amid the voluptuous glories of a summer sunset.

Lost in these dangerous recollections, he did not at first perceive the approach of Miss Willoughby, who advanced from the shade of the trees with a trepidation in her manner almost alarming, from its contrast with her general assurance. Whatever repugnance Glenroy felt on finding himself so mysteriously alone, with a woman who had always been particularly disagreeable to him, his politeness did not suffer him to manifest it; and lifting his hat respectfully from his brow, he took her hand, which actually trembled from agitation, and led her to a bank, he but too well remembered to have been so differently occupied.

After the usual salutations of the day, an embarrassing silence ensued. Glenroy found it difficult to approach a subject so inexplicable, and Griselda, in attempting to speak, was seized with a sudden and obstinate fit of coughing, which resisted all her efforts to overcome.

"You have conferred upon me an unexpected honour, Miss Willoughby," at length uttered Herbert, after waiting in vain for an explanatory sentence from her. "I shall not, I trust, prove unworthy of your confidence, and though you could not have selected a more unfortunate moment, weighed down as my spirits are with untold anxieties, my services are entirely at your command."

"I know your anxieties, Mr. Glenroy," replied she, gathering courage for her task, "and I come to relieve them."

"Know them!" exclaimed Glenroy, "How is it possible? Do you know Mr. Montford? Has he meanly indulged in premature triumph over our ruin?"

"I do not know Mr. Montford, but a friend, who has been informed through him of his claims upon your estate, and his intended prosecution, has told me all. It was to redeem your family from threatened misery I sought this interview. Mr. Glenroy, I am rich. Fortune has been more than bounteous to me. I pity your misfortune. I—"

She stopped, and perhaps for the first time in her life the cheeks of Griselda Willoughby were mantled with burning blushes. That woman must indeed be made of callous materials who can break through the wall with which native modesty and inculcated propriety has enclosed her sex, with an immoveable countenance and untrembling hand.

The dark glance of Glenroy, which had been fixed upon her in haughty surprise, when she declared her knowledge of their situation, gradually assumed a look of wondering admiration. He did not fathom her secret design—he dreamed not of the return that was expected for the offered bounty; he was struck only with the generosity of her purpose, which, coming from her, had the effect of a miracle, and he upbraided himself for his injustice in having believed her utterly incapable of a magnanimous act.

"Miss Willoughby," said he, with all the respect which was rising in his mind expressed in his manner, "accept a son's and brother's thanks. But we have no claim on your benevolence, and the obligation is of a nature I could not easily cancel. I am too proud to subsist under the insupportable burden of gratitude. While I live, my mother and sisters will, I trust, never want protection or support, and we are already schooled for the destiny before us."

"Oh, hard of comprehension and wilfully blind!" thought Griselda; "can he not read it on my face and save me the shame of a declaration?" But she had put her hand to the plough and she would not go back.

"Mr. Glenroy," she continued, the magnitude of her undertaking calling forth a dignity of language she had never used on any other occasion; "I cannot suffer false delicacy to triumph in a moment like this. Take back the thanks which I merit not. You need not live burdened with the debt of gratitude, for I ask in return, what I shall value more than the gold of Peru. Take all my fortune— ten thousand times more, if I had it to offer; save your mother and sisters from present wretchedness, and give me but the heart, whose worth I have long too faithfully appreciated."

Glenroy started at this overwhelming declaration as if a thunderbolt had struck him. The blood rushed with dizzying rapidity to his pale face, covering it with the intense hue of shame, astonishment, and a thousand other indefinite emotions. These soon became merged in absolute horror at the possibility of such an union. The image of Edith rose before him, covered with the light of beauty and the enchantments of grace. Though for ever separated from her by an impassable gulf, he felt that his heart was irrevocably hers in the sight of God, and that it would be sacrilege to violate the deep though silent vow.

Griselda Willoughby was deficient in every womanly charm, which is attractive to the imagination of man. Her figure was heavy, her cheeks were sallow, and no redeeming ray of genius or sensibility emanated from her leaden eye, to throw an illusory charm over features cast in Nature's plebeian mould. All the adventitious aid of dress and fashion could not atone for the complete absence of personal beauty, or that "something more than beauty," more dear, which the illuminated mind and informing soul can impart. Griselda waited for the first emotions of surprise and gratitude to effervesce, but finding him so slow to acknowledge his sense of her favours, mortification and indignation struggled in her bosom. Making a desperate effort, she rose, and standing directly before him she exclaimed :—

"Herbert Glenroy! am I despised? Am I so repugnant that you prefer all the evils of poverty, all its calamitous effects on your desolate family, to unincumbered wealth? the power of triumphing over your enemy? of making your mother and sisters permanently happy? of retaining the home of your youth? Am I scorned as this?"

Glenroy rose simultaneously. There is something in strong passion which invests those who are under its influence with visible dignity. The uncommonly high tone of her language, the boldness and truth of her appeal, pressed powerfully on his conscience. The self-sacrificing vow he had made, to immolate every selfish feeling to filial duty; the awful injunctions of his dying father, to yield up every thing but integrity for the sake of those committed to his care, rose with commanding influence upon his memory. He thought of the sad, faded countenance of his mother; the tears of Constance; the proud grief of Margaret; of the vindictive temper of Montford, ready to exercise, to the fullest extent, the power given by law. By merely sacrificing himself he might avert all this misery; his mother might still pillow her head in peace, amid the scenes hallowed by the memory of the husband she adored; his sisters might continue to bloom in their native bowers, unchilled by the cold pity of the world, if his father's name could remain untarnished by reproach.

"I have vowed to do it," said he to himself, pressing his hand on his aching brow, "I have vowed before the God that made me, by all that is holy in this world and awful in another, to devote myself to this sacred duty, and shall I perjure my soul, when the fiery ordeal comes? I will be true to my integrity—I will tell her all—and then—"

Griselda saw the storm of conflicting passions in his breast. She saw too her triumph was at hand. She had passed the rubicon, and like a warrior resolved on victory, she waited till the enemy, conscious of his weakness, voluntarily should surrender to her power.

"I cannot deceive you, Miss Willoughby," he cried with an effort almost as terrible as the last struggle of nature, "I cannot be so base a wretch as to repay your generosity with duplicity, or to affect sentiments beyond my control.

have no longer the mastery of my own affections. I have nothing but gratitude to offer for your unmerited favour; and after making such a confession, could you purchase the salvation of my family, by bestowing yourself, and fortune on an ingrate like me?"

"The woman who is willing to do what I have done," replied Griselda, with unwavering resolution, "is not to be judged by common rules. I am willing to accept any place you can now offer me in your affections, hoping that time and unceasing devotion will yet advance me to the first. Again I ask, will you yet spurn the fortune I swear to devote to the interests of your family, and the love that in its strength has humbled itself so low?"

Daniel, when he was cast into the den with the unchained regents of the forests, scarcely needed support more than Glenroy in this bitter hour. He gathered up all the scattering energies of his soul, again repeated to himself the vow of his youth, then without daring to look upon her face, extended his hand to Griselda, and said, in a voice almost suffocated with agitation,—

"If thus steeped in poverty, a bankrupt even in affection, you still generously persevere, I have nought but this hand to pledge, and the word of unsullied honour."

The hand which Griselda clasped was as cold as marble, and its very touch might have chilled the warm glow of love and hope. But it was the seal of a compact for life and death. It was a surety of her success, of her joy, of her triumph. She saw in anticipation the canker-worm of wounded vanity and mortification preying on the vernal cheek of her cousin Alice, and the heart-strings of Edith quivering with agony, and she exulted at the prospective. She feared to prolong the interview, not wishing her absence to be marked, and having accomplished that for which she had sacrificed all that is dearest and best to the unpolluted heart of woman, she intimated her wish to depart, and to depart alone.

"I will acquaint papa with all that is necessary," said she, "and will give you immediate possession of the sum that is due to Mr. Montford. And one request let me make before we part—that what has transpired this morning may never go beyond the bosom of your family. For your own sake of course you will not do it."

"Believe, madam," answered the devoted Glenroy, "your reputation shall ever be sacred in my eyes. Even now I blush to think what the world may say at your having sacrificed yourself so unworthily."

"I do not care what the world may say on that subject," replied she, quickly; "it is enough that I glory in my choice, and I know I shall have papa's full consent. But I deprecate such a respectful title as madam, and when we meet next, I pray you not to address me by such a freezing name."

"I beg your pardon, Miss Willoughby—Griselda—anything—everything you please," stammered he, scarcely knowing what he said, as he walked on with her to the boundary line of Sir Reginald's estate.

"I must leave you here," said she, softening her voice to the tenderest cadence. "Come this evening, and you shall be in readiness to meet Mr. Montford, and to defy his threats. Farewell!"

Another pressure from that cold hand, and a silent bow, and they separated. She walked with guilty speed to her chamber. He returned to the spot they had quitted, and, throwing himself on the solitary seat, gave vent to the bitterness of his soul.

"I have sold myself," he cried, "the world will say I have sold myself for gold, and I shall be branded as a heartless, mercenary wretch, a needy adventurer, and *she* will look down upon me with scorn and contempt. Will she? Let her do it if she dare. She knows not the oath that bound me—the iron hand of duty that grasped my naked conscience, and forced me to the doom. She has not seen the words that are written in my memory, as with a pen of fire. 'Sacrifice everything but integrity—forsake everything but truth.' But is it integrity? Is it truth? I told her I did not love her, and yet she mercilessly rang in my ears 'Redeem your family from ruin—save your mother and sisters from wretchedness.' She knew I could not resist such an appeal as that, e'en at the risk of damnation. Wretch, ingrate that I am! I should rather rejoice that I can return and say to the mourners in my house, ' All that you look upon is yet yours.' Yes, even if I have paid a price more precious than blood. Mercenary! I regard money as I do the dust I trample on, and yet—my wife! Oh misery!—misery!—"

" Who dares talk of misery when I am near?" exclaimed a deep voice by his side, and looking up he saw the maniac Evelyn, rolling his wild, melancholy eyes upon his face. " Is it you who dare to rave about misery—young, unblighted, and unwronged? Rouse yourself, poor dreaming boy, and leave sorrow to one who has a legitimate right to it."

" Blistered be your tongue, vain babbler," cried Glenroy, incapable at that moment of endurance ; and starting up and seizing the arm of the maniac, he shook him from him with violence. " You moon-struck rambler, crazed by your own mad ambition, never knowing what it was to have a breast, to jest and jeer at me, and call me a poor boy!"

This was the unkindest speech that ever fell from Glenroy's lips ; but he was goaded by a kind of desperation, and had as little that was rational in him at that moment as the poor being before him. Evelyn trembled like an aspen in his powerful grasp, and, woefully struck by such a change in one who had ever been to him so sympathising and kind, he stood unresisting as a child, and began to weep piteously.

" Good Heaven!" cried Herbert, pierced with remorse and shame, " what have I done? I have insulted one whom the Almighty has sanctified by irredeemable misfortune. Forgive me, if you can. I know not what I uttered."

Poor Evelyn sat down on the ground, and with the humbling imbecility attendant on his calamity, continued to whine and weep. At length, pacified by the entreaties and protestations of Herbert, he suddenly rose up, and began to assume that expression of dignified solemnity, which was most habitual to him.

" Ay, ay," said he, pressing his hand heavily on his breast, " I had a heart—though it is now almost turned to stone—once warm with glad pulsations, and quick with hope and rapture. Visions of beauty flitted round me, brighter than ever visited the poet's dream. Sometimes they came of marble whiteness, then of all the colours of the rainbow. Sometimes they were a Gothic pillar, at others, a Corinthian capital. They were always five in number, a thousand times more beautiful than the Muses or the Graces. When I was dreaming, they would stand side by side by my pillow, and whisper to me what to do in the morning. Oh! I was happy! when the arch fiend—Heaven curse him—came and despoiled me of all, drove me like a wild beast, to live like Nebuchadnezzar on the grass of the field, and to drink with the cattle of the passing brook. But a day of retribution will come. I have sworn to be revenged, even if the whole valley shares in the blaze of destruction."

Thus he went on with increasing wildness, till the stormy passions of Herbert's bosom subsided, like the dark clouds floating away on the wings of the rising gale. He felt chastened and rebuked, and as a penance for the wound he had inflicted, he rambled with the brain-sick wanderer far on the banks of the river, listening to his grievances, sympathising with his sorrows, and wondering if he should not one day become a madman himself.

As soon as the scene of Miss Willoughby's memorable courtship was fairly vacated, and the echo of footsteps died softly on the grass, a dishevelled-looking head peeped cautiously over the bank, and a figure emerged from the bushes, the strangest *genus loci* that ever visited the groves of Vertumnus. A tumbled head-dress was depending from one side ; the frizzled locks were sticking out in every direction, as if each particular hair had been listening ; the robe was torn by brambles, and the feet bedaubed with mud and clay. In this strange and piteous plight, Miss Tabitha Shanks stood confessed, while the very calves that were frisking among the clover, kicked up their heels and scampered off, as if affrighted at the unexpected apparition. She first gazed around with dismay and apprehension, then put out one miry foot and looked miserably at it, then the other, then at the tattered gown, and at last groaned out, " Oh! if I haven't got a cure for listening ! another pair of shoes spoiled."

In spite of Miss Willoughby's caution, it seems she could not baffle the lynx eyes of Miss Shanks. who, somehow or other, got scent of the note, and guessed the place of its destination. Pretending to be busied with everything about the house, she was thinking of nothing but the manner of satisfying her curiosity. In tying up Sir Reginald's queue, she actually made him scream, by pulling his hair in a contrary direction, as she turned her head to see if it was Griselda, who left the room, she was so fearful of losing her track.

Among the other disasters of the morning, she knocked down his gold-headed cane, and trod on the ears of the shaggy-eared dog. This was the step too much.

" I wish, Miss Shanks," said Sir Reginald Willoughby, in no very honeyed tone, " I wish you would take heed to your steps. I believe you think your hands and feet are both zephyrs ; but my dog, as well as my queue, tell a different story."

When Griselda left the house, it did not excite the attention of her father, who was walking in the garden, in his morning gown ; nor of her cousin Alice, who was reading for the fiftieth time the last new novel to get a stock of nonsense for the day.

But Miss Shanks, after watching from the chamber-window the path she took, slipped out through the kitchen door, saying to the cook as she passed out, " if Sir Reginald inquires for me, you may tell him I have just run down into the lower garden, to see if there are any of his favourite pears ripe." With the sagacity of a hunter, she followed the track of Griselda, but fearful of being discovered, she lingered far behind till she saw her approach the shaded bank, and saw through the trees the figure of a man walking to and fro like a troubled spirit on the green. She recollected a path on the edge of the sand-bank of the river, and terminated near the spot, the centre of her present curiosity, and she thought she could snugly ensconce herself among the bushes there, and overhear all that was said, without the danger of being detected. But as she crept along the margin of the river, like a rat on the edge of a milk-pan, in imminent hazard of falling in, she found her footing so precarious, she was obliged to take a path nearer the turf, where the clay was so soft, she was in danger of leaving her shoes behind her every step. The branches thickened as she went on, and as she scrambled through every interception, her thin muslin robe caught at every step in the brambles ; and while she stood to disentangle herself on one side, her bonnet was hooked up by a crossing twig, and, like a second Absalom, she hung suspended betwixt heaven and earth, by her own abounding locks. In this manner she proceeded, as it was equally impossible to retreat, supported by the unnatural strength of curiosity, till the sound of voices warned that she had arrived near the goal of her wishes. Holding in her breath, till she almost lost the power of respiration, she remained half-imbedded in clay, concealed by the shelving bank and luxuriant underwood, listening to a secret which would have repaid her for the sufferings of martyrdom. She felt that she had Griselda, from this moment, as completely in her power, as the conqueror of millions the poor captive, who lies trembling under his chariot wheels. " Let her taunt me again with my obscure origin—let her threaten to discard me again if she dares," muttered to herself the exulting daughter of Farmer Shanks.

It is true, when she first ascended the bank, as we have described, and had leisure to contemplate her draggled appearance, the fear of detection and a fear of personal mortification, extorted from her the doleful exclamation we have faithfully recorded. She sneaked round through the corn fields and lower garden, without stopping a moment to examine the pear tree, and entering the same door from which she started forth on her momentous expedition, endeavoured to escape the scrutiny of Mrs. Dripping, the cook, by skipping up the back stairs as lightly as her clay clogged slippers would permit. Arrived at her own chamber without interruption, she was just beginning to draw the bolt, with self gratulations, when she espied Griselda standing by the window, half-shaded by the gathered folds the curtain.

" Bless my stars !" exclaimed Miss Shanks.

Griselda turned round at this salutary speech, but her face expressed no blessing upon the stars, or anything ever illumined by their beams. Her large eyes, dilated beyond their usual dimensions, rolled balefully over the shrinking form of Miss

Shanks, while her blue and quivering lips in vain endeavoured to articulate the rage, with which every feature was eloquent.

"Vile eaves-dropper," at last she uttered, giving vent to her rage.   "I missed you, and watched you stealing like a serpent among the long grass.   I know where you have been dabbled up to your neck in clay and slime, and tattered like a beggar as you were born; and if you don't tell me this moment what you have heard——"

"What then?" cried the emboldened spinster, strong in her newly-acquired power, and returning Miss Willoughby's tempestuous glances, with a cool and withering sneer.

"Why, you had better be cast at once to the bottom of the Red Sea, for not a home shall you have another night under my roof."

"Very well, Miss Willoughby, you are welcome to keep your own home and your own secret too, if you can. If I am a born beggar, which is a contemptible lie, I have other friends and other homes to go to.   Mrs. Heathwood never shut her door in my face yet, and Miss Edith Trevanion is a sweet young lady, and I

No. 20.

can tell her something that will make her laugh, I guess, if she never laughed before. He—he—he!"

Miss Shanks walked tittering towards her closet, glancing superior to the thunderstruck Griselda as she passed, who now felt but too keenly that the wheel was turned, and instead of the trampler she was to become the trampled. She tasted the first bitter fruit of transgression (surely she who disregards the dignity and delicacy of her sex may be styled a transgressor), in the degradation of the present moment. She must now fawn, where she had before imperiously governed—she must now soothe and flatter, where she had before been servilely flattered herself, or her secret would be at once revealed to all the babbling tongues in Allendale; and Alice and Edith would glory in her shame. Smoothing as much as possible her contracted brow, and subduing her regal tone, she said,—

"I don't understand you, Miss Shanks. If you are angry at what I said about listening, everybody agrees on that score, and you would only expose yourself by revealing anything learned in such a manner. I think you must value your own reputation too much to do it."

"You have become very fastidious all of a sudden," said Miss Shanks, with the same triumphant sneer. "You hadn't such mean ideas about listening last night, when I came back from Mrs. Glenroy's, and if I hadn't a kind of talent that way, you wouldn't be now secure of the handsome husband you are going to have."

"Well, well," interrupted Griselda, "let us say no more about what's passed. I know your disposition is too amiable to wish to injure me, and I really think I couldn't live without you, my dear Miss Shanks. When I am married you shall live with me, as my own sister, and you shall have a nice little chamber, all to yourself, a great deal handsomer than this. Now, promise me," added she, putting a necklace of transparent amber coaxingly around her dear friend's short thick neck, "promise me that you will never breathe a syllable of this, and I'll put no bounds to my future gifts."

Miss Shanks had not dismissed her bright dreams of matrimony, though she had as yet no encouragement from Sir Reginald, and not having a remote intention of giving up her present sinecure, unless compelled, she admired her new ornament in the mirror, and resolving mentally to draw pretty largely upon Miss Willoughby's generosity in future, she made the most solemn protestations that she would sooner cut off her right hand and throw it into burning coals, than betray the best friend she had in the universe. Griselda, secretly galling under the chains she was now doomed to wear, assumed a contented countenance, and telling her tormentor to attend to her toilet without delay, sought her beautiful cousin, that she might indemnify herself, by her mortification, for what she had just endured.

Alice was reclining on a sofa, in a loose morning wrapper of snow-white muslin, her hair unbound and wandering in beautiful negligence over her fair and partially uncovered shoulders, her eyes still riveted on the impassioned pages of the author, on which her vitiated fancy excessively doted. She pretended not to perceive the entrance of her cousin, nor changed her studied attitude, though Griselda hemmed and coughed, and at last began to sing a favourite song of hers,

"Oh! say not woman's heart is bought."

"Oh! dear Griselda," said Alice, in soft, supplicating accents, "do not interrupt me in this exquisitely interesting scene."

"You have read it a thousand times over," cried Griselda, playfully snatching it from her hands, and putting it behind her. "Do not frown, my lovely coz, I have something of deeper interest to communicate than all that book contains. You know we are like sisters, Alice, and should make confidantes of each other."

"How cruel," said Alice, languidly, "to tantalise me thus. What can you have to say, to recompense me to such a privation?"

"Well, to speak the honest truth, my dear coz, I think of being married."

"Very likely," answered Alice, with a provokingly arch smile; "but does any one think of marrying you?"

"I am too much accustomed to your sarcasms, Miss Alice, to think them of any consequence; but I can tell you there is one, whom many a fair bosom has sighed for in vain."

Alice here clapped her hands, and laughed outright, an act she was seldom vulgar enough to commit.

"Laugh while you may, proud beauty," exclaimed Griselda; her power of endurance completely exhausted by her cousin's contemptuous incredulity. "Know then, to your cost, that I am positively and solemnly engaged to no other than Herbert Glenroy."

"It is a falsehood!" cried Alice, starting vehemently from her chair; "he cares no more for you than the fly over that looking-glass. You know he loves Edith Trevanion—deeply, passionately loves her. You said yourself, after returning from the lake, you never saw two human beings so bound up in each other as Glenroy and Edith Trevanion."

Griselda did know this, yet, with that moral adultery, which, in the eye of the Infinite Purity, is a direct infringement of one of the holiest commandments, she gloried in having extorted a heartless vow from the devoted victim of filial piety and fraternal love. She had not even the excuse of passion to plead in her defence. She admired the beauty of the temple, but she was utterly incapable of appreciating the spirit that it enshrined: her soul was too gross to conceive the fair proportions of the indwelling divinity.

"I repeat it, Alice Cameron," said she; "and if you are not satisfied with my word, take my oath—I swear it. He is mine, and from henceforth I shall consider any allusion to Miss Trevanion an insult to my affection. I am going to inform papa of my engagement, and I'll leave it to you to decide whether I shall be likely to jest with him on such a subject."

"Go, then; run, fly, Griz," retorted Alice, in a scornful tone. "Tell it in Gath, and publish it in Askalon. The days of miracles are returned; gold can win, where beauty failed to charm. But flatter not yourself with a triumph over me, for I have long ceased to waste a thought upon a being so cold to passion, so dead to sentiment and feeling."

She forgot, when she uttered this, her previous remark of his deep and passionate love for Edith Trevanion. Her sole object now was to manifest her contempt of Griselda's pretended conquest, and, taking up her book, she reseated herself, humming, though in rather a husky voice,—

"There are heroes more gallant and handsome by far
For beauty to vanquish than young Lochinvar."

Griselda shut, or rather slammed, the door, and a short time afterwards her confounded and exasperated cousin saw her, with her arm twined most lovingly in her father's, walking up and down in the garden, probably repeating the same odious and incredible communication.

It is unnecessary to relate the conversation that passed between the father and daughter. Sir Reginald, though like the owl in the fable, who described her younglings to the proud queen of the air as winged cherubs, imagined his own daughter most beautiful and loveable, could not but discover that in spite of the additional attraction of wealth, she did not seem to inspire others with the same sentiments. The high respectability of Glenroy's family, his brilliant talents and manly graces, which had gained him such *eclat* in society, made it a desirable union to a man who loved distinction and show as much as Sir Reginald Willoughby. He would have been much more gratified, if he were likewise rich; but he knew that such talents as his would ere long be a revenue in themselves; and as for the present, Griselda had a plenty of her own. Very fortunately Griselda was of age, and was in full possession of her aunt's inheritance; so she was not obliged to make a full confession to her father, who gave her his paternal blessing, and received Glenroy, when he passed through that evening's dreaded ordeal, with much ostentatious and parading condescension. A more penetrating eye would have seen the proud and goaded heart of the young man writhing and twisting beneath the smiles that were lavished upon him. What ages he had lived in that single day!

After having sealed his destiny, and recovered sufficient composure to appear before those beloved beings, for whom he had sacrificed all the warm hopes of manhood, one glance at their pallid and dejected countenances gave him strength to communicate what almost blistered his lips. When Constance clung around him, with the caressing fondness of childhood, and sought to hide the tears, which in spite of all her efforts would gush forth afresh in his bosom, he bade her be comforted and dry up her tears, for her flowers should not wither beneath the tread of the stranger, nor their mother be banished from the home of their youth.

A sudden flash of joyful amazement, bright as a burst of sunlight through a murky cloud, beamed around him. He told them that a benevolent friend who had been made acquainted with their situation, had generously offered to lend them all that was necessary to satisfy Mr. Montford's demands, and had also requested that the world might never know the assistance lent. While they began to bless this unknown friend, and entreat his name, he interrupted them by saying—
'Mother, I have accepted the offer, and it must be the business of my life to endeavour to repay the obligation.

Glenroy had too much delicacy of feeling, too lofty a sense of honour, to disclose the motive of the apparently disinterested act. He would not call the wounded crimson of modesty to his sisters' cheeks, by revealing to them that it was possible for a woman to acknowledge an unsolicited attachment; he resolved to represent her conduct in the fairest admissible light, so that she might be rendered respectable and amiable in their eyes; and more than all—he vowed to himself, they should never know the sacrifice he had made for them.

"They shall believe it voluntary," he mentally cried; "they shall never know the wild passions that are struggling within me. The offering that is purified by fire must ascend unpolluted. Yes," continued he, in a deep, hurried tone, "you need not sink under the burden of gratitude; our benefactor is a woman, and I was vain enough to imagine my proffered hand would not be considered valueless by her; she accepted it at once, and vowed that an honest heart was worth more than all the gold of Peru. This friend——"

"Oh! I know—I know," exclaimed Constance, clasping her hands, with a look of extacy, almost celestial; "it is my dear, sweet, lovely Miss Trevanion! I've wished—I've dreamed."——She stopped suddenly, chilled by the expression of her brother's face. Had a dagger been plunged into his naked heart, it could not have given a more exquisite pang; but despair gives energy. For the first time in his life, he looked sternly on his young sister, as he turned from her, saying,—"Constance, your dreams are folly—madness. Repeat them not. It is to Miss Willoughby you are indebted for your present happiness. It is so strange, so sudden, so unexpected. I feel as if I were in a dream myself. Nay, Constance, I will not have another tear. Bring me some wine, for I am weary. and this day shall be consecrated to mirth."

Constance ran from the room, thinking with Miranda, that she was a fool to weep at what she should be glad of, but she could not help it, and thought she should be happier to live in a mud cabin all her days, knowing that her brother had married Edith Trevanion, whom she was sure Heaven had formed on purpose for him. than dwell in a palace and see him united to Griselda Willoughby.

Mrs. Glenroy, who had passed the glowing era of youth and romance, and looked upon life with the saddened eye of experience, believed it a holy and scriptural duty to receive the offered blessings of Providence, without murmuring at the source from whence they came. She had not selfishly dreaded poverty, but to have her children separated—the golden links of family union rudely severed—her son bowed with the burden of ther support—it was this which had bathed her pillow with tears, and weighed down her spirits to the dust.

She admired Edith Trevanion, but she knew not the mastery she had gained over the affections of her son. Though she felt the want of gentle graces in Miss Willoughby, she was not aware of all her deficiencies; for Griselda had always been particularly amiable to Mrs. Glenroy, as she could not fear her as a rival; and more than all, she was the mother of Herbert.

It is true that Mrs. Glenroy was convinced that she never would have been the object of her son's choice, and that he must have been guided by filial affection ; but the apparent nobleness of her conduct exalted her in her estimation, and she hoped that time would endear her to the heart of her son. Gratitude—deep, heartfelt, religious gratitude filled and overflowed her mind ; with eyes too dimmed with tears to perceive the strange and unnatural expression of his features, she embraced and blessed him ; and that holy blessing fell upon his soul like the dew of heaven on the dry and burning desert.

Margaret's glance pierced deeper through the folds of mystery. She had watched the emotions of Edith and her brother ; she knew that he loved her, and she did not believe that he could love in vain. She had seen so much, too, of Griselda Willoughby—her ostentatious pretensions, her obtrusive manners, her envy and jealousy—she judged her incapable of a really generous action. She understood her motive, and the magnanimous sacrifice her brother had made ; and while her heart secretly bled at the thought, she solemnly determined that she would respect his honour, and that the offering should not be made in vain.

"For my mother's sake—for Constance's sake," thought she, "I will try to be grateful ; but would to God it had been my fate instead of his to be immolated on the altar of duty !"

The next evening Montford returned, and entered the house with the air of a master. He was astonished at the tranquillity and order, unbroken by the least confusion, that still pervaded the dwelling. He had expected to have seen a disordered family, mourning over the ruin of their domestic comfort, ready to become denizens of the wide world, casting "longing, lingering looks" on the blessings of which they were to be for ever deprived.

"You did not look for me so soon, sir, it seems," said he to Glenroy ; "have you supposed my parting words were spoken in badinage ?"

"Indeed, sir, you are most welcome," answered Glenroy ; "and you are mistaken if you suppose we are not fully prepared to meet your return."

"This ease and assurance may be vastly amusing for you to assume," cried Montford, fiercely ; "but it sits upon you with a very ill grace. I am not a man to be trifled with, nor are the iron demands of justice to be baffled with in this manner. I have given fair warning—let the consequences rest upon yourself."

"Examine this paper," cried Glenroy, "before you indulge in premature exultation, Mr. Montford, and after having satisfied yourself that you hold in your hand the full amount of the sum you demand, let me tell you, sir, that the presence of a man who has so basely abused the privileges of fortune, and so entirely forgotten the respect due to an honourable family, is insupportable to me."

Montford unrolled the paper, and actually recoiled with amazement, when he beheld its contents. He at first doubted the evidence of his senses ; but it was no delusion. All that avarice, prompted by personal revenge, had urged him to command, was now within his grasp, and his dream of triumph was dissolved.

"This is strange—unaccountable," he stammered ; "very different from the—"

"Dare not question me, sir," interrupted Glenroy—"your demands are fulfilled and our intercourse is at an end. All I ask is your receipt."

Montford almost mechanically took the pen which was placed before him, and wrote the signature demanded. Since Glenroy had so mysteriously eluded his talons, his natural cowardice assumed the empire of which it had been for awhile dispossessed by the insolence of triumph, and he dwindled before the proud and commanding self-possession of the man he came to humiliate. Pocketing in silence the unlooked-for treasure, he turned towards the door.

"Stop one moment, Mr. Montford," said Glenroy, putting his hand upon the latch. "As a gentleman, and a man of honour, I am bound to resent the insulting language you lavished upon me in a former interview, when unconscious of the resources since opened to our family, I humbled myself to solicitation. But as the son of one who loved and revered your late father, who was for years his grateful debtor, I can forgive, and as far as possible forget it, if an apology is offered."

" When I am convicted of a crime, I may sue for forgiveness," replied Montford, planting his foot upon the hreshold. " I am not surprised at the multi-
p'icity of your resources. You are a most skilful alchemist, and deal in most
subtle magic."

He took care to utter the last sentence in a perfectly unintelligible manner, and
then exclaimed aloud,—

" If you wish for any further interview with me, I shall be found at the inn
till to-morrow evening." He then left the door which Glenroy closed in silent
indignation, and, in spite of the embarrassments, the bondage, the anguish of spirit
attendant on the singular situation in which he was now placed, he could not but
now feel a sensation of unalloyed gratitude towards the being who had enabled him
to free himself from the clutches of so sordid and mercenary a wretch.

CHAPTER XXIII.

Oh, vain deceit! I cannot cozen time;
    Or put off memory; never again to me,
As mirth that wakens joy, the matin chime
    Shall strike a welcome call to field or lea;
My heart no more may mov'd or melted be,
    By old accustom'd scenes and sounds, which erst
Drew tears that happiness might boast to see;
    Of peace, of joy, of comfort, all amerc'd—
Man's doom is well fulfilled, his primal fate revers'd.
                                        THE SOLITARY.

HERBERT GLENROY was seated at the window, looking attentively at his sister
Constance, who was busily engaged with her flowers in the garden, when Gilbert
Stanhope was announced. After the usual salutations of the morning had passed
between them, Glenroy requested the favour of a few minutes' conversation with
him.

As may be supposed, Stanhope had some peculiar feelings, as he followed the son
of his father's injured friend out of the parlour, which were not in any measure
dissipated when Glenroy remarked,—

" If it be not troubling you too much, you would oblige me infinitely by walking
with me for a short distance; I am anxious that we should not be interrupted."

They strolled towards the river in the direction of the glen.

" Mr. Stanhope," asked Glenroy, after some common-place observations, " what
is your opinion of duelling?"

" A singular question, my dear sir, but, in reply, I say, that I have no opinion
of it."

" Then," exclaimed Glenroy, in a very disappointed tone, " you consider it
a crime to fight a duel?"

" Assuredly not; for I should be very loth to submit tamely to an insult, and I
have as yet been unable to discover any reason why two men should not fight their
own quarrel as well as fifty thousand in another's."

" Then, I wish you would second me in a duel I intend fighting to-morrow
morn'ng.'

Gilbert, without appearing to be very much astonished, asked who was the
antagonist. Glenroy, in reply to his question, gave him the particulars of Montford's conduct towards him, without betraying his family secrets, and concluded by
saying—" I have offered to accept an apology, do you think the case admits of one?"

" I do not," replied Stanhope, in a serious thoughtful tone; " it should either
be now noticed in an efficient manner, or not at all; under present circumstances
however (in my opinion), the proper course would be to pass it by; think of your
mother and sisters."

" I have thought of them," said Glenroy, grasping Stanhope by the arm, and speaking in a suppressed voice, " and I have other thoughts too, to deter me from it—but (as he passed his hand over his brow) it is no matter; if my hour has come, it has come early, and all is well; death and honour are intimate friends—but (with a sudden change of voice and manner he again asked) will you second me ?"

" I will."

" Then, I shall trouble you a great deal ; more perhaps than I ought. Should I fall, I will commit to you the unpleasant office of soothing the feelings of those that love me ; I have also a message for you to deliver, which, as it is nearest my heart, I will not communicate to you until to-morrow; it shall be the last act of my life—all this, however, is anticipating the worst; but even if I should be fortunate, I shall, of course, be obliged to leave here, and consequently I resign my mother, Margaret, and Constance to your care; I dare say, you will have reasons for being very attentive."

" But your arrangements for to-morrow ?"

" They are few ; you need not call upon Montford, for I will merely send him a note appointing the hour of meeting at five, up the glen ; those who will be stirring at that hour will be only servants or labourers, and the spot I have selected is at a sufficient distance to prevent the possibility of an interruption."

" Perhaps, Mr. Montford will not accept ?"

" Then, there can be no difficulty : but I know he will. You will oblige me by calling on me at half-past four; I shall have a few arrangements to make before starting, which, in all probability, will detain me some minutes, and I should like to be punctual."

" You may depend upon me; but in case you should be fortunate, how do you propose leaving here ?"

" I shall prepare all ready to start immediately on horseback to Scotland, where I shall be obliged to secrete myself for a time. Shall we retrace our steps ?"

The reader will not be much surprised to learn that Stanhope's mind, during this conference, was far from being so calm as it appeared to be. A thousand tumultuous thoughts crowded upon his brain, as they turned homeward, and rendered him entirely insensible to the conversation addressed to him at intervals by his no less agitated companion. After walking some distance, they both involuntarily paused on a little elevation of the bank, and looked upon the " image of eternity."

" Mr. Stanhope," said Glenroy, breaking through the silence, in a tone that immediately arrested Gilbert's attention, " perhaps, you will think me foolish when I say that I believe you were born to be my friend ; I have already given you an extraordinary proof of my confidence, seeing that we have been acquainted but a short time, and I am now about to communicate that to you which I intended should have remained for ever within the secrecy of my own bosom."

Gilbert hastened to assure him that all his friendly feelings were most heartily reciprocated, and, anticipating the nature of the secret about to be confided, suppressed his emotions under an appearance of curiosity.

" I have obligations upon me," continued Herbert Glenroy, gazing fearfully around, and lowering his voice into a whisper, " that ought to make me play the coward even where my honour has been wounded to the quick ; bonds, before which the tender ties of love and affection shrivel into insignificance, bind me to earth, and bid me live, even if it be in infamy—all these I am to violate and break through to-morrow. I had fancied, that when the moment of trial should arrive, duty would meet with no opposition from the stubborn principle of pride ; but I find now that I have been mistaken, and if I fall, the bitterness of death will be increased by the reflection that I have wilfully despised and disobeyed the last command of an injured father."

Gilbert started.

" Ay, sir, injured by one whom he always considered his bosom friend, while his son, upon whom a sacred commission is charged, is about to expose a life set apart for that purpose, in a quarrel that might easily have been avoided. I see you are surprised ; the story, though long, may be told in a few words. My father once thought he had a friend ; they were educated together, and professed to feel for each other all the affection of which human nature is susceptible. After a lapse of some years, during which they never were one hour asunder, my father married, and fixed his residence in England ; he was then separated from his friend, as he also formed a matrimonial connexion, about the same time in Italy. After a considerable interval, Lovell (for that was his name) returned to England, bereaved of his wife, and by invitation resided with the man whom he pretended to love as his brother, and who, in return, confided his whole soul to him. Serpent-like, he stung the bosom that sympathised with his affected sorrow ; by the most infamous arts he defrauded him of his property, and attempted to seduce my mother from the path of virtue—she disclosed his infamy to her husband, and the villain Lovell fled the country."

Gilbert groaned aloud.

After a short pause, Glenroy continued,—" I see you are affected by this recital, and I will hasten to its close. When the approach of death had rendered everything indistinct before the eyes of him to whom I owe my being, he tcalled me to his side and made his last request, that I should shun the name of Lovell, and prevent the descendants of that man from ever approaching his widow or his children ; it was necessary that such a request should be made ; though but a mere boy, in the presence of my Maker, I vowed to pursue with endless hate the author of my father's ruin, and with a solemn oath I dedicated my life to that purpose. Infinite Purity, who registered the vow, beholds me now wilfully about to violate it ! These circumstances were known only to the parties interested ; the world attributed the quarrel to some trifling cause. I cherished the remembrance of it as the apple of my eye ; my family thought, and think still, that the whole occurrence passed from my mind with the excitement it occasioned—for, till now, I have never spoken of it to any human being ; but it lives in every thought and feeling, waking or sleeping, in moments of pleasure, retirement, or study, it is alike present before me ; it is the ultimate object of all my hopes, the end of all my desires ; though circumstances unconnected with it may for a time occupy my attention, still my mind reverts to it like a pendulum to its centre of motion, and ever—but I see you think this a digression. Years rolled on, and I approached to manhood. I received intelligence that Lovell had died somewhere in the north of France, leaving a son, who by the letter of my oath is to be avoided ;—you seem astonished—but, think you, when a nauseous reptile has stung me, and has been successful in its escape, that I would not crush the young it has left crawling about my feet : the offspring of this villain is in existence somewhere on the earth, and if ever I am so fortunate as to meet him, may the lightnings of heaven strike me, if he be not dashed to atoms, and mingled with the mire in which he was fostered."

Gilbert's hand was involuntarily extended towards his companion's throat, and then suddenly thrust into his bosom, as with a convulsed voice he begged him to proceed.

" You enter into my feelings as I expected," continued Glenroy, " and I am grateful for your sympathy. I hear he is now upon my own soil, and should we ever encounter each other, one or both shall hasten into that world, where it is said, the grand secret shall be revealed. This," continued he, after a pause, during which he gazed wildly on the river, " makes me shudder, when I think of to-morrow :—in every wave that rolls onward towards the shore, I fancy I can see my father's spirit reminding me of my engagements—in every gush of wind, I fancy I can hear my father's voice upbraiding me for their violation. Under ordinary circumstances, perhaps, I would fear death but little—but now I feel that it will be a solemn thing to rush into the Almighty's presence with a lie in my right hand."

" Then, why do you fight ?" said Gilbert, crushing his emotions.

" I am a man," replied Glenroy, " and so foolish a one, that I am willing to encounter eternal infamy and disgrace, rather than allow the least perceptible spot to sully my honour."

There was a pause of some continuance, and both the gentlemen seemed lost in their own reflections;—a passing cloud obscuring the brightness of the sun gave a sudden turn to Glenroy's feelings.

"My father's spirit," said he, in a mournful tone, "wherever it dwells in the immensity of space, hears me now when I say, that I prove false to him with a heavy and unwilling heart;—at this hour to-morrow," and he pressed his hand

upon his brow, "perhaps my naked spirits will be exposed to the blasts of Omnipotence's vengeance; far, far from those that love me, and weep over my untimely end. It is a bitter thing for a youth just entering upon a scene of enjoyment, which he fancies endless, to bid farwell to life, and hope, and love, together— but it must be done—though at the same time, I arraign no one; I go a willing victim to the altar. You see, Mr. Stanhope, I am not the painted buterfly the world gives me credit for being; the disguise was assuumed for some purpose, and that purpose (though not very important) has been fully answered. I have seen that which would otherwise have been completely hidden from me; a desire to have human nature exhibited in its true colours has made me do that, for which many would censure and a few applaud me, while, to-morrow, perhaps their censure and their applause will be alike indifferent, but do not allow my gloomy feelings to affect your spirits,—I fear I have detained you too long."

" Excuse me," he said, as they walked towards their home, " if I again take the liberty of requesting you to be punctual to-morrow morning; several arrangements will, of a necessity, have to be made upon the ground, as the only communication that will pass between Montford and myself, will be the challenge and the acceptance, and I have something farther to confide with you, before we proceed to meet our appointment."

" I will exert myself, in order to be punctual," was Gilbert's short and hurried reply.

The rest of the walk was passed for some time in silence. At length Glenroy exclaimed,—

" You are a happy man, and Margaret is fortunate in the esteem of one who is an honour to her. Stanhope, let us be brothers as soon as may be: to bequeath her to your care, to leave her in your protection, will be my consolation. When I am gone, she may yet find comfort; and in confiding to you the happiness of one so dear to me, I have placed a trust in such hands as will treat it sacredly. Cherish her—protect her, even for my sake——"

He was prevented saying more by the sudden appearance of his sister Constance, who had seen them through the hedge which enclosed the garden, advancing towards the house. She hastened to meet them, and immediately perceived the gloomy air which pervaded the countenance of her brother.

On that night Constance Glenroy delayed and lingered near her brother to the latest hour; but when she bade him good night, the nervous and convulsive pressure with which he held her to his bosom, together with something solemn in his parting from her, provoked, even in her placid mind, an apprehension and a woe as new as it was unaccountable.

CHAPTER XXIV.

It has a strange quick jar upon the ear,
  That cocking of a pistol, when you know
A moment more will bring the sight to bear
  Upon your person, twelve yards off, or so;
A gentlemanly distance, not too near,
  If you have got a former friend for foe.
But after being fired at once or twice,
  The ear becomes more Irish, and less nice.—BYRON.

THE ordinary and too well-deserved lamentation over the fragility of human resolutions was not in general applicable to the determinations of Herbert Glenroy, who was usually very rigid in his adherence to his purposes, whether they were of great or small importance. But it must not be supposed that his pertinacity, if it may be so called, in pursuit of designs he had already formed, proceeded from what the world calls obstinacy. Obstinacy may be defined the act of persisting in error; and the rectitude and precision of his judgment generally kept him from being in error at first, so that he had rarely a legitimate cause for breaking his resolution. Nor was he either of such a hard and tenacious nature as to resist the persuasion, and, like the cement of the Romans, only to grow the stiffer by the action of external things. Far from it ; he was always very willing to sacrifice his purposes—where no moral sacrifice was implied—to the wishes and solicitations of those he loved and esteemed. Nor is there any contradiction in this statement, though it may be inquired, how then did he break his resolutions less frequently than other people? The secret was this, and it is worth while to burden memory with it: he never formed his resolutions without thought, which saved at least one third from fracture; and though he broke them sometimes at the entreaty of others, he never sacrificed them to any whim of his own, which saved very nearly two thirds more; for we may depend upon it that the determinations which we abandon, either from a change of circumstances, or from the persuasion of our friends, form but a very minute fraction, when compared with those that we give up either from original error or after caprice.

It has seemed necessary to give this lecture upon resolutions, because Charles Montford had intended to abandon his determination of stopping at the village inn till the following day, as he expected to hear further from Glenroy. His natural cowardice returned to him, and he was about taking his departure, when the challenge from Glenroy was placed in his hands. Upon reading it a gloom settled on his countenance, and his reflections were not of a very pleasant nature.

He found a second in an acquaintance resident in the neighbouring village, and having no temporary concerns to occupy him, he delivered himself to the mental torture incident upon his situation, and passed the intervening period in all the restless anguish of uncertainty and regret, of passion and despair combined.

In the wood then he spent the better portion of the night, strolling about in restless incertitude. From sunset till about nine o'clock there had been a light refreshing rain—not one of those autumnal showers which leave the whole world dark, and drenched, and dreary; but the soft falling of light, pellucid drops, that scarcely bent the blades of grass on which they rested, and through which, ever and anon, the purple of the evening sky, and—as that faded away—the bright glance of a brilliant star, might be seen amidst the broken clouds. As the night advanced, however, the vapours that rested upon the eastern uplands became tinged with light ; and, as if gifted with the power of scattering darkness from her presence, forth came the resplendent moon, while the dim clouds grew pale and white as she advanced, and rolling away over the hills, left the sky all clear. It required scarcely a fanciful mind to suppose that—in the brilliant shining of the millions of drops, which hung on every leaf and rested on every bough—in the glistening ripple of the river that rolled in waves of silver through the plain—in the chequered dancing of the light and shadow through the trees, and in the sudden brightening up of every object throughout the scene which could reflect her beams—it required scarcely a fanciful mind to suppose that the whole world was rejoicing in the soft splendour of that gentle watcher of the night, and gratulating her triumph over the darkness and the clouds. Montford, dead to the beauties around him, still wandered on, wrapped up in his own gloomy reflections.

It was a beautiful sight on that night, as indeed it ever is, to see the planet thus change the aspect of all things in the sky and on the earth; but, perhaps, the sight was more beautiful in Allendale than anywhere around. The nobleman's park is certainly one of those peculiarly English things which are to be seen nowhere else upon the earth ; at least we venture to say there is nothing at all like it in three out of the four quarters of the globe : the wide grassy slopes, the groups of majestic trees, the dim flankings of forest ground, broken with savannahs, and crossed by many a walk, the occasional rivulet or piece of water, the resting-place, the alcove, the ruins of the old mansion where our fathers dwelt, now lapsed into the domain of time, but carefully guarded from any hands but his, with here and there some slope of the ground or some turn of the path bringing us suddenly upon a bright and unexpected prospect of distant landscapes far beyond,—" All nature and all art !" There is nothing like it on the earth, and few things half so beautiful ; for it is tranquil without being dull, and calm without being cheerless ; but of all times, when one would enjoy the stillness, and the serenity at its highest pitch, go forth into a fine old park by moonlight.

The moon, then, within half an hour after her rise, shone full into Glenmore park, and poured her flood of splendour over the wide slopes, glittering with the late ran, along the winding paths and gravel walks, and between the broad trunks of the oaks and beeches. The autumn had not yet so far advanced as to make any very remarkable difference in the thickness of the foliage ; but still some leaves had fallen from the younger and more tender plants, so that the moonbeams played more at liberty upon the ground beneath, and the trees themselves had been carefully kept so far apart, that any one standing under the shadow, except indeed, in the thickets reserved as coverts for the deer, had a view far over the open parts of the park ; and if the eye took such a direction, could descry the park keeper's cottage, situated on a slight slope that concealed it from the windows of the mansion. At the same time, though any one thus placed beneath the old trees—either the clumps which studded the open ground, or the deeper woods of the extremes, could see for a considerable distance around, yet it would have been scarcely possible for anybody standing in the broad moonlight to distinguish other persons under the shadow of the branches, unless, indeed, they came to the very verge of the wooded ground. This became more particularly the case as the moon rose higher, and the crossing and interlacing of the shadows in the woodland was rendered more intricate and perplexed, while the lawns and savannahs only received the brighter light.

Montford had reached the park, and lingered there under the shadow of a tree in the deep wretchedness of misery. He had been long sunk in his abstraction, the nothingness of entire desolation, when he was roused by hearing footsteps approaching he looked in the direction from whence they proceeded, and distinctly saw, in the broad moonlight, Gilbert Stanhope walking towards the tree against which he was leaning. He shrouded himself more in the shadow, not wishing to be seen, and as Stanhope approached, he heard him distinctly talking to himself— " 'Tis strange that after so many years," said Stanhope, " that Glenroy should still bear enmity towards the name of Lovell— Montford having heard of the connection between Glenroy and the elder Lovell, from his father, now pricked up his ears." " Little does he think," continued Gilbert, " that I am the son of that man, whom he says so greatly injured his father. I would have disclosed my name, to him, but by so doing I should have placed a bar between me and his sister, and perhaps—for he is rather hasty, might have shed his blood unwillingly."

Montford could hear no more, for Gilbert had walked some distance past the tree, so that his words were inaudible ; he now only waited till he could quit the park and get to the inn without being seen by Stanhope. He had become acquainted with a secret, which if he escaped the next morning, he intended using in a manner which he hoped would destroy the man he always hated.

*   *   *   *

I am under the impression (though it may be erroneous) that a man about to fight a duel, would look upon the rising sun with feelings of rather a peculiar nature—especially when so beautiful a spectacle is presented as the mighty orb emerging in glorious magnificence from the bosom of the extended ocean, whose surface, studded and spangled with millions of white capped billows in playful agitation, reflects and refracts the saffron rays until sky and sea seem one dazzeling expanse of fretted gold—but be not alarmed courteous reader, I am not about to enter into an elaborate description of that, to which every novel writer, since the age of novel writing, has devoted a chapter—I am anxious to be on good terms with you—therefore to proceed.

Montford's friend, whom we 7 shall call Mr. Falkland, upon fulfilling his appointment, found him unaccountably gloomy and morose ; with a bare acknowledgment of his second's presence, he insisted upon proceeding immediately to the ground.

"We shall be a great deal too early," said Falkland, in a fidgetty tone, "and will have to wait much longer than will be pleasant; it's not half past-four yet, and we can easily walk there in twenty minutes."

"Without any reply, Montford threw open the room door, and after pausing for a moment in the passage, proceeded at a rapid rate towards the place of meeting; Falkland, with a whimsically cross expression of countenance, followed, and after several unsuccessful attempts at conversation, devoted the whole of his attention to lengthening his steps, so that they might bear some proportion to the tremendous strides of his more lofty companion.

The road which they were pursuing, came down the slope of a long hill, exposing its course to the eye for near a mile. There was a gentle rise on each side, covered with wood, but this rise and its forest burden, did not advance within a hundred yards of the road on either hand, leaving between them—except when it was interrupted by some old sand-pits—a space of open ground covered with short green turf, with here and there an ancient oak standing forward before the other trees, and spreading its branches to the way-side. To the right was a little rivulet gurgling along the deep bed it had worn for itself among the short grass, in its way towards the river, that flowed through the valley at about two miles distance, and, on the left, the eye might range far amidst the tall separate trees—now, perhaps, lighting upon a stag at gaze, or a fellow deer tripping away over the dewy ground as light and gracefully as a lady in a ball-room—till sight became lost in the green shade and the dim wilderness of leaves and branches.

After a long silence, during which they nearly arrived at their place of destination, he made a last and desperate effort to attract his principal's attention, by alluding to the case of pistols under his arm.

"They are the same as an old friend of mine fought with; I was to have been his second in that affair, but I was thrown from a horse the day before, and so much hurt that I couldn't attend; just look at them, they're perfect beauties."

This appeal had the desired effect; Montford stopped, and after gazing for some time at the weapons that were displayed before him, in a hurried tone, exclaimed,—

"I will not be so cursed a fool; what need I care what a few brainless fools here may say?—Honour!—Psha!"

The pistols dropped from the hands of Falkland, when he saw his friend turn and hasten from him at a rate which would soon prevent the necessity of pursuit, and which (after the first shock was over) caused him to exert himself to the utmost, in order to overtake him.

"Montford!" said he, grasping him by the arm, while a flush of indignation passed across his countenance, "If you do not stay to fight Glenroy, I will; and afterwards have you proclaimad a coward in every town and city in England."

Montford paused; for one moment his brow was knit, and his hand was clenched, and then bursting into a loud unnatural laugh, he exclaimed,—

"Well done, my little man of the north! I thought I would succeed; an excellent quiz; a capital quiz; now, do you really believe I was trying to run away?"

"I don't know," replied Falkland, instantly recovering his good humour, but looking a little foolish, "I had no time to think—besides, you carried on the joke so well—I'll be even with you, before long, though."

They now walked on in a very pleasant and communicative manner until they reached a spot where the river, taking an abrupt turn round a salient promontory thrown out from the main body of the hills, left hardly room between the margin and the wood. On the other side of the river, which might be a hundred yards broad, was a narrow green meadow backed by some young fir plantings; and just beyond the first turn of the bank, a deep sombre dell led away to the right; while the shadow of the trees over the water, and the wild uninhabited aspect of the whole scene, gave a sensation of gloom, which was not diminished by a large raven flapping heavily up from the edge of the water, and hovering with a hoarse croak over some carrion it had found amongst the weeds.

"This is a murderous-looking spot enough!" said Montford, turning slightly towards Falkland, who had been silent some minutes, "this is a murderous looking spot enough!" His fit of absence seemed to return, for throwing himself upon the sand, his countenance again was overshadowed, and his mind again engrossed, to the exclusion of all conversation. Falkland, after a remark or two upon the "capital quiz," betook himself to his arrangements—from which occupation, however, he was aroused by the noise of a carriage approaching.

"Here they are," he exclaimed, "coming in the right way too; it was an excellent idea in Glenroy to bring a carriage—for one of the other of you will need it—I suppose—I had quite forgot it."

Montford, still remained absorbed in his reverie, but upon a shout from his companion, of "Stanhope is with him, as I hope to be saved!" he started to his feet, and having satisfied himself of the fact, in a suppressed tone, as he struck his hand upon his forehead, exclaimed,—

"Then all is over, and I suffer justly for my silly cowardice and rashness."

Falkland turned to him with a look of surprise, but all remark was prevented, for Herbert Glenroy and his second were now approaching them.

After the usual unmeaning ceremonies, Falkland opened the business by addressing himself to Gilbert,—

"As the whole of this affair," said he, " owing to the peculiarity of the circumstances, has been of a necessity informal, I take the liberty of apologising for any error that may have crept into these arrangements (handing him the paper), and request the favour of your opinion."

"They are entirely approved of," said Stanhope, speaking in rather a haughty tone (for he was by no means pleased with the professional air of his fellow second), "and I presume the more speedy we are in completing them, the better."

"Yes, sir," replied Mr. Falkland; "but one duty remains yet to be discharged, that of interference, to know if any exertions on our part (addressing himself to the principals, and pointing to Glenroy) can possibly compose this most unhappy difference."

Monford, with a sudden start, cast a glacen of singular meaning at his antagonist, but reading in his countenance (as he fancied) an expression of contemptuous defiance, he hastily resumed an appearance of indifference, and with a haughty tone of acknowledgment, answered.—

"Your interference is friendly, sir, but entirely unnecessary."

Falkland turned to Glenroy, but his look of inquiry was replied to by a formal bow, and the seconds went aside to make the final preparations.

"They are English," said Falkland, while, under Gilbert's inspection, he commenced loading the pistols, " of excellent workmanship, and belonged to my grandfather, Colonel Falkland, who, I suppose you know, was a great duellist. They have been in the service since then two or three times, and I make it a point never to go any distance from home without them. I'm afraid," lowering his voice into a whisper, " that your friend will encounter considerable risk. Montford's more than a dead shot—he hits ten times out of eleven."

"Indeed!" said Gilbert, turning, and walking towards Glenroy.

After a few moments' conversation with their principals, the ground was measured, and the parties took their stand.

The sun now broke out most gloriously, and gilded every object near them with renovated brightness. The two young men had taken their stations, as marked out for them, and here Montford withdrew his gaze from the other, and a thrill of intense agitation passed over him; while Glenroy, lifted up his looks firmly upon his antagonist, and was as suddenly calm, and wrapt in serene composure : there might even be a kindly expression floating upon his countenance.

The signal was given; Glenroy fired a second before his antagonist, his ball glanced from Montford's pistol, and entered that gentleman's side. He fell with a tremendous oath, his pistol exploding in his fall, and the ball penetrated the ground within an inch of Falkland's feet.

After a moment's pause he raised himself upon one arm, rejecting the assistance of the second, who advanced to support him, and, after muttering, "It was my presentiment—I am too weak for another shot," desired his antagonist to approach, and regarding him with a countenance, in which hate and anguish was horribly blended, exclaimed, in a voice enfeebled and convulsed with pain,—

"Do not flatter yourself that my wound is mortal; your fortune is not so ample; I will live, and live to blast you. When you shall have attained the object of all your desires, and when, fool as you are, you shall imagine that you have reached the summit of earthly bliss, I will raise this hand, which you vainly hope will be cold in death, and destruction will mar the scene of your enjoyments, and crush you beneath the fulness of my revenge."

The absence of all colour from the face, the dilated nostril, the quivering of the lips, which, though firmly set against each other, would not be still, showed what fierce emotions were struggling for the mastery with Glenroy. But he kept them down, and with a look of contempt on Montford, he turned towards Stanhope.

"Stay!" cried the wounded man, struggling to raise himself upon his hands, "stay one moment longer: you have the gratification of beholding the man who always hated you, extended at your feet; you part from me now, and think you will never see me again; but you shall—by Heaven you shall—when the blood shall be gushing from your heart—when the crime of murder is upon your head—when you are warm from the embraces of—of—of those that love you. I will laugh in derision at your agony, as you do now at mine," and he sank senseless on the ground.

CHAPTER XXV.

"Thou hast loved, fair girl—thou hast loved full well!
Thou art mourning now o'er a broken spell;
Thou hast pour'd thy heart's rich treasures forth,
And art unrepaid for their priceless worth!"—Mrs. Hemans.

I did not wish to see his face,
    I knew it could not be;
Though not a look had altered there,
    What once it was to me.

Since last we met, a fairy spell
    Had been from each removed;
How strange it is, that those can change
    Who were so much beloved!

It is a bitter thing to know
    The heart's enchantment o'er
But 'tis more bitter still to feel
    It can be charmed no more!—L. E. L.

"There never was so charming a spot as this Elm-grove," said Edith Trevanion to Mrs. Heathwood, as they walked together on the lawn that fronted the mansion, under the shade of the elms that formed a circular row round it, and whose extreme luxuriance and beauty had given name and fame to this distinguished abode.

"You remind me," answered Mrs. Heathwood, "of the ardent boy, who admired each successive season so entirely, that he wished each might last for ever.

How many times have I heard you avow that such and such a scene was the loveliest in the world, and that you would like to locate yourself in it for ever."

" I know I am foolishly enthusiastic, my dear madam, and deal too largely in superlatives ; but perhaps after a few years of discipline and experience I may learn to be as cold and rational as we are led to believe the natives of the northern regions are."

" Nay I spoke not in rebuke, but admiration," replied Mrs. Heathwood. " But, my dear Edith, you promised to tell me about your absent friend Susan Adams, of whom I hear strange reports. They say at Sir Reginald's that she has eloped with the brother of the young lady, to whom she acted as governess."

" It is false," cried Edith with animation, interrupting Mrs. Heathwood, " it is false. I know her heart too well—no, if she is gone, her father has either taken her abroad, or some unfair means have been used towards her."

" How can we account for the disappearance of the young man as well ? They can gain no tidings of him at all, and from certain suspicious circumstances, mentioned by Lady Melton in a letter to Sir Reginald, it appears rather strange that both should be missing at the same time."

It will never be known what reply would have been made to this remark of Mrs. Heathwood's, for at that moment the white gate, that opened into the lawn, turned upon its hinges, and the figure of Tabitha Shanks, like a walking note of admiration, appeared ascending the gravel path. Never did human sounds fall so discordantly on Edith's ear as the short, elaborate words of Miss Shanks, for the words of Mrs. Heathwood were still lingering there. They immediately walked into the house—it was entirely out of keeping to ask their new guest to remain with them in the garden.

Miss Shanks looked exceedingly warm, and sat down pantingly, as if she had walked beyond her breath.

"I hope Sir Reginald's family is well," said Mrs. Heathwood, somewhat alarmed at the hurry and perturbation of her manner.

" Oh, perfectly so, I thank you. They never were in better health or spirits," answered Miss Shanks, with a significant simper. " Indeed, they never had more reason to be."

" Has any joyous event occurred ?" asked Mrs. Heathwood, observing something prophetic in the wonderful vibration of the pendulum of Miss Shanks' body —her foot.

" Haven't you heard of it, Miss Trevanion ?" exclaimed she, with affected amazement. " I thought it was all over the town by this time. Haven't you heard that Miss Willoughby is going to be married ?"

" I plead guilty to just so much ignorance," answered Edith, with provoking indifference, taking at the same time a glass of water from the sideboard, without even asking the name of the favoured individual, who, in wedding himself to Griselda, was clothed in soul with the appropriate livery—sackcloth and ashes.

" Didn't you know," cried Miss Shanks, sharpening her voice to its highest key, " didn't you know she was engaged to Herbert Glenroy ? I'm sure I never was so astonished at anything in all my life."

The glass which Edith held, fell from her hand and broke, in a thousand atoms at her feet.

" You make a very foolish and preposterous jest, Miss Shanks," said Mrs. Heathwood, in an indignant tone. " If you wish to indulge in such, you had better seek auditors more credulous or less discriminating."

"I hope I may die this moment," exclaimed the indignant virgin, at being doubted, lifting up both hands with a solemnity worthy of a better occasion,—" I hope these words may be my last, if I do not speak gospel truth. What good would it do me to lose my soul, for people who would never thank me for it? Bless me, Miss Trevanion, how pale you look. Mercy on me ! she is going to fall."

Mrs. Heathwood hastily approached Edith, alarmed at her excessive paleness, when, with an astonishing effort of self-possession, Edith resumed her seat, saying,—

"It is nothing but a sudden dizziness, occasioned by drinking too freely of cold water, after our long ramble on the lawn. I am sorry your carpet should suffer for the effects of my imprudence, Mrs. Heathwood; I will go and send the servant to gather up the fragments.

Mrs. Heathwood was too benevolently polite to oppose this motion; and Edith was leaving the room with perfect composure of manner, when Miss Shanks called after her, with malicious presumption,—

"Won't you come and offer your congratulations to Miss Willoughby before long, and try to cheer up Miss Alice, who some how or other seems quite in the dumps this day or two?"

I cannot have so little respect for either Miss Willoughby or Miss Cameron, as to suppose they commissioned you to beg congratulations for the one, or sympathy for the other," cried Edith, with irrepressible haughtiness, and casting on her as she departed, a look of such eloquent scorn, as made Miss Shanks' every feature ache, and draw closer to each other, as if they were indeed capable of greater approximation.

It was some time before Edith joined her mother, who, fatigued by the walk to Mrs. Heathwood's, and whose health began to decline, was now reclining on an easy chair, regardless of the deepening beauty of nature's regal hour. Edith drew the curtains of the windows that faced the west, excluding a rich suffusion of crimson light, that mantled, as she entered, her mother's figure, and lent a warm and lovely glow to the chill whiteness of her spotless cheek.

"Do not darken the chamber so early, my child," said Mrs. Trevanion; "I do not care about gazing upon the setting sun, but I love to feel its influence. It is like the memory of other days, sometimes sweet and glorious, but always mournful, and soon covered with darkness, as with a shroud."

"I thought the glare would be oppressive," replied Edith, gathering back the folds, and seating herself in the shade.

"Glare! do you call it?" repeated Mrs. Trevanion, "I never knew anything more soft and mellow."

Edith sat silent a few moments, then declared the room was too close to breathe in, though the pure fresh air was flowing in cool streams on her brow, and waving aside the shading ringlets of her hair. It was a lovely evening—the birds were singing blithely amid the trees—the lowing of the cows resounded from the fields, —a delicious perfume from the garden was wafted through the open window. All these things spoke of peace; but there are seasons when the pleasantest external influences have a depressing effect on the mind, by painfully recalling past happiness. Edith was passing into the passage when her mother's voice arrested her.

"Edith, my child, you must not walk abroad with that flushed cheek and weary look,—you are feverish. Good Heavens! what a pulse!" taking her hand, and counting the quick pulsations of veins, which had never yet been swollen by so tumultuous a current.

"I am perfectly well, mother, but I am getting home-sick—I know not what to do."

"Strange!" cried her mother; "do not indulge in caprice, my dear Edith. In this instance, it assumes the character of ingratitude; for surely never was human being more delicately kind or more hospitable than Mrs. Heathwood. Since I have become her guest, even I, querulous and restless as I am, have learned contentment. Her considerate attentions extend to the comforts of our servant. Do not suffer her to suspect your sudden alienation."

"Heaven forbid I should be ungrateful to Mrs. Heathwood," exclaimed Edith. "For her sake I would endure anything—but—but you appeared so anxious to go to Scarborough, and you are so much better now! and Mrs. Heathwood is to accompany us. Dearest mother," continued she, throwing her arms around her, "do let us start.'"

"What does the girl mean?" asked Mrs. Trevanion of Mrs. Heathwood, who entered while Edith was yet speaking. "You hear her strange request."

"Yes! and stranger still—I back her suit," answered Mrs. Heathwood, with a smile so kind, Edith felt as if she could have worshipped her. "The weather is so delightful now, so appropriate for travelling; and I am sure the exercise would be invigorating to you. And I hope, on your return, you will allow me to claim the remainder of the visit I voluntarily shorten now for our mutual pleasure and benefit."

Mrs. Trevanion saw there was a strange excitement in Edith's manner, and though she was ignorant of the cause, she feared it had some connection with the subject of a former conversation with her, after her return from Mrs. Glenroy's. This apprehension induced her to give her willing consent, and it was soon arranged that the next day should be devoted to preparation—the day succeeding to the commencement of the journey.

Mrs. Heathwood was filled with indignant surprise at the communication of

Miss Shanks, which she could no longer doubt ; and, not being able to find any solution to the mystery, she was compelled to believe him actuated by the basest avarice and perjuring his soul for sordid dross. She could have exclaimed in the language of Scripture,—" Ichabod, thy glory is departed !" for Glenroy seemed to have realised her most exalted dreams of perfection ; and, after having witnessed his intence and evident, though unavowed, admiration for Edith, his surrendering himself to gold became more than despicable, even sacrilegious, in her eyes. She now sincerely regretted her previous conversation with Edith, in which she had penetrated so deeply into the virgin sanctuary of her young affections, and beheld the image of this unworthy idolator of Pluto's altar, enshrined amid incense as pure and holy as ever rose in the temple of Vesta. Her first care was to remove her from the scene of Miss Willoughby's insolent triumph, and the vulgar impertinence of her toad-eating friend ; and the contemplated expedition to Scarborough offered an unsuspected and inviting opening for her purpose.

That night Edith laid her head beside her mother's pillow: she lay listening to her parent's breathing, as if the pulsations of her own being depended on each throb, till she ascertained, by the deepening inspirations, that the slumbers which deserted herself, had settled on lids but seldom closed before her own. Her ideas revolving perpetually in the same circle, seemed like the swift moving wheel, to kindle by their own rapidity. Outward objects ceased to interest her—her face was flushed—the veins of her forehead swelled; and, in the hope that sleep might restore her, she tried to forget, if possible, what she could not remove. But sleep is often shy when we woo it most fervently. Edith would fain have slept ; she sought forcibly to dwell on serener thoughts, wept, prayed, almost raved ; still her ideas, with demoniac activity, alighted like bees in murmuring swarms upon the campaign of fancy multiplying—crossing each other, maintaining a constant din and turmoil, as in the brain of a maniac.

CHAPTER XXVI.

Oh ! I come not to upbraid thee,
Nor to woo thee am I here ;
Though in peril I would aid thee,
Though in sorrow I would cheer.

It will be a source of wonder,
When we part—I know it well;
Why our hearts were torn asunder,
None shall ever hear me tell.

I would peril life to save thee,
For no other do I live ;
And the love I freely gave thee,
To no other can I give.

Edith, unable to endure any longer the agony of her feelings, rose softly from the couch, and folding the sheets as lightly as the touch of the west wind on the leaves of the flower, lest she should disturb the slumberer she was leaving, she left the chamber, and passing through the corridor, through whose dim length her eye could scarcely pierce, sought a balcony which looked forth on the beautiful lawn—the rich elm-shaded enclosure described at the commencement of the last chapter. With no covering but her night-robe, she sat down in the chill night air, and baring her temples to its deadly but delicious coolness tried to recollect why she was there, and why the radiant gloom of the hour hung over her like the oppressive weight of a death-pall. Self-reproach and bitter humiliation wounded delicacy and resentment—the consciousness of wasted affections and trampled hopes—all were making fearful warfare in a bosom, whose passions had never before been roused in their strength. She attempted dispassionately to weigh the arguments which her fond fancy urged in his favour, against those which circumstances appeared to suggest on the other side. Sometimes, upon summing up the whole, she seemed to have wronged him. He had never, as she acknowledged, exhibited the slightest aversion to her company, but, on the contrary, was every day more and more assiduous in his visits—more pleased to come—more loth to depart. In his eyes, too, there was often, when the tongue remained silent, an eloquent expression, more impassioned, more persuasive than words. His features, indeed, in their free movements and transparency, seemed to betoken the utmost ingenuousness of character, and a temper too proud and impetuous to conceal its designs behind the dark scenes of guile. There was, moreover, a grandeur in his sentiments incompatible with dissimulation.

There is a rich colouring, an energy, a living power, in the pictures of grief, which none can conceive but those who have passed, with thrilling sympathy, through its sombre majestic galleries. Edith now turned back her inward sight upon the past, and was startled at the vast range and the piercing force of her own vision. Whatever she had done or suffered seemed to be represented, in vivid views, upon the imperishable ground of her fancy ; and innocently as she had lived, there were many scenes, which, when thus reviewed, she could have wished away. Until this moment, a mist appeared to have hung over the landscape of life, hiding, like a veil, the past and future, and showing only the limited horizon of the present. A strong wind, from the great ocean of eternity, had now cleared away this mist, opening a view backward and forward, boundless and appalling. The shame, the degradation of having suffered any human being to gain such ascendancy over her, bowed her proud spirit to the dust ; and then the thought that others had penetrated into her weakness, and that the base spy of Miss Willoughby would carry back the story of her unguarded emotion, stung her to madness. Throwing her arms over the balustrade, she leaned her cheek over one till the muslin sleeve was saturated with her tears. But there was so little of self in her ardent and disinterested nature, that the bitterness of feeling soon diverged into another channel, and she forgot her own self-degradation in the humbling spectacle of another's shame. The idol of moral perfection she had adored, whose divine proportions and spotless purity were the embodied Apollo Belvidere of her imagination, must now be hurled from its shrine—its symmetry marred, and its beauty defaced.

It was in vain she repeated to herself, "He never told me he loved me." Her heart denied the truth of the assertion. There are voiceless vows and unutterred declarations. She recollected the glance of his eye, kindling and flashing when it turned on her, like burnished steel in sunshine—the deep, concentrated gaze, that, darkening in its own intensity, she had so often caught rivetted upon her—the devoted attention with which he hung upon her every accent—the involuntary softening of his voice, whenever he addressed her—ten thousand remembrances dearer to the young romance of passion than all the worded professions of the universe, thronged around her, till conscience vindicated her delicacy and her pride.

The contrasted indifference and cold politeness of his manner to Miss Willoughby, whom he seemed to dislike as much as is consistent with good breeding, rendered his present conduct utterly inexplicable ; for if gold was the allurement, why had he not been earlier drawn into the snare. "Were she gifted with one womanly charm," thought she, "he might be pardoned for the base barter of himself ; but she is so rude and unlovely, so incapable of appreciating the noble, the spiritual —No! I recal the words. Sordid and grovelling as he is, I dismiss him from my esteem. True to the race from which he descends, the calculating spirit of his ancestors triumphs over strength of principle and ardency of love."

If any one is disposed to condemn the rashness and pride of these sentiments, let them be indulgent to Edith in proportion to their knowledge of human nature. Who is not unjust in moments of passion? And Edith had never been taught the most difficult lesson in the world, self-control. The pet of her father, the idol of her mother—her life had been one of unlimited indulgence, and the conscious exercise of power never yet exerted but to bless. As the violence of her emotions subsided, freed from their unnatural restraint, she became sensible of the exposure of her situation, and began to feel that her robe was damp, and her locks heavy with the dews of night. She rose with a shuddering sensation, and turning from the dark glimmer of a moonless sky, and the vapoury shades that rolled grey and gloomy beneath, entered the gallery which led to her chamber.

She thought she heard a kind of groaning sound, issuing from the farther end, but imputing it to her previous excitement, she proceeded—when the sound returned with such added distinctness that it made her blood chill with apprehension. She could discern something which looked like a white moving object, through the truly Radcliffian obscurity of the passage. Her first fear was, that her mother had awakened, and alarmed at her long absence, was seeking her, and overpowered by weakness and anxiety, was uttering those startling moans. Impressed with this idea, she quickened her steps, while the groans grew heavier, and the figure enlarged, and seemed to approach her.

For one moment superstitious terror triumphed over Edith's better reason, as her imagination was in an exalted and feverish state, and it was now that wizard hour, "when injured ghosts complain," and yawning graves are said to release their sheeted tenants, that they may haunt the abodes of the living. But determined, like the princely Dane, "to cross it, though it blasted her," she pressed on till this most mysterious object arrested her passage, and she gazed upon Mrs. Heathwood, who she perceived was walking in her sleep. She saw her wringing her hands in mental anguish, and then talk to herself; she involuntarily listened, fearing to disturb her, and distinctly heard her say,—

"Oh! how many years of penance have I suffered, with the girdle of iron around my soul, the points of accusing conscience piercing deeper and deeper into my heart." She then pressed her hands to her forehead, and exclaimed,—"Oh! the crowding recollections, the dark, imperishing memories that throng around the home of my youth, and coil like serpents amidst the roses of my native bowers. Oh! my dear unfortunate child, may I never live to see the crimes of thy mother visited on thy innocent head—an all-seeing eye has witnessed my guilt and my remorse; but thou, sweet blameless offspring of the most impassioned but ill-fated love, may'st never know how deeply I have sinned, and how bitter has been my expiation."

Bitterly did Edith reproach herself for having selfishly listened to the secrets of another, but still she watched her, till she saw her descend the stairs, and enter her own room: when Edith returned again to hers. The exercise thus taken was the salvation of her health. Had she retired to her bed, damp and shivering as she quitted the balcony, the chill might have penetrated to the depths of vitality, and consumption's "hectic wreath," hereafter have usurped the mutable roses of her cheek; but while busily engaged in watching the steps of her benevolent friend, a kindly glow was communicated to her own frame, and fearful of endangering her mother's health, she exchanged her dew-moistened wrapper for another, and at last fell asleep, with chastened feelings and heroic resolution.

The next day, when Mrs. Heathwood asked Edith if she wished to call upon her friends, before their departure, she was delighted with the readiness with which she replied that she had received too many attentions from Sir Reginald Willoughby's and Mrs. Glenroy's families, to think of leaving Allendale without some acknowledgment of their politeness.

Edith had schooled herself for the task, and she resolved to go on with it unshrinkingly—and it is astonishing what miracles exerted pride, arising from inherent dignity of character, will enable us to perform.

It was late in the afternoon when Mrs. Heathwood ordered her carriage to drive to Sir Reginald's, having been unavoidably detained beyond the hour she had specified. Griselda was excessively chagrined by the graceful self-possession of Edith, and insulted by the unwonted brilliancy of her bloom. She had been feasting her imagination on the marble statue of despair Miss Shanks had described but the fair figure before her was glowing with the warm hues of undiminished beauty.

Alice, who was enacting, like a second Cherubina, the pale, sofa-reclining heroine, was overflowing with tenderness and friendship for her interesting friend, who needed no other lesson to strengthen her in the task.   Their visit was short, and they arose to depart, to the consternation of Miss Willoughby, without alluding to the circumstance of her engagement.   She had no idea of suffering Edith to leave her without enjoying the manifestations of her hidden pangs.

"When I see you next, Miss Trevanion," said she, with a most significant smile, "I hope I shall welcome you to my own house.   It will give me double pleasure as I know Mr. Glenroy also counts you in the number of his friends."

She did enjoy the exquisite happiness of seeing Edith turn as pale as a marble statue at this indelicate address, then as suddenly rival, in depth of complexion, the crimson folds of her piano.   Mrs. Heathwood saved her from sacrificing her sincerity to pride by interrupting her reply.

"Then I must really congratulate you, Miss Willoughby," said she, continuing her movements towards the door; "I thought Miss Shanks was amusing us with a jest of her own, as I have never witnessed any of those preliminary attentions usual on such occasions.   Well, when we return I shall be looking for bridal favours and wedding-cake, as I presume you are too well pleased with your choice to incur the danger of delay."

Griselda writhed in spirit beneath Mrs. Heathwood's clear, searching glance, but she had the hardihood to answer, that she feared no danger after having received such proofs of affection.

"Thank Heaven!" thought Edith, as they re-entered the carriage; "one ordeal is over."   Her increased disgust of Miss Willoughby deepened her indignation for Glenroy's conduct and diminished her dread of the trial before her; but still her breathing became thick and oppressive when she actually found herself in the mansion associated with recollections as sweet and hallowed as ever entwined round the heart of youth, purity and feeling.

Mrs. Glenroy and her daughters were sitting in the room that looked into the garden, but Herbert was not with them.   It was one of those beautiful evenings in autumn, when the busy scenes of our existence are withdrawn,—when the descending sun leaves the world to silence and to the soothing influence of twilight. Evening has always been a favourite portion of the day with the wise and good of all nations.   There appears to be shed over the universal face of nature at this period, a calmness and tranquillity, a peace and sanctity, as it were, which almost insensibly steals into the breast of man, and disposes him to solitude and meditation.   He naturally compares the decline of light and animation with that which attaches to the lot of humanity; and the evening of the day and the evening of life become deeply assimilated in his mind.   It is an association from which, where vice and guilt have not hardened the heart, the most beneficial result has ever been experienced.   It is one which, while it forcibly suggests to us the transient tenure of our stay here, teaches us at the same time how we may best prepare for that which awards us hereafter.   The sun is descending, but descending after a course of beneficence and utility, in dignity and glory, whilst all around him, as he sinks, there is a diffusive air of blessedness and repose.   It is a scene which teaches the way we ought to go.   It tells us that, after having past the fervour of our customs, the morning and noon of our appointed pilgrimage, thus should the rest of our days set in; mild and generous in their close, with every circumstance softened or subdued, and with the loveliest hues of heaven just shedding their farewell light.   It is a scene, moreover, which almost instinctively speaks of another world; the one we are yet inhabiting is gradually receding from our view, the shades of night are beginning to gather round our heads, we are thoughtful and alone, whilst the blessed luminary now parting from us, and yet glowing with such ineffable majesty and beauty, seems about to travel into regions of ineffable happiness and splendour.   We follow him with a pensive and melancholy eye in the vales of glory, which appear to open round his setting beams, we behold mansions of everlasting peace, seats of ever-enduring delight. It is then that our thoughts are carried forward to a Being infinitely good and great, the God and Father of us all, who, distant though he seem to be, and immeasurably beyond the power of our faculties to comprehend, we yet know is about our path and about our bed, and careth for us all; who has prepared for those who love Him scenes of unutterable joy; scenes, to which while rejoicing in the brightness of His presence, the effulgence we have faintly attempted to describe shall be but as the glimmering of a distant star. If associations such as these be often the result of our meditation, as the evening of day comes on, with how much more weight and solemnity must they be felt as pressing on our hearts, when to the influence of this silent hour shall be added the further consciousness that it is also the evening of the year.

I said that Mrs. Glenroy and her daughters were sitting,—but Edith saw, with deep concern, that Constance was supported by pillows on the sofa, with an appearance of debility on her sweet pale face, painfully interesting.

"I am not sick," said she, with a kind of shadowy smile, as Edith took her hand in silent solicitude. "I was well this morning, but it seemed as if all my strength left me instantaneously; I shall be better soon, I am sure I shall, since you are near me."

Edith dared not trust her voice to reply, so much was she affected by the expression of ardent affection, glistening through the languid eyes of this lovely but fragile young creature. She remembered the hour when the sickly light of the moon fell on her brow, as the withering garland loosened, which she had twined; and the beautiful prophetic line of Waller, then quoted, came chillingly to her memory.

Neither Mrs. Glenroy nor Margaret appeared alarmed, for they were accustomed to the delicacy of Constance's constitution, and always called her their green-house plant, which seemed created to be sunned in the smile of affection, and cherished by the dews of kindness. But there is an unutterable something in the eye, that tells when the malady comes from the depths of the fountain of life, then,

————"Like holy revealings
From innermost shrines, comes the light of the feelings."

The spirit rises from its lone recesses, clothes itself in its holiest radiance and looks steadily forth on a world, from which it is ere long to be summoned. No one could be long in the presence of Constance, even in her most joyous moments, without thinking of a purer, better land. The pale violet of her eyes reminded one less of the mountain flower than the hue of heaven, and the same associations were blended with the cerulean veins, that tracked like wandering rills the fair transparency of her complexion. Everything about her breathed of purity, and yet warned you of decay; and this warning was derived from the cold consciousness that all that is sweetest and fairest of the works of creation, are at the same time the frailest and most fleeting.

Edith was so completely absorbed in the contemplation of Constance, and the reflections arising from it, that she was not aware of the entrance of Glenroy till she heard his voice addressing Mrs. Heathwood. Edith felt as if a mist were covering her sight; but she would rather have died in the effort to master her emotion, than allow any to be visible at this moment.

When he extended the customary salutations of the day to her, she was obliged to look up, and did so with an unfaltering glance, though the beatings of her heart were almost audible. Politeness required but a glance, but her previous agitation was composure to that excited by this single glance upon the face of one whom she so cruelly, but unconsciously wronged.

The wrestling of imprisoned passions for a few days, or even hours, will work a greater change on the brow of youth than the lapse of peaceful years, as the wild dashing billows of the ocean leave, from a moment's wrath, traces of desolation, the silent flow of water for ages could not make. He looked pale and heavy. His hair fell neglected on his temples, and an expression almost of sternness darkened a countenance usually remarkable for its sunniness and glow. Even Mrs. Heathwood's indignation was softened, and she almost began to believe him under the spell of some malignant enchanter. She was more than ever convinced of his love for Edith. Then why had he imposed on himself a bondage so inglorious, beneath which his spirit so visibly and wearingly chafed? The more she questioned herself, the more dense the mystery seemed; but while she was thus buried in conjecture, she did not forget that she was the self-elected guardian of Edith, and believing it would be kindness to her to shorten the scene, she mentioned the object of their visit, and the necessity of an early departure, in consequence of their contemplated journey. Constance started painfully at the mention of Edith's departure, and holding both her hands in her own,—

"Oh! do not leave me yet," she said, beseechingly. "When shall I see you again? If Mrs. Heathwood must go, I know she will send the carriage for you if it is only for my sake; I know you will not refuse me, with my head on this pillow, and my eyes looking so beggaringly into yours."

Edith felt as if a request from an invalid friend had the authority of a command, and urged in such a manner it would seem cruel to have denied it. Perhaps she was even willing to have an excuse to linger longer on the spot she had before found enchanted ground; and it is possible, the hope of penetrating into the mystery that surrounded her, might have insinuated itself into her motives of compliance.

"What shall I do?" asked she, hesitatingly, of Mrs. Heathwood.

"I know you will do that which is kindest and best," replied Mrs. Heathwood.

"Then she will remain with me," said Constance, encircling her waist with her gentle arms. In a few moments Mrs. Heathwood was gone, and Edith left by the side of the warm-hearted and affectionate being from whom she was so soon to be separated. The strong interest she had always manifested in Constance, sufficiently accounting for the seriousness that shaded her manners, was the safeguard of her apprehensive pride. So completely did she seem absorbed in the interesting young invalid, that even Margaret's penetrating glance could not discover the wound her peace had received. Herbert, who had left the room with Mrs. Heathwood, did not return again till supper was commenced, when he exerted himself, with some success, to sustain his former character of graceful hospitality; but Mrs. Glenroy's heart was beginning to be painfully enlightened on the subject of her son's affections. All the preceding day she had watched his altered countenance and abstracted air; at night she heard him walking with troubled steps, while he imagined her eyes were closed in slumber, and now she saw him with Edith, and noticed the change in his deportment towards her, from gallantry to coldness, from frankness to reserve, she experienced an aching consciousness that all was not right. She thought of her own blissful union, unclouded in love, gliding on, " like the long, sunny lapse of summer day-light," and while tears of recollecting tenderness suffused her eyes, she inwardly shuddered at the possibility that her son might be the self-devoted martyr of filial love. With her mind filled with these reflections, she turned an earnest gaze on the impassioned, yet spiritual loveliness of Edith, mentally contrasting it with the unattractive image of the plighted heiress, till she scarcely refrained from exclaiming aloud, " Alas! it cannot be otherwise."

Edith felt some very uneasy sensations as the night began to close in, and no carriage arrived, particularly after Dr. Rovington came in and said he thought the clouds were gathering for a tempestuous night. She looked anxiously from the window and saw the clouds drifting along, as if hastening each to bear a tribute to the treasury of the rain and storm. Fearing some accident had prevented Mrs. Heathwood from fulfilling her intention, and shrinking from the prospect of being detained where she was, she would immediately have started on foot, but from the conviction that Glenroy must be her escort. She determined to wait another half hour, and if her expectations were not then realised to request the attendance of the doctor. He pronounced Constance better, and attributed her amendment to Edith's restorative powers. He spoke so cheeringly, it was impossible to attach the idea of danger to any one under his influence. and though his spirits had les[s] than their usual hilarity, his presence acted with talismanic power in banishing restraint, wherever he appeared.   He begged of Mrs. Glenroy a glass of her inimitable cherry bounce, that he might have the pleasure of taking one parting

glass with Edith, for the sake of "auld l[a]n[g] syne."   Though he was gifted with one of the best hearts in the universe, he never troubled himself about the niceties of sensibility, and sometimes cast random shafts where they were least aimed.   He was as much astonished as the rest of the world at Herbert's strange engagement, after the observations he had noted, but, said he to himself, " every one to their taste, as the old woman said when she kissed her cow."   He thought he was now exercising the privilege of a familiar friend, by calling upon him to toast his chosen beatitude.

Glenroy poured out the deep red generous cordial with an eager hand, and drank at one draught, what the doctor called the cup of penitence, to its dregs. Edith actually trembled at the bright flashings of his restless eye, as again and again he filled and drained the brimming glass, and finding her situation becoming more and more intolerable, she rose to claim the services of Dr. Rovington as a protector to Mrs. Heathwood's.   Just as he was professing himself the most
        No. 23.

honoured of human beings, a sudden rap at the door, and an earnest inquiry, "Whether the doctor was there," gave warning that his professional attendance was immediately required elsewhere. He was thus compelled to transfer the intended honour to Glenroy, and took leave of her with reiterated assurances that he would see them in the morning. Edith now had no alternative. To shrink from the companionship of Glenroy would be a silent acknowledgment of his power; and convinced that she must soon meet the carriage, she bade farewell to the interesting inmates of the cottage, and it was long before the night wind dried the tears of Constance, which were left glittering on her cheek.

They walked fast and silently on. Edith anxiously listened to catch the sound of rumbling wheels, mid the hollow rustling of the gale through the distant trees. Not long after, this was succeeded by the ominous sound of distant thunder, heralded by quick, vivid flashes of lightning, that severed the gloom of the congregating vapours. Glenroy entreated her to return and wait till the shower was over, but her apprehensions respecting her mother were becoming so intense, all other fears were weak in comparison, and she expressed so earnest a desire to proceed, he no longer attempted to dissuade her from her purpose. There was something in the dark magnificence of the scene congenial to the feelings of those who walked through the shades. The grey sweeping of the clouds rolled heavy and grand, till they folded themselves up, like a warlike banner in the west, ready to be unfolded at the storm-spirit's will— the dazzling pomp of the lightning as it spanned with a fiery, evanescent chain, the leaden-coloured arch, or covered the heavens with one mantle of pale glory, the deep voice of the thunder, the prophet of the skies, all formed a kind of dreadful harmony, to which the tone of their spirits thrillingly responded. The effort of speaking was unnecessary. Their silence was unheeded amid the solemn eloquence of nature. But soon the clouds gathered their strength with fearful rapidity, the rain began to fall in those big, splashing drops, peculiar to the summer shower, and still the dazzled eyes of Edith watched in vain for the approaching carriage.

"How rash I have been!" she exclaimed, compelled from exhaustion to slacken her speed, while the increasing rain, from which Glenroy in vain endeavoured to shelter her, was fast drenching her light mantle and driving heavily against her face.

"None but a madman, like myself," cried he, "would have permitted you to have ventured abroad under such a heaven as this. You cannot, you must not proceed; we must turn back to the nearest place of shelter, for the common is before us."

Just as he spoke, a burning flash illuminated the portico of the old village church, that stood in the centre of the very common they were now passing. It seemed like an immediate ray from heaven, pointing out this spot of sacred refuge from the bursting storm.

Without waiting for her consent he directed their course to this sanctuary, and in a few moments they stood alone in the blazing darkness, beneath the hallowed arches of the portico of the temple, which, though now superseded by one of ampler dimensions, and nobler architecture, was still venerable from association, while, as if in fulfilment of ancient prophecy, the Almighty seemed bowing the heavens, and coming down over the spot once consecrated to his earthly praise.

Edith, breathless and weary, incapable of sustaining the weight of these solemnities, leaned heavily against the damp side of the archway, while the incessant glare of the lightning, quivering on her face, showed it of a colour as pale as the white wall that supported her. Till now Glenroy had steadily persevered in the only line honour permitted him to pursue. He had avoided her presence, and removed himself from the sound of her voice, and the glance of her eye, as indulgences from which the flaming sword of duty guarded him; but destiny seemed resolved to triumph over the stern dictates of prudence and honour. Providence had united them at this moment, so lone and august, in a spot hallowed by the memories of religion—had thrown her upon his sole protection, in a spot before which the strength of manhood often quails, being one of the grandest manifestations of divine power and elemental vassalage.

It seemed as if they were alone in creation—that the voice of nature and truth was alone heard through the gloom, where she, the object of all the unwasted tenderness and ardour of his glowing youth, stood pale, and apparently sinking before him. For a moment he forgot his extorted vow, its bitter consequences, the moral barriers that separated him from her, and yielding to the irresistible impulse, he threw around her his shielding arms, and called her by all those dear and impassioned names the eloquence of love has taught its votaries.

The oblivion might have been mutual, but the unslumbering guardian of her soul's rectitude did not prove faithless to its trust. Her exhaustion was forgotten in her pride, and, liberating herself from his arms, she proudly asked him,—

" By what right has he dared to humiliate her by such protestations, and desecrate in such a manner the walls that sheltered them ?"

" By the right of despair," cried he, recalled at once to himself, and smitten with remorse and horror by the recollection of his guilty rashness. " Forgive me," he continued, " I did not mean to pain you ; but there are times when I know not what I say—what I mean."

Edith could not speak, but she motioned to be gone. Glenroy's agitation seemed little less than her own ; but he still held her hand, and several times attempted to speak, but emotion choked his utterance. At last he said,—

" Edith, this state of things is not to be endured—I would fain speak to you— tell you of what I have suffered since. No, Edith, you must hear me—dishonoured as I am in your eyes—cold and estranged as you are become—it's but justice you should hear me."

" I have nothing to hear," said Edith. " You have sealed your own destiny. Passion and deceit are alike sacrilegious here."

" I have indeed sealed it," he bitterly replied ; " and I have now lost all that dignified it—the consciousness of my own integrity. But you have to hear me exculpate myself from the very suspicion of cold-blooded perfidy. My crime—if crime it was—was an involuntary one ; so was the avowal of it. I cannot recal it —the words have gone forth, and are registered in heaven's record. Here, beneath God's own temple—blasphemy, as you call it, perjury, if you will—I have told you that I loved you. I thought that death itself could not wrest the secret from my bosom, but I have been mastered by a power, controlling and uncontrollable. I had been more than man to have resisted the agony, the omnipotence of this hour. I have been tried beyond endurance, and remorse is now added to my bitter portion. I would have died a thousand deaths rather than have wronged you, Edith. Would to Heaven," he exclaimed wildly, " would I had died, rather than have lived to suffer as I do."

" Why recur to what has passed—to what cannot be recalled ?" said Edith. " I scorn to deceive you, sir,"—and all the native pride and frankness of her nature rallying round her heart, and buoying it above even the fear of the surrounding elements,—" I scorn to deceive you ; you know it. I *could* have loved you, as woman seldom loves. I *could* have returned all you now dare to profess, for I believed you above all base and sordid passion—superior to hypocrisy and avarice. I would have considered gold as dust, when weighed in the balance with a true and faithful heart. But it is past, sir ; you have forfeited even my esteem, and my forgiveness can only be purchased by everlasting silence on a subject which never should have profaned this sacred shelter."

" Edith, I would yet ask you to forgive—to forget"—(he stopped, and paused in extreme agitation, then proceeded)—" to suffer me to expiate, by a life devoted to you, the involuntary error into which I have fallen."

The pride of woman for a moment mantled Edith's pale cheek with a deep glow at this proposal, and she remained silent ; but it was plain her silence was not that of doubt or timidity, but of deeply-wounded feeling. Glenroy's colour also rose. " If there is more you would have me do, and that I can do, speak, and it shall be done."

"You might have spared me this, had you known me better," said Edith; "such professions must be painful to you—to me they are degrading."

"Degrading !" and he paused for a moment, "I would not renew it, madam,'for the wealth of worlds," and the conviction of being high above the sordid motives she ascribed to him, imparted to his manner all its native dignity. "Your indignation is just : I have acted like a madman. But there is one charge of which at least I am innocent. Mercenary! All the coffered gold that misers ever told could not tempt me from my allegiance to nature and truth. Yet how can you think otherwise ? I cannot vindicate myself if I would ; and I must bear through life, the chilling burden of your contempt."

A human voice rose at this moment, with a wild distinctness on the wailing gale. So sudden and startling near was the sound, it seemed as if it issued from the lonely aisles of the church, to rebuke the beings who dared to disturb the echoes of the deserted sanctuary, with the accents of earth-born passion. Their eyes simultaneously following its direction the crinkling flame revealed a tall, dark figure, standing beneath an elm, that overshadowed the building, and stretching its arms towards heaven. By the fantastic habiliments, the maniac gestures, and black gipsy locks, streaming back from his uncovered head, they recognised the unfortunate Evelyn, so singularly associated with their first meeting, and now ominously breaking on their parting hour.

"There, there," raved he, shaking his right hand towards that point of the horizon where the idol of his frenzied imagination was defined on the dark background of an angry sky ; " the arrow comes winged from the bow of the Almighty. Its point is dipped in unquenchable fire. Ah ! ah ! it is passed. But another shall come, for the quiver of vengeance is full. Yes, the oppressor shall be oppressed, for it is sworn. In the blackness of midnight I had a dream, and laughed till the echoes answered. I saw an army of thunder-spirits, in chariots of sulphur, and with banners of wind, and I marched at their head—and we sat on the roof of that house, and it rocked like a cradle. Then we took a bolt, hissing hot from the forge, and shouting,—the destroyer shall be destroyed, sent it smoking through his heart. It is coming, but not yet. The mansion is cursed,—all that belongs to it is cursed,—for the prayer of the injured is heard, and the doom of Gomorrah is over the land."

"Cease, cease, blasphemer," exclaimed Glenroy, rushing from the side of Edith to the spot where the maniac breathed forth his anathema. "What have I done that you arrogate to yourself the right of omnipotence, and wither me with your curse ? Hence, boding raven, if you would not make me a raving dotard like thyself." The frenzy of Evelyn, which was always dreadfully excited by electrical phenomena, even in its wildest vehemence, was invariably quelled by the voice of Glenroy.

"I uttered no ban against thee," he answered, in a subdued and mournful tone; "I told but the doom that was given. Alas! what have *you* to do with the wicked ? You are the only being who ever pitied my sufferings, and offered to relieve them. No, no, the poor despised outcast blesses you, when no one but God is near to listen."

He paused, weeping and sobbing, for as the violence of the tempest subsides as the rain-drops fall, his paroxysms of frenzy usually melted in a passion of tears.

"Surely," thought Glenroy, "this man is ordained to chasten and rebuke me. Come, poor wretch," he cried, taking his unresisting arm, and leading him into the vestibule, "come to a safer shelter."

The rattling of wheels was now distinctly heard through the abating tumult ot the elements ; a carriage was seen rapidly advancing, and it needed nothing more than the form mounted on the coach-box to identify it as Mrs. Heathwood's. The coachman, upon hearing his name loudly called from the church, with the natural feeling of superstition, thought at first it was a supernatural summons, and instead of slackening his horses, he plied his whip most merrily. His terror was not diminished, when a figure, which seemed to have dropped from the clouds, stood near the horses' heads, like the spectre in the vision of Marmion, and commanded him to stop. He was at length made to understand, that Miss Trevanion was waiting for him in the portico of the old church, and that he must drive up to its arches.

"Tell me," cried Edith, scarcely waiting for the steps to be unfolded, and springing in before Glenroy could proffer his aid, "tell me what has happened? is my mother ill? is Mrs. Heathwood sick? or have I been forgotten?"

"No such thing, Miss," answered the sturdy coachman, shaking the rain from his garments with no very gentle motion. "Misses is well, for aught I know, and so was all the rest, when I left the house. But there's a plank broke in that bridge yonder, and I was obliged to come a long way round."

Glenroy, after having warned the coachman to drive very slowly and cautiously, closed the door of the carriage with a silent bow ; the coachman's whistle went piercing through Edith's ear, who, conscious of her security from observation, threw herself back on the solitary seat, in an agitation of mind which baffles description. She felt as if the scorching lightning had passed over her naked heart, so blighted and withered were its young green affections, just too as she began to be conscious of the sweetness of their bloom.

The coach stopped at Elmgrove before she was aware of it. The door was opened, and the lights streaming from the windows of the house shone full upon a figure, standing by the steps ready to assist her, whose lineaments could never be mistaken.

"Why and wherefore, sir," cried she, forgetting in her amazement that the rays reflected on him also trembled on her own agitated countenance, why have you done this?"

"You would not refuse me the privilege of walking near the carriage as your protector, since I had not the presumption to claim a higher," replied he, with a look of sad yet proud humility.

In spite of Edith's just resentment, she could not but be pierced by the thought that he had thus exposed himself for her, in a night when she would have pitied her "enemy's dog," where he houseless; and hastily extending her hand, she exclaimed, "This is cruel—unnecessary. I needed no protection."

Glenroy did not answer. The hand he took was as cold as a wreath of snow, and he silently prayed that it might be the last time that he ever held it within his own, since he could not retain it for ever.

"You will not walk back," said Edith, as soon as they had reached the threshold. "The coach is entirely at your command. I cannot suffer any farther exposure of your health on my account."

"Health! repeated Glenroy. "The elements are impotent without; when the storm is raging within, Miss Trevanion, there are but two things in this world that I ask ; to believe that you can forgive me—and then—to forget you."

"I do forgive, with my whole heart," said Edith with emotion.

"And the proof?" demanded Glenroy, bitterly.

"That I wish you all happiness," said Edith in a faltering accent ; and, unable to restrain her tears, she was again moving away.

"Stay, Edith," cried Glenroy ; "we must not—we shall not—part thus. 'Tis mockery to talk of happiness to one so wretched as I. My happiness must ever be involved in yours"—his tone softened, and after pausing for awhile, he said, "Edith, 'tis best for both that we should part—at least for the present. Hearts once so dear —still so dear to each other—Edith we are still too much, and yet not enough to each other—if the time should ever come"—He stopped, for he would fain have added, " when we may be more;" but his lips refused to utter so false a supposition—" should the time ever come, Edith," he added with confusion, "when your present sentiments may change—" Edith could not speak, but she waved her hand to repel such a supposition—"At least you cannot prevent me from thinking it *possible* they may," said Glenroy—" God bless you Edith !" A tear was in his eye as he held her hand in his, and looked anxiously, fondly, upon her, as though he waited her parting word. Edith's breast heaved—her lips moved—but no sound passed them. She felt her fortitude giving way but she made a strong effort, and said, with the calmness of agony,— "May you be happy !"   He wrung her hand in silence ; and thus they parted—under what different circunstances again to meet !

Edith hastily closed the door, and not daring to appear before her mother, in such agitation, yet shrinking from the presence of Mrs. Heathwood, she stood irresolute, when Mrs. Heathwood herself came into the ante-room to greet her.

"Do not come near me, Mrs. Heathwood," cried she, retreating from her approach, "I shall chill you to death.   I am drenched with rain.   Let me but throw off these wet garments."

She endeavoured as she spoke to untie the ribbons of her bonnet, but her hands were powerless and the knot was only more closely drawn.   Shocked by the tremulous tones of her voice, and the trepidation of her manner, Mrs. Heathwood drew near in spite of her prohibition, and Edith was compelled to look into her anxious and searching eyes.   She felt as if they could read into the depths of her soul, and unable to resist the impulse, she threw her arms around Mrs. Heathwood's neck, who felt, with inexpressible concern, that other drops than those of the chill night-shower moistened the lace that covered it.

"Ask me nothing now," cried Edith ; "to-merrow you shall know all my weakness, and all its excuse."

CHAPTER XXVII.

"Yes, we must part, since fate has so decreed it,
  And far I'll rove, my fettered heart to free ;
For love should die when hope no more can feed it,—
  And I as yet too fondly think on thee.

Nor think that I'm in search of pleasure roving !
  By thee unshared all joys are vain to me ;
I go in hopes, the power of absence proving,
  I, with less pain, may learn to think on thee.

Judge by thyself, where'er the past recalling,
  Thy pensive memory fondly turns to me ;
Judge by thy tears, in spite of manhood falling,
  What I endure whene'er I think on thee.

But Heaven forbid that thou, like me, shouldst languish !
  So well I love, from selfish views so free ;
I wish thee, Henry, ne'er to know such anguish,
  As tears my heart whene'er I think on thee."

"WELL," said General Trevanion, addressing himself to his wife that evening, ' I know not how it is, but our house is broken up, love ; and, instead of gathering together, as formerly, round the tea table, or the fire-side, we fly each other, hide our thoughts and are unhappy."

"Indeed, Trevanion, you wrong me," answered his wife, " Edith only is changed."

"True, true.   Or rather, she is the cause of change in us : for we are none of us the same.   From the day she first sat upright on my knee, and smiled in my face, until now, I have always looked forward with a sadness and shrinking to the time when, by marriage or otherwise, my child should be removed from my side, and her voice no longer be heard around me, like the echoes of my youth, making my heart glad, and rendering musical the funeral tramp of years.   That house, my love, is desolate, from which the children are departed, each his own way, to be lost to each other among the tumultuous crowds of the world, and never perchance to meet again.   And, long after they are gone, the father's ear listens tremblingly for their well-known footsteps, and, as he paces to and fro, instead of their light and springy tread, hears the dull and joyless sound of his own feet, he first feels the touch of death, and like the last solitary tree of the forest, almost longs for the stroke that shall render him insensible to the loss of those in whom he once delighted. Such have often been my thoughts; but, trust me, I never foresaw that we should be disunited while yet together, and that want of confidence, not distance, should draw between us the line of separation."

"Oh, Trevanion!" replied the mother, bursting into tears, "let us hope this is only temporary. Nothing has and nothing shall be wanting on my part, to restore the happiness of your fire-side. Hitherto Edith has obstinately concealed the cause of her sadness, whatever it may be, both from myself and Mrs. Heathwood."

"I will go to her," said the General, "and bring her hither. This, were it in my nature, is not a time for harshness. To-morrow, or some other day, when she shall be more calm, I will reason with her, and prove the folly of keeping aught secret from her parents."

So saying, he rose from his chair, and sought his daughter in the library. Edith, when he entered, was sitting beside the table, on which her elbow was resting, with her fingers pressed upon her temples, as if to still the violence of their beating. She heeded not the opening of the door, but was suddenly startled by something touching her hand as it hung lifelessly by her side; on perceiving her father, she started from her chair.

"My dear Edith," said he in a kind soothing tone, "why are you thus sad and lonely? Have I, by any lack of paternal tenderness, lost your affection, my child? Or do I seem, in any other way, to have forfeited my right to sympathize with your sorrow, or avenge the injuries which any one may have offered you?"

"Oh, no! dearest father. I revere you next to my God. But bear with me a little while. My thoughts are exceedingly troubled—I am sick at heart; the world seems no longer what it was. But, press me not now. I am very, very much disturbed. Hereafter you shall know all."

"Well, I shall not press you, Edith. But come and join us in the drawing-room. Your mother expects you."

"Nay, excuse me to-night."

"No, no. A little talk will cheer you. Come, take my arm, child."

"I beseech you, father, excuse me this once. I will never disobey you more."

"Why, you have never, that I remember, disobeyed me in your life, Edith, and I am persuaded never will."

"Thank you, dearest father, for that testimony," said Edith, throwing herself on his neck; "it lightens my heart—indeed, indeed it does—and I have need, at this moment, of some comfort."

"Child, child!" said he, striving to command his feelings, "say no more. Kiss me, and go to bed. To-morrow, if you will, we will proceed to Scarboro'; and, never mind—there shall be company, and the change of scene will divert you. Now, ring for your maid and go to bed. Good night. God bless you!"

"A thousand, and a thousand blessings on you, my father. Good night!"

And her heart was rent, for she saw the tears on his cheeks, as he turned away, and marked the broken trembling voice in which he blessed her. Her maid answering her summons, she retired to her own chamber, and immediately dismissing her, resolved, in the softened temper in which her mind now was, to write to Glenroy. He shall know me for what I am, by my own confession, hereafter, if we should ever meet again, he must come to this knowledge, whether I desire it or not."

While this inclination prevailed, she wrote a few sentences, indistinct, blotted, illegible; like the writing of extreme old age. Then, pausing suddenly, she cast away the pen, and rising from her seat, paced the room in violent perturbation. Her hands burned like those of a person in a raging fever, her heart palpitated and fluttered in her breast, and the big drops of perturbation, wrung forth by agony, stood thick on her brow. "Idiot that I am," she exclaimed, "that by self-humiliation and submissiveness would recal the past—for such, it is clear, is his love for me. What would he say, on receiving such a letter? perhaps, if in a gentle mood, he would pity me; perhaps, he would laugh, and show my fond raving to Miss Willoughby. Oh! let me die, ere it comes to this. Let me see, how move the hours. Ten o'clock. No more! Why, it seems an age since we parted. Yet the flame hath scarcely devoured an inch of yon taper, and what a world of agony I have endured! And how long may I live? Sixty or seventy years, perhaps, and wretched all the while as now—an unmarried woman—a thing forsaken and despised—a mark for the rude and jeering world to point the finger at; while the whisper goes round that Glenroy thinks of Edith Trevanion only as a wild girl, whose heart he once played with for amusement.''

"I will write: 'twere well he knew that I am no longer the dupe of his feigning. I will reproach him with what I have sacrificed, with what I have undergone; I will draw,—wherefore should I not?—a parellel between this form and face, and those for which they have been scorned; he shall learn the extent of my contempt for his dishonourable conduct; and my resolution, even at the hazard or sacrifice of my life, to be revenged. Yes, vengeance—the destruction —the perdition of both; nothing less can satisfy my fierce resentment. Vengeance!—what, on the man I loved?—Nay,—oh, break, my heart!—on him whom I still, in spite of all, most passionately love? No, no, no! Let me rather die. Do I not own it to him that my heart ever felt the warmth of passion? Till I saw him I was no better than an image. My life was posting by in one profound unbroken sleep, and I might have descended into the tomb without waking, had he not appeared, and with his sweet voice roused me from the trance. Vengeance! oh, no—let the dark thought be for ever erased from my mind, and the moment accursed in which it was convinced. Can love and revenge dwell together? Can heaven and hell exist in the same breast?"

She knelt by her bedside, and prayed to her Maker to strengthen her in this hour of trial. She prayed long and fervently; and then tried to forget the past in sleep.

To a mind so excited as hers had been, it was not the daily routine of common duties and petty cares that could fill that aching void, that desolation of heart, which, of all human miseries, is perhaps the most insupportable.

*   *   *   *

Though it would be tedious to describe the minutiæ of a journey, during which, the horses were monotonously steady, and the roads uninterestingly smooth and safe, the ride along the celebrated Scarborough beach, that leads to the principal hotel, may constitute an exception to the general remark.

Owing to the debility of Mrs. Trevanion, they had divided the journey into several days, for the weather was most oppressively sultry, and the sun poured down his burning noon-day beams, with all his intensity and power. There was that quivering heat and brightness in the atmosphere which every one has felt and seen when panting under the fervour of a summer sky, when not a cloud softens the dazzling depth of blue, nor a gale flutters through the languid foliage, and each expanded and transparent particle of air seems to shine with a trembling consciousness of its individual existence. Our travellers arrived at Scarborough on the afternoon of one of those fervid days, and the cool sound of the tide, as it flowed gently up the beach, with the refreshing breeze that came softly fluttering over the sparkling waves, had an instantaneous influence, both soothing and exhilarating. The clear sea green of the waters was here and there tinged with the roseate reflection of the western sky, whose sultry glow was given back with a subdued willow tint, beautiful as the lights of memory through the mists of time; and the snowy wreaths they caught up and sported in their refluent motion, lit up by the same oblique resplendence, resembled the diamond crest of royalty. The eye, dazzled by these occasional flashes, sent its glances over the far-beaming expanse, but wherever it turned, it met the brilliant coruscations sparkling over its bosom—the glorious but evanescent jewelry of the ocean.

Edith felt a thrill of strange delight, as she gazed on the loneliness of the scene, whose wild sublimity was far more in accordance with the gloomy excitement of her feelings, than the fair smiling valley she had left behind ; and, leaning from the window, she repeated to herself, with a slight alteration, these magnificent lines :—

" There is a pleasure on the pathless deep,
  There is a rapture in the lonely shore ;
There is society where none intrude,
  By the deep sea, and music in its roar."

And now she felt as though her destiny was sealed. Never more did it seem could her heart awaken to the love of aught that life could bestow. The idol her imagination had fashioned, had fallen ; but even while it lay in shivers at her feet, still her fond credulous heart had unconsciously hovered amid the broken fragments, in the vain hope that the image it had so adored might again rise, to receive the homage of a still enslaved soul. She felt her trials, but she no longer felt them as the cruel mockings or wayward caprices of chance or fortune ; for now she believed that all human trials, painful as they may be in their endurance, transcient and perishable in their existence, are nevertheless designed by Divine wisdom to exercise a purifying and a permanent influence on the immortal
No. 24.

soul, by bringing it to seek happiness in Him who alone is the fountain of happiness, and with whom it is destined for ever to dwell.

> " Oh sacred sorrow ! by whom hearts are tried,
> Sent not to punish mortals, but to guide ;
> If thou art mine, (and who shall proudly dare
> To tell his Maker he has had his share ?)
> Still let me feel for what thy pangs are sent,
> And be my guide, and not my punishment."

With this prayer at her heart, and in the discharge of the daily duties of life thus passed the even tenour of two, to her, long months ; until her thoughts were called home by the arrival of a packet from Allandale, in which was a letter from Constance Glenroy to her.

Leaving for the commencement of some future chapter the letter from the beautiful enthusiast, we will again return to Graham and his daughter, leaving for awhile the fair valley of Allandale, and the destinies of the unhappy Glenroy.

CHAPTER XXVIII.

> " Famine, despair, cold, thirst, and heat had done
>   Their work on them by turns, and thinn'd them to
> Such things a mother had not known her son,
>   Amidst the skeletons of that gaunt crew ;
> By night chill'd, by day scorched, thus one by one
>   They perish'd, until wither'd to these few."

SUSAN, on recovering her senses, beheld the clear firmament above her ; she was still on the raft with her father and Jones, floating peacefully upon the bosom of the vast ocean. The two men looked at each other—the very gaze of despair was appalling to her : as far as the eye could reach, no object could be discerned ; the bright haze of the morning added to the strong refraction of light ; one smooth interminable plain, one endless ocean, one cloudless sky, and one burning sun were all they had to gaze upon. The raft lay like the ark in a world alone ! They had no oar, no mast, no sail—nothing but the bare planks and themselves, without provisions or water. They lay upon the calm ocean, hopeless, friendless, miserable. It was a time of intense anxiety ; their eyes rested upon each other in silent pity not unmixed with fear. Each knew the dreadful alternative to which nature would urge them. The cannibal was already in their looks, and fearful would have been the first attack on either side, for they were both brave and stout men, and equals in strength and courage.

"Father," said Susan timidly, " you see God could preserve us."

An ironical smile was Graham's only reply.

" All danger from storm is past," said she, pointing to the skies.

" But death is still beneath us," said he, looking upon the sea, as the dark and pointed fins of three or four sharks, were seen gliding above the surface of the water, and in so fearful a proximity to their persons, as to render their situation on the low spars, over which the water was washing and retiring at each rise and fall of the waves, doubly dangerous.

Susan cast her fair arms around her father's neck.

" In the name of Him who sees our smallest actions," said she, in a supplicating voice, " grant your child the first favour she has asked of you : dearest father, let us pray together."

When a man has grown old in crime, and hackneyed in the ways of evil, the voice of his conscience is stifled ; but in the early days of life, after the first crime, remorse has an agonising effect. A fearful struggle rages in that bosom where the Prince of Darkness disputes his prey with Heaven—a hellish contest tekes place in the human heart, like a frightful abyss.

Graham's eyes wandered—the horrible fantasies of delirium passed before him; then a void, darkness, and shadows, succeeded them—he was deeply oppressed.

"Pray!" he cried, "and to whom? the Immortal Exterminator. No, never." He hid his face in his hands. He endeavoured to steel his soul, and seemed to dread any soft emotion like the forerunner of disaster.

A long silence now ensued, which was at length broken by Jones, who said, "'Tis a bad business, captain, a very bad business indeed! I think I am sorry I had not fallen in the battle, with some of our brave fellows, and then I should ever have known the misery of this moment."

"It is, indeed," said Graham, "here we are, doomed to die of thirst and hunger! —nothing to eat, Jones, nothing!"

The word "nothing" was repeated by Jones, who pausing for awhile, exclaimed, "Well, well, many's the ship that floats upon the sea; so that if one of us can but live a little—and I dare say we can find food for two—why, then you know your daughter may be saved."

"Food for two!" re-echoed Graham, and advanced a little to Jones, with a look of savage determination. Both understood the allusion: there was no doubt but that they could have outlived the day without resorting to the last resource! but they stood afraid of each other. Although not driven to the alternative, they anticipated the worst results! they could not both long survive the awful situation in which they were placed. If no ship passed within four-and-twenty hours, it was evident that one must have been murdered to save the others.

The hours glided away, and Graham passed the night in dreadful alternatives of fear and hope, tenderness and fury. The stars faded and morning appeared. Not a breath stirred! no shore was to be seen! the sun rose, and soon from the high south it darted its burning rays upon the unsheltered pair, who seemed abandoned by all nature. The ocean slept in lethargic siumber—the blue of the sea blended itself afar off with that of the horizon. All around the unfortunate beings was dread and silence, No food, no refreshing water, no help, not even a cooling breeze. The hot sun shed its penetrating fires upon the exposed head of Susan. Her dazzled and glazed eyes could not bear the bright beams, nor the brilliant reflection of the boundless ocean's waves; she clung for support to the stump of the broken oar which had served for a mast. With the mist sublime courage Susan, though borne down by the excess of her sufferings, uttered not a single complaint. She was afraid to increase her father's sorrow by displaying her own; she wished for darkness that it might hide her sufferings from her father! for a wild blast, that it might prevent him hearing those last sighs which nature might wring from her. The salt water she had drank, and at which her stomach revolted, had scorched her inside, and thirst added its tortures to those of famine.

Who could paint the horrible agony of Graham? all the punishments of hell were at once within and around him, raging in his soul, and spread before his eyes. He ground his teeth with rage, but turned aside his head, that his companion might not behold his despair; he dared not open his mouth, lest blasphemies should escape him, and his daughter, who was still more to be pitied, should load him with her expiring curse.

In all times of tribulation and danger, men turn their thoughts to their Maker and earnestly solicit that support for which, when in health and security, they omitted to pray. There is a delightful calm which generally comes over the mind of the hardened, after they have been induced to pray for support and forgiveness; and few there are who, having once experienced the consolations of religion, totally abandon it afterwards.

Jones fell upon his knees, and, lifting his clasped hands to Heaven, silently began his prayer. The throb of religion reached the heart of his companion, who, fearing to approach the only human being he imagined was now alive with him on wide waste of waters, knelt down at the extremity of the raft; and thus in silence the joined with his prayer for support, and a happy issue out of all their afflictions.

The sea was as smooth as a looking glass; and, saving now and then, the slight cats-paw of air, which ruffled the face of the water for a few yards, all was calm and hushed. In vain they strained their eyes—in vain they turned from side to side to escape the burning rays of the sun; it was useless, for it still shed upon them its burning power. Jones had long complained of thirst, and had frequently dipped his hand into the water, and sucked the fluid; this was hastily done, for, not unfrequently, the sharp fin of a shark was seen rising from the water as if the monster had made a dart at his hand. In the midst of the excruciating torments of thirst, heightened by the salt water and the irritable temple of Graham, as he stamped his impatient foot against the boards, and tore his hair with rage, he suddenly stopped, and called out,—" By Heavens there's a sail!" The extravagance of his joy was now equal to his former despair; he knelt by his daughter's side, who now lay extended upon the wet raft, exclaiming, " Susan, my child, look up, we shall be saved"—she replied not; he took her hands between his own, and said, —" Susan, Susan, speak to me!" the hapless maiden did not answer. She was without utterance but not without existence. Her eyes looked upon Graham. " I see a vessel," he cried, with a sudden transport, " my beloved child—we are saved!"

" It is too late," she murmured, and her head fell back upon the boards. " Oh, death! one moment yet," said Graham, while the hour of safety seemed the very summit of his misfortune. His hands were stretched towards the ship, seeking, as it were, to draw it through the space towards the raft. Every means of making a signal were resorted to; one flung his jacket in the air, whilst the other, although the vessel was miles distant, endeavoured to hail her. Sometimes they hailed together, in order to produce a louder sound, and occasionally both stood up to make some signal.

Whilst they stood, watching in silence the approach of they ship, which slowly made her way through the water,—and, at the very instant they were assuring each other that they were seen, and that the vessel was purposely steered on the course she was keeping to reach them, the whole fabric of hope was destroyed in a second; the brig kept away about three points, and began to make more sail. Then it was an awful moment—their countenances saddened as they looked at each other; for in vain they hailed—in vain they threw their jackets in the air— it was evident they had not been seen, and that the ship was steering her proper course.

It was after a long, deep-drawn sigh from Jones, and after wiping away a stream of tears which flowed down his rugged cheeks as he looked at the vessel, then about two miles distant, that he broke into loud lamentations on the utter hopelessness of their condition if they were not seen. In vain they declared that the ship had purposely altered her course to avoid them—in vain they pointed to a man going aloft, whom they could distinctly see—and in vain they waved their jackets, and assisted the signal with speech. The time was slipping away, and if once they got abaft the beams of the ship, every second would lessen the chance of being seen; besides, the sea-breeze might come down, and then she would be far away, and beyond all hope, in a quarter of an hour. Now was it that the man who had been so loudly lamenting his fate seemed suddenly inspired with fresh hope and courage; he looked attentively at the ship, then at his companion, and said,—" By Heavens I'll do it, or we are lost."

" Do what?" said Graham.

" Though," said Jones, " it is no trifle to do, when I look upon the monsters of the deep floating around us," and he pointed to the sharks, which were swimming about the raft; " yet I will try, for if she passes us, what can we do? I may as well die one death as another. I tell you what, captain, my mind's made up— I'll swim to her: if I get safe to her we are all saved; if not I shall die without adding another to my long list of crimes." Then falling on his knees, and saying, " God protect me!" he jumped overboard with as much calmness as if he was about to bathe in security. No sooner had he begun to strike out in the direction he intended than Graham turned towards the sharks. The fins had disappeared, and it was evident they had heard the splash, and would soon follow their prey. It is difficult to say which suffered the greatest. Graham, on the raft, looked towards the ship, and kept waving his jacket—then turned towards the sharks. His horror may be imagined when he saw three of these terrific monsters swim past the raft, exactly in the direction of Jones; he splashed his jacket in the water to scare them away, but they seemed quite aware of the impotency of the attack, and lazily pursued their course.

Jones being an excellent swimmer, there seemed no doubt he would pass within hail of the ship, provided the sharks did not interfere; and he, knowing that they would not be long in following him, kept kicking the water and splashing as he swam. It was not until a great distance had been accomplished that the swimmer became apprised of his danger, and saw by his side one of the terrific creatures; still, however, he bravely swam, and kicked—his mind was made up for the worst, and he had little hope of success. In the meantime the breeze had gradually freshened, and the ship passed with greater velocity through the water; every stitch of canvass was spread. To the poor swimmer the sails seemed bursting with the breeze; and as he used the utmost endeavour to propel himself, so as to cut off the vessel, the spray appeared to dash from the bow, and the ship to fly through the water. He was now close enough to hope his voice might be heard; but he hailed and hailed in vain—not a soul was to be seen on deck: the man who steered was too intent upon his avocation to listen to the call of mercy. The ship passed, and Jones was every second getting farther in the distance; every hope was gone, not a ray of that bright divinity remained; the fatigue had nearly exhausted him, and the sharks only waited for the first quiet moment to swallow their victim.

It was in vain he thought of returning towards the raft, for he never could have reached her, and Graham had no means of assisting him. In the act of offering up his last prayer, he was seized by a shark and drawn beneath the surface. A cry of horror was heard, and the despairing glance of Jones was witnessed by Graham. The mutilated body floated for an instant in its blood, with the look of agony and terror still imprinted on the conscious countenance. At the next moment it had become food for the monsters of the deep.

Graham could not doubt his misery. His child, he fancied, was no more. His companion was gone—nothing in the universe was left him. "Now I may blaspheme," he murmured between his teeth; but he was silent, for he gazed upon his daughter, and his thoughts of her restrained his fury.

The ship was now but at a small distance, the cry of horror which had bee uttered by Jones had attracted notice, and the attention of the crew was drawn towards the distant raft, upon which Graham now sat motionless, and, with his back turned towards the ship, would not even look upon it. The future had no promise for him. "Let them leave me," he said, "let them pursue their voyage, —I will live and die here!"

The boat from the ship arrived alongside, and as one of the crew boarded the raft, Graham turned his head contemptuously. "What would you?" said he, "what brings you to this sepulchre?—Mankind! leave me in peace."

"Unfortunate man," replied the sailor, "we come to preserve you."

"You," interrupted Graham, with frantic irony, and pointing to Susan. "There, look, do you come in time to preserve her?"

"Follow us," cried the seaman, and he lifted the inanimate form of the maiden in his arms.

"No," replied Graham, "I am well in this place; I choose it,—let me remain here."

The seaman appeared moved with his sufferings and his distraction. "Man," said he, "grief has clouded your reason. Misery has fallen upon you, but every misfortune has its end. God—"

Graham interrupted him by a cry of execration. "God," repeated he, "I have said, and I say again—there is none, or it is a monster. The creation is but a disordered mass. The earth is only a chaos of horror and malediction. Mankind are only the frightful productions of darkness and chance, and the breath of life is nothing more than an infernal curse which pervades immensity."

At these words the seamen were convinced of his madness, and ceased to interrogate him. Notwithstanding his resistance, they bore him to their ship. Their cares and remedies were successfully bestowed upon Susan. The period of her existence had not yet terminated.

Days passed, nay weeks, before she perfectly recovered, and not till the white cliffs of Albion came in sight was she restored to health.

Graham had recounted to the captain of the ship, which was a homeward-bound Indiaman, the loss of his vessel by fire, and the sufferings of himself and crew upon the raft; and upon the arrival of the vessel in the Thames, from whence Susan had sailed in the smuggler's vessel, he offered to remunerate him, from a well-filled bag which he drew from his bosom, for his passage in the ship. This the captain indignantly refused.

After staying for a short time in London, Graham informed his daughter, that it was his intention to proceed to Hexham, where he ascertained his aunt Lady Maxwell then was, and place her under the protection of one who had before offered her a kindness. To this Susan raised no objection, being anxious to be again with her beloved friends in Allendale. She could not entirely divest herself of the faint idea that he actually sough ther happiness, however mistaken might be the measures he resorted to, when she saw the ray of satisfaction that illumined his face as she consented to his proposal. Fortitude, even when displayed in a bad cause, and bearing the stamp of impenitence, is apt to create a momentary emotion of admiration : for it impresses the belief, that though blighted by vice in the issue it had at first been conjoined with honour and virtue.

Such were the ideas that floated on the mind of Susan as she watched her fear-inspiring parent, during the recital of his past life, which he now fully disclosed to his unhappy daughter. He for the first time informed her of her connection with lady Maxwell, of her real name, which he told her was Florence Graham, and which he had ascertained from the casket which he took from old Mary Adams. He also informed her, that from a visit he had made at the island of Madeira, he had discovered that her mother still lived, and that she had quitted that island some years back for England; but was unable to discover what part she had fixed upon as her residence. Upon arriving thus far in his narrative, she perceived that he appeared deeply affected, probably upon his recalling past scenes which now became vividly pictured in his imagination. She had seen him—a man whose every lineament evinced depravity—gazing with a cold and undaunted eye at the waves which threatened to engulf him; while others, whose crimes bore no comparison in atrocity, were shivering under the influence of terror, and pouring out tears and supplications to him who alone could protect them : it was nothing singular, therefore, that she began to look upon him as the wreck of a great and lofty character. She was, as yet, a stranger to the callousness of heart which habitual exposure to peril and privation too generally occasions, or that cold apathy, even to personal safety, which arises from being long accustomed to the sight of human blood. Graham had so often believed his last hour come that he almost began to doubt whether it would ever arrive; but had he actually experienced penitence and timidity, that ferocious pride, which formed the chief characteristic in his nature, would have induced him to withhold the avowal, though a single hint would have purchased lasting security.

They arrived at Hexham, shortly after Constance Glenroy had written to Edith Trevanion the letter mentioned at the end of the last chapter; and Graham immediately sought an interview with Lady Maxwell. We will pass over the astonishment of the dowager, when she found that the daughter now presented by her nephew, as Florence Graham, was no other than Susan Adams, the friend of Edith Trevanion.

Graham, after Lady Maxwell had promised to give Susan, whom we shall henceforth call Florence, that protection in her house, which her near relationship entitled her to, embraced his daughter, and departed again to wander, and by a life of repentance, to expiate his many crimes.

With a look of friendly sincerity Lady Maxwell approached Florence, after her grief occasioned by the parting with her father had subsided, and, extending her hand, said in a tone more fervent than her words—" I will dispense with all introduction, my young friend, and suppose us already intimate with each other ; for though almost strangers, we have been long acquainted by description. I have often heard Susan Adams held up as a character worthy of imitation and love ; nor shall Florence Graham's worth be less highly appreciated by friends who are biassed to value her for her innate qualities alone, not for the name she bears, or the race she is descended from."

Florence pressed the hand she held to her lips, while tears of affection fell upon it.—" This goodness overpowers me," she exclaimed, " for a long series of calamities has weakened my mind, and left me little more self-command than an infant. To your friendship I am already indebted for more than I shall ever be able to express my sense of; but, believe me, I am grateful, truly grateful."

" I do believe it," returned the dowager ; " and, to prove that I do not assert a falsity, mean to make an instantaneous claim on you, so as to give you an opportunity of placing me on the debtor side of the book. Your father has communicated all he knows of your eventful history, to which he has added his own private comments, electing me, at the same time, as grand inquisitor over your conduct; when, after duly weighing the case, I have come to the conclusion, that a tissue of unfortunate events alone has brought you under the censure of the world, and that personally you have done nothing to merit the neglect of your friends, or the calumnies which have been propagated. It is not in our power to sever the ties of relationship which bind you to the wretched man who has occasioned all your misfortunes, but we are able to show that we believe you innocent, and still entitled to the countenance of society. Henceforth Glanmore Abbey must be your home."

Florence for a moment made no reply ; she saw that Lady Maxwell was aware of the happy change which a few days had occasioned in her prospects, and the conviction that sincerity prompted the invitation, induced her to reply,—" You are much—much too good, thus to interest yourself in the welfare of an individual who appears before you in so doubtful a character, but indeed—indeed—"

" There must be no buts in the matter, Florence," interrupted Lady Maxwell, with gentle authority. " We are allied by blood, and, until deprived of the charge, I look upon myself as entitled to counsel and direct you.' "

" I have done," returned Florence, while a sigh of blended sorrow and joy rose from her heart ; " l have suffered much ; but, thank Heaven ! the darkest cloud is passing away, and the time coming, when you shall find your generous reliance on me not misplaced."

" I will not detain you now, my young friend, you must need some repose, and be anxious to see your friends. Good night, and remember that you are under a roof where repining is a stranger, and where wordly jarring seldom ventures to intrude; therefore dismiss all gloomy retrospection, and look only to the future."

Notwithstanding all these incentives to forget the past, Florence, nevertheless, found it an arduous task ; for when the blighted hopes of our early days begin to revive, the mind is nearly as far from tranquillity as when the barb of misery is festering in the heart. The same anxiety for the flight of time is also experienced, but different, very different, are the feelings which occasion the wish to shorten it; for when hope lends its light to the future, we desire to skim over the intermediate days, as the traveller accelerates his pace while crossing a monotonous waste, beyond which rise the glittering spires of some far-famed city ; while in grief, the broken down spirit desires only to arrive at the gate of eternity, the only haven which a relentless fate assures him he shall be able to attain.

CHAPTER XXIX.

A dazzling mass of artificial light,
Which showed all things, but nothing as they were;
The music, and the banquet, and the wine;
The garlands, the rose odours, and the flowers;
The sparkling eyes and flashing ornaments;
The white arms and the raven hair; the braids
And bracelets: swan-like bosoms, and the necklaces,
An India in itself, yet dazzling not
The eye like what it circled;
The many twinkling feet, so small and sylph-like;
All the delusion of the busy scene;
Its false and true enchantments—art and nature."—BYRON.

FLORENCE awoke the next morning at the accustomed hour of six, and the novelty of her situation banishing all remains of fatigue, she arose, and determined to employ the time which might elapse before the family assembled in strolling in the garden. She wandered with delight through grounds laid out by the finest taste, and gazed on the various prospects they commanded, till her eyes filled with tears of rapture.

Her reflections were interrupted by Matilda Maxwell, who seemed delighted at their meeting.—"Ah, Florence!" she exclaimed; "my anxiety for your welfare has kept me waking all night, and brought me thus early to seek you. I found you had left your room, and conjectured that I should find you in the garden. Come, my mother waits us in the breakfast room."

When Matilda heard how long she had been walking—"Oh, lazy girl that I am!" she cried; "I thought I exerted the most praiseworthy resolution when I started from disturbed repose at eight o'clock."

When they reached the house, Lady Maxwell, extending her hand in the most friendly manner to Florence, said,—"I find I must take care not to lose the fame I have acquired for my early rising: I assure you I am quoted as an example to half the ladies in the country, and that by much less activity than you seem to be in the habit of practising."

They sat down to breakfast, and a "merry war of words" was maintained between them, and displayed throughout the contest a nicely balanced share of wit and satire, whilst the more serious parts of the conversation abounded with reflections, judiciously combined, from an equal study of books and actual observations upon life.

Florence soon felt completely at ease in the presence of her new protectress; and with all the amiable and unsuspecting confidence of her sex, made her acquainted, in the course of the conversation, with the dearest sentiments and wishes of her heart.

Lady Maxwell was delighted with her warmth of feeling, and the purity of all her views. When she spoke of Margaret Glenroy, it was with an earnestness, a simplicity that was more impressive than the most studied eloquence.—"She has been everything to me," said she—"my guide, my monitress, my friend."

"You shall have the carriage this morning," said the dowager, and with Matilda visit your friends, as to-morrow you will have no time, as I intend you to go to the ball given by Sir Reginald Willoughby in honour of his daughter's birthday."

The bosom of Florence was filled with delight, as she pictured to herself the surprise of Margaret and Constance Glenroy at her unexpected arrival amongst them; and she retired to prepare herself for her visit.

What was the astonishmhnt of the Glenroys at again beholding one whom they never expected to see more, but their amazement and horror cannot be described, as they listened to the account given by Florence of the brutal manner in which she had been carried off by young Melton, and the sufferings she had endured, and the perils she had escaped at sea.

But their astonishment was nothing in comparison to that expressed on the features of Florence, as she listened to the recital of events which had transpired at Allendale since her departure, the absence of Edith Trevanion, and the intended marriage of Herbert Glenroy and Griselda Willoughby. Like the rest of their friends it was a mystery to her.

She found the beautiful Constance ill ; and her situation cannot better be described than in the words of the poet,—

"Gently, most gently, on thy victim's head,
    Consumption, lay thine hand !—let me decay,
Like the expiring lamp, unseen, away,
    And softly go to slumber with the dead.
And if 'tis true what holy men have said,
    That strains angelic oft foretel the day

> Of death, to those good men who fell thy prey,
> O let the aerial music round my bed
> Dissolving sad in dying symphony,
> Whisper the solemn warning in mine ear:
> That I may bid my weeping friends good-bye
> Ere I depart upon my journey drear:
> And, smiling faintly on the painful past,
> Compose my decent head, and breathe my last."

FLORENCE was deeply affected, at seeing her former companion so reduced by sickness, and expressed a hope that she would still recover. On taking her departure she promised to be unremitting in her calls, now that she was once more among her friends.

On their way home, Matilda Maxwell expressed her regret that her brother was not with them, but was in hopes he would arrive in time for the ball.—"I declare," she said, "dearly as I love my brother, I am intolerably angry with him for staying so long in London, where he must be choked with dust. He leaves Glanmore Abbey in all the beauties of summer, and then in the winter he will remain under its leafless trees, and rail against all its gregarious animals who go to town. But this ball will bring him down, and we shall soon see him."

Lady Maxwell had anticipated her protegee's wants for a ball room appearance, but discarding every thing of finery from the catalogue of Florence Graham's toilet, had merely placed there a white muslin dress, of somewhat finer texture than the dresses usually worn by her neighbours, and perhaps more fashionably formed by the waiting woman of the dowager, who fortunately for Florence, having nothing of the modern fine gentlewoman's "gentlewoman" in her composition, readily adopted her mistress's wishes in her favour, and exerted herself to dispose of the already elegant maiden to the greatest advantage.

"Miss Graham, my lady," said the waiting-woman Dowager, "wants little of finery to set herself off. In my opinion, finery, on her, would but serve to hide one of the finest works of nature."

Lady Maxwell smiled.—"You are eloquent on the subject, Myrtle, Miss Graham is indeed a lovely young woman, and stands less in want of ornaments, than many I have seen, of even reputed beauty. I almost wish she were not so! Beauty, Myrtle, is often a dangerous gift—under some circumstances peculiarly so. Miss Graham is indeed an object for admiration, for pursuit, for envy, for—in short there are many evils attending a young woman in her situation of life; deprived of the protection of her parents——"

"But I think, my lady," said Myrtle respectfully, "you would advise her; and——"

"I would be her friend, Myrtle, though no friend can supply the place of a parent; but, my son William, is not, as you know, Myrtle, and I grieve to say, very scrupulous on many subjects. He admired her very much, about two years ago, if you recollect when she met with an accident; and to speak my mind to you freely, Myrtle, I hope he may not stay long in the country while she is with me; not from any objection I should have to Miss Graham becoming his wife, because it would secure the estates to which she is entitled, in the family; but that I think William is not more refined in his ideas of matrimony, than in any thing else."

"Mr. William is a very fine young gentleman, however," observed Myrtle.

"Fine enough, Myrtle, to look at, and specious enough in his manners too. There would be the danger, to an unprotected female. His principles, Myrtle," and Lady Maxwell looked exceedingly grave, and sighed heavily—"his principles—yet he may have sown his wild oats, to call them no worse—radically bad I trust he is not, and, if he is, I only wonder whence the seeds sprang."

A pause ensued in the conversation.

Lady Maxwell took up the muslin Myrtle was working on—"I think, as Mis

Graham is about your size, Myrtle," said she, "this dress, made to fit yourself, will just answer for her. No ornaments, if you please, but a bit of lace on the bosom and sleeves, and a plain white satin band round the waist, with a diamond clasp of mine."

Passing over several minor occurrences, together with the arrival of William Maxwell and a friend, we will at once proceed with the ball, which was expected to be too gay a thing for any one to decline the invitation who had the power of accepting it, and at eleven o'clock the rooms were brilliant with handsome dresses, and lovely, or at least animated, faces. We will say nothing of aching hearts and aching heads, veiled by wreathed smiles and gay tones. Happy for us, in some sense, that the fabled ring, whose touch revealed the inmost thoughts, is only to be found in Eastern story; that humanbeings have no windows in their breasts; that every house is not a palace of Truth. Some few simple people may now gaze on smiling faces, and listen to the laugh, and the jest, and the repartee, and never guess :—

> " That laughter is a veil that's thrown,
> To hide from every eye despair."

The kind-hearted may never imagine that envy and malice can lurk under soft words and gentle tones ; and the young and unerring may dream for awhile that the world is indeed the Paradise it looks. The delusion will end soon enough to pleasure even the most rigid.

Not that we think a ball-room either awakens or displays such evil sentiments more than any other assembly. Those feelings and passions are in the human heart, and they may rule in the open air or in the quiet parlour, as well as in the splendid saloon. There may be a spirit of pride and display in a hovel; humility in a palace; content in a peasant's hut; envy in a court; vanity under the decent grey and sober cut of the quakeress ; and modesty in the splendid and elegantly fashioned dress. It is the heart, and not the station, the mind, and not the circumstance, that makes the difference. Yet is the ball-room an epitome of the world. How many enter it with high expectations, and leave it with blighted hopes! and then what a jaundiced account do we all allow ourselves to give of the " accidents of the hour,"—the rooms were dark—the people looked out of humour, the hostess was inattentive—the music was execrable; whilst we kept back the real cause of our discomfiture. Ask another. A soft light pervaded the apartment—all looked happy—the hostess indefatigable—the music beautiful : and this one also reveals not the real cause of her pleasure. And is it not thus in life ? Our adversity, or our prosperity; our sorrows, or our pleasures ; our prejudices, or our affections ; do they not give the colour to our descriptions of what has been—the hopes of what may be ? What office more thankless than the giver of a fete, if we pique our vanity on universal applause. To hope to pass through life unscathed, unblamed—to find the philosopher's stone, the waters of oblivion, or the sense of a madman, are hopes possessed of equal wisdom. But he who gives a fete from ostentation, cannot complain if the criticisms of the guests are withheld by no friendly feeling. The entertainment is given to please the inviter and the invited, and the former must not expect the latter to be grateful. And such a fete was this. Sir Reginald Willoughby availed himself of the excuse of his daughter's birthday to astonish the natives with his magnificence. There were men to chalk the floors, men to decorate the rooms, a grand supper, and splendid music. As may be imagined every thing was grand, from the anxious vanity of old Sir Reginald to the chicken for the supper, and the old Scotch tunes for the quadrilles.

Who could resist such a combination ? Feet which had been allowed to hope for repose were practised to rival others. Milliners and dress makers who had been on the point of giving up business in despair, were obliged to assume the midnight lamp to complete their orders ; flies had new wheels ; chaises new poles ; mammas had new turbans ; young ladies new dresses, whilst papas, in the anticipation of pines and champagne, furnished brooches and chains. In short the rooms were crowded to excess, and were dazzling with an unparalleled display of rank, beauty and fashion. Sir Reginald received his guests with a sort of splendid courtesy, awakening awe, ridicule, pity or contempt, according to the moods of his visitors.

As the company congregated, dancing commenced ; the ball room was of extensive dimensions, and eight sets of quadrilles stood up at once without inconvenience.

"Gentlemen, will you lead your partners to the dancing room, if you please ?" said Sir Reginald ; and the young beauties prepared to look demure, and thinking of anything rather than being asked for their hands, whilst the young gentlemen ran their fingers through their hair for the last time, and drew on their white gloves.

"Now, Miss Graham," said William Maxwell, "may I presume to request the honour of your hand ?"

"It would be impossible to refuse !" was her laughing reply ; and entering, they took place opposite Glenroy and Miss Willoughby. Waltzing succeeded the quadrilles,—"Now," whispered Maxwell to Florence, "do justice to my opinion. If you move in a waltz as you do in a quadrille, I'll pronounce you unrivalled every way."

"I'll do my best not to disgrace it," answered she, smiling.

Florence possessed neither affectation nor weakness. She was as light as a wood-nymph, and in the spirit of the dance she thought but of its pleasures. William Maxwell, tall, elegant, and as graceful as his lovely partner, moved with all the ease and elegance that dance requires, and saw only the charming object encircled in its mazes.

Florence too, whirling in the vortex of its evolutions, noticed nothing but the dance itself, during some moments that she whirled through it, when suddenly pausing on her step, she perceived at a glance, they were the only couple moving. William Maxwell observed it also, and likewise that a complete circle had formed round to look at them. More embarrassed on the account of Florence than his own, and desirous that she should not notice the admiration he was aware she had awakened, which he judged might distress her, he by another circle of the room drew her in its evolutions completely out of it, and, without any aparent design, they mixed in the general mass. The manœuvre was so delicately and neatly effected, that Florence had no idea of having attracted general notice ; and, situated as she was had she done so, her delicacy and her pride had taken the alarm, lest it should be thought she designedly made an exhibition of her graces.

Maxwell led her through the crowd, to another apartment, where, seating her on a sofa near a lady, he retired to bring her some refreshment; he did not stay long, and returned with a glass of negus. Florence smiled as she took it, and said,—"I have done your bidding, in the dance."

"Yes," he answered, "you have, and by Heavens, I am as far gone as might rationally be expected, from such a hair-brained fellow as me."

"Gone where, or how ?" inquired Florence, with curiosity.

"Gone where—upon my soul, I don't know, and gone how—I'm shot if I can tell."

"I don't comprehend you, sir," said Florence.

"How the deuce should you," he cried, "when I can't comprehend myself."

"Then, sir, you deal in riddles."

"And woman's a riddle, they say," added he ; "if not, she's a witch, and has witched and bewitched me."

"I hope not !" replied Florence laughing. "Let me hear all about it ; I never could resist a love tale, and cried when I was five years old, when I read of the Beast, who took up his tail in his paws to wipe his eyes because Beauty refused him."

"Umph !" And he looked the vexation he felt. "However. don't waltz any more to-night, Florence : kick your heels in as many quadrilles as you please : but that other thing will set your head spinning."

"Like it has done yours, sir," replied Florence, as he darted from her side and joined his sister, who was conversing with Sir Reginald Willoughby,

"Ah! Sir Reginald," said young Maxwell as he joined them, "I saw you ride by me yesterday on your mare as I arrived from London."

"Yes," said Sir Reginald, " I was going to see some very pretty young ladies," and he smiled at Matilda,

"Some very pretty young ladies? Well, who could they be?" asked Maxwell "I don't think there are many pretty young ladies in this neighbourhood.

"Oh, pardon me, sir, but I think I could name two or three."

"Dear me, could you!" said he laughing, and evidently thinking his sister and Florence must be included in the number. "Well, now, really, with the exception of my sister and your daughter, and Miss Alice, I should be puzzled to find any. Miss Shanks, to be sure, may be a beauty some of these days, but I think it will be a long while first," and he smiled. "I should hardly think you alluded to any young ladies that were not in their teens."

"Oh, but indeed I did—to one."

"Ha, ha, ha!—Well, at any rate your pretty young ladies yesterday were not in the immediate neighbourhood, or else you would not have gone on horseback."

"That's a clever guess of yours. Now try then if you can guess their names."

"Let me see. The Browns!"

"You don't call them beauties, I hope?"

Oh, there's no accounting you know for tastes—I dare say they have their admirers. Well then—the Thompsons?"

"Out again."

"The Miss Wellfords?"

"No."

"Tell me in which direction you rode—east, west, north or south?"

"Oh that would be telling you at once."

"Not the Wellfords?"

"No."

"Nor the Thompsons?"

"No."

"Nor the Browns?

"No."

"Well, I give it up."

"The Miss Glenroys."

"Was it indeed!"

Sir Reginald had now exhausted his "agreeable nothings," so he walked off.

At the other end of the sofa where Florence was seated, sat a lady, who had been and still remained in conversation with a party near her. They quitted almost at the same time that William Maxwell retired, and the lady, who was no other than Alice Cameron, drew near Florence and entered into conversation with her. This room, equally with the others of the suite, was continually filled with the influx and reflux of the company, passing to and fro, and as they revolved, "nods and becks and wreathed smiles," passed alternately from one and the other.

After chatting together a few minutes, Alice, who for some time had been shewing symptoms of wearing a smile at her own thoughts, said suddenly—" Do you think, Miss Graham, I shall ever be married?"

The question was so opposite to what they had been talking, and so sudden, that Florence could not help smiling also, as she replied :—

"Indeed, Miss Cameron, that is a question impossible for me to determine on; but I dare say you may if you like.'

"Well, come, that's faovurable, however," returned the other. "Now, you would not have me refuse one of the handsomest, finest, and to all that I know, one of the most delightful creatures in the world."

"Even that is a matter entirely depending on your own opinion, Miss Cameron," said Florence; "and if he is all you say of him, it is not likely—that is, you may probably think the gentleman deserving your favourable sentiments."

" Vastly correct and proper your replies no doubt, Miss Graham," observed her companion, with much becoming gravity. "The gentleman has not yet made his proposals ; but I expect he'll be very much inclined to do so as soon as he can ; and what though he may be a few years my senior—that's no consequence, you know. We hear of ladies marrying their grandfathers in point of age."

" And that is another matter of opinion," said Florence.

" Upon my word," resumed Alice, " it would almost appear to me as though you were destined for the old maid's list, you are so dry and circumspect in your answers. But would you not like to see this admirer of mine ?"

" I should have no objection certainly," said Florence ; " only as he is such an Apollo, I must shield my heart within an iceberg."

" Then you shall be gratified," returned Alice. " But I first caution you—be as circumspect in your actions as you have just now been in your words—and turn your head cautiously to the left, rather behind you : you cannot mistake the person ; for though he is not directly near us, he is the first gentleman this way."

Florence strictly obeyed the words of Alice, and having taken her words in a literal sense, she did not feel at all embarrassed in turning her head to look at a gentleman under the circumstances stated. Her eyes rested on the figure of a man, whose face struck her as being familiar. His were intensely directed towards her (as she thought, towards Miss Cameron). When removing hers a minute or two through innate modesty, she again raised them, he was still in the same position, and Florence dared not look again.

" Well, cried Alice, as Florence turned round, " what do you think now, Miss Graham ?"

" Think !" repeated Florence with warmth, " that with respect to outward appearance, whoever the gentleman may be, he has not his prototype on earth."

Alice burst into an immoderate fit of laughter—

" Bravo !" she exclaimed. " Well, if I am not caught, you are ; and it's all fair, for, upon my honour, my dear Florence, the gentleman has been this hour endeavouring with all his might to get a sly peep at your full front ; and I manœuvered to help the poor fellow out of his difficulty."

" Good Heavens, Miss Cameron !" cried Florence, " you don't say so ?"

" Oh, but I do though," replied she ; " and not only say, but I have given proof positive that I do what I say, and now you can't help yourself. Alas ! poor Maxwell !"

" What of him, pray ?" said Florence ; " I suppose you fancy now, because we were dancing together——"

" I don't fancy it at all," returned Alice. " All the company are talking about it."

" Then I wish the company had something better to engage their conversation," said Florence. " But assure yourself, Miss Cameron, I think no more of William Maxwell than I would of a brother—I have neither the vanity nor the inclination ; and for any nonsense he may talk, it's just his character—*badinage* and *plaisantrie*. For Heaven's sake contradict such an idle story, wherever you hear it ! It's a falsity, I positively assure you."

" Well then," cried Alice, " there is no danger of a duel between these nonsuches about you ; because, you know, that would bring your name at once into notoriety."

" I have no such ambition I assure you," said Florence. " But, *apropos* of names—do you know this strange gentleman's ?"

" That's a good one !" laughed out Alice ; " inquisitive about him already. But, upon my honour I don't ; only I think he seems rather a stranger, and I should likewise suppose him to be a foreigner. He's rather dark, I think ; and what magnificent eyes the fellow has got ! if he had any grace about him, seeing two poor damsels here, stuck to the wall like fixtures,——"

" Lumber, you mean," interrupted Florence.

" Any thing," continued Alice,—" he'd ask us to dance."

"He is not assuming," remarked Florence.

"Not presuming," added Alice. "But upon my honour I believe he has heard me, for he is moving this way."

"I'll be off," cried Florence, starting from the sofa, but without turning her looks towards him. "If he has overheard our conversation, I would not meet his eyes for worlds."

"Don't go," cried Alice, holding her dress; "if you do I'll play you such a trick as you'll not forget. Don't leave me to brave it out myself. But he has made a halt; he may not be intending to come."

"Perhaps through politeness," observed Florence, "from seeing us in debate about some great question," and she laughed. "But I would not stay the chance of his coming on any account."

Alice Cameron let go her hold.

"I'll see you again in the course of the night," added Florence, moving off quickly.

"Remember!" called out Alice, holding up her finger in threat, "only remember!"

Florence found Matilda and her brother in earnest conversation with Doctor Rovington, who had been amusing them with a description of the party on the lake, and the disaster of himself and Miss Shanks. After the introduction had been gone through between Florence and the doctor, and an explanation of the change in her name, as he at once recognised in her his former patient, William Maxwell resumed the conversation.

"Your amusing disaster, doctor, reminds me of a ridiculous accident which happened to an old lady several years back—you remember, Matilda, when we were going up to Richmond!"

"For shame, William!" exclaimed Matilda, "the woman was almost drowned."

"This old lady, Mrs. Francis," pursued William, laughing, "measured nearly two yards in circumference, and probably weighed a ton. How any one could think of inviting her to partake of an aquatic excursion, I cannot imagine. She was terrified lest every barge and bridge on the river should fall foul of us; and when one happened to come near, good heavens! how she was alarmed. At length we hoisted a sail,—ha! ha—I think I see her now—she shut her eyes, clenched her hands, and thought every moment would launch her into eternity. At every tack she fell nearly into convulsions; and at length a squall overtook us, —she set up one to match it, and was launched into the river!"

"Shocking!" cried Doctor Rovington, "and what became of her?"

"Her pelisse," continued Maxwell, "her orange-coloured pelisse, stiffened with whalebone and buckram, for a time bore up—her parasol—Ha! ha! ha!—she grasped vigorously with both hands, caught the wind, and conveyed her like a majestic barge, right towards the Wandsworth shore; rich, as you know, in slime and rushes; and there, among the congregated mud of ages, she was safely deposited, howling most piteously, while all who beheld her were in convulsions."

"Pray, Matilda," said Florence, "how much of this tale may we credit?"

"Indeed, Florence," said Matilda, laughing, "nearly the whole of it is true. We were not far, however, from shore, and the parasol was an umbrella, so that the adventure was not quite so miraculous."

"And did none of you gentlemen try to save her?" inquired the doctor.

"Not one of us," returned William, "she would have sunk any one who had taken her in tow. I, indeed, thought of jumping in, just for the look of the thing; but by the time I had taken off, and folded up my coat and waistcoat, she was safely landed. Good lack, what a pickle she was in!"

"Indeed she was!" ejaculated Matilda. "Such a pelisse!"

"And such legs!" exclaimed William.

"Poor woman," said Florence.

"How very ridiculous!" ejaculated the Doctor.

"I begged her umbrella as a memento of the catastrophe," said Maxwell, "and the print of her nails is to be seen in its handle to this day."

"Oh, William, William!—"

"To finish the scene, she lifted up her voice and wept so vociferously that the household of Lord Egmont and the Archbishop of Dublin rushed down to the water side to see what was the matter."

"William! William!"

Ha, ha, ha!"and Maxwell laughed convulsively, "I shall never forget that day. The party was unique in every respect. Mrs. Francis and her son with her, he was a puny little fellow that put one exactly in mind of a Vauxhall sandwich, she called him Jemmy. Then there was a girl who played off a great many fine airs on me, and was continually placing her foot in my way, for no other reason that I could perceive than to show me that for once she had on silk stockings; for she had prodigiously thick ancles. There was a pair of lovers too, billing and cooing amazingly, of which I, sitting directly opposite, had the full benefit; and never was I more annoyed in my life—I don't patronize love-making."

Florence had hardly disappeared from the side of Alice Cameron, when the stranger advanced. He bowed to Alice, as if soliciting to occupy part of the sofa; which she politely returning, he seated himself beside her.—"I don't intrude I hope, madam?" said he.

"Certainly not, sir," replied Alice. "You are no foreigner, however," thought she. "I wish, sir, you had taken advantage of the seat before," she good-naturedly added.

"I wish I had, madam," he very pointedly answered; "But I feared being presumptuous."

"Aye," thought Alice again, "love is always diffident.—In an assembly of persons like this," said she aloud, "we are never very strict to our technicals—we scramble at every thing we can catch, whether it be the convenience of a chair or the attributes of the table."

"Fashion is a child of caprice," said he, and his accent appeared to be rather foreign.

"So, thought Alice again, you're a Frenchman, no doubt; an emigrant perhaps; or no, the French ambassador may-be, whom I have not yet seen.—"You will pardon me, sir," resumed Alice, addressing herself to him again, "but perhaps you are not of this country."

"Why, do I appear like a foreigner?" said he.

Alice smiled.—"I should almost have my doubts that you were not an Irishman," she cried, "from your answering my question by putting another."

"I am a citizen of the world at present," he replied, in a lively tone; "and all mankind my brothers."

"And all women your sisters," subjoined Alice. "Well, that's liberal of you, however. I claim that honour, and that young lady just gone from here—"

"No, if you please," he hastily interrupted her, "not my sister; I acknowledged no relationship to that young lady.'

Humph! thought Alice; there's more there than meets the ear!

"Might I ask you, madam," and he seemed afraid to get his words out, "who she is—What is her name?"

"Her name!" said Alice—"who she is! she's a tolerably prettyish, well-looking girl enough—I believe a young person—not over young either—because you must not take every one by their good looks of a gala night. Now I look—no matter what I look. But this person—you were asking—what was it?—something of the lady who just quitted me; I am so forgetful."

"I asked you, madam, the name of that lovely creature, who just went from hence," said he emphatically, "and with whom you seemed in earnest conversation."

"Oh, that lady; I thought it might be a lady who was—who had just been sitting here," and she looked slyly at him, while she thus played on his curiosity.

"That last young lady, madam," he impatiently expressed; "you cannot mistake her; she is the perfection of every beauty."

" Upon my honour, sir," said Alice laughing, "you need give no greater proof of your being a plain substantial John Bull, or Pat, than your extravagant compliment to one lady, at the expense of the whole sex besides. A foreigner would have sworn, and no doubt in many instances, excepting the present, foresworn himself, that the beauty present excelled her who quitted here not many minutes ago."

" I shall not dispute, in this instance," said he, good-naturedly, "that the lad ⌐ present may be the superior Pallas ; but I must say the other is the Venus."

"Perhaps, though your gallantry, sir, might not permit it," returned Alice, with a cunning smile, "you give me that appellation, because you think there may be some resemblance between the owl, the emblem of the wise goddess, and me."

"Pardon me," he exclaimed, laughing ; "such a thought never entered my head ; but I see you want to evade my question of—what is the lady's name ?"

No. 26.

"Oh, the lady's name," said she, standing up; "the name of the lady who just now sat on the sofa—Cameron—Miss Cameron. You'll excuse me going just now—I see my party expecting me. I may have the pleasure of meeting you again."

"I am sorry you a e removing hence, madam," he replied, rising likewise from the sofa; "but I am extremely obliged to you for your information."

"If you knew but all," thought she; but it was all in joke that Alice Cameron gave her own name, because Florence had sneaked off like a culprit; "and I said I'd be revenged," thought she; "and now the fine fellow will vow and declare he's over head and ears in love with Miss Cameron, and we shall have a fine laugh at the expense of both."

Alice after playing this trick did not dare to remain on this seat any longer, lest some untoward interloper should approach her, and let out her name; notwithstanding she would have had no objection to continue in conversation with this gentleman, and, true woman-like, learn a little more of himself; but she durst not develop her own plot; therefore, with a smile from her, and a bow from him, they parted for the present.

Quadrilles were going forward—and looking round, she soon espied William Maxwell among the dancers. Florence was standing by herself, but was soon joined by the stranger, of whom she had just then been thinking, and endeavouring to call his features to her recollection.

She felt the warm blood tinge her cheek as he approached her; yet why should it? She would again have moved away from him, but having done so before, it would now look pointed; she therefore kept her ground; but her heart beat in a very unusual, indeed in rather a new, way to her.

He came nearer, and with evident embarrassment addressed her—"If I could dare solicit the honour of your hand, madam, in a quadrille, or a waltz—yet can I expect it is disengaged, though I should be so presumptuous?"

Florence startled at his voice, which sounded familiarly to her ears, and gazing rather earnestly at his features, said,—"I certainly am not engaged, sir, at present, and should with much pleasure accept you; but you see the quadrille sets are all formed."

"The next party, madam ——"

"Will be waltzes," said she; "and I have already set my head nearly afloat; therefore, I dare not venture one again."

"Well, madam," he delicately, but pointedly, expressed, "there may have been more heads than your own thrown into confusion by that waltz to-night."

Florence did not comprehend the allusion, which was too evidently made, not to know where and what it meant; yet that tell-tale cheek of hers manifested, to herself at least, that it was understood.

"The next set of quadrilles?" said he to her.

She bowed in the affirmative, and a slight occasional conversation ensued.

In the midst of it, and as the intermediate couples of the dance stood still a minute or two, William Maxwell sprang towards where Florence stood; he had been watching her some time—and whispering her, but no longer inert or affected, his eyes darted fire: "If you dance with that fellow, by Jove! I'll shoot him and you!" and off he was again to his place.

Florence stood petrified. What could she think of this menace, or what did it mean?—for what was it? Could it be that William Maxwell had any doubtful opinion of the stranger? But no—had it been so, he would have been ordered out of the company. No; and for the first time the pride, if not the vanity, of Florence awoke with the idea that Maxwell had thought proper to cast an eye upon her, under some licentious pursuit, and dignify it perhaps with the name of love; for justly she must think her rank in life, "A PIRATE'S DAUGHTER," could never give her pretensions to him; fortune she had none, although entitled to her father's property; and Lady Maxwell had, no doubt, rather see him a breathless corpse before her, than disgrace himself by an union with the daughter of a man proscribed by his country; she could not therefore bring herself for a moment to think he meditated any honourable design, and this apparent jealousy could not proceed from the mere warmth of a well-wisher; and yet, Florence, without being able to establish truth on her conjectures, thought that, placed as she was, it would be wrong of her to evoke any public controversy on her conduct, by perhaps causing a dispute between the two gentlemen, by her dancing with the stranger. It was a matter of little consequence to her that she danced any more; and as she had already said her head was a little affected, she would, before the other set of quadrilles was formed, manage to get off her engagement, when she would leave the ball-room entirely. She still remained where she was, however, now and then speaking to this gentleman. He could not but have noticed the action and private whisper of William Maxwell, and if he made any particular reflection on the matter, it was not for him, at this early period, to offer any observation on it, turning therefore to the stranger,—"The ball room is quite oppressive," she said; "if you please I should wish to retire to one of the other rooms—my head I feel is not quite right."

A polite assent to her intimation was instantly attended to. The gentleman conducted, or rather accompanied, her to where she wished, when having procured her a seat, he remained standing near it.

"I must get off from dancing with him," she thought; and, while her heart revolted at the truth, and her inclination against the pleasure of being his partner, she believed she had no other alternative to avoid that which she could not tell, yet still apprehended; and, at all events, guarding against possibilities, could not implicate her correctness, or her judgment, whatever might be her wishes; but even those she must, in her circumstances, sacrifice to prudence.

While debating within herself, she observed Miss Willoughby, on whose arm leaned Alice Cameron, with William Maxwell and some other ladies and gentlemen, forming a group in conversation not far from where she was seated; but the crowd, passing and repassing, hid her from their view. Florence really feared Maxwell's noticing her, with the stranger in attendance, and became anxious the latter should remove from his station.—"I should almost, sir," said she, colouring deeply as she addressed the stranger, "be tempted to submit myself to your kindness, and solicit your permission for declining to dance any more to-night."

The stranger's countenance instantly changed from the glow of animation which had previously lighted it up, to the deepest mark of disappointment. "You are not serious, madam?" said he, in somewhat an agitated tone of voice.

"I am indeed, sir," replied Florence, and her words were hardly more steady, for she was averring a direct falsity to her wishes and her feelings; "my head, I think, gets worse; but, should I ever again have the pleasure of meeting you in a ball-room, I shall feel honoured in the opportunity of redeeming my word."

He bowed very coolly to her compliment.

"As a stranger almost here, madam," he as formally answered, "but still familiar to your features, ay, and those features, which yours so strongly call to recollection, will never be forgotten; but no matter—I cannot expect the same influence over you as an acquaintance or a friend may have: I regret your indisposition; but, should it go off, and you feel yourself inclined to join the dancers with some more fortunate partner, do not suffer any engagement you may think yourself bound in to me, to prevent your wishes—I shall not interfere to disturb them. We may meet again, but it is not very probable." He again bowed politely, but with the most marked coldness, and immediately retired.

Florence, had it not been through shame, had absolutely cried through vexation: her state of mind became far from enviable; for what did the stranger's words imply? —that William Maxwell held control over her in some way or another; for he must have observed his whisper and behaviour to her, and her own subsequent conduct spoke what, not comprehended fully, must appear at best doubtful. She would have withdrawn entirely from the party, did she not fear to offend Lady Maxwell, and she would have sought her ladyship in the card-room, were she not apprehensive of again meeting the stranger : she therefore still remained where she was; but her eyes involuntarily wandered round the room. No object met their view, on whom she could bestow a second look—no person in the company who could bear a comparison with her rejected partner !—To a figure, tall, graceful, and proportioned, he added a faultless countenance, his features being noble as well as fine— his complexion by no means florid, yet wholly divested of a sallow hue; it was dark, however ; but his noble forehead, round which and his fine shaped head the clustering curls of his glossy brown hair sported, was fair and delicate as his hand. His eyes, as Alice Cameron observed, were magnificent, and his smile captivating. In fact the term magnificent was never more happily applied to the *tout ensemble*. Yet he appeared wholly and entirely divested of all personal vanity (though he showed some symptoms of pride as he parted from Florence): he seemed to have passed the inexperienced days of youth, as he appeared to be a few years the senior of William Maxwell. He was dressed in deep mourning, yet wore no other sombre insignia about him, until Florence's demurrer struck the deathblow to his hopes of dancing with her. What further he might be inclined, most probably, would depend on a thousand things— but that he was sadly disappointed, the expression of his countenance told plainer than even his words could.

Having kept her seat some time, Florence, conceiving she had paid sufficient deference to prudential reasonings for retaining it so long, rose to seek Lady Maxwell, when in doing so William caught sight of her, and saying something to the party he directly advanced to her. Had he been any other person, and under existing circumstances, she would hardly have spoken to him ; but being who he was, she must keep her ill-humour and spleen to herself.

"Will you permit me," said he, on coming up, "to introduce you to Miss Willoughby: she's dying to renew acquaintance with you once more." And then he continued in a very low key, almost a whisper, though it did not wear the appearance of one, "If you knew how you have gratified me, my dear Florence !"

"How so, sir?" asked Florence, though she thought the question superfluous, only she would not let it appear so.

"By not dancing with that gentleman," he replied.

"I confess, sir," returned Florence, "I feel surprised, that in a select company of the higher classes, no matter how large, and in the house of a knight, there should be admitted a person of such reprehensible character, as to find it necessary to caution even so humble an individual as myself against forming the temporary engagement of a dance with him."

Maxwell looked at her with astonishment. "Good Heaven, Florence!" said he, "what is it you have supposed my reason for that prohibition?"

"What I have said, sir," she answered.

"You have totally and entirely mistaken it," said he; and whether his manner betrayed irritability or pettishness, Florence could not tell, but it seemed something of both. "You might have danced with him, if you pleased, Miss Graham, —only for Heaven's sake, say nothing about it to Miss Willoughby; that gentleman came with the Wellfords, who are old city friends of Sir Reginald."

The eyes of Florence rested on the floor, in deep abstraction of place and circumstances save the last possible one, when her attention was again roused by the voice of Griselda, saying,—"My dear Florence, how happy am I in claiming you once more as my friend. Alice has told me your history, and I hope you will stay amongst us for good ; but, dear me, what have you done with the foreign don?"

"That gentleman, Miss Willoughby," repeated Florence, rather confusedly—"I really—that is, I—how should I know? He did me the honour of addressing a few words to me."

"I thought you had been going to dance with him," said Griselda, "and then—'

"I rather think," hastily observed Maxwell, "that I prevented Miss Graham; I—I—had not the honour—I did not know who the gentleman might be,"

"Oh," said Alice, looking knowingly at Florence, "I guess."

William Maxwell was not at all pleased with himself for what he had done, having found this stranger to belong to the Wellford party; and so much mortified did he feel, he made no attempt to inquire respecting him, nor learn who he was.

Florence did not dare open her lips,—"Conscience makes cowards of us all;" and the party continued to lounge about the room, and were their thoughts made known, Alice Cameron and Florence Graham's had been found again to agree, for both were busily employing their eyes in looking for the same object, yet not from the same causes. Both, however, were for the present doomed to disappointment. The stranger appeared not again.

CHAPTER XXX.

Leaves have their time to fall,
    And flowers to wither at the north wind's breath,
And stars to set; but all—
    Thou hast all seasons for thine own, oh Death!

Youth and the rose,
    May look like things too lovely for decay,
And smile at thee. But thou art not of those
    Who wait the ripened bloom to seize thy prey.—MRS. HEMANS.

"Allendale.

"DEAR MISS TREVANION,—I would say dear Edith, and I know you will grant me that privilege, for you are as kind as I am encroaching. You did not ask me to write you, but something tells me you will welcome tidings from your invalid friend, and the sweet valley you loved so well. You left me lying on the sofa, in our little parlour that looks into the garden, languid and useless, a fading plant amid the bright coloured blossoms of summer. Here still I lie, though I sometimes feel strong enough to walk into the piazza and even into the garden, through the flowers I have planted and watered; and when I look on them in their frail beauty, their fragrant voices seem to say to me, ' Constance, you are fading faster than we.' Do not smile at the expression 'fragrant voice.' The odour of flowers was always eloquent to me. It is their language, and breathes of heaven to the children of earth. It may not be as glorious as the dialect of the stars, but it is as divine, and prolaims as clearly that they were made by an almighty hand. I believe I have been an idolatrous worshipper of Flora, and loved too well what is only sweet, fair, and perishing; but now when I gaze on their rainbow tints, I think only of Him, 'whose breath perfumes them, and whose pencil paints;' or, if my thoughts take an earthly direction, I reflect on the hour when their leaves shall strew my early grave, and another spring be weeping in dewy stillness over the young votary of Nature. Dear Edith, forgive the tear that falls trembling on my paper as I write. I am very young to die; and it is so natural for youth and hope to shrink from the cold sods of the valley—the lone and voiceless tomb! Then my mother looks on me with such mournful love; my sister watches over me as if her existence hung on my wasting life; and Herbert my brother—Oh, Edith, I cannot speak of him.

*   *   *   *   *   *   *

"Two or three days are passed since I laid down my pen; but I am better now, and will not weary you with sad repinings. Do you remember that beautiful sonnet, commencing,—

    " ' Gently, most gently, on thy victim's head,
      Consumption! lay thine hand—let me decay,
      Like the expiring lamp, unseen away,
      And softly go to slumber with the dead.'

"That prayer is answered in me. Soft as the touch of infancy is the dooming hand that is laid on my heart; and I only know that it is that of death, by the pulsation that grows every day weaker and weaker, and the current that flows more and more slowly in my veins. I am writing with my portfolio resting on my knee, and you see that it is but an unsteady writing-desk. They would fain deprive me of my pen, but it is such a pleasure to recal myself to your recollection, I must be indulged. I imagine you at my side, just as I saw you last, looking at me so like a pitying angel, I almost welcomed the weakness that made me an object of such interest in your eyes.

"There is one thing I yearn to utter. I thought—I feared that you esteemed my brother less than you once did. I know not how to express what I would; but do not judge him unkindly. He never lived for himself, but us; and when I think what my weak murmurs may have induced him to, I dare not go on. It may be wrong; if so, may Heaven forgive me! But to see him look so pale and altered, and know he never can be happy—it almost breaks my heart. Oh, if you knew what dreams, what sweet visions had brightened my fancy, what garlands of happiness I have sometimes woven—visionary creature that I am! But the dreams are fled, the garlands are scentless. Yet, thanks to the mercy of my heavenly Father, through the dimness that is gathering over the things of earth, a holy radiance is shining on my soul—the healing rays of the Sun of Righteousness.

"Dearest Edith, return, that I may look on you again before I pass away, and am seen no more. Tell my beloved Mrs. Heathwood, her little favourite mourns for her presence. I cannot write more. Send me one line, saying that you do not forget me, and I will lay it under my pillow as a charm against weariness; and when I lie awake, looking at the stars, which are to me the 'flowers of the sky,' I will pray for you, and bless you. CONSTANCE."

Edith's tears fell fast as rain-drops on the letter, whose unsteady lines showed the weakness of the hand that traced them. Notwithstanding her previous presentiments, she was not prepared for such a confirmation of her worst fears. She thought she saw her pale, transparent countenance glimmering through the shades of death. She followed her in imagination down the dark valley—she whom she first and so lately saw in all the loveliness of her innocent girlhood—and her soul sickened at the contemplation. Even love, that lingered on the words that alluded to the object of its forbidden devotion, was chilled as if the cold breath of mortality was passing over it. With more purity, but equal intenseness of feeling, she could have exclaimed with the recluse of—

"Oh, Death, all eloquent, you only prove,
What dust we dote on, when 'tis man we love."

Fortunately she was alone, and the anxious eye of maternal tenderness was not witness to her emotion. The moment she broke the seal, she had retired, distrusting her fortitude, though ignorant of the contents. The broken sentences which spoke of the wretchedness of her brother—the visions she had once indulged in—that which she could, he dared not reveal—all mysterious as they were—conveyed to her words of meaning; and though nothing was explained, contained volumes of vindication. A ray of conjecture darted through the gloom, but it rather served to bewilder than to enlighten her. Strange paradox of the human heart! The knowledge of his wretchedness was her only consolation; and the image of Glenroy, as it was now presented to her, pale and saddened, was a thousand times more attractive to her imagination than as she had first beheld him, in the unshorn brightness of his manhood. Then came the shuddering conviction, that such memories were sins; that he was the plighted husband of another, and that other Griselda Willoughby.

A light step entered the apartment. The next moment she found herself clasped in the arms of Alice Cameron.

"Ah! my sweet friend!" exclaimed she, in the same melting tone of affected sensibility, "have I found you at last? How sweet is the reunion of congenial souls after the pangs of separation!"

Edith was more surprised than pleased at this unexpected meeting, and was too honest to profess a rapture that she did not feel.

"Are you alone?" said she, after expressing all the pleasure sincerity admitted, and trembling at the thought that her cousin might be her companion.

"No; I came with Lady Maxwell and some friends: they asked me to join their party to this romantic spot. I was enraptured with the proposal, for I was dying with *ennui*, in a state of perfect stagnation. Griselda is so engrossed with her *cher ami*, she forgot my existence, nor could I upbraid her. When woman loves, she sees nothing but the idolised object of her adoration,—the external world is annihilated. She is soon to be bound in the silken fetters of Hymen, when I shall return to officiate as bridesmaid, on the interesting occasion."

Poor Edith was doomed to sit and hear this, and many other speeches of a similar nature, and try to wear an unmoved countenance and calm demeanour, but in vain. Her colour came and went, quick as summer lightning, and her troubled eye sought to evade the cold bright glance that revelled in its anguish. Alice revenged herself for her slighted charms, on the rival who had cast them in the shade, and she went on describing Glenroy as a happy and devoted lover, and Griselda the most enviable of her sex, till Edith's tortured spirit writhed in agony. She at last turned the conversation, by speaking of Constance's danger.

"Ah! yes, poor sweet young creature!" continued Alice, putting her white handkerchief to her eyes, with as much feeling as Tilburina, "she is too pure for this unethereal world, too spiritualised for converse with gross mortals. Oh, she looks so lovely in decay, with that bright death-rose on her cheek!"

Nature here drew from her the unaffected tribute of a sigh, for she thought that the vernal roses of her own cheek might one day be changed to the same wasting brightness, nor was her heart so demoralised by vanity, as to be incapable of sympathy for one so young and unpretending, so early doomed as Constance.

In the full current of sympathy, the more selfish sorrows of Edith became merged; and, though conscious herself that the waters of bitterness mingled with the stream, they had, at least, a legitimate channel. She looked forward to a species of martyrdom, during the remainder of their visit, for she knew every flower of romance and sentiment the fair Alice lavished upon her would contain some lurking thorn, and she must take them, and smile too, though with bleeding fingers and an aching heart. But the same sickly love of admiration, which engendered the feelings of envy and jealousy, of which Edith was the victim, became in this instance her safeguard from persecution. She rejoiced when Alice took her departure, and, stealing away unobserved, wandered round the rocky coast: she knew they were soon to leave.

There was a rock that projected far into the sea, which was almost rent from the original mass, and was only accessible by some irregular stepping-stones, usually covered when the tide ran high. It had not yet been dignified by a name, nor was it pointed out to every visitor, as an object worthy of particular admiration; but this very circumstance made it doubly interesting to Edith, for she felt that she was the discoverer of its beauty, or rather sublimity, it having undoubted claims to the latter, being insulated, grey, irregular, and moreover, almost surrounded by the most ancient element in the world.

Here she sat, glorying in her solitude; and tried to think steadily of all that had transpired during the last few months. Had she quitted Allendale after hearing of Glenroy's engagement with Miss Willoughby, without seeing him again, scorn and resentment might, ere long, have annihilated the sentiments she blushed to have cherished. But the scene in the thunderstorm, where she received the conviction, that, in spite of everything, he loved her even to despair, confirmed his empire, or rather re-enthroned him in her heart; one moment she contemned, another she palliated his conduct; then she despised herself that she could not hate him and banish him from her thoughts.

Perhaps there was more real humility in her mind at this moment than she had ever felt before; and the tears that she suffered to escape from her eyes had their source in a purified fountain.

She sat watching the swelling tide, as it rolled slowly and regularly against the rock, dashing the spray so high as to throw occasional moisture on her face, then calmly subsiding, with that gurgling, monotonous sound, which might well be called the lullaby of Nature. She was no poet, but she had, nevertheless, a kind of poetic ambition to know what inspiration the baptism of ocean's spray could impart; and, without looking behind to observe how much the tide had already encroached on the path which led to her present elevation, she continued to count the waves, as she saw the billows gradually swell and enlarge, till they paused as if exhausted with their own efforts.

The sky was overcast, so that the sea did not present the magnificent reflection of the sunbeams, which had so often shone dazzlingly in her eyes, and she was comparing its present dull green, feathered with white foam, to the emerald hue and diamond sparkles of yesterday, when a phenomenon as unexpected and unaccountable as it was sublime, arrested her attention, and soon riveted it in awe. Rolling on, from where it was bounded by the horizon alone, the ocean assumed that bright fiery tint, often witnessed near the tropics, but of rare occurrence in these regions, gathering intensity of colour, as it flowed nearer and nearer, till it broke against the very rock on which she was seated.

Perfectly unprepared for such a splendid exhibition, and believing it an unprecedented phenomenon there, it is not surprising that a sensation of terror should have prevented her from enjoying the grandeur of the spectacle, and that she involuntarily turned to retrace her steps back to the hotel. With surprise and alarm, she saw the path over the stepping-stones covered with water; so rapid had been the rising of the tide—a circumstance which she had thoughtlessly and unpardonably disregarded. She could not discern a trace of the rocks to guide her return; the chasm was too wide to permit a hope of springing over it; no one was near to afford her relief. Though she fully believed the brightness of her spirit was dimmed for ever, she had not the least inclination to follow the example of the Lesbian songstress, nor make the rocks of Scarborough as memorable as the cliffs of Leucadia. She did not stretch out her arms to the advancing billows and welcome their approach, as a true despairing heroine should have done, but with an unaffected shudder of dismay, pressed her hands together, and upbraided herself for her unguarded folly. The thought of her parents, and the anxiety they would suffer on her account, brought with it a consolation even in its anguish.

"They will think of me, and send some one to my assistance. Mrs. Heathwood will not forget me."

Unfortunately the ledge of rocks which formed the bank she had descended was higher than the one which was her footing-ground, so that she could not ascertain whether any messenger was approaching, nor could she make any others conscious of the real danger of her situation. What convulsion of nature the sudden ignition of the dull, cold waters portended, she knew not; but it was awful to see them stretching, rolling, and dashing round her, a liquid conflagration, a foaming blaze, uniting in idea and similitude two of the most powerful and destructive elements in creation.

Every time they chafed sullenly against the coast, tossing over her head the spray, which her imagination converted into particles of living fire; chilling as they were, she started with increasing apprehension, and becoming sick and dizzy from the intenseness of her feelings, and the incessant motion of the sea around her, she believed herself doomed to find her grave in the boiling surge, whose hoarse murmurs sounded in her ear like the dirge of her own soul. It would be impossible to analyse all her emotions; but notwithstanding the fear of death, the regret of life, the thought of her mother's agony, and whatever other remembrances pressed upon her heart, an overpowering yet supporting sense of the glory of God, and a trembling reliance on his mercy, at length pervaded her being, and bore up her spirit as on the wings of the cherubim. She remembered those words of Scripture, where the prophet exclaims,—"I will hide myself in the hollow of the rock, till the glory of the Lord has passed by;" and feeling, as she had never done before, the omnipresence of the Deity, she covered her eyes with her hand, to shut out the sublime incomprehensibility of the scene; and kneeling down on the rock, commended herself to Him, who holds the world's oceans in the hollow of His hands. The fervour of faith, and the stillness of resignation, were interrupted

by the sudden, earnest sound of a human voice calling upon her; and all the hopes of life rushed warmly through her veins, when, looking up, she saw a man standing on the ledge above, for she knew he would not leave her to the consequences of her own rashness.

Edith, a few days previous to this, had noticed a stranger, who she supposed had recently arrived at Scarborough, pacing the beach, and gazing intently on the ocean. He was already on the shady side of manhood, as the slight tinge of grey that here and there dimmed the lustre of his dark brown hair, and the occasional lines that marked the smoothness of his pale, high brow, evidently showed ; yet it was equally evident that sorrow or ill-health had anticipated the touches of time, and left traces deeper than those of age on a face which must have been handsome in its prime. When he looked down on the beach as he walked, Edith thought she had never seen an expression of more prevailing melancholy, concentrated and unrelieved by one ray of gladness ; but when he suddenly raised his deep piercing eyes, the intellect that flashed from every glance seemed to disperse the shades that gathered on his brow. The effect was as instantaneous and powerful as the illumination caused by a lantern gleaming on the shadows of night.

Such was the appearance of the stranger, who now called to her from the ledge of rocks above.

"Good Heaven !" he exclaimed ; "what could induce you to expose yourself in this manner ? The tide rises at this hour, and has often covered the rocks where you are. Such a sea as this too !"

"I have indeed been most foolish and mad," she answered, ashamed of her danger, divested as it was of moral dignity. "I deserve to suffer all the consequences of such wild self-oblivion. I forgot the tide till it was too late—and this awful phenomenon."

"Be not alarmed, there is nothing to be apprehended from it : I have often seen it in other climes. One moment—I will return and release you. Thank Heaven ! the means are hard by."

It seemed but a moment, even to the expecting Edith, before he reappeared with a fishing-rod, which most fortunately some weary angler had thrown upon the beach, not far from the spot where he witnessed her isolated situation. To ascertain by this rod the locality of the stepping stones, and thus guided to wade through the tide to the place of her retreat, were acts which involved no danger to himself, while it secured her rescue, by means too simple and common-place to be strictly romantic. She hardly knew whether gratitude or shame was predominant in her mind ; when the stranger, bearing her on one arm, as if she were the child she resembled in thoughtless imprudence, while he directed his course by the staff he bore in his other hand, ascended in safety the precipitous path, over which the surge now dashed and foamed with increasing violence. It was some moments before she could realise her security ; for to her dizzy senses the ground seemed to rock and heave like the ocean she had escaped, and to be clothed with the same fiery radiance. She looked back on the rock she had just quitted, and shuddered at the wild tossing of the spray, which had lately wrapped her as with a mantle.

"How much do I owe you, sir ?" said she, with all her characteristic ardour of manner. "Yet I fear you think me a very foolish girl. How like a poor forlorn sea-gull I must have looked, perched on such an eyry ;" and she could not forbear laughing at the image her fancy drew of herself, assisted as it was by the sight of her ruffles, which fell in flimsy folds on her neck, and her uncurled locks, which, damp with the spray, and disordered by the strong sea breeze, hung heavily round her face.

"No ! you remind me of the halcyon," replied he, "sent there to soothe the troubled waves. Though, to speak truly, I was too much alarmed at your real danger, to compare you either to the bird of peace or rapine. You owe me nothing ; 'tis I who am your debtor, for you show me there is something in the world still precious—something that breathes of hope in a life of memory."

Edith, whose eyes were turned in grateful acknowledgment towards him, was suddenly embarrassed by the fervour that lighted up his gloomy countenance, and the marked emphasis of his words. Anxious to divert his thoughts from herself, she alluded to the ominous and almost supernatural appearance of the ocean.

"To your inexperienced eye," said he, "this appears supernatural, and it is, indeed, imposingly sublime. But I have been a mariner on the Indian Ocean, when the whole expanse around me was involved in an intolerable brightness.

You know it is a kind of phosphorescent glory; whether proceeding in this instance from the glowworm of the sea, or the decomposition of matter, I do not pretend to determine. I have observed, for a few days past, that the weather has been unusually sultry, and the sea, of a waveless calm, circumstances which generally herald this light in the tropical climes."

Edith knew enough of natural science to understand the nature of phosphorus, but she had never made very deep or acurate researches. The additional remarks she elicited from the stranger, though they might be uninteresting to the reader, familiarly acquainted with the secrets of science, were received by her with enthuiasm, and, continuing their conversation upon the same subject, they walked towards the hotel.

CHAPTER XXXI.

The past, the future—all that fate
Can bring, of dark or desperate,
Around such hours, but makes them cast
Intenser radiance while they last.—FIRE WORSHIPPERS.

I dare not raise my eyes to Heaven,
Nor mercy ask for me;
My soul despairs to be forgiven,
Unpardoned, love, by thee.—THE STRANGER.

DURING the events described in the last chapter, a far different scene occurred at the hotel. Florence Graham had accompanied Lady Maxwell to Scarborough; and, upon being informed by Alice Cameron, that her friend Edith was in the same house with them, she quitted the room where she had been sitting with Alice to seek her friend. The door of this room opened, as well as most of the entrances to the different apartments, into a large passage. Just as she had quitted the room, the door of another chamber opened, and there came forward Mrs. Heathwood.

Her eye caught that of Florence, and seemed to fascinate her. She suddenly became motionless; wildly she stared upon Mrs. Heathwood, who, in her turn, seemed arrested in her progress, and stood still as a statue, with her eyes fixed with absorbing interest on the beautiful apparition before her. An expression of perplexity and pain flitted over the amazed features of Florence; and then it seemed that by some almost supernatural effort, confusion, amounting to stupefaction, suddenly brightened and expanded into keen and overwhelming intelligence. Exclaiming in a frenzied tone,—" My mother !" Florence sprang forward, and fell senseless in Mrs. Heathwood's arms.

Such, after so much mystery, so many aspirations, so much anxiety, and so much suffering,—such was the first meeting of Florence Graham with her mother. She recognised in Mrs. Heathwood the features, though much older, of the portrait shown her by her father, as the likeness of her mother.

Mrs. Heathwood herself, trembling and speechless, bore the apparently lifeless Florence into her apartment. Not permitting her for a moment to quit her embrace, she seated herself, and gazed silently on the inanimate and unknown form she held so strangely within her arms. Those lips now closed as if in death had uttered, however, one word which thrilled to her heart, and still echoed, like a supernatural communication, within her ear. She examined with an eye of agitated scrutiny the fair features no longer sensible of her presence. She gazed upon that transparent brow, as if she would read some secret in its pellucid veins;

and touched those long locks of raven hair, with a trembling finger, that seemed to be wildly seeking for some vague and miraculous proof of inexpressible identity. The fair creature had called her "mother!" she dared not think whom she might be. Her thoughts were wandering in a distant land; visions of another life, another country, rose before her, troubled and obscure. Baffled aspirations, and hopes blighted in the bud, and the cherished secrets of her lorn existence, clustered like clouds upon her perplexed, yet creative brain. It was a word to make her mad. This beautiful being had called her by that name; and seemed to have expired, as it were, in the irresistible expression. Her heart yearned to her; she had met her embrace with an inexplicable sympathy; her devotion had seemed, as it were, her duty and her right. Yet who was she? She was a parent. It was a fact—a fact alike full of solace and mortification, the consciousness of which never deserted her. But she was the mother of an unknown child, to her the child of her poetic dreams, rather than her reality. And now there came this radiant creature, who called her by that name. Was she awake, and in the harsh busy world, or was it the apparition of an over-excited imagination, brooding too constantly on one fond idea, on which she now gazed so fixedly? Was this some spirit? Would that she would speak again! Would but those sealed lips part and utter but one word—would but again call her mother, and she asked no more.

Mother!—to be called so by one whom she could not name, by one over whom she mused in solitude, by one to whom she had poured forth all the passion of her desolate soul; to be called so by this being was the aspiring secret of her life. She had painted her to herself in her loneliness, she had conjured up dreams of ineffable loveliness, and inexpressible love; she had led with her an imaginary life of thrilling tenderness; she had indulged in a delicious fancy of mutual interchange of the most exquisite offices of our nature; and then when she had sometimes looked around her, and found no daughter there, no beaming countenance of purity to greet her with its constant smile, and receive the quick and ceaseless tribute of her vigilant affection, the tears had stolen down her lately excited features, all the consoling beauty of her visions had vanished into air, she had felt the deep curse of her desolation, and had anathematised the cunning brain that made her misery a thousand-fold keener by the mockery of its transporting illusions.

Mrs. Heathwood looked up to heaven as if waiting for some fresh miracle to terminate the harrowing suspense of her tortured mind; she looked down upon her mysterious companion; the rose was gradually returning to her cheek, her lips seemed to tremble with reviving breath. There was only one word more strange to her ear than that which she had uttered, but an irresistible impulse sent forth the sound.

"Florence!" exclaimed Mrs. Heathwood.

The eyes of the maiden slowly opened; she stared around her with a vague glance of perplexity, not unmingled with pain; she looked up; she caught the rapt gaze of her mother, bending over her with fondness, yet with fear; her lips moved i for a moment they refused to articulate, yet at length they again uttered "Florence!" And the only response she made was to cling to her with nervous energy, and hide her face in her bosom.

Mrs. Heathwood pressed her to her heart. Yet even now she hesitated to credit the incredible union. Again she called her by her name, but added with rising confidence, "My child!"

"Your child, your child," she murmured. "Your own Florence."

She pressed her lips to hers, which it then seemed they would never again quit; she breathed over her a thousand blessings; and she felt the tears of her mother trickling on her neck.

At length Florence looked up and sighed; she was exhausted by the violence of her emotions; her mother relaxed her grasp with infinite tenderness, and watching her with the most delicate solicitude, rested her on her knee; she leaned her arm upon her mother's shoulder, and sat with downcast eyes.

Mrs. Heathwood gently took her disengaged hand, and pressed it to her lips. "I am as in a dream," murmured Florence.

"The daughter of my heart has found her mother," said Mrs. Heathwood in an impassioned voice, "the mother who has long lived upon her fancied image."

At that moment the room door opened, and Edith Trevanion accompanied by her preserver entered. Mrs. Heathwood looked up, and beheld her husband.

She was rooted to the earth. She turned deadly pale; for a moment her countenance expressed only terror, but the terror quickly turned into aversion. The moment she had recognised her husband, she had dexterously disengaged herself from the grasp of Florence, and advancing towards Graham, she said, "Malcolm Graham, we meet at last, this is my child!"

"It is," replied Graham, and at that moment Edith quitted the room.

"Then respect for a few moments the feelings of a mother who has met her only child in a manner so unforeseen," and she turned from him towards her daughter.

The presence of her father instantaneously restored Florence to herself. Her mind was in a moment cleared and settled. Her past and peculiar life, and all its incidents, recurred to her with their accustomed order, vividness, and truth. She thoroughly comprehended her present situation. Actuated by long-cherished feelings, and the necessity of the occasion, she threw herself at her mother's feet, and exclaimed, "Oh! mother, he is my father, love him!"

Mrs. Heathwood stood with an averted countenance, Florence clinging to her hand, which she had caught when she came forward, and which now fell passive by Mrs. Heathwood's side, giving no sign by any pressure or motion, of the slightest sympathy with her daughter, or feeling for the strange and agonising situation in which they were both placed.

"Florence Velasquez," said Graham, in a voice that trembled, though the speaker struggled to appear calm, "be charitable! Accident, or some diviner motive, has brought us together this day. If you will not treat me with kindness, look not upon me with aversion before your child."

She was silent and motionless, her countenance hidden from her husband and her daughter, but her erect form betokening her inexorable mind. "Florence," said Graham, who had now withdrawn to some distance, and leant against the wall, "will not more than twenty years of desolation purchase one moment of intercourse! I have injured you. Be it so. This is not the moment I will defend myself. But have I not suffered? Is not this meeting a punishment deeper even than vengeance could devise? Is it nothing to behold this beautiful maiden, and feel that she is only yours? Florence Velasquez, look on me, look on me only one moment! My frame is bowed, my hair is grey, my heart is withered—the principle of existence waxes faint and slack in this attenuated frame. I am no longer that Malcolm Graham on whom you once smiled, but a man stricken with many sorrows. The odious conviction of my life cannot long haunt you; yet a little while and my memory will alone remain. Think of this, Florence, I beseech you, think of it. Oh! believe me when the speedy hour arrives that will consign me to the grave, where I shall at least find peace, it will not be utterly without satisfaction that you will remember that we met if even by accident, and parted at least not with harshness!"

"Mother, dearest mother!" murmured her daughter, "speak to him, look on him."

"Florence," said her mother, without turning her head, but in a calm, firm tone, "between your father and myself, there can be nothing to communicate, either of fact or feeling. Now let us depart."

"No, no, not depart!" said Florence, frantically. "You did not say depart, dear mother! I cannot go," she added in a low and half-hysterical voice.

"Desert me, then," said the mother, and Mrs. Heathwood moved to depart, but Florence, still kneeling, clung to her convulsively.

"Mother, you shall not go; you shall not leave me; we will never part,' continued Florence, in a tone almost of violence, as she perceived her mother give no indication of yielding to her wish. "Are my feelings then nothing?" she then exclaimed. "Am I for ever to be a victim?" She loosened her hold from her mother's hand, her mother moved on, Florence fell upon her forehead, and uttered a faint scream. The heart of Mrs. Heathwood relented when she fancied her daughter suffered pain, however slight; she hesitated, she turned, she hastened to her child; her husband had simultaneously advanced; in the rapid movement and confusion her hand touched that of Graham's.

'I yield her to you, Florence," said Graham, placing his daughter in her mother's arms. "You mistake me, if you think I seek to practise on the feelings of my child. She is yours; may she compensate you for the misery I have caused you, but never sought to occasion."

"I am not hurt, dear mother," said Florence, as her mother tenderly examined her forehead. "Dear, dear mother, why did you reproach me?"

"Forget it," said Mrs. Heathwood, in a softened tone; "for indeed you are irreproachable."

"Oh! Florence," said Graham, turning to his wife, "may not this maiden be some atonement—this girl, of whom I solemnly declare I would not deprive you, though I would willingly forfeit my life for a year of her affection; and your—your sufferance," he added.

"Mother! speak to him," said Florence, with her head on her mother's bosom, who still, however, remained rigidly standing. But Mrs. Heathwood was silent.

"Florence!" exclaimed Graham to his wife, rapidly advancing, with an imploring gesture, and speaking in a tone of infinite anguish, "Florence, even now we can be happy!"

The countenance of his wife was troubled, but its stern expression had disappeared. The long-concealed, yet at length irrepressible emotion, of her daughter had touched her heart. In the conflict of affection between the claims of her two parents, Mrs. Heathwood had observed with a sentiment of sweet emotion, in spite of all the fearfulness of the meeting, that Florence had not faltered in her devotion to her mother. The mental torture of her child touched her to the quick. She had too long and too fondly schooled herself to look upon the outraged wife as the only victim. There was, then, at length it appeared even to her, another. She had laboured in the flattering delusion that the devotion of a mother's love might compensate to Florence for the loss of that other parent, for the worthless husband, had she chosen to tolerate the degrading connection, even now that she knew his character, might nevertheless prove a tender father. The seeds of affection for the father of her being were mystically implanted in the bosom of his child. And, thinking of these things, she wept.

This evidence of emotion, which in such a spirit Graham knew how to estimate, emboldened him to advance; he fell on one knee before her and her daughter; gently he stole her hand, and pressed it to his lips. It was not withdrawn, and Florence laid her hand upon theirs, and would have bound them together, had her mother been relentless. It seemed to Florence that she was at length happy, but she would not speak: she would not disturb the still and silent bliss of the impending reconciliation. Was it then, indeed, at hand? In truth the deportment of Graham throughout the whole interview, so delicate, so subdued, so studiously avoiding the slightest rivalry with his wife in the affections of their child, and so carefully abstaining from attempting 'in the slightest degree to control the feelings of his daughter, had not been lost upon Mrs. Heathwood. And when she thought of him, so changed from what he had been, grey, bent, and careworn, with all the lustre that had once so fascinated her, faded, and talking of that impending fate which his wan though spiritual countenance too clearly intimated, her heart melted. At that moment the door was thrown violently open, and Black Will the Pedlar entered, who, our readers will recollect, wished the landlord of the little inn at Allendale, to give up Graham to the magistrates: he was accompanied by a constable.

"Now," said Will, "my fortune's made. Graham the Pirate, you are our prisoner."

"Never," said Graham, and he attempted to quit the room, but was seized by the Pedlar, who presented a pistol at his head; a scuffle now ensued between the two, and the constable was about laying his hand on Graham when the pistol held by the Pedlar exploded; the constable started back, and Black Will lay a corpse upon the floor. In a moment Graham darted to the window, which Florence had opened, and standing on the sill, exclaimed,—" Farewell; Florence! forget me for a while, I will return when least expected," and jumped to the ground.

Leaving for some future chapter the recital of Mrs. Heathwood's preservation from the earthquake, and her subsequent life, we will precede our friends on their return to Allendale.

———

CHAPTER XXXII.

—————————" Yes, 'tis the hand
Of death I feel press heavy on my vitals,
Slow sapping the warm current of existence.
My moments now are few—the sand of life
Ebbs fastly to its finish. Yet a little,
And the last fleeting particle will fall,
Silent, unseen, unnoticed, unlamented.
Come then, sad thought, and let us meditate
While meditate we may. We have now
But a small portion of what men call time
To hold communion: for even now the knife,
The separating knife, I feel divide
The tender bond that binds my soul to earth.
Yes, I must die—I feel that I must die;
And though to me has life been dark and dreary,
Though hope for me has smiled but to deceive,
And disappointment still pursued her blandishments,
Yet do I feel my soul recoil within me
As I contemplate the dim gulf of death,
The shuddering void, the awful blank—futurity.
Ay, I had planned full many a sanguine scheme
Of earthly happiness—romantic schemes,
All fraught with loveliness; and it is hard
To feel the hand of death arrest one's steps,
Throw a chill blight o'er all our budding hopes,
And hurl one's soul untimely to the shades,
Lost in the gaping gulf of blank oblivion.
Fifty years hence and who will hear of Constance?
Oh! none;—another busy brood of beings
Will shoot up in the interim, and none
Will hold her in remembrance. I shall sink
As sinks a stranger in the crowded streets
Of busy London: some short bustle's caused,
A few inquiries, and the crowds close in,
And all's forgotten. On my grassy grave
The men of future times will careless tread,
And read my name upon the sculptured stone;
Nor will the sound, familiar to their ears,
Recal my vanish'd memory. I did hope
For better things! I hoped I should not leave

The earth without a vestige ;—Fate decrees
It shall be otherwise, and I submit.
Henceforth, oh world, no more of thy desires !
No more of hope ! the wanton vagrant hope !
I abjure all. Now other cares engross me ;
And my tired soul, with emulative haste,
Looks to its God, and plumes its wings to heaven.
                                        KIRKE WHITE.

THE white muslin curtains of that window at the Glenroys, which looked down into the garden, were drawn together, so as to exclude the dazzling rays of the sun, which fall with such oppressive brightness on the sad and dying eye.   Children were seen leaning over the white railing, and looking up with silent awe towards the chamber, which their young imaginations invested with the pomp and solemnities of death; for it had been told them, and they whispered it to each other, that Constance Glenroy was dying.   There are few who have not felt the dim, religious grandeur associated with the scene, where a human being is known to be passing through the mysterious change which separates that breath which is the inspiration of the Almighty, from the cold particles of earth it lately warmed and informed.   We pass the mud-walled hovel, where death holds his gloomy yet magnificent court, with a sensation of thrilling veneration, which the purple and gold of royalty never could awaken; for the spot where our immortal spirit is taking its invisible flight, is the most fearful, the most glorious, in the universe.

Pale and shadowy, no vestige of her former self remaining, but her spiritual blue eyes and fair soft locks, which had been cut during her illness, and fell in short thick clusters on her brow, Constance lay half reclining in the arms of her brother, feeling that death itself was divested of its horrors, while thus upheld over the dark, misty valley.   Her mother was kneeling in prayer by her bedside, in a humiliation of sorrow and depth of resignation, which none but those who have passed through the refiner's fire are capable of feeling; and Margaret's face was bowed on the pillow in speechless anguish, all its living roses wasted by watching, weariness, and woe.

"Is the sun near setting ?" asked Constance, in a faint, difficult voice, lifting her eyes to the darkened windows.

"Not yet, my sister," answered Herbert; while the conviction that it would never rise again for her pressed cold and heavy as iron on his heart.

"I fear she will not come," continued she, still more faintly ; "at least till I am gone.   Yet I loved her so entirely, my spirit would linger here a little longer, that my parting eyes may look on her once more.   All that I love on earth will then be round me ; and I can die, Herbert—oh, I can die so happy !"

A smile, wan, yet beautiful as a moon-beam shining through mist, flitted over her ashy features, for at that moment, with footsteps "soft as snow on snow," she, whose presence she had just so affectionately desired, entered the apartment.   It was indeed Edith, of whose return to Allendale they had that day been made conscious, and who, at the earnest request of Constance, had been summoned to her dying bed.   The expiring girl feebly extended her arms towards her, with a low exclamation of mingled joy and pain ; and Edith, absorbed by sympathy and awe, scarcely perceived, while locked in her embrace, that the pillow on which Constance leaned was the bosom of Glenroy.   The tumults of earthly passion were stilled and rebuked by the immediate and solemnising presence of death; and when the eyes of Herbert and Edith met, over a face on which the damps of dissolution were beginning to gather, no conscious blushes stained their cheeks, no faltering glance told of forbidden memories. It was a sad, steadfast look, chastened by the disappointments of this world, but purified by the best hopes of another—a silent, mutual acknowledgment of blighted but imperishable affections, which, however chilled on earth, were destined to be entwined for ever, where mystery and distrust have no admittance.   Time seemed annihilated ; and eternity—God and eternity—pervaded every thought.   It was the first time Edith had ever stood by the bed " where parting life was laid," and she was oppressed by the awful reality. It was the first time she had ever truly realised she was herself a child of the dust, and doomed to decay; for she saw the consuming of beauty, the vanishing of all those fair tints which constitute the loveliness of ife. Poetry and painting may throw illusive colours around such scenes, but there

is no delusion in nature; and there is always something in the last moments of the dying, which fills the living with a kind of holy dread. Edith gazed on the sunken cheek, hueless lips, and glazing eye of the young and late beautiful Constance. She watched the labouring breath growing shorter and shorter, the damp, pallid hands closed closely together, till her own eyes grew dim and her own limbs powerless, and sinking on her knees by Mrs. Glenroy's side, the sobs of sorrow and the prayer of faith blended together by the couch of death.

No. 28.

All at length became so hushed and still, the mother rose to look upon the face of the dead ; but with one of those sudden illuminations of life's wasting lamp, Constance opened her eyes, and exclaimed with startling distinctness,—

"Mother, dear mother, bend over me. I have something to tell you. Let not Herbert marry that woman. He does not love her, and a voice just whispered to me that it was wicked. If I had not wept so much, he never would have done it. For us—for me—and now I am going to die. O God, forgive me!"

She paused a moment, and her wandering reason, mistaking the silence of powerless grief for assent, kindled into joy at the supposition.

"Oh, mother," she continued, with an angelic smile, "I knew it could not be. In my Father's house are many mansions. Then let them rake our cottage from us. We'll live in the palaces of heaven. The flowers will never wither there ; and there, Herbert, your poor Constance's tears will never grieve you more ; and Edith will comfort you for all I've made you shed on earth. For she's kind and gentle ; and then she loves you too."

The voice of the sweet enthusiast died on the ear; the unlocked hands fell heavily by her side, and the lips, just parted with a bewildered smile, were fixed in the immobility of everlasting sleep. The spirit was travelling its unseen path, and the mourners were gazing on dust and ashes.

＊　　　　＊　　　　＊　　　　＊　　　　＊　　　　＊

Who can tell the anguish of a parent's heart sorrowing for the loss of her child? He only to whom all hearts are open, and who, remembering we are clay, forbids not those fond and mournful recollections with which we invest the perished form of the object of our love. Alas! how does our startled fancy recoil from the first dread thought, and seek to cheat itself, by conjuring up, and enthroning anew, that image in our hearts which our reason sternly tells us is no more. No!—the being all life and motion, and strength and beauty, whom we have so lately held to our breasts—whose voice even now sounds as sweetest music in our ear—in whose eyes we were wont to read as in a book—whose vacant seat still stands before use—whose thousand mementos lie scattered around us—is that being indeed gone from the face of this bright earth for ever? Still—still would we seek the living among the dead! In vain does human sympathy seek to pour its oil on the dark and troubled waters of affliction. 'Tis a hand divine can alone stem the torrent which overflows our soul—'tis a voice from heaven alone can speak peace to our stricken hearts, when it tells us the dust we so loved on earth, whether it be scattered o'er the trackless desert, or be buried in the dark and fathomless abysses of the ocean, He will again build up in immortal beauty, and restore to that divine inheritance, where there is no more sorrow or death. Oh, blessed are they, who, even in the anguish of their spirits, can bring their fainting hearts to His footstool, and there, with meek submission say, "Not my will, but thine be done." With such, "weeping may endure for a night, but joy cometh in the morning."

CHAPTER XXXIII.

Those clasped hands—that look, that thrilling tone—
Oh! who of old e'er braced his armour on
For holier, higher deed—for hope more bright—
To succour age, and revel in the light
Of a young spirit's loving, grateful mood—
Sole monarch of her heart's rich solitude!
That shriek—that touch—those words that bid him stay—
But urge and light him on his onward way.
Fond heart, be still! the sacrifice must be;
And that high soul prove worthy even thee;
Although the world's loud praise—Fame's brightest guile—
Are but as tinsel to the glowing smile.—ANON.

It was the lone hour of midnight; the clouds swept darkly o'er a moonless sky; the wind had that low mysterious murmur which breathes through the pale leaves of autumn when the gale rustles through the forest; while by the dim light of a lamp that glimmered on the table, Herbert Glenroy watched by the shrouded body of Constance. The eyes of maternal and sisterly affection, that had for many a weary night kept their unslumbering vigils over her, were at length closed in a troubled sleep; but he felt as neither " poppy, nor mandragona, nor all the drowsy drugs in the world," would ever medicine him into repose. In the deep stillness of the scene, unbroken save by the sullen sweeping of the night-blast against the windows, the throbbing of his own heart assumed a sound fearful and distinct. He placed his hand on the innocent heart, now cold and pulseless as marble, so late the uncontaminated residence of vitality, and he loathed the consciousness of existence. He bent over the still and placid lips, pale and pure as the fallen snow-drop's leaves, and it seemed that he still heard the solemn prohibition breathed forth as her soul was departing—"Let not Herbert marry that woman." Then the seraphic strains that followed—" Edith shall comfort him for all the tears he has shed on earth," floated like angel symphonies on his ear.

" Never, never, sweet cherub!" he exclaimed, in irrepressible anguish of spirit; then finding the contrast chill utter lifelessness with his own stormy emotions too oppressively appalling, he rose, and throwing up the sash leaned his feverish brow against the casement, and looked steadily on the heavens, then gloomy and heavy as a funeral pall, almost wondering that he could not trace on the night arch the luminous track of his sister's ascended spirit.

While he thus gazed, a sudden flash of light flitted across his face; but dazzled by the unexpected brightness he could not ascertain its source. Again the coruscation darted through the gloom, and he distinctly saw the turret of Hexham Hall illumined by a quivering radiance, at first glimmering and uncertain, but soon shining with a steady glow, and rising like a pharos through the sea of midnight darkness.

" Sir Reginald Willoughby's house is on fire!" was his sudden exclamation of horror and surprise.

To close the sash, draw the white curtains closely round the virgin clay, descend the staircase, and rush into the street, was the work of an instant. The alarm of " fire! fire!" burst clear and high as a trumpet's call from his lips, and echoed far through the dense atmosphere. It was answered from the upper end of the street, and before he had reached the avenue of tall poplar trees, that led to the dwelling, the bell of the village church was ringing its deafening peal.

The sky, which had been overcast with heavy clouds, was brightly illumined in that part of the horizon, and reflected a glowing and ruddy light on the black scene below; while the surrounding scenery in every other direction appeared by th contrast to be wrapped in tenfold darkness; and the frequent flashes of livid light which at times shone around, left no doubt on the mind of Glenroy that the fire was rapidly consuming the dwelling.

A sudden turn of the path, and an opening among the trees, gave to his view the fire, which was each moment increasing in fury. First rose a thick volume of smoke, broken, as it were, into clouds of various shapes and shade; dense and narrow at the bottom, but expanding as it rose, and spreading wide its misty wreaths, till at length they floated over the clear grey sky like the snow flakes of a giant world. Then there was a change in the shape and colour of the smoke; forked darts of vivid flame ever and anon burst through the misty column—there seemed a mighty struggle which should gain the mastery: then the smoke partly passed away, and the vapoury pillar gave place to a bright pyramid of dazzling fire—the blaze of Truth dispelling the mist of Error. He hurried on, and the next turning in the path hid it from his view. As he came near and in full sight of the house, the flames rolled in gathering volumes from the roof of the left wing, mixed with black coils of smoke, twining like hideous serpents with the burning wreaths, undulating in the heavens.

Glenroy's blood froze in his veins, when, by the lurid light surrounding him, he saw a dark figure standing in an archway beneath the roof, which had been made as a niche for some sculptured divinity; and through the noise of the rushing flames, a shout of wild exultation was distinctly audible.

"The oppressor is oppressed," screamed the maniac voice of Evelyn; "the bolt is fallen from Heaven's own armoury, and hisses in the heart of the destroyer."

Glenroy rushed on with the speed of desperation. He understood but too well the words of the maddened prophet; and the scene in the thunder shower, beneath the portico of the old church, was brought fearfully to his memory. Notwithstanding his repugnance to his unhappy nuptials, the thought of the imminent danger to which Griselda was exposed, moved all the energies of humanity within him. He could not have winged his way with more breathless rapidity if he had seen Edith herself in the midst of conflagration, than he now did to that wing of the building which contained the chamber of Griselda Willoughby. With a strength he had never exerted before, he burst open the folding doors, and ran up the first flight of steps calling on Sir Reginald's name in a voice which might have pierced the dull, cold ear of Constance. Sir Reginald, who slept in the lower apartment of the same wing, heard the startling summons, and opening his door, exclaimed,—

"Who calls? Good Heaven! what is the matter?"

"Your house is in flames," said Glenroy, "save yourself, Sir Reginald, I'll save your daughter."

"Oh, save her!" cried the miserable father, scarcely conscious of the extent of the calamity. "For God's sake find her—in that room above—there——"

He attempted to follow the flying steps of Glenroy; but his knees knocked together, and he clung to the banisters for support, while cold clammy sweat gathered on his brow.

When Glenroy reached the landing-place, volumes of smoke rolled down through the upper gallery, reddening as they rolled, thickening and heating the atmosphere, so as to threaten instant suffocation. Smothering, groping in the darkness, he felt, by the vibration of the wood, that his hand was upon the door, but the resisting latch showed that it had been locked by the tenant.

"Griselda! Griselda!" cried he, "rouse for your life! Wake, or you perish! The flames are around you, but I'll bear you through them at life's peril."

A horrible shriek, so wild a shrill that it seemed as if the agony of years were concentrated in one breath, pierced through the barrier that separated them, followed by the sound of a heavy body falling near the door. Another effort, and he wrenched it from its hinges, but gasping and choking was driven back a moment by the flames that bursting through the other end of the apartment, were rushing with hideous roaring to find a downward passage. His reeling senses could barely distinguish a white object prone on the floor, which he conceived mus be the unfortunate Griselda, probably lifeless through fear. How he lifted the leaden weight, bore it down the staircase fast filling with smoke, while billows of fire rolled fiercely behind him, he knew not—felt not. He was only conscious that he was flying from something terrible, and that the existence of another, dependant on him for protection, was at stake.

At the foot of the marble steps in front of the devoted mansion, he staggered and fell, breathless from preternatural exertion, and gasping from the burning atmosphere he had so long inhaled. A crowd was now gathered round the spot, making fruitless endeavours to avert the progress of the o'er-mastering element. Through the confused and jarring sounds, he could hear the voice of the wretched father calling upon his child.

"My child, my child! Merciful Heaven! has she perished in the flames? Glenroy! where is he? Good God! is he too lost?"

In vain did Glenroy endeavour to answer the heartrending appeal; his parched lips and dry throat could articulate no sound; he tried to rise and bring the father to his rescued, though still insensible, daughter, but his stiffened limbs refused to obey his volition. While he thus remained, his spirit, galled by the bondage of the flesh, his eyes, blinded by the smoke and glare, were fixed by a kind of fascination on the supernatural figure that still kept its perilous station in the lofty archway. The fire was raging in the wings of the building and in the rear, but had not yet reached the post, where, like a triumphant demon, he stood shouting and laughing over the ruin he had wrought. Enveloped in the cadaverous light of the surrounding flames, his long black hair, seemingly ignited and sparkling as it streamed back in serpent coils from his brow—his unearthly accents mingling with the sullen roar of the conflagration, it is impossible for the imagination to conceive a more awful personification of a spirit of darkness, in the regions of despair.

"I've done it, I've done it," howled the maniac, "yes! pitiless wretch! the houseless and homeless has found vengeance at last. The hour is come. I waited till the mandate was given. Here I stand till the flames wrap me in their winding sheet. Here I shout till the pillars of the temple bow down beneath me, and crush me in its fall. Then, ha! ha! I'll rise immortal o'er the blazing wreck and laugh at your desolation.

Just as he had finished the last exulting sentence, a tremendous roll of flame burst through the arch over his head; the roof fell with a terrible crash, while the deluded avenger of his imagined wrongs was seen clinging for a moment to the burning rafters, then plunging, sinking down, down into a fiery grave. This horrible sight roused the paralysed senses of Glenroy. He felt as if chains were fallen from him, and the hot, deadly weight heaved from his lungs.

Far and near the surrounding scene lay strongly and magnificently visible in the deep red glare. Street and house—roof and chimney—the huge dense crowd, and the mantle of cloud and storm that veiled the heavens, all glowed like objects in the near reflection of some heated furnace. So might have gleamed the buried Pompeii, when the mountain heaved its fiery tempest to the night.

Terrified at the long and total insensibility of Griselda, Glenroy sprung upon his feet, in the hope of finding at least a draught of water in the confusion to rouse her from her deadly swoon. The voice of Dr. Rovington sounded like a preserving angel's, and he was soon by the side of his unconscious patient, followed by the half-distracted father, who, true to the holy impulses of nature, forgot the wealth he had prized so dearly, in anxiety for his only child.

"You have saved her, then, Glenroy," cried he; "God bless you, my son; God bless you!" and overcome by the sudden revulsion of his feelings, the late proud and stately Sir Reginald Willoughby sat down on the ground and wept like a boy.

"We must convey her to the nearest dwelling," said the doctor, "where we can find proper restoratives." It seemed but the space of a moment, when they entered a cottage near the late princely residence, whose female inmates were gazing in terror and admiration on the magnificent spectacle adjacent. Glenroy laid his apparently reviving burden on a bed indicated by one compassionate woman, while another ran for a candle and camphor. The moment the light shone full upon the features of the rescued victim, Glenroy recoiled with horror and amazement, exclaiming—" Gracious Providence! what have I done?"—while the miserable father, with a cry of piercing agony, fell prostrate on the floor and grovelled in the dust. It was indeed no other than Miss Tabitha Shanks, who, by a strange providence, had that night slept in the room so lately occupied by Griselda, who had taken possession of another, in a different part of the building, and Tabitha had thus received the succour intended for the unfortunate heiress.

" Is it yet too late ?" cried Glenroy, rushing again into the road, whither Sir Reginald, clinging to the hope excited by his words, immediately pursued him.

They had scarcely reached the building, when a piercing shriek of anguish and despair smote on their ears, and rivetted them to the spot, and which at the same time drew the attention of all the spectators to that part of the building from which the heartrending shriek proceeded. The cause was but too evident.

At one of the upper windows was seen dimly, amid the smoke and flames which appeared to surround her, the form of a female, who, with frantic cries, and distracted gestures, vainly entreated for assistance. Scarcely was there time to behold the awful situation of this unhappy being, before she suddenly disappeared, and the intervening columns of smoke shrouded her from their view.

A simultaneous exclamation of horror now burst from every spectator : " Gracious Heaven! she has fallen into the devouring flames—she's lost for ever." A sudden silence ensued ; every eye was anxiously bent on the spot where she appeared, when a gentle breeze blowing aside the smoke, she was again discovered with clasped hands and uplifted eyes, supplicating from Heaven that consolation and succour which no human aid could afford. A sight so distressing could not but touch even the most frozen heart. A cry of horror again burst forth from the spectators ; but there was no head sufficiently collected to devise, nor hand bold enough to execute, any expedient for relief from her impending fate.

At this moment—a moment so replete with bitter anguish—her self-possession had not entirely forsaken her. The activity of Glenroy, who was eagerly urging some of the country people to procure a ladder, had fixed her attention—in him she recognised the form of one in whom had centred all her hopes of happiness, whose presence now only served to increase the agony of her soul. With eagerness she stretched out her hands, and called upon him to save her from her perilous situation ; the recognition had been mutual—when the circling smoke again obscured Griselda from view.

With frantic impetuosity Herbert Glenroy forced his way through the gazing crowd, and, in defiance of all opposition, attempted to enter the flaming house, but, fortunately for him, in vain—the fire continued to rage with unabated fury, and the half-burnt beams obstructed the entrance ! the stairs were already partly consumed—to reach the apartment that contained the unhappy Griselda by that way was impossible. Equally unavailing were the liberal offers of Sir Reginald to that person who could devise the means for her escape.

" A thousand pounds to any one who will save her," cried he.

" Life is as dear to us as to you, sir !" said several voices.

" Will no one save her, then ?" said Sir Reginald, wildly, as the screams of his daughter became more dreadful. " Will no one save her ?"

" I will, Sir Reginald !" It was the voice of a young peasant ; but his mother clung around him.

" Oh, Sir Reginald ! bid him stay here ! Rob not the widow of her only prop!"

" Is it certain death, then ?"

" Certain !" cried several voices.

" I will venture ! You will take care of my mother, Sir Reginald, if I die. Keep her back, some one ;" but the mother clung the more wildly to her son.

" Sir Reginald, bid him stay. Why should one life be lost for another, or both —the poor for the rich ?"

Sir Reginald paused in silent agony. What right had he to rob the widow of her only stay? He felt the force of the appeal, and waved him back.

Glenroy had rapidly inspected the whole of the building, in hope of finding some other place of entrance, with as little success. Equally useless were his repeated entreaties that she would throw her herself from the window, and trust to him alone for her safety. But she was either too much confused, and too irresolute, to follow his advice, or noise and the crackling of the burning timber prevented her from hearing him distinctly.

The progress of the fire admitted no delay—something must be instantly attempted, or she must inevitably perish. To preserve her life at the hazard of his own, required no second thought. It is only under cogent circumstances of such extremity, that we are able to ascertain what we can perform. Had Glenroy been an uninterested observer, the calls of humanity would have been sufficient to have displayed his firmness and intrepidity; but at this moment, his was the courage of desperation. Having determined to rescue her, he resolved to make some attempt, however perilous, for her preservation. He had observed some out-houses, almost adjoining, though detached from the burning on that side where Griselda had been seen, and imagined, that if some communication could be formed between them and the window at which she had appeared, there was still a possibility of saving her from destruction.

Every one at his suggestion was busy in endeavouring to find something that could be employed for this purpose. At length encouraging shouts proclaimed that assistance was at hand. A ladder, which had been found in the garden, was immediately raised for the purpose on the roof of these out-buildings; but the dismay of the spectators was, if possible, still increased, on finding that it was too short to reach the window. All was again despair—the flames suddenly burst from the window beneath that at which Griselda was awaiting assistance; they raged for a short time, when the floor gave way beneath her, and she was precipitated in the burning mass—a shriek told her fate, and as she was seen falling through from the lower windows, Sir Reginald exclaimed,—

" Oh! look there, look there, Glenroy!" and he groaned with anguish, " burning—burning—childless! houseless! Merciless judge! I ask but to die."

Nature does not portion its affections in proportion to the worth of the object; and with all her imperfections, Griselda was very dear to her father's heart. She was his only child, and all his earthly love was garnered up in her, even as if she were a treasury of " Heaven's own influences." This selfish and high-minded man, who had imagined prosperity immortal, and adversity of plebeian rank, humbled, crushed beneath the hand of the Almighty, felt, for the first time, the powerlessness of earth, and the omnipotence of Heaven. Transfixed like a statue, he gazed on the broad mass of living flame now wrapping every outline of the dwelling, the certain grave of his child, over whose rescue he had so recently wept in the impotence of joy; then covering his face with his hands, he would again have bowed himself to the dust, had not the arm of Glenroy sustained him, and supported him back to the shelter they had formed; where Miss Shanks, bewildered and aghast, was yet rejoicing in the consciousness of her recovered existence.

No thought of self entered the breast of Glenroy in this hour of unlooked-for dismay. Every feeling of former repugnance was merged in commiseration for the awful doom of his affianced wife; and remembering only the devoted affection she had avowed for him, and the relief his family had received through her instrumentality, he upbraided himself for his coldness and aversion, his selfishness and ingratitude. He had done all that man could do; he had perilled his own life to save hers, as freely as if she had been the dearest object in the universe, but destiny had rendered his efforts futile. Never, without a shivering sensation, could he recal the shriek that pierced hs ears, which he fervently hoped might have been her death-shriek, so dreadful was the image of the agonies that must have succeeded.

Through the remainder of that disastrous night, he remained with the wretched Sir Reginald, by a sympathy deeper than words, affording him a consolation words are impotent to convey. Thus smitten by calamity, he was an object of reverence in his eyes, far greater than he had ever been in his hour of pride and prosperity,—for sorrow is Heaven's anointing oil, and sanctifies the being on whom its influence is shed.

The morning sunbeams, undimmed by the woes of man, shone dazzingly down on the smouldering wreck of Hexham Hall, where the ashes of the maniac Evelyn and the unfortunate Griselda Willoughby, mingled undistinguished from the ruins of lifeless matter, save by some bleached and ghastly bones.

CHAPTER XXXIV.

Let wretches loaded hard with guilt as I am,
Bow with the weight, and groan beneath the burden;
Creep, with the remnant of the strength they've left,
Before the footstool of the Heaven they've injured.—OTWAY.

ALTHOUGH business increases on our hands, and the plot of our story thickens, we must for awhile leave Glenroy and return to our heroine; but were we disposed to exercise the art of bookmaking, we could furnish a long chapter in detailing the gossip among the villagers occasioned by the recent occurrences at Allendale; but we have neither time nor inclination for having recourse to such mean artifices; the great events of this veritable history which we have still to relate, and the plots which remain to be unfolded, are more than sufficient to extend this work to the size originally intended.

Winter had now set in, not in his terrors, but in that gloomy desolation which saddens the face of nature. By day, the sun, skirting along the horizon, scarcely showed his blunted beams through the dense haze which hovered around; the leafless trees were covered with glittering gems, which sometimes seemed dissolved in tears; at others, were shaken off by the blast, rattling as they fell among the withered leaves, as the clods of the valley rattle on the coffin, when deposited in the dark chambers of the "narrow house." The song of the woodlands was now silent, except when the cushat still complained in her deep recess. High in air the clamorous crows, in wild and irregular flight, wheeled in mingled confusion and with ceaseless noise, as they winged their way in quest of scanty food. Cutting their way in wedge line, as if their course had been directed by a drill-sergeant, or as if they sailed through the air upon the system of Clerks Naval Tactics, came the geese from the hills, and the wild ducks from the lakes; while the solitary wail of the curlew, and the wild scream of the heron, were heard in the marshes. Robin hopped around the cottage door, or twittered on the leafless spray, brushing off the hoar frost with his wings, as he fluttered among the branches. Dark louring clouds ushered in the long and dreary night; the torrent resounded from the valley; the watch-dog bayed the twilight passenger; the fox howled the heath-clad hill, and owl hooted from the thicket.

A bright fire burned on the hearth of the sitting room at Heathwood, and before it sat Florence and her mother, whose head rested on the table in an attitude of deep dejection; her face was deadly pale, and her lips quivered with suppressed emotion. She had been relating to her daughter her history from the time she first became acquainted with Graham, to the time she gave to old Mary Adams her infant daughter, with the packet containing the history of her birth, with which the reader is well acquainted.

After a few minutes spent in endeavouring to compose herself, Mrs. Heathwood again commenced.

"Let me—let me, I conjure you, hurry over the sad remnant of my calamitous

ttory.   Horrors on horrors crowd on my memory—my brain turns at the recollec-
ion—I will proceed—but briefly.

" My father had intended to send me far in the country, on the night when I
gave you to Mary Adams, but, on the morning when he found I had contrived to
send you away, he altered his intentions.   What was my consternation, when he
bade me prepare to receive the son of an ancient friend, who had just arrived from

England, as my future husband, declaring that we had been betrothed to each
other by our parents from infancy.   When in dismay and trembling, I shrank
from the proposition, and besought him never to mention his name again, he fell
nto a fearful passion, and commanded me to obey him as a daughter.   What secret
bond united him to the father of Mr. Heathwood, I know not.   It is one of those
secrets which will never be revealed till the judgment-day; but, I believe this
union had dependencies, which were never to be divulged to the world.

No. 29.

" He spurned my prayers and my tears, and, when driven to despair, I fell at his feet and pleaded my marriage with your father—Righteous Powers! how terrible is man in his wrath! The tempest swept over me, but it did not crush me. He declared our nuptial vows null and illegitimate. The priest who united us was dead—there was no witness left on earth—the record was only in heaven. He breathed forth dark threats against you; he made your life the condition of my obedience; and I, child that I was, believed that he had the power of life and death in his hands, although I knew that you were far from him. I would have thrown myself on the compassion of my destined husband, but I was not permitted to be with him alone. The stern eye of parental despotism was for ever upon me. Let me not curse a father's memory: in all else he was kind. That some awful oath bound him to the dead father of Heathwood, I must ever believe; and the happiness and rectitude of his child was to be the devoted sacrifice. Oh! how can I recal the agonies of the past?

" I saw the preparations for bridal festivity—the paraphernalia more dreadful to me than the winding sheet of the grave. My senses seemed paralysed—a nightmare brooded over my soul—I was passive and despairing, a kind of connecting link between the living and the dead. With a shivering heart and a fiery brain, I was carried to the altar.

" Let me hasten to the close, while my failing strength is yet equal to the task. I remember nothing, till I found myself alone with Mr. Heathwood, for the first time, on the evening of the fatal ceremony. He addressed me in the language of gentleness and persuasion. He drew near me, and taking my cold and trembling hand in his, vowed to devote his life to my felicity. The lethargy of madness and despair was broken up; with a maniac shriek I snatched my hand from his grasp, and throwing myself wildly on the ground, implored his malediction instead of his blessing. I knelt in the strong prostration of agony at his feet, and told him the wretch I had made myself and him. Unhappy Heathwood—he was worthy of a better fate; I blighted his opening manhood—I doomed him to an early grave. He did not mock me in my humiliation and woe. He saw that my brain was smitten —my reason wavering; he gave me back my unhallowed vows; he forswore his own in the name of the all-hearing God, raised me, forgave me, and left me—I never saw him more."

Mrs. Heathwood paused, overcome by the intensity of her recollections. Florence was dreadfully agitated. " And did he never return?" she asked; " did my father never come back to claim you as his own?"

" Never," was the reply. " My father had circulated a report that I had perished in the earthquake which visited the island a short time after you were born. Being anxious to recover you, and being now my own mistress, I quitted Madeira for England. We were driven on our voyage by distress of weather to remain several days at a port in France; here we found the vessel in which I had taken my passage so violently shattered and impaired, that it was near two months ere we could proceed on our voyage. Another vessel put in; it brought intelligence of the most awful nature—the death of my parents.

" I arrived in England, deprived of father—mother—child! reft of every stay on earth. Vain were my inquiries after you and my nurse, Mary Adams; I advertised in all the papers for weeks, but without effect. All hope of seeing my little lost one became extinct, and I determined to trust to Providence to bring us together, as I felt fully convinced that we should certainly meet again. I sought out my father's man of business in London, by whose honesty I became possessed of immense wealth, far beyond my most sanguine expectations. I remained in London some years, and then, hearing that this beautiful residence was for sale, I purchased it, and have ever since resided here; except when I have occasionally gone to London, or upon visits to the neighbouring gentry."

It is curious to recal our feelings at a moment when a great event is impending over us, and we are utterly unconscious of its probable occurrence. How often does it happen that a subject which almost unceasingly engages our mind, is least thought of at the very instant that the agitating suspense involved in its consideration is perhaps about to be terminated for ever!

That very moment, as Mrs. Heathwood had concluded her narrative, the servant entered and laid before her a letter; what was her agitation when she recognised the handwriting of her husband—that handwriting which in her early years had ofttimes infused joy in her young heart! Her first thought was to save Florence from sharing that agitation. She rose quickly; she commanded herself sufficiently to advise her daughter, in a calm tone, to remain seated, while for a moment she refreshed herself by a stroll. She had not quitted Florence many paces, when she broke the seal and read these lines:—

"Tremble not, Florence, when you recognise this handwriting. It is that of one whose only aspiration is to contribute to your happiness; and, although the fulfilment of that fond desire may be denied him, it never shall be said, even by you, that any conduct of his should now occasion you annoyance. I am in Hexham—start not, in Hexham gaol. I have gazed at night upon your house, and watched the form of my wife and child; but a little help from you, and I quit England for ever, and it shall not be my fault if you are ever again disturbed by the memory of the miserable Graham. But to accomplish my escape, I make this one appeal, if not to your justice, at least to your mercy. After the fatal separation of a life, we have once more met: you have looked upon me not with hatred; my hand has once more pressed yours; for a moment I indulged the impossible hope that this weary and exhausted spirit might at length be blessed. With agony I allude to the incident that dispelled the rapture of this vision. The bloodhounds never gave over the pursuit; they tracked me day by day, and although compelled to hide in the woods, and subsist for awhile upon the wild berries from the hedges, they captured me at last.

"Whatever may have been my errors, whatever my crimes—for I will not attempt to justify to you a single circumstance of my life—I humble myself in the dust before you, and solicit only mercy; yet whatever may have been my career, oh! Florence, in the infinite softness of your soul, was it not for a moment pardoned? You are a woman with a brain as clear as your heart is pure. Judge me with calmness; and surely, Florence, when I kneel before you full of deep repentance and long remorse, if you could pardon the past, however mortifying, I will for ever bless you!

"Once you loved me; I ask you not to love me now. There is nothing about me now that can touch the heart of woman. I am old before my time; bent with the blended influence of action and of thought, and of physical and moral suffering. The play of my spirit has gone for ever. My passions have expired like my hopes. The remaining sands of my life are few. Once it was otherwise. You can recal a different picture of the Malcolm Graham on whom you smiled, and of whom you were the first love. Oh, Florence!—grey, feeble, exhausted, penitent—let me escape from here and die! I ask no more—I will not even count on your pity; but do not, oh, do not leave me to die upon a scaffold!"

It was read again and again—dim as was the sight of Mrs. Heathwood with fast flowing tears. Still holding the letter, but with hands fallen, she gazed upon the heavens before her in a fit of abstraction. It was the voice of her daughter that roused her.

"Mother," said Florence, in a tone of some decision, "you are troubled, and we have only one cause of trouble. That letter is from my father."

Mrs. Heathwood gave her the letter in silence.

Florence withdrew almost unconsciously a few paces from her mother. She felt this to be the crisis of her life. There never was a moment which she believed required more fully the presence of all her energies. Before she had addressed Mrs. Heathwood, she had endeavoured to steel her mind to great exertion. Yet now that she held the letter, she could not command herself sufficiently to read it. Her breath deserted her; her hand lost its power; she could not even open the lines on which life depended. Suddenly, with a rapid effort, she glanced at the contents. The blood returned to her cheek—her eye became bright with excitement—she gasped for breath—she advanced to her mother. "You will grant all that he desires !"

Still gazing on the heavens, Mrs. Heathwood continued silent.

"Mother," said Florence, "my beloved mother, you hesitate." She approached Mrs. Heathwood, and, with one arm round her neck grasped with the other her parent's hand. "I implore you, by all that affection which you lavish on me, yield to this supplication. Tell me so—I beseech you tell me so. You loved him when you deemed he had forgotten you ; when you pictured him to yourself in all the pride of health, wanton and daring, and now that he writes to you from a prison, penitent, perhaps dying, more like a remorseful spirit than a breathing being, and humbles himself before you, and appeals only to your mercy,—you cannot desert him—no, no, mother, you will not—for his sake, for your own sake, and for your child's, you will not !"

"My child ! my child ! all my hopes were in my child," murmured Mrs. Heathwood.

" Is she not by your side ?" said Florence.

"You know not what you ask; you know not what you counsel." said her mother. "It has been the prayer and effort of my life that I should never see him more ; he deceived me, cruelly deceived me, and left me to struggle as I might. There is a bitterness in the reconciliation which follows long estrangement, tha yields a pang more acute even than the first disunion."

"The pang is already felt, mother, " said Florence. "Reject my father, but you cannot resume the feelings of a month back. You have seen him—you have listened to him. His image has entered your soul; your heart is softened. Leave him to die upon the scaffold, and you will remain the most miserable of women."

" Florence," said Mrs. Heathwood, with a great effort, " I am miserable."

This unprecedented confession of suffering from the strong mind of her mother melted Florence to the heart. She advanced, and threw her arms round her mother's neck, and buried her weeping face in her bosom.

"Speak to me, my daughter," said Mrs. Heathwood ; "counsel me, for my mind trembles ; anxiety has weakened it. Nay, I beseech you speak—speak, Florence—what shall I do?"

"Render my father that assistance which he requires."

Ear'y the following morning Mrs. Heathwood and her daughter proceeded to the prison at Hexham ; and soon found themselves in one of its gloomy cells. A mist seemed to fall over the sight of Mrs. Heathwood as the ponderous door closed on her, and she trembled so violently, that she was compelled to lean against the wall for support.

As she recovered her self-possession, she looked around the miserable place in which she stood. In one corner, on a heap of straw, sat a man with his wrists and ankles heavily ironed. He appeared to be labouring under strong agitation, and, rising with difficulty, he slipped one of his hands from the iron ring that confined it, and threw back the hair from his forehead. At the same moment he advanced, so that the light from the solitary window fell on his features. Mrs. Heathwood uttered one wild, heart-piercing shriek, and sunk nearly insensible on his bosom. When she recovered consciousness, she started from his supporting arm, and exclaimed, " Misery—misery to find you thus !" and she covered her face with her hands, and wept bitterly.

"Florence," said Graham, "you do indeed find me wretchedly situated. Had not necessity compelled me to unfold it, you should never have known it."

"Oh, Graham,—what could so darken your once kind heart,—why did you follow such a dreadful life ?"

"Desperation," replied he ; " I found myself despised by my father, while my elder brother was looked upon with affection—fortune I had none, that also went to my brother. In an evil hour, a savage joy broke every link that bound me to my species, and I became a pirate—I have seen the proud man kneel for mercy, and the coward shriek in his agony, and I laughed as I heard the death-rattle in their throats—I knew it was death to be loved by such a wretch as I was—I changed my name, I wooed and won you—your father discovered my real character—I tore myself away from you, and tried to cease to love you—since then my career has been one of strife and bloodshed." He paused for a moment, and then continued :—" The love of life is strong, and I knew it was only through your means, that I could obtain the means of escape. All I require of you is, to visit me this evening, and bring a file, a countryman's frock and a piece of rope, and my escape is certain."

Mrs. Heathwood listened in bewildered silence. She was too much overwhelmed to have the power of thought. Graham did not understand the cause of her silence.

" Do you shrink from assisting?" he inquired in a stern tone : then softening, he continued, "If so, I can but die."

" Die !" almost shrieked the distracted wife. "Die! when I save you! No—no—if you do not wish to drive me quite mad, do not use such reproachful language. I would—indeed I would, give my life to rescue you from impending fate."

The unfortunate man again approached her, and drawing her towards him, threw his arm around her.

* * * * * *

That night Graham with a small file cut through the manacles that encircled his ankles, and then proceeded to file the iron bars at the window. To conceal the noise made by the file he began to sing, and when he had got half through the last bar the file broke. He endeavoured to wrench the bars from their place ; he exerted his strength to the utmost in repeated trials, but apparently not the slightest effect followed.

He threw himself upon the straw, exhausted by his continued exertions.

" Am I to be baffled at last? What mean these fearful forebodings, which now press with benumbing weight upon my soul? Have I forgotten my motto?

' Fate wills that I should conquer.'

Let me gaze once more upon the heavens. The star of destiny has mounted stil higher, and methinks smiles upon me. One more effort for safety."

Nerving himself for a desperate exertion of strength, Graham again approached the window. He was now more successful. The iron gradually yielded, and in another moment bent, and the window was open for his escape. Hastily putting on the countryman's frock, he tied the rope to part of the iron-work of the window, and slid gently down to the ground; but at that moment, the watch-man approached. The night was dark and chilly. A solitary star twinkled in the heavens. A thick pall of clouds overspread the firmament, shrouding all Nature in blackness and gloom.

As the watchman came near, Graham assumed the stagger and appearance of a drunken countryman.

" Who goes there ?" exclaimed the watchman, as Graham approached him.

" I say mi—mister, what the de—devil is the reason that you—you build your streets so cur—cursed crooked in this town. A man ca—can't walk straight without coming slap against a house every fi—five minutes, de—devilish provoking."

" Who are you, friend ?"

" Who am I—ah—who am I ?—ah—ah. I'll be hanged if I know who I am —but who the devil are you?" and he advanced another step, but unhappily stumbled against a stone, which nearly laid him sprawling on the ground.

' Keep your distance, friend, and answer my question."

"Answer your question your—yourself," and he sung a stanza of a drinking-song, very popular in those days,—

"Drink, boys, drink—here's to the foe—
And may the devil get them—

> Drink, boys, drink—here's to our friends,
> And may no harm beset them!—ugh—ugh.
> Hurra—the glass
> Shall merrily pass—
> Drink, boys, drink!"

"Well, I ho-hope not. The night's as black as a nigger's face. Where is my te-team; or the ta-tavern where I left my te-team; or the town where I left my team and the ta-tavern?"

"Here's the prison," said the watchman laughing; "and unless you become a little more quiet, I shall provide you with quarters here for to-night."

"Oh, oh! this is Hex-Hexham then,—and the cour-court house sure'enough. Well, then, the tavern is a li-little way above—I say, mister, where is the ta-tavern?"

"Which tavern?"

"Why, the ta-tavern where I left my te-team. I wonder if my te-team has lost its place too."

"There is a tavern a few rods below this place, which is much frequented."

"Ay, ay, below—let-let me see;" and Graham imitating to perfection the drunken man, looked around him—an operation which his apparent want of balance rendered sufficiently ludicrous; this was done to ascertain the road least frequented. "Below—well, that isn't above—damme if I know which is be-below; when it's so dark and clo-cloudy how can a man see his way?"

"I am to understand, then, that you are from the country?"

"Ay, that am I—and I am go-going back again to mor-morrow."

"Where do you live?"

"Don't you know old Tom Wilson? well tha-that's a good one—ah, ah—come give us your flipper.

> "Come, all ye covenanters,
> I'd have you for to know,
> That for to fight the enemy,
> We're going for to go.
>
> Then shoulder on your muskets, boys,
> All loaded for to fight;
> We'll conquer, and march home again
> Before to-morrow night!"

By this time they had got a long way past the rope, which Graham was fearful the watchman would notice, but his apparent drunkenness had the desired effect, and kept the watchman's attention to himself.

"Well, march about your business now, we have had enough of this foolery," said the watchman, and turned from him. This was all Graham wanted, staggering in a different direction to keep up the farce, until the darkness rendered them indistinct to each other; ne approached the rope, and taking a small knife from his pocket, he cut a piece off, high as his arms could reach, so that it should not be observable in the darkness. He then, casting a hasty glance behind him, quitted Hexham for ever.

CHAPTER XXXV.

I've seen thee in the sunset beams,
I've loved thee as a thing divine:
How have I shunned thee? but thine eye
Hangs o'er me like a watching sphere,
Star of my solitary sky,
Where'er my spirit turns, 'tis there;
For life, for death, the chain is twin'd.—CROLY.

THE master of fiction has compared he course of a supposititious history to the career of a stone, rolled down the side of a mountain which at first labouring and stumbling along in a slow and hesitating manner, as if on the point of being arrested by every petty obstruction, gathers force as it descends, and at last pitches onwards with impetuous leaps, which soon conduct it to the bottom. To give the figure the completeness of an allegory, it may be added, that when the moving body has once acquired a little superfluous momentum of its own, it communicates it to other stones, and these again to others, which increasing in number as they grow in velocity, are at last seen rattling down to the vale below, in a perfect avalanche, as confounding to the senses as it is hurrying to the spirits. In this manner, a single incident begins its weary course along the declivity of story, stirring up others as it rolls onward; until, in the end, there is such a mass in motion, that if all were to be described as fully as at the starting, it would require a Briareus himself to do them justice. It is, then, difficult to keep pace even with the original event, the course of which is as violent as the others; and this can be done only by imitating the hurry of the moving body, and marching in great leaps to the end.

We must pass over the confusion caused throughout Hexham by the escape of Graham; the steps that were taken to follow him; and the joy that pervaded the bosoms of Florence and her mother at his success, and proceed on with that part of the story which pertains to the Glenroys.

It was a short time after the destruction of Hexham Hall and the burial of Constance that the following letter was received by Herbert Glenroy:—

"SIR,—I would not intrude on you at such an hour, did not the motive that actuates me lift me above the cold ceremonies of society. We are about proceeding to London; let this circumstance be my apology for invading the sanctuary of domestic affliction. I could not depart and leave a question, in which my own happiness is deeply interested, undecided. As the guardian of a daughter's delicacy I cannot now add more. But favour me with an interview, and I shall then learn whether I shall hereafter regret having in this instance expressed so much.
"TREVANION."

In consequence of this note Glenroy presented himself at the general's, and, on entering the drawing-room, found himself in the presence of Trevanion.

After the usual salutations the general commenced:—

"I do not ask you to pardon the intrusion of my note. I know too well the desolation caused by severed affections to allow fastidious scruples to triumph over what I consider my first and holiest duties. I would not violate the respect due to the memory of the departed, but the feelings of a father are sacred. Suffer me to ask you one question, and your answer will determine my future conduct. Do you still love my daughter?"

"He alone who made me knows how fervently I love her," answered Glenroy, the blood rushing high into his temples as he spoke; "but I cannot even claim a place in her esteem. Bewildered at your unexpected kindness, I marvel at its source."

"To be candid with you at once," replied Trevanion, "I know your history. Jealous of my daughter's felicity, I marked a cloud upon her sunshiny spirit, and learned from her all her heart. The mystery that obscured your character has since been dispersed, and you are fully vindicated in your estimation. The woman whom you rescued from the flames is now a guest of mine, and in gratitude to you has related a conversation which occurred on the banks of the river, to which she was an unseen listener. My daughter feels that she has unconsciously wronged you, and does honour to the rectitude of your principles, and the strength of your filial devotion."

Not all the joys which Glenroy felt, at being once more reinstated in Edith's esteem, could overpower the pain he experienced, that Griselda's shameful secret had not been buried in her untimely grave. He never would have justified himself at the expense of her reputation, and, little aware of Miss Shanks' listening capabilities, believed his own honourable bosom its only depository. For one moment, however, he yielded with tumultuous ecstasy to the conviction of Edith's love, and the hope that dawned upon his destiny; but a cold recollection came over him like a death frost, and holding down the throbbings of his heart, he sought to answer the piercing glance of General Trevanion with one that shrunk not from his scrutiny.

"I am most unfortunate, sir," said Glenroy. "You have learned the mysteries of my past life, and I know they will be sacred in your keeping; for not only my own honour, but that of a most respectable individual is inevitably involved. That I love your daughter, even to idolatry, I dare not deny; but it is in the utter hopelessness of passion, for shackled on every side, weighed down by obligations it must be the business of my life to cancel, I know that I have but one difficult path to tread. No! sir, prouder than I am poor, I must be content to adore, lone and remote, the excellencies I can never claim as my own."

"Not so," answered Trevanion, vehemently; "I am rich by the decease of a distant relative, who has bequeathed to me immense wealth, and you have that to which gold is but dust. Edith," continued he suddenly opening the door, which led into the library, "Edith, my child, come hither."

Startled by the unexpected summons, Edith came with instant obedience, unconscious that she was called into the presence of him, who at that moment was occupying all her thoughts. Arrested by surprise and emotion, she stood before him, the beautiful colour of modesty mantling her cheek, while the face of Glenroy became as pale as the marble bust placed over the mantel-piece on which he leaned.

"My daughter shall be the umpire," said the general, taking her hand into his and drawing her towards him; "Edith, this young man is a paradox. He professes he lives but to adore you, while his pride forbids him to claim alliance with your virtues. What think you of the strength of that love that yields without a struggle to the empire of pride?"

"Without a struggle!" exclaimed Glenroy—"Heaven be my witness that you wrong me. Edith, Miss Trevanion, since first I have known you, my life has been one continual conflict between love and duty. Were I the master of thousands, I should still deem myself unworthy of your acceptance, but now— there is a bond upon my soul." Here Glenroy's proud blood flowed back with painful revulsion even to his brows. "Spare me," he continued, "spare the memory of the dead." In bitter humiliation of spirit, he knelt at her feet, oppressed by the greatness of the sacrifice he was making. "Pride! Edith, does this look like pride? I have never knelt but in prayer before, and now, while I know I must resign you for ever, my soul prostrates itself in the dust before you, to vindicate its adoration."

"No! inestimable young man, you shall never resign her," exclaimed Trevanion. "I had rather a daughter of mine were united to such high and honourable worth, than see her placed upon a throne. Consider me from this moment in the light of a father, and as such, responsible for every obligation you have imposed on yourself. You will still leave me your debtor, if you prove a faithful guardian to my child. And now, Edith, bid him rise, and tell him as he once sacrificed love to filial duty, he must now immolate his pride to his love."

"If he deem me worthy of a sacrifice," said Edith, holding out her hand to

Glenroy, with a 'smile] so lovely in its bashful archness, it would have conferred value on a much meaner offering.

"I am used to despair, but not to happiness," cried Glenroy, bending his head over the trembling hand that raised him from the earth. "I cannot sustain such a weight of gratitude, a bankrupt even in words."

He remembered the moment when he had parted from Edith, on the threshold of Mrs. Heathwood's door—and holding her icy hand in his, had prayed that he

might never again clasp it, unless he could retain it for ever—and now, as its yielding softness thrilled to his inmost heart, he felt the blissful assurance, that it might be his, by every sanction that paternal authority and maiden truth could give. Even pride, rebelling against the burthen of obligation from the father, became merged in a consciousness of unutterable joy.

"You have rebuked my haughty spirit, sir," said he, turning towards General

No. 30.

Trevanion a countenance luminous with feeling. I will not blush to be your debtor, in the confidence of one day redeeming what I may owe ; for in England the path of honourable distinction is open to all. That path I have sworn to tread, and when I have travelled so far as to secure even the reversion of fame and fortune, then, sir, and not till then, I will claim your daughter."

"You have the reversion now ; you have a security in your talents and present reputation. But I cannot for the present part with my daughter ; nor would I have you fail in any respect due to the unfortunate family, with which you are in honour connected. To-morrow we go to London, and in one year from this time we shall return, and then we can talk about those worldly trifles, fame and fortune."

He approached the door as he was speaking, and opening it as he uttered the last words, turned upon Edith a benign smile, and left the apartment.

*   *   *   *   *   *

Winter, as we said in the last chapter, had commenced, and miry ways, sullen skies, and chilling winds, bespoke the presence of December. Dreary as was the outward face of things, no less dreary were the feelings of the Glenroys.

Winter, indeed, is dark and unlovely, yet it had generally been welcomed with cheerfulness. Allendale was not more gloomy, more leafless, or more clouded than usual at the fall of the year. What then made it appear so changed ? Passion had been there. Tranquillity ceases to be valued when we have recently known delight ; it is only after the turbulence of grief that it can be again appreciated. The last few months had been a period of unceasing excitement ; and now that the little circle once more closed round its hearth, the charm of domestic privacy was not immediately felt. There was much more to think of with regret in the past, than to enjoy in the present, or hope for in the future.

Mrs. Glenroy, indeed, as she made up the evening blaze, would exclaim, "How long it is since we have enjoyed a nice, uninterrupted winter evening !" And then, casting her eyes upon the vacant seat of her much-loved Constance, a tear would roll down her aged cheeks, and she would remain silent for the greater portion of the evening, thinking of her once beautiful child ; or probably meditating upon her loneliness, when Margaret and Herbert should be married, and her household completely broken up ; as it was decided that Margaret should be wedded to Gilbert Stanhope on the same day that the destinies of Edith and Herbert Glenroy should become united.

CHAPTER XXXVI.

Oh, blame her not ! When zephyrs wake,
The aspen's trembling leaves must shake ;
When beams the sun through April's shower,
It needs must bloom the violet flower ;
And love, howe'er the maiden strive,
Must with reviving hope revive.—SCOTT.

COULD Florence have drank a Lethean draught, and buried in oblivion the events of a few past months, she had been happy; for she had everything within her reach that could then conduce to it—friends, admirers, youth, talents, and beauty. The natural vivacity of her disposition was certainly clouded from recent causes, yet neither the goodness of her heart nor the affability of her temper had undergone any change ; and, notwithstanding the glowing tint, which a short time back dwelt unrivalled on her cheek, became, sometimes, superseded by a varying tinge of paler hue, when, in spite of her mother's precautions, thoughts would obtrude themselves, to the disturbance of happier moments, still the early bud of promise was ripening into perfection. Florence's innate modesty repressed the bold stare of admiration, but she could not repel the admirer. The notice she attracted gave her no pleasure; and the desire she evinced in her manners to avoid it but attracted it to her the more.

Winter and spring both passed; and summer was making rapid advances, with its calm, placid evenings; with its crimson glories; and its warm, glowing magnificence; its gentle breezes, and its deepening shadows. Oh, it is then that memory riots in its power, and the heart writhes in agony!

Though so many months had passed over, the heart of Florence would sometimes beat stronger when the reccollection of the noble stranger, whom she had seen at the ball given by Sir Reginald Willoughby, crossed her mind. But it was a vain recollection; he had passed away, like a beam of the sun, bright, but evanescent. Not the most remote hope existed of her ever again beholding him; yet, while she acknowledged her thoughts to pursue a shadow, she could not drive from them that she had seen those features before; but the thought was as a passing meteor of resplendent lustre.

"And is it possible," she apostrophised to herself one evening, as from the window of her chamber she gazed upon the beautiful landscape before her, while the calm, light breeze wafted the ringlets round her face—"is it possible the human heart can be so perverse as to suffer its feelings to linger on an object lost to it for ever? Death—death leaves behind it regrets, which recal to the soul virtues we once knew, and happiness we once shared in, blesssings dear, though painful, to recollection, on which the memory loves to dwell, and anticipates a reunion in a world of bliss hereafter. But here, here are no recollections to dwell on; no imagery to trace virtues or vices; no hope to anticipate; all is blank and hopeless. I will, yes, I will, summon common reason to my aid; I will banish his remembrance from my thoughts; I will, if I can—if I can, I will think of him no more. And yet, has he ever thought of me? I may be a guilty creature in my thoughts," and she chased away a falling tear. "Oh, that this stranger should so strongly remind me of him who, in my happiest days, would stroll with me in the wild woods of America, and who now holds captive this beating heart, which, alas, may be too fatally influenced for the husband of some happy wife. Oh, Heaven forbid! Not even in ignorance would I be the guilty creature. Yes, I will exert my reason, and forget I ever saw him. But, still we may meet again,—" and she paused for some time; and then again continued,—"No, no, how is it possible he should find me here—here, in Florence Graham, the once happy and simple Susan Adams?" again she paused, when a sudden thought flashed across her brain, and she exclaimed, "but my poor old nurse must have told them who I was."

Again the truant tears strayed on her cheek, while, resting her head against the side of the window, she occasionally wiped them off with her handkerchief, she suffered them to flow as the last trbiute to an attachment which had not even the shadow of being again renewed.

"What a fool! what a vain, silly, silly fool I am!" cried she again.

"Oh! I should indeed be deservedly an object of his contempt and scorn, did he know I could be so weak as to give one moment's thought to him; and yet," added she, with a fresh fall of tears, "I have, since I left America, oft thought of him!"

Florence was wiping the truant tears from her cheeks, when, without any ceremonious notice to say some person wanted entrance, the door was flung open and in bounced Alice Cameron.

While at Scarborough, the dazzling beauty of Alice attracted attention, and the report of her being an heiress,—which her relationship to Sir Reginald Willoughby sanctioned—was a great additional attraction. Amongst her host of admirers, there was one, who was highly distinguished for his excessively fashionable appearance, and particularly for the elegant moustaches which shaded his upper lip. He boasted of having noble blood in his veins, announcing himself as the descendant of the Earl of Somebody, and assuming all the airs of titled aristocracy. Alice was happy and honoured enough to fix the notice of this self-styled sprig of nobility, (and it may be that his claims were legitimate,) and weak enough to feel herself flattered. He became her shadow by day and her reflection by night, while her sweet friend, who was cherished in the deep foldings of her heart, was neglected, and in that respect blessed. She had almost imagined him some prince in disguise, who had been allured from foreign lands by the fame of her beauty, like those in the Arabian Tales, for she told Florence that she had been struck at the first glance " with the imperial roll of his eye, and the imperial curl of his moustache."

Alice, after expatiat'ng upon the merits of this fashionable descendant of an earl, said :—" I am returned, Florence, because I have now no fear of your robbing me of my sweetheart and my hopes. But I have had my revenge of you, however. I don't know whether you ever found it out or not ; but I have laughed a hundred times myself at it since."

" How ?" said Florence—" I don't understand you."

" Do you remember the *preux* gallant, the magnificent-eyed fellow, that eyed you instead of me at Sir Reginald's grand ball?" asked Alice, laughing.

Florence would have betrayed the tenacity of her recollection, by the blush on her cheek, without uttering a word ; but she contrived to stammer out—" I—I think I do remember something of the gentleman you mean."

" Do you indeed !" said Alice, archly looking at her. " And, no doubt, he may remember you too. And so, when I found him very inquisitive about you, and thinking no more about me than if I was the Delphic oracle to answer his questions, 'I'll be even with you, my *beau garcon*,' said I, 'and make you fancy yourself in love with me instead of her.' So when he asked, and pressed me to tell the name of the lady who had just been sitting on the sofa, with a famous *ruse de guerre*, I jumped up and said—'Cameron, sir!'—Ha, ha, ha! it was a capital hit of mine. So, of course, he adored Miss Cameron, and knew nothing of Miss Graham."

The blush on the cheek of Florence was succeeded by the hue of the lily ; and Alice Cameron, the best-hearted creature on earth, had, in the exuberance of her vivacity, unfortunately injured the best feelings of her she really admired, esteemed and loved.

Alice, in the enjoyment of her good-natured laugh, not aware of the mischief she had done, turned to Florence, with a sly peep, intending to say something lively ; but the laugh and the jest sank into sudden astonishment and anxiety, when she beheld the pale countenance of Florence, and the silent tear stealing from beneath her eye-lashes. " Great God !" exclaimed Alice ; " Florence, my dear Florence, what is the matter? have I done wrong? has my foolish whim been productive of any unpleasant consequence to you? Speak to me, my dear girl ; I shall never forgive myself. I am sure it's well said, some people never come to years of discretion."

" My dear Miss Cameron," said Florence, " forgive me, I am very low spirited ; I cannot be angry with or against you ; you would not injure an enemy."

" But I might a friend," rejoined Alice, " by the simple privilege of being able to make more free with them. But tell me candidly, my dear Florence, have I been the cause of bringing you any uneasiness or disappointment?"

Florence thus called on, told Alice of her lover in America, which this stranger so strongly reminded her of, although so many years had elapsed since she had seen him, and that he had perhaps recognized her; but upon being told a different name to that which he expected to hear, after his first interview when she refused to dance with him, had perhaps thought no more about the matter.

Her manner of giving this statement convinced Alice that she had (very innocently) been the cause of very acutely implicating the dearest feelings of Florence Indeed her vivacity was considerably abated since making this discovery, and she thought much more of her untimely wit than she expressed about it. She took her leave of Florence, promising to call again on the following day.

The residence of Mrs. Heathwood was most desirably situated within a short distance of many beautiful and romantic scenes, independent of those in its immediate vicinage; and amongst others the famous old Abbey of St. Hildebert's stood prominent in the landscape.

Florence had long wished to see this abbey, as well as some others that embellished the banks of the Tyne ; and now that a congi   eason permitted the gratification of this laudable curiosity, a party consisting of her old friends was formed for that purpose.

On the edge of a steep rock, whose feet were washed by the Tyne, and to which there was access but by a small bridge, stood the remains of the venerable abbey ; the lofty banks at either side displaying the feathered foliage of various beautiful trees, intermixed with shrubs and luxuriant ground plants, the clear river winding its course over polished rocks and pebbles, pleasing the eye by its transcient lustre, and the ear by its sound; while birds carolled about, and joined their melodious notes to the flowing murmurs—the objects altogether harmonised into a scene at once grand, romantic, and beautiful.

After examining the various beauties which the place presented to the eye, Mrs. Heathwood proposed paying a visit to a romantic glen, not far from the abbey, to which none of the party seemed disinclined, and they all walked on thither, Florence leaning on the arm of William Maxwell.

The path leading from the old abbey, exhibited at each step such scenes of beauty, and every succeeding one so different to the former, that, to the eye of a stranger, it appeared like a land of enchantment or fairyism. The banks, high, broken, and irregular, clothed in wood, with here and there an interval of bare rock peeping beneath the trees, and an accidental vista through which the "silvered waters" were seen to roam, and the loftier hills in the distance meeting the clouds, altogether presented such a sylvan scene as only the beholder could form a just conception of.

William Maxwell, while in earnest conversation, or from some unlucky chance, took a wrong turn, and so interesting was the subject that neither remarked the increased wildness and beauty of the path, and both started in the most innocent surprise, on the brink of a dead smooth stream. They looked round on each other, and then on the ground, but neither spoke.

Silence may proceed from various causes ; from terror, or awkwardness, or dislike, or delight, or from a feeling not exactly any of these, yet partaking of all. Who shall decide from what cause this silence was unbroken ? It was a beautiful spot to which they had wandered thus unconsciously. They stood on a bank overlooking the silent stream, with a rich old wood above and around them. No spendthrift heir had levelled the pride of his ancestors ; no speedy proprietor had walked the echoes, with the hollow sound of the destroying axe.

On the opposite side, the ground sloped upwards, richly but partially wooded; and admitted occasionally, glimpses of the country beyond. The variety of the trees, and their different styles of growth, prevented monotony, and increased the beauty. Some rose stately and tall, as if disdaining the soil from whence they sprang; some spread their branches far and wide, as if in gratitude to the earth, and the dews of heaven ; whilst others laved their boughs in the dark stream, some with the abandonment of sanctioned love, and some with the light and flickering movement of coquetry. The overhanging trees threw a deep shade over the stream ; but there were spots where it seemed, in every joy, to mirror the grey and sometimes lightly clouded sky,—bright glimpses of a purer world, like our early dreams of heaven.

It was, as we have said, a wild and lovely scene, with nothing to break its chantment; for not a sound was heard, save the melancholy note of the woodpigeon, and the deep breathing of the two beings, who stood with linked arms and downcast eyes. They spoke not to, they looked not at, each other. But are there not senses more delicate, more intense, and more acute than sight and hearing ? There are but senses of the body; the heart has finer senses of its own; and, without a word or look, spirits mingle. Ay, and those feelings may become too exquisitely intense, and the heart may seek relief in more earthly thoughts.

A sigh startled both, and they looked inquiringly to learn from whom it proceeded, and then again both looked down. But the spell had been broken, and Florence spoke hurriedly too. Did she fear a longer silence, or did she fear her companion's speech?

"Conversing about the beauties of the place, we have taken a wrong turn."

This was no wonderful discovery, and might have been made some minutes sooner, but of course the gentleman was too polite to say so; after a slight pause she continued,—" our friends will miss us, let us seek then?"

Maxwell offered no objection; yet he cast "one long and lingering look behind."

He might never have such an opportunity again—they walked on in silence, brushing aside the branches that overhung the wild and lovely path. The silent scene had lost some of its beauty in their eyes, as we said before; for inward thought and melancholy presentiment had thrown its shadow over the present.

I hate presentiment! It is a two-edged sword, marring the beauty of the present and the future.

Perhaps Florence hated too, or perhaps she had a better reason for speaking. It might be the silence was getting awful, or perhaps awkward; or she might speak from that strong and strange impulse which forces us to tell things long kept secret.

"How silent and how solemn is this place!" said Florence, "it throws an indefinable awe over me!—it seems as though all nature were hushed to repose, and only we two awake in creation."

"Oh! Florence—Miss Graham," cried William Maxwell, induced by the opportunity and the scene itself to hazard a declaration, "that I might hope to be the one in creation most favoured by you! This sweet and silent grove seems formed by nature as the calm retirement of a youthful pair, where, apart from the world, the trembling lover might lay his heart at the feet of his beloved mistress, as I now do mine at yours."

The action, the manner, the words, so forcibly recalled to her mind the first declaration of Musgrove, who had obtained her first and only disinterested love, (which our reader will recollect was witnessed by little Bob Stanly,) that though she expected this avowal, and on Maxwell's own account wished it made, that she might have the opportunity of terminating whatever hopes he might form, she burst into tears, and applying her handkerchief to her eyes, rested her face against it for a few minutes, and allowed him to proceed.

"But why should I say now?" continued Maxwell; "it has been yours from the first moment almost I beheld you—it is he who has been its master that now presents himself, his name, his hand, to your acceptance! Ah! dearest Florence, avert not that sweet face! Hope does indeed but feebly tremble in my bosom; those who greatly love must greatly fear. Are my fears only those of a lover, or must I call that hour fatal which first presented you to my view?"

"Oh! I hope not, William," cried Florence, with a strong marked expression of distress and concern, "I hope—I trust not! Let me not be the cause of giving unhappiness to an amiable man. Recal this declaration,—say I have your friendship, your esteem—but your love—oh no—not your love. Rise, sir—rise. I entreat you; do not kneel to me—it but aggravates the wretchedness I already too severely feel, for I am most—most unhappy!"

William Maxwell rose instantly, and seated himself on a bank. He took her passive hand—it was cold and trembling; her cheeks were nearly colourless, and she sighed and wept alternately. Neither was he free from emotion, he too surely saw his fate in her manner, and his apprehensions now were, that a premature disclosure had caused a disappointment, by making his sentiments known to their object ere he had secured an interest in her good opinion.

"Were my fears then prophetic, Florence?" he resumed, after awhile; "are my hopes blasted for ever? Yet shall I confess, that with a cautious eye I have watched each man who approached you? I have tried to read on your countenance whether a favourable one was nigh. I observed nothing that could warrant a suspicion of it. Yet—yes! still and ever beloved Florence, I have frequently traced a tear, heard a sigh suppressed as it rose, observed your thoughts abstracted, and have sometimes seen you start from your reverie as if suddenly recollecting yourself. From these symptoms have arisen my doubt, though I could not command my affections; they are yours, Florence, wholly and for ever. If time, if assiduity, if love, pure, ardent, and perfect, can have room to hope, only give me the shadow of it. I will await your own time; and, should a hopeless attachment be yours—but forgive me, dearest Florence, my words accord not with my firm persuasion that such a misfortune could never attend you, for the man blessed by your love must find his earthly heaven in it.

"William Maxwell!" cried Florence, "urge not a subject which I must turn from. You know not—you cannot form a judgment how deeply it distresses me. Short as is the period of my acquaintance with you, I yet fully appreciate the worth of your character; it is brought before me every day in stronger colours. The world speaks of you with esteem and respect; your friends are vain of being called such, and strangers are anxious to be numbered in your acquaintance; and were it possible I could accept the distinctions you offer me, I should be the most honoured, as well as the most enviable woman in the country. But as it is, I deeply, truly, most sincerely regret the predilection should be in my favour."

"Yet say not, Florence," cried William, "that it never will be in your power to return it. If, indeed, your affections are not engaged, only suffer me to be your slave: I will be so in every sense. Your word shall be my law—your time mine; I will serve you as did the lover of Rebecca, and only look impatiently to the dear reward. Florence, my mother was the pride and glory of her family, the admiration of all who knew her; yet not more vain of his wife could have been my father, than should be his son, if permitted to present you to the world a s a Maxwell."

"It is but common-place language to say I feel honoured by your partiality," replied Florence. "I do so; yet I am not gratified by it. Your friendship I had been vain of—your love can only give me regret, since it is unfortunately placed; for honour, justice, your own merits, compel me to say, the heart you sue for is not mine to bestow. Long ere I saw you, ere I knew Allendale, it was disposed of."

Maxwell took her hand tenderly and respectfully. "Forgive me, most beloved of human beings," said he, "forgive me that adoring you as I do, as I must do, I yet experience, in the frailties incidental to man's nature, a sentiment bordering on indignation, even while I dread being obliged to revoke that sentiment, against the apparent tardiness of him who holds the invaluable gift of your affections. Ah, why comes he not to claim the blissful treasure? Oh, Florence! pardon me that I dare to impeach his tenderness; but such a being as you!—the very air you breathe should be to the enviable object of your selection as the sole essence his existence."

Florence burst into tears.

"Oh," he exclaimed, "why should I touch the chord of your unhappiness, and not have the power of alleviating it! Florence! Florence! is he indeed faithless? Yet why do I ask that question? We are not willingly the enemies of our own happiness. Oh, would you but permit me to devote my life to you—would you but allow me the most distant prospect of some day calling you mine; if, indeed, this dreaded, I could almost say hated, rival is undeserving of you—how incoherently I talk—how wildly! My excuse is that which we wish to be true, we wish to believe. Yet, yet, Florence, if I am indeed in error, and circumstances keep you apart, I will endeavour to subdue the dearest feelings of my heart, and restore happiness to yours. Those tears distract me; speak, dear Florence—if I am not to be your lover, give me all your confidence as a friend."

"William Maxwell," said Florence, "thos tearse bespeak at once my unhappiness and my gratitude. I am indeed unhappy; and, while I acknowledge myself grateful, most grateful for your noble disinterestedness, let me solemnly assure you it is not within the power of your generous friendship to alter the character of my fate."

"Florence!" he impatiently cried, " do you reject both my love and friendship? Am I fated to see the woman as dear to me as my own existence, not yet in her prime, and wasting her youth in solitary, hopeless melancholy? Do not drive me mad, Florence—tell me why you reject me—for whom? Am I myself an object of dislike to you? Rank may to a mind such as yours be but a secondary consideration; in the world's estimation mine is not contemptible. Were it the first that worldly power could bestow, it should be laid at your feet."

" I believe you," said Florence, impressively, " and had I been disengaged when first I saw you, 'tis more than probable your attentions had gained for you your wishes ; yet, in justice to your worth, and the sentiments of respect which that worth has not failed to impress on my mind, your rank had most truly been but a second consideration in the scale of my happiness. More than my respect, blended with the esteem so justly your due, I cannot bestow; nor would I have you build a hope on any probable contingency or event, for not time itself can change my present sentiments, or give you from me the shadow of having such a hope accomplished."

" Alas! Florence," he mournfully returned, " how sad must be that destiny which brings no prospect of hope through a long life of misery! Have you really set the seal on mine? Is there an eternal barrier to my wishes, of which I can form no conjecture? or do you establish your conviction in the belief of your own immutable faith?"

Florence stood up, and for a few moments seemed to hold council with her own thoughts, as she slowly paced to and fro, when again turning to Maxwell, she rested one hand impressively on his arm, and in a tone of voice which gave energy to the action, as well as to her words—" It is true," said she, " I have not yet attained the prime of life, yet ere I knew the term love scarcely by name, my affections were disposed of—irrevocably, unchangeably given. Though years silvered my head, still would they be the same ; I gave my heart once and for ever."

" Gracious Heaven!" cried Maxwell, " can it be possible? But I will not urge you further, dearest Florence. I will hover near you, I will watch over you; at a future period you may think me worthy your confidence—till then, and for ever consider me as a friend, warm, ardent, sincere. Do not slight me wholly, Florence, lest you drive me to despair, perhaps to destruction."

" Heaven forbid!" she solemnly ejaculated, extending her hand to him, which he kissed. The action was an involuntary impulse, and she did not notice it, nor withdraw her hand." " Be my friend, then," she added ; " I accept with pride and gratitude, the permission of calling you such, and, at some future period, perhaps not a far distant one, you shall know how impossible it is you can be more."

With this treaty of friendship, William Maxwell saw he must for the present at least endeavour to rest satisfied. One sentiment he understood was near akin to the other between the two sexes, and though Florence had said her affections were engaged, still it might be that esteem for the friend present would supersede affection for the absent indifferent lover. Indifferent ! alas! there was too surely no question on that subject. He might be absent in another climate, in another world ; but indifferent! No; the man who had once professed an attachment for Florence could never afterwards feel for a colder sentiment.

They rejoined their party, and it required not any wonderful penetration of those who were acquainted with the nature of his sentiment to discover that William Maxwell had met with something which oppressed his spirits considerably; and the cause was soon traced to its true source in his dejected mien and altered appearance ; and, from being the first to propose and promote amusement, his total indifference towards it; whilst to Florence he evidently strove to suppress the ardour of the lover, while yet he was solicitous in observing her every wish.

CHAPTER XXXVII.

My own loved Zayda! do we meet once more?
She starts—she turns. The lightning of surprise,
Of sudden rapture, flashes from her eyes!—HEMANS.

A CALM moonlight evening succeeded the eventful day named in the last chapter :—a perfect stillness reigned throughout Elmgrove, a stillness {so

unbroken, many might have imagined its inhabitants sunk in peaceful slumbers— occasionally a light gleamed from the windows of Mrs. Heathwood's apartment, who, it would seem, did not contemplate the night as one of peculiar loveliness.

Florence had extinguished her light, but had not retired to rest ;—she softly opened the sash, and contemplated the tranquil scene before her with a degree of nervous depression quite unusual to her—the air, though cold, appeared to revive her as it entered the window, impregnated with the odour of the flowers growing beneath it ; and the foliage of the shrubbery skirting the walks, formed a dark body of the gloom which just then her fancy esteemed and admired. As she sat by the opened window, the room illuminated by the beams of the moon, her sad range of thoughts brought to her remembrance the days of former tranquil happiness that she had spent while an uneducated girl in the woods of America : —she retraced those untroubled hours, when she had been innocent in her amusements, and happy in tranquil pleasures—she had before her imagination those brilliant times, which all perhaps can recal as belonging to their early youth ; but those ideas only made the present more exquisitely painful. Her father and her mother by turns occupied her thoughts—and as she thought upon the wandering life which her father must lead, and of his probable fate, she wept with a violence amounting to despair—and then in humility of spirit only wept meekly whilst she prayed.

The stillness which prevailed for some time was broken only by the sighs of Florence, or the gentle undulating leaves, as they waved to the soft evening breeze. At one time she fancied something more than the slight rustling of the trees struck on her hearing ; she arose, and stood a few seconds at the open window to listen, but all was silent : still, and undisturbed.

Again she flung herself on a seat, her arm rested on the window sill, and her head reclined over the delicate white hand ; the other hung carelessly by her side. A long lock of her beautiful waving hair had escaped its fastening and fell over her shoulder and bosom ; and the glossy ringlets from her forehead and temples shaded, though they did not conceal, her pale but lovely countenance. The rays of the moon shone full upon her. An interval of some minutes elapsed, when again the same rustling movement she had heard before sounded on her ear, and she turned her head in the direction it came from. Good Heavens ! her quivering lips moved, and she exclaimed aloud, " William Musgrove." He stood with folded arms, leaning against a tree, as if he had been deeply contemplating her, but no sooner did he hear his name pronounced, than he came forward.

It was impossible for Florence to conceal her emotion ; she had not power to move, and the tears of joy, shame, and the long-cherished feelings of her heart stole over her burning blushes, and she was compelled to hide her face in her handkerchief, to conceal, if possible, the strong, the vivid emotions expressed on it.

After a silence of some minutes, Musgrove exclaimed—" Miss Cameron !"

" No, no," said Florence—" that name belongs not to me : it was given you in a moment of playfulness by Miss Cameron herself."

" And for what purpose ?" cried Musgrove.

" Merely in frolic," said Florence, " for my running away from my seat, and—leaving her to—sit alone, I believe."

If the explanation was not very correct, it was very passable, considering she could not declare the absolute truth at this moment.

" Do you then forget me ?" said Florence, after a pause, " has time completely blotted me from your memory ?"

" No, no," said Musgrove, " I have not indeed forgotten my own Susan Adams. I recognised you the first moment I saw you in the ball-room, but upon being told a different name from that which I expected to hear, I thought at the time I might be mistaken, and your refusal to dance with me seemed to confirm my opinion that you were not her whom I had been so long seeking. I heard the name of Alice Cameron oft repeated by the company as I passed through the room, which I quitted immediately ; since then I have visited the Castle of Lochallan, and ascertained from an old fisherman there certain particulars, which brought me again to Allendale. I arrived here this afternoon, and after making a few inquiries of the villagers, most of whom seemed well acquainted with your history, I had determined to call here in the morning. Chance led me here this evening, and seeing you sittiug at the window with the moon shining full upon you, I at once recognised you, and was determined, if possible, to obtain an interview. I have succeeded, dearest Florence, in my wishes—I ask not if you have loved others since we parted—I ask only if you love me now?"

"More, oh, immeasurably more, than when you first obtained my love," said Florence; "but, dearest William, this is not proper at this hour of the night—leave me now, and in the morning I will introduce you to my mother, and all can be explained to her."

Musgrove, bidding an affectionate good night, departed, and Florence retired to bed. Oh, what a change within so short a space! To have seen Musgrove—to know he was still the same adoring lover, unchanged in faith or affection, to whom she had given every tender sentiment the heart of woman could bestow—to know he was deserving that tenderness, and to find she might again indulge that dear affection for him—filled her soul with such exquisite, and at the same time such sudden and unhoped-for bliss, that she seemed as if transported to a better world. The certainty of being still the object of Musgrove's tender affection gave such renovation to her mind, such rapture to her bosom, such a conviction to her heart of his meriting all the dear and tender sentiments that her heart could bestow, that happiness was expressed in the returning smile which played on her lip, in the mild radiance of her eye, in the elasticity of her step.

Mrs. Heathwood looked with earnest inquiry on the eloquent countenance of her daughter, where all was struggling to reveal itself.

"Florence," said she, taking her hand, "your spirit seems strangely stirred. If it is with joy, you will surely share it with me; if it is grief or anxiety, will you not suffer me to share it with you?"

"Oh, it is something that differs from all," replied Florence, with emotion. "It is joy; but joy so strange—so—"

Mrs. Heathwood looked at her with surprise.

"It seems strange that any joy could have such an effect upon you."

"No, oh, no! You would not say so if you knew—if you could guess." Her heart throbbed violently, and her colour went and came with the quickness of lightning.

"Then, will you not tell me, my love, what it is that thus strangely moves you?"

After a struggle to repress her feelings, Florence succeeded. She became perfectly calm, and gave to her mother a long account of her attachment to Musgrove; she gave her such explanations to all her questions, that when he arrived, and was introduced by Florence to her mother, he had little to explain.

CHAPTER XXXVIII.

" Farewell, my native land, a long farewell ;
   The anchor's up, why do I lingering stay ?
Wide in the favouring breeze the white sails swell,
   Farewell, farewell, I must at once away!

" How swift from land the gallant vessel steers!
   Woods, meads and hills, are fading from my sight ;
But while I strive to laugh away my tears,
   My heart feels dark, as is the starless night.

" Away regret ! and now to brave the world,
   With stern resolve, and feelings buried deep,
That ne'er again, wherever I am hurl'd,
   Shall wake from apathy's benumbing sleep.

" Deep let me drink of dull oblivion's wave ;
   Again, and deeper, I'd the draught renew :
The pang is past, and now my heart is brave—
   Farewell my native land, farewell to you !"

How little do they know of true woman who speak lightly of a woman's love; and yet it is a fashion among poets and novelists, and essayists and philosophers, to compare female hearts and affections to anything that is light, and volatile, and ephemeral in nature! Thus woman's love has been compared to the evanescent sweetness of the fast fading flower, to the inconstancy of the moon, which " monthly changes in her circled orb," to the ever shifting wind, and, in short, to everything of which nature is variable. Impressions made upon their hearts have been successively likened to the letters which the contemplation or the idle have traced in the sand, or to the bubbles and waves created upon the lake by a stone, which subside in a minute or two, and leave the surface as clear, and as bright, and as calm as ever.

But how little do they know of women who write and speak of them in this manner! How little do they know the deep and concentrated feeling, and never-ending memory of first impressions, of which a true woman's heart is capable ; and how many are there whom we see persuing and performing all the duties of a wife, who, having married from parental command, have never ceased involuntarily to cherish the fond memory of some early love, which they are supposed to have forgotten, because duty and propriety command that its influence should remain unperceived ! How little do we appreciate that generous burst of feeling which a first love creates in a woman's breast, and which is seldom, if ever, completely forgotten amidst all the subsequent scenes of her life !

A man may have many passions, because his passions are generally the effects of his senses. He is captivated by beauty—he lends himself the willing slave of a feeling which he is in the habit of encouraging, and which he takes every means to cherish and to gratify. He succeeds—the gratification is past—beauty palls upon the senses, and loses its charms by being gazed upon as his own—another complexion, or another form, or another pair of bright eyes, and other flowing tresses, attract his attention—the same feeling is again excited—his senses are again led temporary captives to be again gratified, and disenthralled as before, by gratification. With man half his passions are caprices. But with woman it is different. Education fences round her heart with the almost impregnable guards which the conventional forms of society prescribe. If her heart feel a preference, it is her duty to repress it, unless that preference be sought by the attentions of another. Her feelings are germs in the bud, which require attention, care and cultivation, to call into flower—they are blossoms which require the warmth of man's admiration and love to ripen into fruit. A woman's love is therefore seldom excited by temporary or sudden admiration. Her mind is too delicately constructed, for persons to have much to do with the origin of love in her heart; and it is that makes the love of Desdemona a much more natural passion for a female than that of Juliet.

Passion springs up in a man's heart spontaneously and quickly, like those flowers which we see by the way side, where accident may have scattered the seed in a light though fertile soil, and lying close to the surface, they blossom, and are blighted by the very sun which called them into existence. But in a woman's heart they require to be sown with a careful hand, and cultivated with a kindly attention; but when once they have taken root, the fibres strike downwards; and though the flowers may be blighted by after circumstances, or chilled by coldness or unkindness, the roots are seldom eradicated. Like the vase in which roses have once been distilled:—

> "You may break, you may ruin the vase, if you will,
> But the scent of the roses will hang round it still."

It was thus with Florence. Her early love had been cherished, and had remained at the bottom of her heart, deeply hidden.

Young and inexperienced as it was, Musgrove's was no common mind; his heart had not been hardened by those intrigues into which the youth of the present day plunge so early, and from which too many of them unfortunately form their opinions of the whole female sex.

He had loved with all the vigour of a young and first love. There was none of the namby-pamby sentimentality—none of that frittered feeling which so often characterises passion at his age; it was pure, wholesome, manly love, founded on a thorough knowledge of the worth of the object; a love that promised to stand the test of years, and was not to be conquered even by disappointment; and which would have guided a woman through all the storms of life; that would have grappled with ill fortune for the sake of her protection, and have mastered her in the hopes of procuring independence for the object of his affection.

At the time Florence had been carried off from Philadelphia by her father, an appointment had been just procured for William Musgrove in India, which at that time presented a wide field for exertion—a mass of cases and actions had accumulated from the extension of territory, and from commercial and territorial disputes of all kinds. The oriental vineyard presented a plentiful harvest, and there were but few labourers to divide the toil and the profits.

Musgrove quitted Philadelphia, uncertain of the destination of his first love and of his dearest hopes, to seek for power and fortune in a distant country. No time had been lost by his father in preparation, and he left the Delaware only a few days after the abduction of Florence, and without being able to ascertain whither her father had taken her; he only knew that her name was "Florence Graham, and that she was a Pirate's Daughter."

The hurry and bustle of departure occupied his mind; and the first moment of silent reflection was that in which he found himself on the deck—and felt the motion of the vessel that rode proudly over the waves to fetch the produce of the East, to pour into the lap of the industrious denizens of the New World; and as he saw the sails unfurled, and watched the fast receding shore, he became almost careless of his fate, and could have exclaimed with the poet:—

> " Sail on, sail on, thou fearless bark—
> Wherever blows the welcome wind,
> It cannot lead to scenes more dark,
> More sad than those I leave behind.
> Sail on, sail on, through endless space—
> Through calm—through tempest—stop no more;—
> The stormiest sea's a resting-place,
> To him who leaves a heart on shore."

For a moment he gave himself up to the bitterness of his feelings—for a moment dissolved into all the softness of sorrow. He soon, however, recollected how useless it was thus to give way to sentiments that ought to be buried in oblivion : he roused himself into energy—cast one last and lingering look at the receding shores of his native land, and breathing a fervent prayer for the happiness of Florence, as they seemed to melt in the horizon and mingle in the distance, he turned with a determined though despairing heart, to the contemplation of a scene which it is ever the pride of man to behold—the active energy of a ship's crew, and that admirable discipline of a number of tempestuous and warlike spirits, which has tended more to the high character of the navy, than the stout oak of which its vessels are constructed.

There is something exhilarating in the activity and cheerfulness of seamen as they climb the yards, unfurl the sails, and perform with dexterity all those evolutions which give to man almost the mastership of the winds and waves—something inspiring in the hearty cheering and vigorous yeo, yeo, that echoes as the various ropes of the complicated machinery are hauled into their proper places ; and as the white sails spread their swelling bosoms to the winds, and bear the vessel proudly on through the blue waters.

Musgrove felt it; it roused his sinking heart to energy; he contemplated the power of man ; and as he observed that it controlled even the winds and waves, he determined that it should also control and direct the feelings and passions of his own heart.

A long monotonous voyage was, however, a dangerous trial ; the want of variety in external objects is too apt to throw the heart and mind back upon the resources of memory for occupation ; and the contemplation of the vast solitude of the deep, in which the single vessel that floated him on its surface seemed but as an atom, was rather calculated to encourage than to repress the feelings of Musgrove.

A determined mind can, however, accomplish anything that it undertakes with energy: he knew that employment was the grand panacea ; he, therefore, devoted himself to the attainment of all kinds of knowledge connected with the country to which he was going.   These pursuits, together with the conversation of the intelligent officers of the Indiaman in which he had taken his passage, occupied his time, if not his heart, and left him little room for reflection on past circumstances.

Sometimes, in the silence of the night, as he watched the rapid waters rolling beneath him, he gave a solitary thought to past times.   The name of Florence would appear to his imagination written in the dark blue wave that rolled beneath him, or among the stars which shone so brilliantly and passively in the clear, blue sky above him : her beauties, her softness, the recollection of the first hours of their love, would then steal into his mind : his heart would melt as memory poured forth her store of scenes and circumstances connected with his disappointment, tears would rush into his eyes, he would forget himself, and for a moment give way to fancies of what might have been, and resign himself to a dreamy existence, from which he would suddenly rouse his mind, address a silent prayer for strength to assist the softening influence of these recollections, and betake himself to the studies of his profession.

Madras was the place of their destination, and our young voyager looked eagerly out for a view of that scene he had often heard spoken of with delight.   A brilliant morning drew all the passengers on deck, and the splendour of the scene which gradually opened to the view no person could form a judgment of, unless having before seen it.   The celestial blue above, the sun yet below the horizon, but pointing its golden beams in advance, the clear but deepened reflection of the objects on the element which bore the stately vessel along, with all her paraphernalia floating in the light breeze that propelled it ; while in front, as she drew near shore, the attention was arrested by the splendid display which land and water presented to the admiring senses.

Nothing of the kind, perhaps, can be more enchanting, or more imposing to the eye of a stranger, than the entrance into Madras.   The town, in a splendid amphitheatre, presents itself in front of the finest bay imagination can conceive. The colonnaded buildings, light, airy, and graceful, and stuccoed with the beautiful plaster clunam, which bears the lustre and polish of the purest white marble, is not to be surpassed by any comparison ; nor can any composition bear a proportion with this peculiar ornament, for it belongs only to its own eastern soil, and is used for its own particular purposes ; the brilliancy of its tint, when the sun sheds his rays on it, is not to be beholden by the unaccustomed eye of a European ; yet, when he turns from its lustre, the decline of that orb is anxiously looked for to admit a more attentive view of this splendid outline.

The anchor was scarcely dropped, when the boats came dancing alongside the vessel, some to convey the passengers on shore, and others bringing many of the natives to examine the new arrivals : the suavity and politeness of those people was discernible in all their actions—grace and elegance attended their motions, which with the splendour of their costume, so different from Europe, the polished beautiful black countenance, brilliant eyes, pearly teeth, flowing robe of purest white, and graceful turban of the same delicate hue, struck the astonished sight of our young novice with wonder and delight.

Musgrove was landed from the vessel in a mussoulah-boat, which is purposely built for running through the surf, flat-bottomed, light and elastic : it dances like a cork on the surface of the water, bounds over the rolling waves as a feather in the breeze, and in safety reaches the shore. He was landed on one of the finest beaches in the world, where he was immediately surrounded by the most polite, obsequious, and friendly attention, as, in fact, were all the passengers who came in from his, and some other of the ships that had sailed in company. He brought with him some letters of introduction to many distinguished persons residing at Madras, which having in proper time delivered, he was soon encompassed by a host of friends. Hospitality threw her fascinating wreath of roses, divested of thorns and scattered by the hand of taste and elegance through the paths of pleasure.

William Musgrove was soon a general favourite ; handsome, lively, generous, ardent—the young American's company was everywhere sought, and everywhere looked for. He was followed, flattered, and admired ; but the luxurious habit of a luxuriant tropical climate, the smile of beauty, the blandishments of favour, or the allurements of distinction above his compeers, could not, nor did divest his mind of one single particle of its own brilliant intrinsic worth. He might, and no doubt did, in his more silent thoughts appreciate those marks of partiality with some degree of self-complacency, for youth is not the season of humility—but he manifested no outward tokens of consequence for them, nor arrogated the slightest feeling of superiority in this general and very visible distinction of him. He was esteemed by his own sex, as well as admired ; nay, loved by the other—for many a heart sent a secret sigh after the elegant young American, and many a bright eye followed his footsteps, or watched his approach. His unaffected manners, however, preserved him from the enmity or envy of those of his own sex, who would even wish to rival him in the good opinion of some favourite fair one ; his general deportment was alike to all ; affable and courteous, he selected no particular favourite among the young ladies ; and those of riper years could hardly be thought to create much jealousy : those had already had their day, and beaux of their time had sighed at their feet with the same fervour, admiration, and adoration, as did now more modern and youthful ones at the feet of their own or their granddaughters.

At the period of Musgrove's going to India, Nadir Shah, the usurper of the Persian throne, had been invited by the Nizam to invade Hindostan, hoping to profit by the confusion which would thus be occasioned. Tumults, massacres, and famine were the result ; and all that part of the country was in commotion and convulsed. Musgrove, who to his other good qualities united bravery without impetuosity, was ardent to signalise himself ; and his wish of doing so remained not long ungratified. He was sent into the Mysore country, where he was stationed a considerable length of time, and earned his laurels in many a severe and dangerous contest. But his humanity kept pace with his bravery : the thirst of wealth never allured him to the thirst of blood ; he never put an unfortunate creature to the sword, that he might plunder him of his riches: he met his adversary like a man, no matter what his colour might be, and fought like a hero ; but, when the battle was over, the foe was no longer an enemy, the wounded were assisted, the vanquished were respected, and the hero was adored.

A peace soon after being established, the conduct of Musgrove was ac nowledged to be such as entitled him to particular attention : he was therefore nominated, in a kind of diplomatic agency to the Carnatic, the dominions of the Nabob of Arcot—an appointment at once lucrative and distinguished, and which circumstance eventually paved his way to wealth and fortune, although not immediately attaching to the situation itself. His personal attractions brought him into marked notice : he was caressed by all ranks ; and the nabob, though a haughty sovereign, from the first time of seeing, became strongly attached to him. Musgrove received innumerable proofs of his highness's esteem; he presented him with the most costly tokens of his favour, and had him near him whenever he could.

After remaining here several years, he received information of his father's death ; he at once made up his mind to leave India and proceed to England. Having formed an acquaintance with a rich merchant of the name of Welford, who was also about quitting India, he took a passage in the same ship with him, and after a prosperous voyage touched at the island of Madeira ; here to his great surprise he met Don Lopez, who was also waiting for a vessel to England, and accordingly embarked in the same vessel, which soon reached England in safety.

Upon their arrival in London, Don Lopez having some business to arrange, took up his abode with his agent, while Musgrove accepted the invitation of Welford to spend a few weeks at his brother's, at Hexham, and while here received the invitation to the ball given on the birth day of the unfortunate Griselda Willoughby. The reader knows the rest.

Musgrove, after meeting with Florence as related in the last chapter, immediately wrote to Don Lopez, who in a few days arrived at Allendale and was received with every mark of joy and respect by Florence and her mother.

Leaving Don Lopez relating the changes which had taken place at Madeira in a few short years, the death of his brother, the father of Mrs. Heathwood, and all her relatives, we will transport our readers to a fresh chapter, and there make them, through the medium of the fashionable milliners of the place, acquainted with several particulars which no doubt they are anxious to know.

CHAPTER XXXIX.

Which is the villain ?   Let me see his eyes;
That when I note another man like him,
I may avoid him.—SHAKSPEARE.

WHAT a month November is in London ! Such a clatter about deaths and engagements ; such a display of ladies and winter fashions; such an exhibition of visiting cards and whiskers ; such an interchange of invitations and cashmeres; such admiration of pretty necks and waltzing ; such a confusion of dates and acceptances ; such an evaporation of love and—but I forget myself. The whole of the young ladies, in and near Allendale and Hexham, were thrown into terrible confusion, by the announcement of the intended marriages between Herbert Glenroy and Edith Trevanion, Gilbert Stanhope and Margaret Glenroy, and William Musgrove and Florence Graham, which were to be celebrated on the—instant, at Hexham church, in accordance with the ancient rule and custom.

I wish I possessed the ability to describe the commotion excited by the publication of this important intelligence, for it assuredly would afford our readers source of considerable amusement. I must be contented, however, with introducing them (in order that they may not be entirely ignorant) into a very exclusive *coterie* of ladies, assembled at the far-famed millinery establishment of Miss Mary Moody, in —— street, Hexham, where they may be enabled to form some idea of the interest felt and expressed upon this singular occasion.

"Bless me, Harriet," exclaimed Miss Williams, a lively-looking girl, who was

attitudinising before a mirror, with the last pattern hat upon her head, "what an ugly thing this is; what could Miss Moody be thinking about when she made it up?"

"I don't think so," replied Miss Roberts, the lady addressed, very Frenchified in her appearance, "it is exceedingly becoming, and I intend to have one just like it."

No. 32.

"I wonder what the price is," said Miss Williams, and her attention was immediately attracted to another object, by Miss Roberts exclaiming,—

"Mercy upon me, what a perfect beauty!" as she uncovered a box that stood upon a table, and exhibited an article which immediately rivetted the attention of both.

"Oh, Miss Moody," exclaimed Miss Williams, as that important personage entered, "do tell me whose dress this is."

"It is Miss Grahams," replied Miss Moody, smiling at an attempt made by Miss Williams to conceal an indentation the pattern hat had received while under her inspection, "for her wedding."

The dress had nearly suffered from the particular attentions bestowed upon it, after this interesting communication.

"Has she seen it since it was finished?" inquired Miss Williams after the first burst of admiration was over.

"Not yet; here is Miss Glenroy's and Miss Trevanion's (opening another box); they are exactly alike, and in excellent taste."

"They're charming," exclaimed Miss Roberts, "without a single fault; I called to see Miss Welford yesterday; she tells me that all the bridesmaids are to be dressed alike; what a delightful wedding it will be."

"Oh! enchanting," said Miss Williams, who had replaced the hat upon the stand very much to Miss Moody's satisfaction, "and I should have no objection to be one of them."

"Just to think," exclaimed Miss Roberts, in a very disappointed tone, "that I have never seen Mr. Musgrove. I went to Mr. Welford's a few nights ago, and he had been just gone about five minutes, and though I have watched for him every day, I have not been able to get a single glimpse."

"He is perfectly elegant," said Miss Moody, casting a side glance at Miss Williams, who was again before the mirror, "his manners are princely, and he has the handsomest hair I ever saw in my life."

"I don't like either him or his," remarked Miss Williams, rather sharply; "he is quite a disagreeable character."

"Mr. Musgrove a disagreeable character!" exclaimed Miss Moody, in astonishment; "you are the first person I ever heard speak ill of him."

"There are many beside myself of the same opinion," said Miss Williams, as she retreated backward from the mirror; "and I'm sure no body can be pleased with his cold, haughty formality."

"Cold, haughty formality! where did you ever see him?"

"At two or three places; and I was tired enough of him before he made himself so agreeable as to evaporate—he has not an extraordinarily low opinion of himself."

"I would not undertake to judge of a person's character," observed Miss Moody, somewhat irritated, "from having seen him but once, during a morning visit; I I dare say you did not exchange a single word with him? Mr. Musgrove however——"

"Is not half so agreeable as Mr. Glenroy," interrupted Miss Williams, again examining the pattern hat, "and, though I dare say Florence thinks him every thing, I would not be in her place for the world."

"If you could, that is," retorted Miss Moody, in a low tone; and then raising her voice inquired of Alice Cameron, who entered the room at the moment, "whether she had ever seen Mr. Musgrove waltz?"

"No, never," said Alice, and then suddenly casting her eyes upon the dresses, she exclaimed—"I wonder who will look the prettiest in the dresses, they all have dark eyes and hair, but the expression of their faces is as different as day and night."

"Entirely so," said Miss Moody, "and I think I give the preference to Miss Graham, but I see she is coming here accompanied by Miss Trevanion," continued Miss Moody looking out of the window.

* * * * *

One year, from the time General Trevanion quitted Allendale, had glided away, and during its silent lapse, the village experienced those vicissitudes incident to a mutable world. There had been the records of births, marriages, and deaths—the three grand events of human life.

Glenroy, his year of probation having expired, claimed the reward for which he had toiled with unremitting ardour. He had fulfilled his promise to General Trevanion, for fortune and fame already beamed with reversionary brightness upon his path. In the proud confidence of future independence, obtained by honourable exertion, his spirit ceased to chafe under the remembrance of uncancelled obligations.

Sir Reginald Willoughby, humbled by misfortune, yet retaining many traces of his former aristocracy, lingered for awhile near the scene of his calamities ; but at length, unable to endure their remembrance, left the valley, and returned to the metropolis, leaving his ward, Alice Cameron, at Mrs. Heathwood's, who promised to join them in a few weeks. It would be an omission not to remark here, that General Trevanion, before his departure, had sought an interview with Sir Reginald, and with the delicacy which the subject demanded, made known the debt of Glenroy, which he immediately cancelled. Sir Reginald was surprised and agitated, but he did not refuse the offering. He never mentioned the subject to Glenroy, who was fully aware of all he owed to the general.

The approach of the wedding afforded matter of rejoicing to many of the worthy inhabitants of the quiet village of Allendale. The parties themselves (it is to be hoped) were very well pleased : the bridesmaids and their attendants anticipated choice opportunities for flirtations of the most approved description,—some of them had serious thoughts upon the subject. The fortunate mother with a long string of yellow-faced daughters was sure that one at least would be taken off in all the hurry and confusion attendant upon the gaiety that would follow the anxiously expected nuptials. The blooming girl whose entry had been fixed for the coming winter was perfectly enraptured that circumstance should have proved so favourable —there would be such a continual succession of delightful balls and parties,— very often she dreamed she was a *belle*, and awoke once in an agony of tears, because she thought she had been left by mistake to sit and look at a cotillon. The matured beauty indulged the hope that the coming winter would put an end to her disagreeable walks by night with no attendant but a servant maid. The epicure thought of dinners and old-fashioned balls, and took a walk to sharpen his appetite. The milliners bled their fingers. The tailors forgot to send in their bills. The servant maids tried on their mistresses, dresses. The—in short every-body talked, and thought, and dreamt of nothing else but the treble wedding.

A splendid dinner awaited the company of Mrs. Heathwood's, after the marriage ceremony had been performed, and harmony and mirth presided at the board. When the courses were removed, and the dessert set, Don Lopez told the servants as they withdrew, to make merry, as they needed not come again till they were summoned. When the wine had gone round to the health of their respected hostess, Don Lopez addressing himself in general terms to the company, to thank them for the honour of their presence on that day, continued—"And to comme-morate it, when by course of years I shall be no longer a sojourner here, I claim the privilege of a parent, and presenting General Trevanion with this authority," handing him a sealed packet, "request his good office."

General Trevanion opened it, and smiled ; William Maxwell who stood near him looked over his shoulder, and smiled also ; Musgrove pressed the trembling hand of Florence, and Don Lopez rising, it was a signal all obeyed. The packet contained the will of Don Lopez, by which, after giving a few small legacies, he left the remainder of his large property to Florence.

It was read aloud by the general at the request of Don Lopez, and when he had concluded, William Musgrove, in the name of his wife, warmly thanked Don Lopez for his kindness and liberality. Lady Maxwell as a mark of her esteem, presented her also with the deeds of the estate which belonged to her father, saying after a few words, "That Florence had a greater right to them than she had."

*   *   *   *   *   *   *

Being a bachelor, I of course cannot pretend to describe a gentleman's feelings directly after marriage, but I am informed, they are of a very peculiar nature, and can be but partially communicated: at any rate on the evening of the fourth day after the celebration of his nuptials, Herbert Glenroy was sitting alone in his dressing-room.

"Alone!" exclaims the sentimental reader, in astonishment.

Yes, sir, alone—but he was thinking about going through the operation of dressing, before accompanying his lovely bride and sister to a ball to be given that night by Lady Maxwell, in honour of the occasion. He had actually brought his courage to the sticking place, and had gone so far as to take a hair-brush in his hand, when the door opened, and a note was brought in.

"The ladies send word they will soon be ready, sir," said the servant.

"Why, what o'clock is it?"

"Just nine, sir."

"Indeed! say I'll not keep them waiting a moment; who brought this note?"

"I don't know, sir,"

"Very well," said Glenroy, and the door closed; he opened the note; it was as follows:—

"Gilbert Lovell will be in the murderer's glen to-night, at twelve. Unless your oath has passed from your memory, go armed to meet your hereditary enemy. Take a friend with you: I should name one who has before rendered you a similar service,—Gilbert Stanhope."

It was without date or signature, and the writing, though not in the least disguised, was entirely unknown to him to whom it was addressed.

"How lovely the brides look to-night," said our old friend Alice Cameron to Matilda Maxwell, who was seated beside her upon a sofa in a recess of the ball-room at Glanmore Abbey; "I am at a loss to know which is the handsomest.

"It is hard to decide," replied Matilda Maxwell, "their style is so entirely different; but look at Herbert Glenroy, I've been observing him two or three times this evening, he does not look so happy as he ought, and now and then he knits his brow as if he were very angry at something."

"Perhaps he has a headache," replied Alice, "he used to complain of it; I declare they are going to waltz."

At half-past eleven, Herbert Glenroy left the ball-room accompanied by the husband of his sister, and walked towards the glen; the night had been clear, but occasional gusts of wind had collected the scattered clouds, which, pursuing their trackless flight across the glittering face of the heavens, concealed at intervals the melancholy rays of the moon, and rendered objects more indistinct than they would have been, had the light or darkness been steady or continued.

On reaching the place of appointment, Glenroy paused and looked round him—all was death-like silence and stillness; he scarcely thought of his companion; the contrast with the scene he had just left, and the nature of the business upon which he came, disposed him for reflections peculiarly solemn; he was startled from these observations by the sound of a footstep, and, on turning, indistinctly saw the figure of a man enveloped in a cloak, advancing towards him from the opposite end of the glen.

The stranger paused within a few feet of them, looked intently upon Gilbert Stanhope, and slowly muttered to himself, "It is as I expected."

"What means this?" said Glenroy, "you are——"

"Charles Montford!" said the stranger.

"For what purpose are you here?"

"Said I not," replied Montford, "when we last met, that we should meet again; and that I would laugh in derision at your agony as you did then at mine—behold him," and he pointed to Gilbert, "whom you swore to be revenged upon—the enemy to your house—Gilbert Lovell," and he burst into a loud laugh as he saw Glenroy fix his steadfast gaze upon his friend.

"Villain!" said Gilbert, darting upon Montford, "damned villain, what injury have I done you, that you should thus seek revenge?"

Montford without answering him endeavoured to liberate himself from the grasp of him whom we must now recognise as Gilbert Lovell; the struggle was fierce: both were active men, but Lovell had the mastery, when Montford suddenly drew a pistol from his bosom, and fired full upon his adversary—his grasp relaxed—Montford darted away from him, and was immediately lost among the trees—the stillness of the night was startled by his loud laugh, which was wild and scornful.

The injury sustained by Lovell was trifling—the ball had passed through the fleshy part of the arm. Hastily binding his handkerchief round the wounded part, he turned towards Glenroy.

It was a long death-like silence that ensued. Glenroy stood rivetted to the spot, with his eyes fixed immoveably upon Lovell; not a muscle seemed to stir, as if he scarcely drew a breath; and when he did, it was a deep convulsive gasp, that might be heard—it was almost a groan—and all was again still. There was a sign of anguish, and he spoke.

"Gilbert Lovell!" he said, "you have heard my oath," and he paused for a moment; "but as the husband of my sister, I forgive you. Had I known you before the connection had taken place, our meeting would have been different—but as it is—all—all shall be forgotten." He placed his hand in that of Lovell's, who grasped it fervently, and they returned to the ball-room in a far different mood to that in which they had quitted it.

———

CHAPTER XL.

Man, I have loved you; 'tis not in words to tell
How much, how deeply I have loved; 'tis past,
And now my soul has but one passion, one
Desire—revenge, great as my injuries.—BYRON.

———

Crime! there is one will trace thee!
Crime! there is one will face thee!
   Hide where thou wilt,
   The record of guilt,
The avenger still will chase thee!
When the day of alarm is ending,
And thy dark career seems tending
   To brighter ways,
   And innocent days,
Detection is impending.—HAYNES BAYLEY.

In the most romantic history there must be mere matters of fact untinged by the least shade of romance, and so it must be with our's; for it must be truly said the great sum of human life—the great accounts of happiness and misery—are made up of trifles. In short, to speak more plainly, a long life is like a tailor's or a lawyer's bill, there is a great sum total at the end, made up of very insignificant items in its progress.

The history of the lives of most people are included in their births, marriages, and deaths. The only biographer the generality of human beings deserve, is the journalist; and the whole story of their lives is contained in the paragraphs which record the above events.

How seldom, in perusing those daily records of births, marriages, and deaths, which the newspapers contain, do we ever calculate on the importance of the events recorded to the persons themselves. How seldom do we think, when reading the paragraph that announces the birth of an infant son, that there is another being thrown into the world, at all events to struggle through its difficulties, perhaps to regulate its destinies! or of a daughter, that there is another victim to be added to the many—many—who have been and are daily immolated at the shrine of licentious passion! When we read of a marriage, how little do we know of the heart-burnings and breakings that it may occasion; of the violations of filial duty which have preceded it; or think of that violation of the conjugal ones which it may produce! And when we read of death after death in the daily obituary, how few are there that say to themselves, " There is another and another soul gone to its last account,—

> "To that bourne from whence no traveller returns,"

to answer for all the actions of a life passed in the midst of temptations and passions, and pains and pleasures, to which the event recorded in the carelessly perused paragraph has put an end, and opened to the ethereal and undying spirit a new existence."

Yet still all these events must take place in a common as well as in a romantic life; and thus it was with Charles Montford, for whose further career this chapter is particularly devoted.

A character with some determined propensities to vice of its own is not half so dangerous, half so little to be depended upon, as that vacillating temper, which is led away by the imitation of others; and which, chamelion-like, takes its colours from those by which it is surrounded.

In the one instance, a man is only misled by his own vice; in the other by the vices of many, pursuing them all by turns.

Such a character was Montford's: with no decided propensity to any particular vice, he was completely led by those with whom he associated. Infirm of purpose, with a great dread of ridicule, mixed with a strong passion for pleasure, he was subject to the variation of every pressing wind.

At college he had imitated the follies of others. He went to the continent because every young man of fortune had done the same thing. He travelled, because he found some of his old companions had determined on making the tour of Europe; and he indulged in all the vices of all the capitals he passed through, first to imitate the set with which he lived, and, secondly, to escape the ridicule with which any qualm of conscience would inevitably have been visited.

In some of the places where he had stopped in Italy, he had been the participator in a number of intrigues, one of which he was obliged to break off, and return to England in consequence of the death of his father.

After the affairs of his father had been settled, he plunged into all the vices and follies of the metropolis, and but a short time after the payment of the bond to him by Glenroy, he found himself almost a beggar. Determined to retrieve his fortune by marriage with some wealthy heiress, he disguised his person with a pair of handsome moustaches, and set off to the then fashionable place of resort—Scarborough, and became acquainted with Alice Cameron, and effectually subdued her heart.

A few days after the events recorded in the last chapter, Alice joined her father in London, and thither Montford followed her. After innumerable private meetings, he prevailed upon her to ask the consent of Sir Reginald to their union, as a part of her property could not be touched unless she was married with the consent of her guardian.

Sir Reginald avowed his decided disapprobation to the union. Montford's principles—his morals, were highly displeasing to him, his character became known to Sir Reginald from General Trevanion, when he was made acquainted with the affair of the bond, which his daughter's money discharged. Prejudiced and disgusted with his character, Sir Reginald now also became deaf to his niece's solicitations, who, little aware of the unworthiness of her plea, urged on her knees the hitherto indulgent guardian to give his consent to the alliance. In vain she pleaded. Sir Reginald, impatient that his ward should renew a subject he was so much averse to, and one to which he had frequently pointed out insurmountable objections, with his own rooted dislike to the person, for the first time in his life spurned her angrily from him, and with evident trepidation hastily quitted the room, leaving Alice in her supplicating posture, and overwhelmed with tears.

At this unlucky moment Montford entered, and while duty forsook her seat, he at once took advantage of the opportunity so propitious to his cause. Well versed in artful insinuations, while he soothed her affection, he awakened her feelings to the harsh severity she endured ; and with an apparent disinterested affection, like a wolf watching the moment to seize his harmless prey, varied his discourse at pleasure. Not ignorant that real virtue is most likely to be subdued by the appearance of superior worth, this accomplished masterpiece of deceit knew the part he must act to its full extent.

Sometimes he threatened vengeance on the author of her sorrows, avowing that the man should not exist capable of giving her pain.

"Should," he would continue, in language which he knew would be most acceptable to her, " those eyes that have the power only by a look to pronounce my happiness or misery be dimmed by floods of tears ? By Heaven, they shall not ?" Then changing his tone and manner, " What does my unruly passion prompt me to say? Speak I not of the uncle of my Alice? And shall one of his white hairs be ruffled by my unwarranted hand ? Impious declaration ! No; it is he who shall put a period to a life become irksome to me—where he has pointed the dagger, there let it bleed. Nay, Alice, you have no cause to shudder; when my fate is decided, your uncle's unkind advice will flourish in your fair form in renovating perfection. Yes, Alice, I am indeed well aware of all the impending horrors of suicide. Equally am I convinced, that as long as this heart beats with vital fire, it will throb for you ; and well am I apprised of what your sufferings will be while I exist, unless you condescend to claim by marriage my protection. If your affection is so trifling that you choose to reject this last and only expedient, mine is too powerful to wilfully give a moment's anguish ; therefore I will no longer hesitate to extricate you, and avert the impending danger. Sit not thus, Alice, absorbed in grief; speak, dear girl—flatter me at least with hope ; look upon me—speak, I conjure you. Rack not my tortured brain with despair ; all the furies have taken possession of my soul, and I feel now fit to perpetrate the blackest crime. What is life bereft of the object of our love ? A wide dreary heath, replete with chasms of dark revenge, on which we stumble incessantly. Come, death—come surrounded with thy keenest pointed arrows ; I resign myself to thy fatal sting, and I wait thy javelin without dismay—welcome ! welcome ! farewell, Alice ! loved, adored Alice, farewell ! Eternal felicity shower on thy head ; and may the torments I feel dart through my veins, extenuated fall on thee in drops of honeyed love, then Alice will too late pity her Montford's wrongs."

Alice, bathed in tears, and terrified at his wild and incoherent language, scarcely knew what to say or how to act ; and after an effort to hush her own perturbations, stammered out in broken accents something about her uncle ; but her feelings were too much exhausted to suffer her to express accurately the sentiments she wished, and Montford replied with impassioned enthusiasm,—

" Talk not of your uncle's consent—he will never consent to our union. Say you will be mine, and this night I will release you from tyranny. Ah ! Alice, you hesitate ; if so, you see me no more ; nor shall these eyes again behold to-morrow's sun."

" My soul, Montford," rejoined Alice, with emphasis, " recoils at the mean artifice ; steal from my home in the dead of night like a guilty thief, and plunge my uncle into misery—it cannot be !"

" No, madam, no—you are right ; but to plunge the dagger in your Montford's heart is justifiable. Be it so ; 'tis done—you have pronounced my doom ; it comes from your lips. 'Tis sufficient—eternally farewell."

" Ah ! how cruelly you injure a heart you know your own," said Alice. " Stay—hear me, Montford ; whither do you go ? Stay! I entreat you, hear me."

With apparent composure Montford returned, and resumed his plea. " What has the darling of my soul to impart ? Will she reprieve her harsh decree ?

Fear not, my love, your guardian's anger, still less his sorrow. When he learns you are irretrievably mine, he will forgive and receive you to his arms."

"Dare I believe you?" cried Alice. "That thought emboldens me!"

Hapless, inconsiderate maid! Had a heart less romantic, less sanguine, been thine, too plainly it had perceived the extravagant part he played was put on and off at will, just as thy countenance varied; void of guile, thy heart suspected not deceit, nor conceived that he snatched at thy charming person for thy more charming fortune. Assured that the present moment was too critical to lose, he made the most of it to carry his point, concluding that his schemes might be entirely frustrated on another interview with her uncle, who could not behold the traces of sorrow on a face he now tenderly loved, and whose smiles supported his declining years, without erasing their marks with that affection which knows no interest—that Alice had too much good sense to withstand the argumentative solicitations of the best of uncles—and that were she once to learn the imperfections of her lover, she would not only cease to esteem, but dismiss him, whatever pain it might give her at the moment.

Love held the veil of pity over her good sense, and Alice at length yielded to Montford's protestations of everlasting affection and gratitude.

"Love," says Mrs. Inchbald, whose knowledge of human nature can be equalled only by the humour with which she describes its follies, and the unrivalled pathos with which she exhibits its distresses—"love, however rated by many as the chief passion of the heart, is but a poor dependant, a retainer on the other passions—admiration, gratitude, respect, esteem, pride in the object; divest the boasted sensation of these, and it is no more than the impression of a twelvemonth, by courtesy, or a vulgar error, called love."

At the appointed hour Montford arrived to hurry off triumphantly his lovely prize, fearful the expedition of four horses would be insufficient to secure his treasure. Alice, trembling, awaited him; but ere she had crossed the threshold of her uncle's door, the inconsistency of the step she was taking, the indelicacy of elopement, rushed on her mind in colours of the blackest ingratitude; in the same moment her uncle's tender care, his unbounded affection, his unlimited indulgence on all occasions awakened her too faithful memory; and she stood fixed to the spot. Rectitude and filial love at that instant powerfully predominated; and, with a firm voice and resolute tone, she declared she would not proceed farther, while, with a positive and determined manner, she urged Montford to renew his suit with her uncle, adding, till which time he must suffer her to return unmolested to her apartment.

For a short interval, Montford remained as one thunderstruck, speechless and motionless; but, too deep in cunning to continue long off his guard, he quickly foresaw that if duty once reassumed its empire, he was for ever discarded; consequently, at that crisis, something must be done to the purpose, and no means seemed more likely, in his opinion, than immediately asserting his authority, and thus by force compel her into compliance, since she appeared too resolute and collected to listen to soft words and fair promises. Judging rightly, it was more probable a sudden transition of temper, while it surprised her, might sooner induce her to forget the impropriety of the act, than all the entreaties he could suggest, whilst she was so powerfully supported by the dictates of duty.

With these ideas, he retorted, with a stern countenance and angry tone,—

"No, madam, I shall not most assuredly, with my consent, allow you to return. You were not forced to meet me; you have voluntarily resigned yourself to my protection, and I look upon you from this moment as my wife; or did you, madam, appoint to meet me here only to make a fool of me, and sport with my passion? to tantalise me with the vague hope that your obdurate guardian will consent to an union, you perfectly know is his decided aversion? and why? Because the humble name of Charles Montford is not emblazoned with the temporal distinction of lord, or duke, or some such other nonsense. No, Alice, trust me I will not throw my happiness away, nor shall a woman's fears daunt my courage. There is no time for remonstrance, which can tend to little purpose; your tears are ineffectual. Am I become odious to you? For shame, Alice! these ridiculous scruples are beneath you. This reluctance to realise my happiness proves the strength of your affection, and is a grateful recompense for the tortures I have endured, lest anything should ruffle yours; it is a pleasing specimen of what I may expect hereafter. S'death, madam, this thought carries perdition with it; these coquettish airs are ill judged after once making an assignation at this hour; in fact, there is no expedient now

left; if you positively refuse to become my lawful wife, your fame is eternally blasted, and you are no stranger to my other alternative. To-morrow's sun, I repeat and swear by Heaven, I never behold from your side. And this, madam, you may rely I will fulfil."

The inefficacy of all she suggested, and the impatient manner in which he listened to her prayers and entreaties, then on a retrospection of meeting him at this late hour, what might be reported to her disadvantage were it known, which in all probability it would be, strongly induced her to reject the little degree of reason she had collected, and she was on the point of telling him so, when her agitated frame fell lifeless in his arms : the contending passions of love, duty, fear, and pride, for a short time invigorated her strength ; but, the instant they ceased to combat, her spirits, already exhausted, failed her.

During the time Alice lay lifeless in the arms of Montford, he had time to compose his ungovernable temper, which from feigned choler had actually degenerated into real anger, and, on her recovery, to act the part of the fond, compassioned lover. This easy deceit, powerfully favoured by his truly handsome face and alluring deportment, that even to a heart less susceptible than Alice's, must have pleaded in his behalf, soon succeeded with Alice, who, awakening from her swoon, found herself some miles on her journey, with Montford only by her side, using every art to bring her to herself; pleading his love with all the tenderness and energy that words could enforce, and, though too weak to convey the effusions of real love, they shortly reinstated him in her good opinion, as they served to lull her recollection to the present moment only, and make the journey pass swift on the wings of love. Nay, they were hammered together by the blacksmith with her full consent, giving with her hand her heart, while it bounded with affection, and she looked to the receiver for all its future happiness.

They returned to London by easy stages, and, after they had taken up their residence in lodgings at the west end of the town, eagerly sought the forgiveness of Sir Reginald Willoughby ; but their efforts were fruitless—he peremptorily refused to see them.

They had resided but a few short months at their lodgings. Montford's temper, since his marriage, ever unkind, even morose, and being no longer constrained by hope, no point to gain, no curb to check its impetuosity, grew daily more insufferable. Alice had again sought an interview with Sir Reginald, but was again repulsed, and, upon her return home, high words passed between her and Montford, who, vowing vengeance against Sir Reginald for withholding his consent, quitted the house.

Alice, wrapping her shawl about her, took a walk in the garden. Her thoughts were sad, the evening breeze felt cold, and she drew her shawl more closely round her. Seating herself upon a rustic bench, the scene around her, far as the eye could reach, seemed to repose in tranquil beauty ; but the heart of Alice felt uneasy sensations of sorrow, as she thought of the unkindness of her husband, and of the step she had taken. A rustling noise among the trees made her look behind her, and she was about leaving the place, as she perceived a tall female issue from among the trees, when she was commanded to stay. Alice fearfully raised her eyes at this command, for it was not the tone of entreaty. The dress of the stranger was that of an Italian peasant, her figure was graceful, her hair, which retained its blackness, was braided on her high forehead, and her dark eyes, in her present mood, seemed to flash fire. She must have been a very fine woman, and still retained traces of beauty ; but ill-health or violent passions had utterly obliterated the expression which once perhaps gave a charm to her fine features, and, without it, they became repulsive rather than agreeable.

"Here," said Alice, offering her some money, supposing her to be one of those numerous women who beg about the streets of London, "this will relieve your present necessities."

"I am no beggar," replied the stranger, scornfully putting aside the trembling hand that presented the money ; "I need none of your charity, but I have much to say that you must hear."

"Come, then, to-morrow to the house," said Alice.

"To-morrow!" repeated the stranger, with a frantic laugh ; "ay, that was his word—to-morrow I will come, but he came not—he consigned me to perpetual penance and confinement—he deserted me. You must, you shall hear me now. I have crossed the stony defile, the rugged mountain, and the stormy sea, to seek him—to teach him how a woman can avenge her injuries."

"Of whom do you speak?" asked Alice, a fearful suspicion glancing on her mind; "who has injured you?"

"Charles Montford," replied the stranger, "your worthless husband; it was he who wooed me with tender words and sweet persuasions—who swore to love me while he had existence; yes, it was Charles Montford who won my young heart, and destroyed my innocence and peace. Before he came to my native valley, I laboured all day, and was content; I slept tranquilly and sweetly on my humble pallet, and rose with the sun to milk our goats, and spin the cotton for our garments. I was happy, though I was the drudge of a harsh and sordid mother, for at sunset I bound my dark tresses with a garland of flowers, wishing for no richer gems, and danced on the green margin of the lake with my young companions, and my laugh and my song spoke the cheerfulness of my heart; but when I saw Charles Montford, a change came over me; I was no longer satisfied with my condition, nor content to labour, for he called me beautiful; he said I was not suited to a peasant's life, nor fit for the rude occupations in which he saw me employed. His flattery made me proud and idle. I despised the humble cabin in which I was born; I detested the mean garments in which I was clad; and rebelled against the commands of my mother, whom I had hitherto obeyed without demur or contradiction. But a cloud, dark as that which now crosses the heavens, had fallen upon my spirits, the precursor of gloom and tempest. Yet, had he then left me, I should have grieved but for a time; I might have forgotten his flatteries; I might have returned again to my goats and my reel, and been happy with my former companions. But he bought me of my unnatural parent for a purse of gold, and I gladly consented to go with him from my native valley. Yes, I left my young companions, all that had once been dear to me, without regret, for I was going to reside with him, whom my fancy painted the best and most beautiful of human kind. Montford placed me in splendid apartments, where I was instructed to adorn my person, to move more gracefully in the dance, and join my voice to the soft notes of the lute and mandolin. Would that my attainments had rested there! But, woe for me, I was taught to read; books brought reflection, and I felt and knew the value of the virtue I had lost, and the degradation into which I had fallen."

"Unhappy creature! from my soul I pity you," said Alice. "But, alas! I fear you have little to hope from the justice or humanity of your seducer."

"I have neither hope nor expectation, but of revenge," replied the stranger. "Look not impatient, my tale is almost told."

"To-morrow, I will hear the rest to-morrow," returned the deeply-agitated Alice; "suffer me now to depart."

"Remain," said the female, sternly. "To-morrow is a word of deep and fatal import! What know ye of to-morrow? Can you be certain you shall see to-morrow? The sun will shine, and the blue sky canopy the earth to-morrow, but your eyes may not behold them; they may be closed in death."

"Most true," replied Alice, her blood chilling at the deep tone and wild look of the stranger, whose gaze was fixed upon her, "most true; life and death are at the disposal of the Almighty, and we know not how soon we may be summoned hence."

"Stay, then, and hear me," resumed the stranger; "I beheld, with horror, the snare into which love had led me; my dishonour preyed upon my spirits; I became pale, languid, and melancholy; and the holy father, to whom I made confession, told me I was in the road to perdition; he bade me fast, pray, and repent; and refused to absolve me, unless I forsook my sin. My lost condition frenzied my brain. I knelt at the feet of Montford,—he had told me he loved me as man never loved woman, and I believed him—I pictured his faith pure as my own, the offspring of the fondest, truest love that ever warmed a human bosom,—I told him all the anguish of my heart, the fearful doom I had been menaced with, and I implored him to restore me to self-esteem—to make me his wife, that I might continue to love and reside with him, without incurring the peril of my soul."

The stranger paused for a moment, and the trembling Alice would have fled to the house, but the woman held her by the wrist, and she was compelled to listen

to her.   Again she continued her narrative :—"But he laughed at my distress, he
scoffed at my religious fears, he ridiculed my remorse, and called my confessor a
canting, meddling hypocrite, who, if I would offer him a few pieces of gold, would
sell me indulgence and absolution.   I found growing up in myself a new energy—
a new power—a fire equal to his own.   I clung to his knees; I entreated, I begged,
I pray'd him to marry me; but, with a look of disdain, he shook me off, and
haughtily bade me remember the immeasurable distance between a rich Englishman
and a low-born peasant girl, whose person he had purchased with his gold, and
honoured by taking to his bed."

"If you have any pity, mercy—tell me no more, said Alice.

"I once had both," resumed the stranger; "but they are now extinct in my
heart.   Pity, mercy, neither was shown to me.   I spoke of my injuries, of the
vengeance of offended Heaven; but he bade me restrain the insolence of my
speech, and leave him to settle his accounts with Heaven, as it best suited his
opinions and belief; he sternly bade me trouble him no more with artful
representations of a wounded conscience, for he was convinced my tears and well-
acted agonies were employed to bring about the ambitious design I had formed of
winning him to marry me.   'But the saintly father who has set you on this
extravagant scheme,' said Montford, 'will find I am not so mean in spirit, nor so
weak in understanding, as to sacrifice my name with her who has forfeited all
claim to the world's respect, and whose proudest boast is a tolerable person.'
I shrieked, I tore my hair, as I heard the destroyer of my virtue thus insult me;
but with barbarous coldness he bade me not deprive myself of my chief charm.
'Preserve those raven tresses,' said he, 'to attract another lover when I am
gone, which will shortly be the case, for to be plain with you I intend leaving
here for my own country.'   'You cannot,' said I, 'you will not be so base as
to abandon me!'   'I will take care you shall not want the necessaries of life;
I leave you now to recollect your own lowly condition, and when you are reasonable
enough to confess your folly, and sufficiently humble to acknowledge the honour
I have done you by taking you from a life of drudgery and poverty, I may be
induced to pardon your presumption, and take you again to my favour.'   I started
to my feet, with flashing eyes I threatened him.   It was the first unfolding of
that character which neither he nor I knew belonged to my nature.   It was the
first uncoiling of the basilisk within me.   He gazed on me incredulously, and
coolly smiled.   I fainted. When I recovered recollection, I found myself laid on a
couch in my own apartment; about half an hour had elapsed, when I heard a
carriage drive up to the door of the house ; and supposing it to be that kept for my
use, I desired my attendant to go and dismiss it.   In a few moments she returned,
and presented a billet; it was addressed to me; I knew the characters; they were
Montford's.   Here," continued the stranger, drawing it from her bosom, "here
is the written record of his unequalled treachery—to me the characters are
flame——"

As she spoke, her large dark eyes fell on the paper, and in a tone of bitterness
she read,—"Rosalie, I am willing to believe the artful representations of your
confessor have disordered your brain, and impelled you to an act which I am
persuaded you now deeply repent; influenced by this belief, I will forget it,
provided you suffer Paulo to conduct you immediately to the villa which I inhabit,
where the cool air will be of service to your health, and repose will tranquillise
your spirits.   Your attendant can go with you, with the hope that you will be
as wishful as myself for reconciliation.   Adieu till to-morrow evening, when you
shall find that your remonstrances and representations have had due effect; that
I am not regardless of your soul's peace, but have resolved to restore you to virtue."

"What could I believe?" said the stranger, as she crushed the billet together,
"but that he repented of my seduction, and designed to repair the injury he had
done me by the sacred rite of marriage, for by no other means did it appear to me
that he could satisfy my upbraiding conscience, and restore me to peace.   Fool!
credulous fool to be again deceived; I pressed the letter to my lips and shed over
it tears of transport.   My attendant hastily collected a few necessary articles of

apparel, and I joyfully departed for the villa—a little romantic place Montford had lately hired, a retreat for the sultry heat of summer, when it became fashionable to prefer nature, in her beautiful simplicity, rather than the crowded assemblies and conversaziones."

The way seemed rough and tedious, but it was beguiled by Paulo's description of the groves and fountains that enriched the domain to which we were travelling. The sun had sunk, and the evening had set in heavy and gloomy, when a sudden turn in the road, which had wound between two hills, brought us close to the ponderous gates of a monastery. There, to my astonishment and consternation, the carriage stopped, and I was forced, in spite of my shrieks and resistance, to enter a dismal apartment, where, as I cast my eyes despairingly round, I beheld only frightful figures carved in black oak, and narrow grated casements, that seemed as if they were designed to exclude, rather than admit, the cheerful rays of the sun. Here I was left alone with Paulo, while my attendant was conducted to the presence of the abbess, to whom she was the bearer of Montford's instructions respecting me.

" In the meantime, Paulo, invested with full powers by my betrayer, insolently informed me, that Montford would never see me more; but that, believing my brain was unsettled, he had generously provided an asylum for me in the convent; to which I had, by his orders, been safely conducted, where I was to remain during life, and where my betrayer trusted I should recover peace and virtue; that my outrageous conduct had only precipitated our parting, for in a few days Montford would quit Italy for ever; and as it was impossible to make me the companion of his travels, it was best we should separate at once.

" It matters not to relate the reproaches I poured upon my treacherous attendants, by whom I was left to rave and lament too late my credulity and desertion. When I arrived at the convent, I had valuable jewels about my person; these I contrived to conceal from the eyes of the abbess. With some of them I bribed the gardener of the convent to assist my escape, and convey me back to my late residence; but my purpose was utterly disappointed; for when I reached the house I found it shut up, and learned that Montford had departed for England. 'I will follow the perfidious wretch,' said I, 'to the farthest extremity of the globe!'

" Stimulated by the revenge I determined to obtain, I overcame incredible difficulties; despising peril and fatigue I traced h'm to London, and have wandered here to ——''

" Not to commit murder!" said Alice, shrinking from the flashing eye of the stranger; "no, as you hope to be forgiven, though Montford has deceived and abandoned you, do not perpetrate a deed that will provoke Heaven to forsake you; none are absolutely miserable, who dare hope for Heaven's mercy and forgiveness. Let not your own act sever this blessed hope from your soul; forbear to nourish a revengeful spirit."

" Never!" interrupted the stranger, " I have sworn to be revenged—ha! see; here he comes," and at that moment Montford made his appearance, but suddenly stopped upon recognising the features of the stranger, who stood in silence gazing on him with a horrid, unnatural smile of exultation.

" I am here at last!" she cried, " I have followed you for months; and now coward, villain, liar, you are not again likely to escape me."

Montford's attitude was unchanged; his eyes still glared upon her: blood trickled from his under lip, caused by the unnatural pressure of his teeth; his cheeks seemed burning with fever; and so violently did he tremble, that Alice every moment expected he would fall.

" Villain!" exclaimed Rosalie, after steadfastly gazing at him for a moment, " we meet once more. I loved you once, with all weak woman's devoted tenderness, and how did you repay it? By trampling on the warm affection of my heart; by insult, injury, and treachery. I have suffered through you the misery of scorn and disgrace; think you that any particle of love can be cherished with rhese remembrances? Know me truly; I hate you with a deep, inveterate abhorence, and I have sought you here, for a deeply deadly vengeance."

"Not," said Montford, drawing a pistol, which he always carried with him from his coat pocket, "not while I have the power to repulse you, thou femal devil! quit this place instantly," and he pointed the pistol towards her; she rushed forward, grasped his right hand with hers, and with her left, she plunged a smal stiletto, which she had concealed up her sleeve, up to the hilt in his side.

Montford staggered and fell, while with a frantic laugh, Rosalie exclaimed,—

"Perfidious villain! I am revenged, for never shall the poison with which my stiletto is embued be extracted from thy blood; for myself, I care not; the officers of justice will be here, and should I be taken, my life will be forfeited; but thus— thus, I disappoint them." She plunged the stiletto deep into her bosom, and fell lifeless by the side of her seducer—a dreadful proof of Italian vengeance.

The servants, attracted by the cries of Alice, now hastened to the spot, and found her kneeling by the side of Montford. Every spark of resentment which she had felt towards him, vanished on viewing the affecting spectacle. She gazed on him with melancholy concern, such as cannot but affect the feelings of every considerate being who sees an unprepared, unrepenting sinner depart this world suddenly—"Unhappy rash man," she cried, with uplifted hands bending over the bleeding corpse! "unhappy husband! is this thy wretched doom?" Then falling on her knees, emphatically addressed her broken prayer to Heaven.

"O God of mercies! look down with tender pity, hear the widow's prayer,— and, oh! forgive! forgive his numberless offences; receive his departed soul; and, if it be thy pleasure, suffer me to expiate his sins on earth. Pardon him, O Lord! as I—Let not my husband,—let him not encounter thy severe wrath; inflict sooner his punishment on me, left in this wide world of woe!"

An agony of grief bereft her of speech. The painful remembrance of what she once believed him; the direful contrast, the livid image exhibited before her, with the tender affection she had borne him, now overpowered her busy memory; and, rejecting his imperfections, she only recollected their past love, which overbalanced for the moment every other sensation, and quickly operated so violently on her feeble nerves, as to render her situation distracted.

*   *   *   *   *   *   *

Alice was now forgiven by Sir Reginald Willoughby, who took her again to his house. Doomed to the sad realities of life, poor Alice wept over her dreams of romance, and turned for consolation to the very pages that had led to the ruin she deplored. The ruling passion governed still.

———

CHAPTER XLI.

Do not forget, o'er other scenes
  The while thine eyes delighted rove,
The hours of youth, thy childhood's home
  Of innocence and love!

Oft let the joys that once were thine,
  In fancy's dreams revisit thee—
Oh, they shall prove a plenteous source
  Of blissful memory!

But there are joys that never fade—
  The joys that virtue can impart;
And there's a treasure nought can spoil—
  An uncorrupted heart!—CHARLES MAY.

RETURN we once more to Graham, whom we left making the best use of his legs to carry him from Hexham, nor did he slacken his pace until he was a considerable way from the town. He was now miserable. The night was dark as a dungeon; but not half so dark as his own thoughts. He trembled at the first appearance of day, lest he should be again apprehended and committed to prison. Dawn found him on the borders of Westmoreland. Cold and weary as he was, he dared not approach a house or the public road, but lay concealed in a wood all day under sensations of the utmost fear. Towards evening he cautiously emerged from his hiding-place; compelled by hunger he entered a lonely house at a distance from the public road, obtained some refreshment, and warmed his benumbed limbs. Under cover of the night he again pursued his way, and reached Appleby early the following morning. Entering the first pot-house which he came to, he obtained a warm breakfast and a bed, of both of which he stood greatly in need. He soon fell asleep, in spite of the agitation of his mind; but his dreams were far more horrifying than his waking thoughts, dreadful as they were. He awoke early in the afternoon, feverish and unrefreshed.

Starting again when darkness covered the earth, he proceeded on the road which he thought would take him to the coast; he felt it would be imprudent in him to ask the road, as that might create suspicion. In the morning he found himself some miles advanced among the mountains, ignorant of the situation of the country where he then was. He saw no appearance of neighbourhood, no cottage where he could obtain rest, nor any one from which he could beg or buy a little refreshment. He seemed alone in the world; and giving way to the oppression of his mind, asked himself very seriously why he should continue to " cumber the earth," or why he might not end at once a life for which no one cared, and which everything tended to embitter? Dreadful thoughts rose rapidly in his mind, and a torrent which foamed at his feet, through a dark and gloomy ravine, seemed to present means of deliverance from the evils with which he believed himself surrounded. Such was the distraction of his soul, that every softer remembrance was lost.

Those friends, his wife and daughter, of whose fidelity and affection he was assured when reason was suffered to act, were forgotten; even love itself ceased to actuate, or was recalled only to add to his despair, by showing him a blessing which this last outrage of his feelings deprived him of for ever. In gloomy desperation he believed no one in the wide world would lament him, for on no one inhabitant of that cold and selfish world had he a single claim, save upon his daughter, and he felt that all further connection with her proscribed father would only degrade her in the eyes of her friends.

From thoughts thus subversive of reason and principle, he was roused at length by a shout from the heights above the low valley, where he had continued for hours to pursue his weary way, unmindful of bodily fatigue. He looked up, and beheld two men of singular appearance, who, perceiving they had fixed his attention, called to him to turn from his present path, or death would indeed be the consequence.

He looked forward as the men spoke, and observed that the deep valley he had so long traversed, without observing whither it led, ended in a dark and gloomy gulf, into which a few more steps would have inevitably precipitated him. With a clear sense of its immediate danger, the instinctive love of life returned; and shuddering at the abyss before him, and still more at the full sense of his own impious despair, he fell on his knees, and his softened heart swelled with kindlier feelings.

To leave this dismal valley now became his earnest wish, but no path was apparent. He looked up, and observed the men still gazing at him; his voice scarcely reached them as he inquired by what means he could extricate himself; but they judged from his gestures that such was the purport of his words, and pointing to a turning of the rock, he retraced his steps a short distance, and found a steep and narrow path, which he feared, when found, would to him be inaccessible.

The honest peasants above saw his distress, and one of them descending, assisted him, till Graham, after immense fatigue and labour, which his exhausted state of mind and body rendered greater, at last reached the plain above in safety.

The peasants observed the agitation and feebleness which pervaded his whole frame, and pointing to a miserable cabin at some distance, invited him to proceed with them to it, where food and rest, though coarse and humble, might be procured. Graham, gratefully accepting their offered kindness, followed them to their hut; and after some coarse refreshment, which greatly revived him, he sought to lose the fatigue and oppression he felt in a transcient slumber. Repose, though on so hard a pallet, befriended and revived him, and he awoke soothed and tranquillised. His hosts, rude and unpolished as they were, possessed plain good sense, and that kind of philosophy which is unconnected with learning, and incompatible with sensibility; and easily perceiving that their guest laboured under some heavy affliction, they endeavoured, by arguments of genuine truth and judgment, to prove the folly of immoderate grieving for irremediable evils, and the propriety of more active measures, as more effectually assisting to overcome them.

Graham listened with attention to their homely arguments, and paid them the compliment of profiting by them. He spent three days in the gloomy hut on these dreary mountains, and then with firmer nerves, and a less wild appearance, followed the instructions of his humble friends, who had pointed out the readiest way to the coast, from whence he might embark to Ireland, and there procure a passage to any part of the continent. He rewarded these men as well as his purse, which had been given him by Mrs. Heathcote, would afford, and then commenced his lonely tour.

The result of Graham's three days of solitary reflection was beneficial to both mind and body, for they showed him the folly and guilt of yielding to despair by suicide. He, therefore, determined to go to France, and there seek some employment by which he might drag out the remainder of his miserable existence, and in some way atone for his former crimes.

He proceeded in this mood for several hours, and was turning into the road which led to ——, when he was stopped by hearing a rough voice exclaim,—

"God bless your honour, spare a copper for poor Jack, who has lost his precious limbs in fighting for his king and country."

Turning his eyes to the road-side, Graham saw, seated upon a bank, two strange objects, a tall ungainly-looking man, in a tattered seaman's dress, with one arm off by the elbow, a young, good-looking, but tattered female by his side. In a moment Graham stopped, and drew from his pocket a penny, which he gave to the female, saying at the same time, "It's for Jack!"

"Bless your honour," said the tall seaman, "it's all one. That there young one, I calculate, is my wife; poor thing, she was struck dumb, in real earnest, when she saw me come home to her with the loss of my fin. Bless her pretty face, she didn't forsake her poor Jeptha for all that."

While he spoke, a strong feeling came upon Graham that he had seen his face before; but when or where, he could not call to mind. As Graham stood gazing into his face, the beggar looked as scrutinisingly at him.

"Were you ever in America?" inquired Graham.

"Martha's Vineyard! but I guess I have been," replied the tall sailor.

"Then you must be Jeptha Dobbs, formerly the mate of the Santaclaus," replied Graham.

"I reckon," replied Jeptha, "that you have guessed right for once in your life. I was once mate of the good old ship. Ah! those times are past, I am now Jeptha Dobbs the Gipsy; but who may you be?"

"No matter," replied Graham, "you know me not."

"But I think I do," said Jeptha, "you are——" and he whispered in Graham's ear.

"I am," said Graham, "but you see me now, destitute of everything, a wanderer upon the face of the earth, not knowing which way to escape from the officers of justice. I have recently escaped from——. Can I trust you?"

"You can."

Graham paused for a few moments, and then continued, "I have escaped from Hexham prison, and wish for some means of escaping from England."

"Never strike to an enemy, nor quit the pumps while the vessel can float," said Jeptha. "There are many ways of doing that, but suppose you join us for a short time; you can live a jovial life, and escape notice: see here." And Jeptha drew his arm from his jacket, which had been forced in elbow first, doubling up the arm to give it the appearance of being maimed.

"No, no," said Graham, "my determination is fixed; but how is it I see you following this life?"

"I'll tell you," said Jeptha. "I came to England in the old Santaclaus, and after staying some time in London, I made up my mind to go to India, but when I got there, I soon found India was no place for me. I could not abide the black, lazy, cowardly rascals of lascars; and there were crowds of them in all the vessels I could find. They are all well enough in fair weather; but when it blows, the heart is blown out of them. They are either in the way, or skulking in corners: so I took the first opportunity of returning to England. When I got to London, I

No. 34.

had a tarnation good spree, and got into all kinds of mischief, and I reckon the guineas went like smoke, and in about a fortnight I was a beggar; my clothes and all went, for I opened my blinkers one morning in a watchhouse in Wapping, and found only a watchman's great coat thrown over me. I had now time to reflect, but nothing to reflect upon, for all I had in the world was a shirt and pair of trousers. There was no charge against me, so I walked from the watchhouse, like a man adrift in an old boat without oars or food. I went to the water-side, for pity or employ. I got fitted in a kind of way; but could not find a vessel, for there were too many like myself. What to do I knew not. More than once I thought of doing as I had been done by—that is, helping myself where I could; but although I was often without food, and slept in the street or under a boat, I, somehow, could not bring my mind to that. I often wished I was again in my own country; but how to get there I knew not. At length the thought came into my mind—I might get a sum of money together by begging about the country as a poor tar. I should not at any rate, I thought, be worse off than in London—and where was the odds? So off I set, but was poorly enough off, for I was not then up to the trade; so my stout look and honest truth met nothing but unkindness and insult. At length one day, as I was almost dying of starvation, I retired under some trees and laid me down to rest. The sun had sunk when I awoke; but, as ill-fortune would have it, the night was gloomy and overcast; not a star was visible; after wandering about for more than an hour without knowing in what direction I was going, I espied a light, which I hoped might be that of some house, where I might procure a crust of bread, for I was nigh famishing. This lent me fresh strength, and I pushed on; but on approaching close, I found it proceeded from the tents of some gipsies, who were encamped under the shelter of a shady lane.

"Balancing between my dread of these lawless people, and my fears of perishing from cold and hunger, I crept behind a tree to examine the party, which consisted of several men and women, and two children. Much time was not afforded me for reflection; for of a sudden I heard the rush of footsteps, a brawny hand seized me by the throat, and I was dragged towards the tents by a tall, powerful gipsy, who, it seems, had been watching me. In an instant I was immediately surrounded, and my captor threw from his back a fine young kid. 'Hilloa!' said one of the men, 'who hast there, lad?' Without waiting for the tall gipsy to answer, I made known my destitute condition, and was kindly and hospitably invited to share their repast. Fan there was one of the troop. From the moment I saw her, I took a liking to her pretty face—I joined the gang for her sake, and soon won her regard and love. I was now content and happy. We had victuals of the best and plenty, and roamed where we pleased, with no restraint but our own wills. I found there was some tough work before my hands. Fan had one or two pretenders to her love, in her own and other gangs, and my rivals were not to be lightly thought of, for in their minds none but the brave deserve the fair. It was win your bride, and keep her while you can. The one whom her parents intended for her husband, was the tall gipsy who first collared me; but Fan had no inclination for the match, and my arrival confirmed her dislike to him. Our loves were only known to ourselves, and our interviews stolen, until my services had gained me the esteem of her father.

"Under the tuition of Fan, I became a most expert beggar, and my contributions to the common stock often equalled the amount of all the others put together. I became the pride of the gang; and no wonder—for I strove for Fan, and was cheered on by her acclaim, while I was scowled at by my rivals, who were quick enough, though her parents had no suspicion of it, to see her preference for me. When we thought it proper time, I proposed to the father for the hand of his daughter. He had no objection to me as a son-in-law, further than that he had all but promised her to the other, but would leave it to Fan and myself to manage the affair as we best could, and would interfere no farther with his authority than for the good of the gang. If Fan was pleased, he cared not who had her. When I told her the result of my conference with her father, she was as well pleased as myself, and arm in arm we returned to the tents.

"The tall gipsy, who was called Long Gabriel, had just come home after an excursion; so, as soon as he saw u, his rage knew no bounds, and his dark eyes flashed fire, as he came forward and ordered me to quit my hold of the girl. There were few words passed between us; every one knew what was to take place, so no one interfered further than to see fair play. So the short and the long of it is, Long Gabriel was beaten, and I was married to Fan the next day, agreeably to the gipsy fashion—that is, a feast was given to all the gang; and her father delivered her up to me with a long harangue, concluding by declaring us man and wife, and the others wishing us joy.

"Fan and I did not remain long with the gang after this. Long Gabriel and his mother were our implacable enemies, and neither of us were safe from their revenge; not that I cared a straw for them openly, but I knew their character too well to be at ease. Fan and I left them, have lived well and comfortably since, and could save money, only there is no occasion for it. We, like all people of superior minds in the world, live by our wits; there is no occasion for working when we can live without. I never want money and a good dinner. From experience I can assure you, no trade is so easy, or quickly learned, as begging. The first day is the worst; after that, it comes quite natural and agreeable. So what say you, captain? Be one of us."

"No, no!" said Graham, "I must leave England; all I want is to reach the coast, so that I may get to the continent."

"Well, well!" said Jeptha, "I'll put you in the road."

This Jeptha did, and in two days Graham stood on the sea beach; he soon obtained a passage to Ireland, and from thence to France. Having successfully overcome the dangers and difficulties of his long and tedious progress, Graham found himself in Austria, where he entered the army as a common soldier.

He was engaged in a number of those sanguinary actions which achieved wonders by dint of perseverance and a reckless sacrifice of human blood, and by the pouring in of fresh levies, to fill up the vacant ranks of men mowed down by the scythe of war, in carrying on these arduous enterprises.

Battle after battle inured him to his new life, and promotion on promotion followed his wounds, and deeds of daring in the different awful encounters which he had to sustain against experienced and intrepid foes. The grades of non-commissioned officer, subaltern, captain, and lieutenant-colonel, followed each other in rapid succession; but many a year and many a peril, the earth his resting-place, and the clouds his curtains, sleepless nights and fasting days, were the price he paid for all this glory and promotion; honour, and to retrieve the disgrace of his past life, was now the phantom that attracted him—the glowworm which led on his weary steps, in fine, the object of his idolatry; still wife and home, his daughter, and early sympathies, were not entirely obliterated from the tablets of his memory; and as peace approached, they acquired a fresh colouring, as a neglected picture, covered with dust and placed in the shade and damp of obscurity and distance, regains its former appearance on nearer approach, and on being relieved of the cobwebs and mildews which have formerly defaced it.

For twelve years he had continued totally ignorant of their fortune, and even of their existence. He felt that one of the most exquisite gratifications the earth could afford him, was to behold his wife and child. What a multitude of adventures and incidents might they not have encountered in the space of twelve years? Imagination and affection dwell impatiently on the interval; nor can anything quiet the conjectures of him that loves, short of the most complete information. What a difference must twelve years have produced? With what mingled and exquisite emotions does the father contemplate the daughter whom he left! He sees her with astonishment and rapture displaying maturer beauties, discovering in her countenance new traces of knowledge and sentiment, and in her gesture and manners a character finished, matronly, and sedate.

He determined not to make himself known to them; and anticipated with eager transport the hour at which he should revisit the place of his birth, wander amidst the shades where his careless infancy had strayed, recognise objects made sacred to his heart by associations, and steal a joy, unsuspected and unknown, to which the very secrecy with which it was ravished would give a tenfold zest.

FLORENCE GRAHAM; OR,

CHAPTER XLII.

ONWARD and still onward speeds the flight of Time. Deaf, blind, relentless—for nothing he stays his wing. Ever with the same eternal haste he presses on. Events that might astound an universe, prayers that might pierce a fiend, never delay, never melt him; cities roar, and are silent; empires rise and fall; mountains bow their ice-crowned thrones; seas advance from their unfathomed beds; and yet, ever unpausing, unpitying, unwondering, his course is on, and still on.

Twelve years!—twelve eventful years had passed like a breath. So startlingly rapid passed time. Yesterday—only yesterday—were noisy children on the green; images were around all bright and dear: look you now what a transformation! Youth is vanished; years—how we know not, are on our foreheads, and in our hearts. As in a theatre the scene is changed, other objects, new characters, are before us. They call us by different names; they woo us to strange enterprises. Go to the haunt of your boyhood—go—with your grave, cold face, your wearied and melancholy heart. Stand amid the careless and happy forms that sport there to-day. You will strike them with awe. The unshaded glance, the joyous laugh, the high, happy shout, will be hushed till you pass.

Many changes had taken place in Allendale in twelve years. Glenroy had been presented with a living in London. His friend and brother, Gilbert Lovell, also accompanied him to the metropolis; their friendship was inseparable; their hearts and tastes, and, what was of far greater importance, their religious principles in unison; they might almost be said to commence on earth a foretaste of those immortal joys they were humbly preparing themselves to participate in hereafter.

Mrs. Glenroy was the guest of both alternately, dividing her time between them; but, in her old age, her thoughts were constantly on her poor Constance, and oft as she sat alone, thinking of past times, a tear might be seen stealing slowly down her furrowed cheek.

Lady Maxwell was Lady Maxwell still; spending her time in the summer at Hexham, and the winter in London, unwilling to believe that she had yet lost all her former attractions. It is difficult, indeed, for the wisest of us to remark the advances which Time, that silent destroyer, makes upon all human creatures.

Miss Shanks continued for several years a resident at Elmgrove, paying many a long visit to the Glenroys, to show her gratitude to her preserver. But, when they quitted Allendale, and Mrs. Hathwood accompanied Florence to her father's family estate Lochallan, which had undergone a thorough repair, poor Tabitha was at last obliged to accept of a home with her despised and neglected sister, where she repined at the degradation of her lot—the fretful ghost of departed gentility—and took to her virgin arms a stout English yeoman, thus fulfilling the prediction of her father—" That her top knot must come,

' To a linsey, woollen gown,
And she should marry a farmer.' "

Reader! our tale is nearly told; but one more scene, and it is finished.

Seated around a comfortable log fire, in one of the handsomest rooms of Lochallan Castle, was a snug family party. In an arm chair sat a silver headed dame, whose person possessed all the mellow charm which beauty receives from age. Her white locks were smoothed over her brow, with a majesty that at once won respect and reverence. Her face was mild and happy, but years had impressed it with heavy marks, and yet more than years—sorrow.

A graceful form hung over her chair, with her arm affectionately upon her shoulder, and by her side a gentleman had drawn familiarly.

It required no more than a glance to discover in the two latter, Florence and Musgrove, and in their aged companion, the still noble but changed form of Mrs. Heathwood.

Opposite to this group, on the other side the of fire-place, sat Don Lopez, a hearty old man, who had been reading from a book. On his knee sat a fair young girl, and by his side was standing a stout, rosy-cheeked boy—the children of Florence.

The day had been a dreary one, and the sea, which could be plainly seen from the windows of the castle, was lashed into rage by the power of the wind, and presented one of those terrific scenes which speak desolation to the seaman's heart.

"Hark!" said Don Lopez, "I think there's a signal gun firing." As he finished speaking, the firing of guns was distinctly heard.

"Let us to the beach," said Musgrove, "we may be of assistance."

He quitted the apartment, accompanied by Don Lopez ; summoning the servants, they procured lights, and many minutes did not elapse before they reached the steepest part of the headland which overhung the bay.

Gun after gun was fired, but at such a distance that they despaired of being useful. They knew not how nor whither to direct their efforts, but stood close together, trying to resist the force of the tempest, and endeavouring to catch any sound that might guide them to the scene of distress.

Musgrove directed a fire to be kindled, which after a time burnt brightly, and at length discovered to them the situation of the vessel, which was fast drifting on a lee shore, without the most remote chance of salvation.

Shipwreck, even to those who behold it in security, is a tremendous scene, accompanied, as it almost invariably is, by the tumult of the elements and the waste of human life ; and never did a suffering crew witness a more tempestuous night than that which we are now attempting to describe ; for, buffeted by a merciless sea, every stitch of canvass torn into shreds by the fury of the wind, and close in with a perilous coast, which the intensity of the darkness completely concealed, all hope of escape was impossible, from the first moment the vessel found herself embayed in the unexpected hurricane, and her complete destruction was inevitable.

Fresh fuel was piled upon the fire ; and as the flames rose with increased brightness, the black hull and tall bare masts of a stately vessel driving swiftly towards the beach, was distinctly visible.

"What has she to expect?" asked Musgrove, after all had been intently watching her for some time in silence.

"She must go down, sir," replied an old fisherman, with the cold, determined tone of one certain of the truth of his assertion, and too familiar with wrecks to deem one more than a common accident of life.

"Can none be saved?" he eagerly demanded.

"Impossible, sir. See, one mast is gone, and she pitches dreadfully."

"Is there no hope, then?" inquired Musgrove, still more anxiously, for his was not a mind to contemplate the sufferings of his fellow men unmoved.

"She drives on still, but not so quickly as at first," observed the fisherman, without directly answering Musgrove's question.

"Then is there hope?" eagerly demanded Musgrove.

"No, no ; only she rides the waves less lightly. The sea will have her—she must go down."

"Should she gain the beach?"

"She will not, or, if she should, it's all one—she would be dashed in pieces. Her crew will sail in no other ship."

It is a fearful thing for man to pass from life with no loving voice to soothe, no friendly arm to aid ; with dark waves rushing and roaring all around—the swimmer's art of no avail—the outworn strength fading, failing—the writhing frame struggling till the flood flows over him. It is an awful thing to pass from life at any time, but doubly so in such an hour, in such a scene as this. To stand before his Maker without one hour's calm to breathe the prayer—to commune with his sinful heart.

"See!" said the fisherman, "the ship is driven furiously towards the beach, and now whirled round by those meeting waves. How she pitches! she cannot rise on the waves! A few minutes more and she will go down—we shall have seen the last of her. The storm is getting wilder—we can scarcely keep our feet even on this side of the beach."

The man said truly. The storm was indeed growing wilder every moment, the gusts of wind more frequent and furious, the surf higher and in greater volume, whilst the sea beyond looked like an immense boiling caldron heated by subterraneous fires. The clouds became darker and heavier—occasionally a faint light played along the gloom, succeeded by the rumbling of distant thunder, and some large drops of rain fell on the upturned face; but the fury of the tempest was not to be vented in a shower.

The vessel now pitched fearfully; and instead of riding on the top of the long dark furrows, rolled helplessly into their hollows. A cross sea struck her bows— those on shore thought they saw her stagger beneath the shock.

The surf rose higher—a sheet of blinding spray obscured the sight for some moments. When they looked again, the vessel was no longer there, and a wailing cry, only low from the distance and the ocean's roar, came on their ears.

"It's all over," said several—some in the quiet tone of habitude, some with an exaltation of the voice. Did those last, overlooking the death of many, think of the treasure that the wreck might bring them?

All, then, had gone to stand before their Maker. There was no more time for trial or probation. Age and youth—the sinewy and the feeble—the sad and the light-hearted—the suffering and the happy—the loved and the unloved—had all gone down to their long and dreamless rest in that one moment.

Leaving directions with the servants and fishermen to attend to any of the crew that might be washed ashore, Musgrove and Don Lopez returned to the castle.

It was only with the dawn the storm abated; and the painted sides and lofty masts, and the gallant crew, were promiscuously floating amid the foam of the ocean, or sleeping beneath its pitiless waves. Who that had looked upon that sea the following week could have deemed it the agent of such fearful suffering.

The wind was hushed—the water lulled in its mighty cradle—its surface smooth as a summer sea—its waves, advancing with a gentle and graceful swell, broke with a soothing murmur on the shingly beach, as if paying homage, not asserting rule. Another week, and the events here recorded were forgotten, or its wonders superseded by some newer marvel.

It was a few days after the fatal hurricane when one grey and lowering morning Florence sat at her window gazing vacantly at the sea; for sometimes she continued wrapped up in forgetfulness of passing time, until her attention was caught by some unusual appearance floating on the surface of the water. At first she took it for a mass of weed; but as it approached the shore a vague apprehension crossed her mind that it was a human form, and, hastily summoning an attendant, she proceeded to the shore. She watched with breathless emotion till the tide washed it slowly to the beach. Her attendant, an old retainer, drew it on the shore high and dry; it was a dead body enveloped in an old sail.

Florence grew sick, and staggered unconsciously to a projecting point of rock for support. Her head seemed to turn round—her sight failed her; and many minutes elapsed before she recovered her senses sufficiently to make further examination. What language is capable of conveying, even in the faintest degree, an idea of the horror which thrilled through her frame, as the old man lifted the sail-cloth from the body, and she beheld the countenance of her father!

*   *   *   *   *   *

In a shaded spot of the kirkyard, formed by one of the angles of the building, in which arises a yew-tree, whose foliage is almost black, in comparison with the neighbouring ivy which rises round it, and the turf which spreads its green and daisied carpet beneath it, is a white stone. It is but a rude attempt to perpetuate the memory of the dead, and upon it are carved these words,—

"MALCOLM GRAHAM."

LONDON: Printed and Published by E. Lloyd, 12, Salisbury Square, Fleet Street.

www.ingramcontent.com/pod-product-compliance
Lightning Source LLC
Chambersburg PA
CBHW081322020726

47506CB00005B/1162